THE COLLEGE

a novel

Dirk Barram

INKWATER PRESS

PORTLAND • OREGON
INKWATERPRESS.COM

THE COLLEGE

PROLOGUE

THANKSGIVING 2001
PINEHURST, NEW HAMPSHIRE

John Phillips died peacefully in his sleep sometime during the early morning hours of Thanksgiving Day 2001, at his beloved country estate, three miles outside the sleepy central New Hampshire town of Pinehurst. His unremarkable passing was in sharp contrast to his life. A physical giant of a man, in 1958 he had assumed control of his father's, and before that, his grandfather's New England woolen mill, Phillips Textiles. A fixture in the New England woolen mill industry, family owned and operated for the entire 110 years of its existence, Phillips Textiles was an economic force in the region. John Phillips ruled with an iron hand. Cold, ruthless, yet fair, and possessing a fine business acumen he successfully guided the business through almost 30 years of unparalleled growth. Upon his death that Thanksgiving morning, Phillips Textiles' assets were a reported $400 million. John Phillips himself would leave behind a personal fortune of $75 million. Upon his death John Phillips left behind a family that loved him, friends who admired him, some enemies and a substantial amount of money.

Behind the 100-year-old stone wall surrounding the family estate, in the large upstairs master bedroom overlooking the fading colors of the late autumn countryside, sometime in the cold gray early morning, John Phillips breathed his final breath. Martha Phillips, his wife of 48 years, discovered his still form, cold to the touch at 7:00 A.M. as she came in to wake him for breakfast, a routine she had done every morning for the entire 48 years of their marriage. Pale and shaking, she picked up the phone and called her granddaughter, Sarah Phillips, who in turn called Dr. Morris Glenn, the Phillips long-time family physician. Dr. Glenn quickly called for an ambulance and then telephoned Thomas Lawton, the family attorney. Within the space of 10 minutes, all three had arrived at the Phillips home. The ambulance was already parked at the front door. In the upstairs bedroom Morris Glenn gently lifted his old friend's wrist and felt for a pulse while at the same time placing a stethoscope on his chest. After several moments he looked up at Martha and sadly shook his head.

"I'm so sorry, Martha."

Sarah held her grandmother, both women crying softly. Glancing at Thomas Lawton, Dr. Glenn instructed the ambulance attendants to give the family a few private moments before removing the body. Outside the bedroom in the upstairs hallway, Dr. Glenn and Thomas Lawton quietly conferred for a few moments before Lawton left for his law office in Pinehurst. Little did the residents of this sleepy New England town realize that within twelve months, Ted Koppel of ABC News would be in their town broadcasting to the country an incredible story of human intrigue and tragedy.

CHAPTER ONE

LESLIE PATTON

Leslie Patton, dressed in dark clothing and a blue hat, carefully parked her old Willys jeep in the darkened and empty parking lot of Taylor Hall, on the Kingston College campus. Getting out, she cautiously looked around before walking briskly to the building's main front door. She had every right to be there and in fact often worked at night. As the Assistant Director of Development for Kingston College she frequently made calls at night from her office. Nighttime was when people were usually home. Her job at the college required her to help manage the planned giving program and to assist in the raising of money for the college's annual fund. She reported directly to Susan Anthony, the Director of Development, who in turn reported to Walton Trent, Vice President for Development. Trent and Dr. James Cannon, Kingston College President, would meet with the heavy hitters as she liked to call them: the people with money. Real money! Cannon and Trent would cultivate these people with the hope that eventually they would write Kingston College into their wills. The college would get them to establish a bequest such that upon death their estate or at least a portion of it would automatically revert to the college. Sometimes it would take years to cultivate people. Leslie's job was to manage the complex details of the planned giving program. At any given time the college had upwards of 30 bequests in process. The taxation and legal documentation process kept her very busy.

Tonight, however, Leslie Patton wasn't anxious for anyone to know she was in the building. She wanted to look at some files that were not in her office. She unlocked the heavy front doors with her key card and after glancing around at the quiet campus and seeing no one she hurriedly closed the massive front doors behind her. She knew campus security might come by especially after seeing the light on in the building. This didn't worry her. She could easily bluff security if they found her in a nearby office. They would check her ID card and be satisfied. She would simply explain she needed the files. They didn't know who worked where. These people weren't the FBI.

Her footsteps echoed loudly in the spacious empty foyer as she made for the stairs to the second floor where she took them two at time. She was in good shape. At the top she turned left and hurried to the development suite. Unlocking the main door she quickly went into her office. She turned her light on and switched on her computer, calling up the planned giving file. She rapidly scrolled down the page to Elisabeth Ann Williams. There it was just as she remembered. Mrs. Williams had died at her summer home on Lake Winnipesaukee, leaving the college $2.8 million. Leslie went out to the outer office and looked in the official department files at the actual document file on Elisabeth Williams. The paperwork was in order. The college's attorney and Mrs. Williams's attorneys had all signed off. The document was notarized. All of the appropriate college signatures were there. It just didn't make sense, she thought. She stood for a long time looking at the file before making up her mind. Her heart was beating faster now. She made up her mind. Earlier in the day she had secretly taken the master key to all of the development offices. She ran down the carpeted hallway to Walton Trent's office at the end of the development suite and opened his door. His office was immaculate. The imposing cherry desk faced visitors. Two small but expensive wingback chairs were in front. To the left on his desk sat a sixteen-inch computer screen with a starry night screensaver glowing in the dark. Looking back and listening for any unfamiliar sounds, she went over and quickly typed in Walton Trent's password. He would kill her if he knew she had stolen it. In a moment the screen showed the planned giving file program similar to hers. The main difference was his file was the official one and the one he used to develop the official donation documents. She scrolled down to Elisabeth Ann Williams's name and moved the cursor over to the amount line. She was stunned. Her legs felt weak. Leslie blinked to make certain she was seeing the correct figure. She was. Her pulse raced. She closed the file and looked carefully around to make sure everything was as she found it.

She backed out of Trent's office and closed the door. A moment later she was safely in her office sitting at her desk pondering what she had just seen. After 10 minutes of sitting she turned to her computer and after a few minutes of rapid typing stood up and turned off her office lights and left the development suite. She walked slowly down the flight of stairs and out the front door of Taylor Hall. The cold fall air helped clear her senses. She climbed into her jeep and headed out Old Vermont Road. The darkness seemed to intensify as she drove along. She felt the car begin to lose speed abruptly. She pumped the accelerator hard but to no avail. A mile out of town the jeep slowed to a dead stop. She looked at an empty gas gauge. Gosh, she must be losing her mind. She was sure she had recently filled it up at the Texaco in Pinehurst. She got out of the jeep and looked up and down at the dark empty road. She felt cold. Suddenly the yellow lights of an oncoming car coming from the direction of Pinehurst bounced off the dark trees. She breathed a sigh of relief. Soon the car's lights illuminated her old jeep and began to slow down. She waved her hands and with an unsuspecting smile stepped into the path of the lights. The approaching car slowed, then inexplicably lunged ahead with unbelievable speed and smashed into Leslie with full force. It all happened in an instant. She had no time to get out of the way. The front bumper hit her legs first, shattering them both before thrusting her upward into the unforgiving windshield where her pelvis, chest and face suffered mortal fractures no surgeon could ever fix. She literally flew up and over the speeding car and hit the cold pavement behind with a horrible thud. The car slowed to a stop fifty yards ahead and paused as if to survey the damage, its engine idling quietly in the darkness. Suddenly, as if satisfied, it quickly sped off. Leslie lay there, in the middle of the country road, a lonely, bleeding and broken mass. Death would only be a few minutes away. Leslie Patton was discovered 30 minutes later by a deputy sheriff who was driving west from Pinehurst. The 29- year-old police officer came upon Leslie and at first thought she was an animal lying in the road. He stepped out of his cruiser and walking closer shone his heavy-duty flashlight on the scene. To his horror he saw it was a human being. His face white from shock, he quickly knelt over by the side of the road and vomited his dinner. The graphic image of a young woman's horribly twisted body with broken bones protruding through the skin and permanently fixed mouth wide open in bewilderment, lying in a widening pool of blood, would stay with him the rest of his life. He had seen accidents but this was the worst. Wiping his face he went back to his car and radioed for assistance from both the police at Pinehurst and the sheriff's dispatch in Concord. After placing the calls he went to his trunk and pulled out three road flares and lit them. Soon their fiery red glow illuminated the country night. Leslie Patton's body grew increasingly cold, as she lay there surrounded by the warmth of the flares. Deputy Sheriff Walter Thompson, a young father of three girls, just stood there in the red glow of the emergency flares guarding the lifeless body of Leslie Patton, contemplating the fragility of life. Soon the wail of approaching sirens made him feel less alone.

CHAPTER TWO

On Monday morning, September 9th, the alarm clock's sudden and rude buzzing jolted Peter Kramer out of a deep sleep. He reached out and hit the snooze button and then pulled the blue comforter over his head and burrowed back into his warm, sleepy cocoon. He fell asleep but 10 minutes later the persistent alarm shook him awake once more. Crawling out of bed, he headed for the bathroom where he turned on the sink's faucet to hot. Soon the water was steaming and he splashed it over his face to both wake himself up and moisten his beard. Reaching for the green can of Gillette shaving cream he lathered his face. He was careful not to nick his face. He didn't want to teach his first college class with dried blood on his face. Finished, he stepped into the shower and turning on the hot water, letting it soothe his back. Hot water seeped into every pore as he stood there fully enjoying the heat. Ten minutes later he turned off the shower and dripping wet blindly reached for the towel on the rack. He dried himself off and began to dress. He put on a pair of tan Dockers and a light blue button down shirt with his favorite tie, which featured MGB cars in a variety of colors. After putting on his casual loafers he went into the kitchen and ate a breakfast of Total cereal and a whole banana. Slinging his blue sport coat over his shoulder, he picked up his knapsack with his teaching materials and stepped outside. The yellow morning sunshine contrasted with the bright blue sky, accompanied by a crispness to the air that warned winter wasn't too far away. It was going to be a gorgeous early fall day. Tossing his stuff into the back seat of his British Racing Green MGB he hopped in and drove out past the elegant brick house and down the immaculate driveway to Green River Road. Turning left, he pushed the gas pedal to the floor and headed for Pinehurst. The sun-dappled trees were just beginning to turn color. Soon the fall foliage would transform the countryside into a brilliant array of colors. The MGB sped past stone walls that appeared to move like shimmering waves paralleling the road. Peter was struck with the unique unevenness of these stone walls, erected long ago by farmers who were not concerned with symmetry. He recalled the poem by Robert Frost, "The Road Less Traveled," in which Frost reminisced about the stone walls of the New England countryside. Peter could now appreciate the meaning of the poem.

After a few minutes he entered the outskirts of Pinehurst. The small New England town was quiet at 7:40 A.M. He approached the campus of Kingston College. The 200-acre campus was undeniably beautiful. Old New England Dutch Elm trees lined the long main entrance leading into the center of campus. Expansive yet neatly maintained green lawns were bisected by brick walkways accented by old-fashioned lightposts with flowered planters atop. Red brick buildings, some 200 years old, most covered in green ivy, gave the campus an Ivy League look. Two recent buildings, the Phillips Fieldhouse and Kenmore Science Center, both built within the last two years, served to enrich an already beautiful campus. Eighty-nine percent of the students lived on campus. Kingston had a small but active fraternity and sorority system. The college belonged to the New England Association of Private Colleges and was a member of the National Collegiate Athletic Association. Three thousand students and 400 full-time faculty members filled the classrooms.

He wound his way along the campus drive bordered by neatly manicured deep green hedges until he came to the Business and Economics building. Parking the MGB, he went directly to his office. The building was empty. He was the only professor with an 8:00 A.M. class and Thelma Grady, the department secretary, didn't arrive until 8:00. He began to feel nervous. This was his first class. The quietness of the office only enhanced his anxiety. No one to distract him from the approaching moment. He glanced at his watch, which read 7:45. He wanted to get to the classroom well ahead of the students. Gathering his materials he walked out of the building and began the short trek across the still campus. He began rehearsing how he would open the class. A couple of students were walking behind him and he wondered if they were in his class. He finally came to Kingston Hall, the main classroom building on campus. The red brick, ivy-covered building looked imposing. He entered the green carpeted lobby and proceeded to the wide stairway, which took him up to the second floor and classroom 215. The classroom looked like it would seat fifty or so students. It was empty. Breathing a sigh of relief he began to arrange his papers on the front desk. He then turned and began writing some instructions on the blackboard. Once he was done he would be ready. Suddenly the door opened and in walked the two students who had been behind him. He twisted around and said hi. They smiled, returned his greeting and took two seats in the third row. They began chattering so he was free to continue writing on the blackboard. Within 10 minutes the class was almost full. It was time to begin. It was 8:00. Peter introduced himself and told the class a little about himself. He felt his heart beating and he knew he was talking too fast. Slow down and relax, he silently thought. He noticed three familiar faces and for an instant couldn't place them and then it dawned on him. They had been in class last spring during his interview. Following his introduction he distributed the course syllabus and reviewed this with the class. He was careful to explain when the mid-term and final exams would be as well as the two five-page papers he expected. With 47 students he would have a lot of grading. He stopped and asked if there were any questions. One student raised her hand and asked if the final exam would be comprehensive. Another wondered about his class attendance policy. Peter then began to talk about the course and his expectations. The students listened with interest. Everything was new, he was new and they were curious about this new faculty member. He was smart, young, athletic looking and very good looking. He had their interest.

The class ended at 8:50. He dismissed them and began gathering his papers. Several students came up to him with further questions and comments. One was Natalie Madison, the young woman he had met last spring during his interview. "I'm glad you decided to come to Kingston," she said. "I hope you enjoy it here." Her smile was genuine.

"Thanks," Peter said in response. "I think I will like it here."

They walked out of the classroom and down the stairs now crammed with students. The downstairs lobby was buzzing with students as they made their way through the crowd. Outside in the warm sun they chatted briefly before parting. Peter was smart enough to keep the conversation short and professional. He was glad to be on his way. He felt good about his first class besides being relieved to have it over. The students seemed interested and attentive. He had a 10:20 Introduction to Business class with mostly freshmen students. Since it was now 9:00 he had time to work in his office. As he entered the Business and Economics building he bumped into Melissa Crane, who was hurriedly walking out the door to her class.

"How was your first class?" she asked.

"Well, I think it went all right. I have 47 students. They seemed interested," he said.

"Wow," exclaimed Melissa. "How did we ever let that happen? That is a lot of students. Well, I gotta get to my Economics class. I'll talk with you later."

Peter turned and went to his office. He checked his phone for messages knowing full well that he would have no messages. He was still too new to Kingston to know many people. He began reviewing preparations for his next class.

CHAPTER THREE

September flew by. Peter's classes were going very well. He was busy with class preparations and grading and had little time for outside activities. He was falling in love with the college, town and countryside. On Saturday afternoons Anne Ashdown would invite Peter for tea and crumpets. In late summer he had answered her ad for someone to rent the small cottage on her large estate a couple miles from town. After just a few minutes on the beautiful estate Peter had signed a one-year lease.

At first he wondered what he was getting into but gradually came to appreciate her company. He was amused by her acerbic wit. As she put it, she had the goods on a lot of people in Pinehurst including many at the college. She thought President Cannon and Randolph Bolles, Chair of the Board of Trustees, were, in her words, "pompous and impractical."

"Cannon doesn't have much personality and Bolles is an idiot," she said one afternoon. "I've known Randolph Bolles all of my life. We grew up together in this town. I remember when he was six he fell off the merry-go-ground at the town fair and hit his head. He hasn't been the same since," she said with a twinkle in her eye. "How he ever became a public utilities executive I'll never know." She thought Elisabeth Rutherford, Dean of the College, was tops. They had been friends for years. Peter knew Mrs. Ashdown loved their afternoon teas. In some ways he thought he was substituting for her son, who rarely came to visit. As time passed their friendship deepened.

One early October Saturday afternoon Peter watched as a blue Mercedes slowly made its way up the driveway and came to a stop. Out stepped a well-dressed attractive older woman. She disappeared into the front of the main house but moments later came out to the back patio with Anne Ashdown. Mrs. Ashdown waved to Peter, who was changing the oil in the MGB. Wiping his dirty hands on an oilcloth he walked over to the patio.

"Peter," she said, "I'd like you to meet a dear friend of mine, Mrs. Martha Phillips. Martha lives a couple of miles from here. We grew up together in Pinehurst."

"It's a pleasure to meet you," said Peter.

"Mr. Kramer," she addressed, "I understand you are a new faculty member at the college." Martha Phillips was a slim woman, beautifully dressed, with gray hair neatly cropped into a bun.

She is elegant, thought Peter. "Yes, I am new at the college," he replied. Something passed between Anne Ashdown and Martha Phillips but Peter couldn't put a finger on it.

She seemed to appraise him as they talked. Peter almost felt like he was on display, like an exotic bird at a pet store.

"Peter, I've invited Mrs. Phillips for tea. Will you join us?" she asked. What could he do?

"Let me wash my hands and I will join you both in a few minutes." He turned to go back to the cottage and felt two pair of eyes watching him as he walked away. They were up to something he thought.

Afternoon tea that Saturday was fascinating. Peter felt

like he was in the presence of two strategic and persuasive women. Martha Phillips asked him a lot of questions. She listened carefully to his answers. Anne simply watched with an amused look on her face. Peter tried to stem the tide and ask Martha Phillips some questions. She deftly avoided answering most of his questions. Maybe wealthy people were like this, he thought. Lots of questions and not much about themselves. He was intrigued. At 4:30 Martha abruptly stood up and declared, "Well I must return home. Mr. Kramer, it has been an utmost pleasure talking with you. I must say you are a bright young man. I truly hope you like teaching at Kingston. You will be an asset."

Peter was surprised but pleased to hear her say this.

"Mrs. Phillips, it has been good to meet you. Thank you for your kind words."

She nodded and began walking to her Mercedes. Peter opened her door and after thanking him she drove off. He turned back to Anne who was standing on the patio watching Martha Phillips drive away.

"She's a lovely woman," said Anne. "We have been friends for a long, long time. Last Thanksgiving her husband, John died in his sleep in the early morning. It was such a shock. He hadn't been sick. Dr. Glenn said that it was just due to old age. His heart just got tired and stopped. He was only 77 years old. He was the majority owner of Phillips Textiles. It's a family owned business and employs many people in and around Pinehurst. She dearly misses him but is a strong woman. She will make it. Just like I did. By the way, have you met her granddaughter, Sarah? She works at the college. She is the Assistant Vice President for Finance."

"No, I haven't met her," said Peter. Things were now coming into focus. These two women were trying to set him up with Martha Phillips's granddaughter.

"So are you trying to get us together?" asked Peter, looking directly into Anne Ashdown's sea-blue eyes.

"Well," she admitted, "the thought has crossed our minds."

"The thought has crossed your minds?" he said laughing. "Why you two have been cooking up something ever since I came to Pinehurst. Between Mrs. Phillips's zillion questions and the twinkle in your eyes, one doesn't have to be an Oxford scholar to know something's up."

"Why haven't you ever married, Peter?" she asked pointedly. The directness of the question caught him unexpectedly. Anne Ashdown could be as blunt as a speeding train.

"I was engaged in college during my senior year but before going off to graduate school I broke it off. I thought I was ready but realized I wasn't ready to settle down. Earning my masters and doctorate was a priority, more so than marriage I guess." Mrs. Ashdown just nodded listening intently. "Graduate school wasn't like college. There wasn't either the time or abundance of women like in college." At this Mrs. Ashdown laughed. "So I focused my attention on my studies at Wharton and Michigan State University. I dated some but nothing serious ever developed. Hey, how come I am sitting here pouring out my sad love life to you?" he asked suddenly.

"Well, Peter, I've grown fond of you and think you are a nice young man who deserves someone just as nice. Anyway, matchmaking is fun. I think you would like Sarah. I've known her since the night she was delivered by Dr. Glenn during a raging blizzard. All the roads were impassable so her father, Thomas, drove a snowmobile to Morris Glenn's house in town and picked him up and took him back to the family farm two miles out of town. At 3:00 in the morning he delivered Sarah. My husband Alan followed in his snowmobile just to make sure they got to the house. I think he thought the whole affair was an adventure. Sarah has had tragedy in her life. Her mother and father were both killed in a small plane crash when she was three years old. Thomas was John and Martha's only son. It was a terrible time. Thomas shouldn't have been trying to fly around Mount Washington in that storm. John and Martha raised Sarah. I better not tell you anymore. It's not my place." So characteristically, Anne Ashdown stopped talking abruptly.

"Mrs. Ashdown, maybe I will meet Sarah on campus one of these days. I'm pretty busy with my fall teaching load and want to do well. Well, I better get back to the car. I need to finish before it gets dark."

She smiled at Peter and made her way back into her house. A remarkable woman, thought Peter. He would at least meet Sarah if for no other reason than for Anne Ashdown.

CHAPTER FOUR

ELISABETH RUTHERFORD

Elisabeth Rutherford stood six feet tall without shoes. At 49 years of age, graying slightly, never married, and with the chiseled face of an aristocrat, she had long ago decided to devote her life to teaching history and eventually working her way into college administration. Born into wealth and raised in Boston, she had graduated from Radcliffe in 1974 with a degree in history. Her parents, unlike those of many of her female friends, encouraged her to pursue her dreams and career aspirations. Her decision to teach history in college was cast in stone as a result of her academic advisor and mentor at Radcliffe, Dr. Theodore Catlidge. Catlidge saw in Elisabeth a grasp of history that he rarely saw in students. Through his encouragement and nurturing she continued pursuing her love of history, entering Harvard's master's program in medieval history and then onto Yale where she completed her doctorate in the same field. Upon graduation from Yale she taught history for 10 years at Wellesley College in Newton, Massachusetts. In 1991 she left Wellesley and came to Kingston as the Associate

Dean of the Faculty and Associate Professor of History. Seven years later in 1998 she was selected to become dean when then dean, James Cannon, became President.

In the years following her appointment as dean, she and Cannon had worked fairly well together. They both shared a deep commitment to building a strong academic program at Kingston. There were some differences. Where Cannon was severe and lacked interpersonal skills, Elisabeth was quiet but warm. Her soft but elegant features contrasted sharply with Cannon's hawk-like angular profile. Their greatest difference was that while both had a vision for Kingston, Cannon lacked the courage to truly fight for it. Elisabeth Rutherford was not lacking in will. The irony was that the widely held campus and public perception was the very opposite. Truth be known Elisabeth Rutherford was not afraid of confrontation and it was this very quality that brought her to President Cannon's office this morning. It was only during the last year that Elisabeth had noticed a subtle change in Cannon. She couldn't put a finger on it, but something was bothering him, very deeply. It was this nagging intuition that propelled Elisabeth to schedule an appointment with Cannon. She entered his office at 9:00 A.M. on a Tuesday still not quite sure how to approach him. His glasses were drooping low on his long nose as he read intently. He was thoroughly fixated on the document before him, so much so that he didn't hear Elisabeth. He felt her presence first and jerked his head up, startled.

"Oh Elisabeth, good morning," he said. "I didn't realize you had walked in."

"Hello, James, how are you this morning?"

He peered at her through his thick glasses, as if looking for a deeper meaning to her pleasantry. Elisabeth's face remained passive, giving nothing away. Her Beacon Hill Bostonian upbringing allowed her to be comfortable with silence.

"I'm doing fine," said Cannon. "The board meeting is approaching. You know the pressure from that," he responded.

"James," she said directly, "I've noticed a change in you these last 10 months or so. You appear bothered and distracted. Are you all right?" Her heart went out to him with this question.

"What do you mean?" he asked with a curious look on his face.

"Well, you seem easily distracted in cabinet meetings, for example. I've known you for seven years and have never seen you like this. It's like you have lost your focus and drive, or at the least they have been diminished. Your mind seems elsewhere."

Cannon was visibility agitated. He resented Elisabeth marching in and saying these things to him.

"Listen, Elisabeth, I'm fine. I really don't know what you are talking about."

She hesitated. This was going nowhere fast. He was rebuffing her attempts to help him. She decided to plow forward.

"James, you are spending an inordinate amount of time with Walton Trent compared with the other vice presidents. You two seem to be always huddled together. Almost secretive! What's going on?"

He bristled.

"I don't know what you are getting at. You know Walton and I have to spend time together to raise money for the college. We are in the middle of a capital campaign. So much depends on this campaign. You and the other vice presidents don't have to worry about money issues except for Dan Miller. Even he doesn't have to raise money. He just manages the budget."

Cannon was getting worked up. She could see he wasn't

going to budge. It was fruitless. She knew something was going on but her timing was premature. No use winning the battle and losing the war. She began backing off.

"James, I'm not trying to pry. If there is anything I can do to help you, please ask."

He nodded a silent thanks. Ten minutes later she was back in her office. What had just happened, she asked herself?

After Elisabeth left, James Cannon sat staring out his office window at the students streaming across the campus on their way to class. He wished he could be a faculty member again. No worries! At least none of the magnitude he now faced. Kingston needed money. It seemed like the college always needed money.

While the capital campaign was picking up steam, they still had a long way to go. How could they ever reach their goal? They desperately needed to if the college was to finance the new library, expensive faculty development program, and add $20 million to the institutional endowment. He felt the familiar pangs of doubt and fear. He simply did not like raising money. He was a scholar, not someone who asked for money. It was almost beneath him. This is where he counted on Walton Trent. And now Elisabeth Rutherford was on his case.

CHAPTER FIVE

The Kingston College Board of Trustees met at least semiannually, once in the fall and again in February. The board came on a Friday morning for committee meetings and met in full session on Saturday beginning at 8:30 A.M. The Friday evening was reserved for a dinner with faculty and staff. The dinner was held in the college dining hall. A program was always planned that traditionally included introductions of new faculty.

At 6:00 on the evening of the board dinner, Peter was back at the cottage grading some papers from his Introduction to Business class. Around 6:15 he stood up, stretching his arms, which ached from writing comments on students' papers. Glancing at the clock he realized it was time to go. After washing his face and brushing his teeth, he put on dress pants and a clean white shirt with a red and blue tie that hopefully matched his navy blue blazer. Quickly running a comb through his wavy brown hair, he ran out the door and jumped into the MGB. The fall air was cold so he kept the top up. After ten minutes he reached town and drove onto the campus and parked in the large lot next to Taylor Hall. People were walking in the direction of the dining hall. He was glad he had dressed up when he saw their suits and ties and dresses.

The college dining hall was decorated in a fall motif with a small platform at one end. A student was playing a piano while people ate hors d'oeuvres and drank punch in a small reception hall adjacent to the dining hall. Peter saw Melissa Crane with her husband Jack, and Ted and Ellen Wilson. He wandered over to say hi to his two teaching colleagues. He wasn't very comfortable in these settings. Small talk was boring. For some reason he always got tired standing around being polite and talking with people. He could play basketball for two hours non-stop but shopping or banquets like this one could tire him out in minutes.

"Hello, Peter," said Melissa. "This is your first board dinner, isn't it?"

Peter greeted Melissa and Jack. "Yes, it is," he replied. "So, what can I expect?"

"Well you can expect the President and board chair to talk about the state of the college. Bolles will talk about academic quality and Cannon will mention Kingston's ranking among other colleges. Same old stuff! Oh, and of course you will be introduced. Good thing you came."

Ted and Ellen moved over and said hello. Peter had never met Ellen so Ted introduced her to him. She was a short, plump woman with a gracious smile. Peter liked her immediately.

The lights dimmed, signaling the crowd to move into the dining room. Peter followed the Cranes and Wilsons. They found a table in the middle and toward the back. Each table had a fall floral arrangement with bright red and yellow fall leaves resting in the center of the table. A yellow candle cast small shadows. Peter sat down. He looked around and saw a sea of unfamiliar faces. He still didn't know very many people at Kingston. The sudden chirping of the microphone silenced the talkative crowd. Heads turned toward the raised platform where President Cannon was standing flicking the mike with one of his fingers to make sure it was functioning. Not very smooth, thought Peter. The crowd soon quieted. Cannon welcomed everyone to the dinner and began with a few remarks. True to Melissa's prediction he talked about Kingston's position within the New England Association of Colleges, and *U.S. News and World Report*'s national ranking of Kingston as one of America's best colleges. He was in his element. To be able to stand there and talk about the recognition and visibility of Kingston was incredibly fulfilling for James Cannon. This was why he had wanted the presidency so badly. After a few minutes he finished. Students dressed in white shirts and black bow ties began serving the dinner. Peter noticed several of his students. The college food service had prepared New England clam chowder and Caesar salad, which was followed by turkey, mashed potatoes and cranberries. Peter ate heartily. He still wasn't the greatest cook so appreciated eating out.

The dinner conversation seemed to center on President Cannon and Walton Trent, the Vice President for Development. Melissa asked Ted Wilson if he knew anymore about Walton Trent's background. Evidently, Peter surmised, Trent's coming to Kingston College had created somewhat of a controversy. He listened carefully.

"Don't you know anything more about Trent?" persisted Melissa.

"Not really," replied Ted. "Just the same stuff you've heard. Some mysterious kind of business in New York with Chemical Bank. It seems he left under less than positive circumstances. But we all know that. I'm sure Cannon knows a lot more but he isn't saying. It's just not like Cannon to hire Trent's type. I've known him for fifteen years and while he may be obstinate, he is a good man. He loves Kingston and wouldn't do anything to hurt the place. This just doesn't make sense."

"What seems to be the problem?" asked Peter innocently.

"Trent doesn't belong here, plain and simple." said Melissa.

"Why?" asked Peter. He was amazed his two colleagues were talking so freely about a senior administrator of the college.

"Well," said Ted with some hesitation, "Walton Trent has never really fit in at Kingston. He is aloof, doesn't truly understand what a liberal arts college is all about, and frankly, he has offended some people."

Peter nodded thoughtfully. "Then why is he here? How could he ever be comfortable in a small community like Pinehurst? Pinehurst isn't New York," he said with some knowledge.

"Good question, Peter," said Melissa. "That's a question we still don't have the answer to, at least not yet."

After dessert, President Cannon stepped back to the microphone and began the evening program. He warmly welcomed the Board of Trustees and their spouses, introducing several prominent ones. Melissa whispered to Peter that he was giving special recognition to some because they were wealthy. She could be cynical, he thought, but she was probably right. Cannon then introduced the college's student music group called Nightspring. Peter was impressed with how good they sounded. When they were finished Cannon asked the five new faculty members to come to the platform to be introduced. Peter was reluctant to go forward. He was by nature a private person and didn't need, let alone seek public recognition. Elisabeth Rutherford had prepared short biographies on each new faculty member. Cannon fiddled with the cards in his hands as the five slowly made their way to the front. Peter wondered why Cannon didn't let the Dean of the Faculty do the introductions. After all, the Academic Affairs Office had done the hiring. Peter was fourth in line as they all faced the audience. The bright lights played on the stage, making it very difficult to see into the crowd. All he could make out was a sea of darkness. When it came time for Peter to be introduced he shyly stepped forward. Cannon read Peter's bio stressing his recently earned Ph.D. at Michigan State and MBA from Wharton. Cannon was impressed with degrees from name universities. The introduction was short given Peter's lack of teaching experience but Cannon made the point that Peter had been a standout doctoral student at Michigan State and held great promise as a teacher. At the end of the five introductions the audience clapped loudly. Peter and the other new faculty gratefully returned to their tables.

"There now, that wasn't so bad," kidded Melissa. "Seriously, we are glad you came to Kingston." Peter could see she meant it.

Ted Wilson, though more reserved than Melissa, smiled and voiced his agreement. He looked at Peter and paused...

"Listen Peter, don't let all of this talk about Walton Trent bother you. Kingston is a good college. It's just that sometimes we faculty types don't understand or maybe even trust some of the administration. Isn't this true at most colleges and universities? I mean, how can someone like Walton Trent ever understand what a liberal arts college is all about? How could we expect him to? He has never taught. His job is to raise money."

Peter was slightly embarrassed. He didn't want to get caught up in campus politics. He had enough to do as a new faculty member. He just wanted to teach.

"Oh I'm fine, Ted," he responded. "I'm really beginning to like being here. As long as I am left to do my job I'll be happy. No politics for me. I'll leave that up to you and the other department chairs."

"Sounds smart, Peter," replied Ted.

They turned their attention in time to hear President Cannon introduce Randolph Bolles, chairman of the Board of Trustees. Peter watched Bolles with his heavy frame lurch to the platform. Peter smiled as he recalled Anne Ashdown's description of Randolph Bolles falling off the town merry-go-round as a six-year-old. Bolles gripped the podium tightly with two strong hands. His eyes squinted out into the darkened room knowing it was full of people but unable to see anyone. Peter almost felt sorry for him. Bolles mumbled something unintelligible and then after clearing his voice loudly began to talk about what was becoming a familiar theme to Peter.

"Kingston College has the chance to become a great college; one with a first-class academic reputation," he spouted to the audience. "We need the best scholars and researchers to come to this campus and make this happen. We can't rest on past accomplishments. We can move to the next level but only when we refocus our energies and commitment to academic quality."

Peter was struck with Bolles's reference to the future. He had said nothing about the current faculty. He remembered the look on Dean Rutherford's face when Bolles had spoken at the new faculty orientation. Peter looked around the dark room for her but couldn't see much. She probably had that same look on her face as Bolles spoke now.

Bolles ended his talk in a mumbled fashion much like he began. The stage shook slightly as he made his way down the short stairs.

"Well, Peter, what do you think of our board chair?" asked Melissa with a twinkle in her eyes as the dinner broke up a few minutes later.

Peter wouldn't bite. "Oh, I heard him at new faculty orientation. He certainly is convinced of what is best for Kingston College." He let it go at this.

"Randolph Bolles is a pretty strong board chair," she said. "He may not always be on track for what's best for Kingston but he is very savvy politically. He is worth keeping an eye on. He can hurt you." She wasn't smiling when she said this.

The crowd of faculty and board members headed for the exits. Peter was walking out with the Wilsons and Cranes when he saw her. He drew in his breath. She was wearing a dark blue coat, which contrasted beautifully with her long flowing blond hair. Her profile as she turned slightly was stunning. Her soft but elegant features almost made his heart stop. She was absolutely beautiful. Who was she, he wondered? She looked vaguely familiar but he couldn't place her. She was walking out with an older man who wore steel-rimmed glasses and had gray-white hair. It had to be her father, he hoped. Melissa noticed Peter looking at the woman and started to laugh.

"Oh, Peter, I see you have discovered the most eligible young woman in Pinehurst." Peter blushed. He didn't think anyone had seen him staring at the woman.

"Who is she?" he asked in a low voice. He didn't want anyone to hear his question.

"Her name is Sarah Phillips and she works right here at the college. She is the Associate Vice President for Finance. That older man is her boss, Dan Miller. The other woman is Dan's wife, June. You probably didn't notice her. Sarah is one of the Phillips clan. Smart as a whip and, as you have already noticed, a strikingly beautiful woman."

It made sense now. She looked like a younger version of Martha Phillips. So this was the young woman Mrs. Ashdown wanted him to meet. Leave it to Mrs. Ashdown.

Out in the lobby the crowd had thinned. Most of the board members had scattered to return to their motels. Peter saw President Cannon and Walton Trent huddled in one corner talking intently with an older man in glasses. Trent seemed to be doing most of the talking. Peter said good night to the Wilsons and Cranes and began making his way across the moonlit campus to his car in Taylor parking lot. The air was cold but refreshing. A small white BMW was parked next to his MGB. As he got closer to his own car he saw someone was in the BMW. He stopped short. It was Sarah Phillips. He hesitated, not quite sure of what to do. He felt like he was in high school again. Suddenly the BMW's electric window rolled down and Sarah leaned her head out. Peter felt his heart stop. She smiled up at him and said hello. Her lovely hair spilled out the open window.

"You must be Dr. Kramer," she said. "I saw you introduced at the dinner tonight. My name is Sarah Phillips. I work here at the college in the business office."

"I know," said Peter. "I met your grandmother last week at Mrs. Ashdown's place. I am renting the cottage out back. Mrs. Ashdown told me you worked at the college and thought I should meet you. I didn't know who you were until tonight when I noticed you at the dinner. Melissa Crane told me who you were." He felt his cheeks reddening. Nothing like telling her everything at once.

"Well, to be honest, Grandmother and Mrs. Ashdown both told me about you too. So when I saw you tonight I decided to say hi."

They talked for a few more minutes before Sarah said she had to go home and let her dog Jamie out for a run. She smiled at him as she sped away.

CHAPTER SIX

One week later Peter saw Sarah Phillips again as he walked out of Taylor Hall. He had just given his first exam in Introduction to Business and was loaded down with 47 tests. They met at the brick crosswalk in the middle of the colorful campus. A warm autumn breeze stirred the red and yellow leaves still clinging to the massive oak trees. The early fall warmth was intoxicating. The smell of burning leaves filled the air. The lawn was full of students studying on the lawn, tossing frisbees and enjoying the last vestiges of the fading late summer sun. She was dressed in an autumn plaid skirt and burgundy sweater.

"Hello, Peter," she said. "How have you been? You look like you have your hands full with those papers. Let me guess, students' tests?"

"I think I got too ambitious trying to find out how much my students know. Now I have a ton of papers to grade." He frowned.

She laughed that easy relaxed laugh.

"Hey, I told my grandmother that we finally met. She said that you had answered all of her questions very well. She also says to say hi. My grandmother is hard to please. You must have done something right. She also says that Anne Ashdown likes you. That's a compliment in and of itself."

Peter said, "You know your grandmother does ask a lot of questions, many more than she answers. She keeps things pretty close to the vest. She managed to evade all of my questions while peppering me with all of hers."

Sarah grinned. "That is vintage Martha Phillips." She hesitated before continuing. Looking Peter straight in the eye she asked. "I was wondering if you would like to come to our home for dinner this Saturday night. Grandmother would love the company and you'd also get to meet my dog Jamie. She doesn't ask any questions, just does a lot of licking."

"I would like that," he answered.

"We live out on Old Vermont Road about two miles from town. Since you live at the Ashdowns', rather than coming back into town you can cut over by taking Canterbury Lane, which connects Green River with Old Vermont Road. When you come to Old Vermont turn left and look for the Phillips place about a half of a mile down on the left. You'll see an old stone wall in front of the place. Actually we are less than one mile as the crow flies. Just a few woods and streams between us. How about coming at 6:30?"

"That sounds great," he said. "I will look forward to it."

"Well, I'm off to a budget meeting. See you Saturday. Good luck with those papers," she said with that same easy smile.

He watched her continue in the direction of Kingston Hall before he turned towards the Business and Economics building. He had plenty of work to do. He didn't want to get behind. He had made a commitment to return student tests and papers back within one week. Forty-seven tests would keep him hopping.

CHAPTER SEVEN

That same day Peter drove slowly out of the campus past the field where the women's varsity soccer team was playing Dartmouth College. Peter stopped for a few minutes along the side of the road. The top was down on the MGB. The scoreboard had Kingston up by two goals. Spectators lined both sides of the field. Evidently this was a big game, he thought. He stayed long enough to watch a tall brown-haired girl kick a spectacular 35-foot shot, like a cannon, straight into the right upper corner of the goal. The crowd roared. Clearly she was a Kingston player. After a few minutes he drove off towards Green River Road. The fall foliage was spectacular. Nothing like this in Michigan he mused. Along the country road century-old stone walls surrounded the ripening apple orchards as if daring the uninvited to enter. He was tempted to stop and jump over a wall and snatch an apple. The autumn aroma was enticing. Why not, he asked himself? He skidded to an abrupt stop and leaped out. Looking up and down the empty road he climbed over the stone wall closest to his car and entered the quiet orchard. Silence greeted him. The limbs were heavy with the red apples. All he had to do was reach up and pick one off. A dog barked in the distance. The dying late after-noon sun cast soft shadows over the still apple orchard. He eyed the best apple and standing on his toes plucked it off the beckoning limb. He had his prize. Turning back towards the road he heard the loud engine of an approaching truck. He froze. What if it was the farmer who owned the orchard? He quickly slipped behind a tree, crouching low, apple still in his left hand. Almost immediately the truck was in sight. An old red Ford pickup with an even older farmer wearing an old Red Sox baseball cap slowed next to the MGB. Peter waited quietly. Moments passed before the farmer gunned the Ford engine and sputtered on down the road. He must have thought I ran out of gas, Peter thought. Looking up and down the road once again and seeing no one else, Peter ran to his car and sped off. The juicy red apple was still clutched in his left hand. He felt a mixture of guilt and excitement.

Five minutes later he turned right into Mrs. Ashdown's estate. He drove slowly up the drive and headed to his cottage. She was out on the back patio tending to her flowers. Parking his car at the cottage, Peter walked towards her to say hi.

She had not heard him drive up, so engrossed was she with her flowers. She heard the crunch of his shoes on the gravel walkway and looked up, a generous smile on her face.

"Mr. Kramer, how delightful to see you," she said warmly. Her eyes twinkled. Peter immediately suspected she already knew he had met Sarah. "And how are things going with you?"

"Fine, Mrs. Ashdown. I've had a good week. I'm glad it's Friday, however."

"Oh, why is that?" she asked. "Do you have any plans for the weekend?"

She did know, he thought.

"Well Mrs. Ashdown, you know I finally met Sarah Phillips last week and she has invited me for dinner tomorrow night over at her grandmother's home."

"Splendid, Mr. Kramer. I am pleased to hear that." Her mischievous face beamed.

"Of course this is news to you, isn't it?" he kidded in good nature.

"Can I expect you for afternoon tea tomorrow?" she asked, avoiding his question. Peter saw the look in her eyes. She loved his company.

"Yes, of course," he said. "I'll be grading papers most of the day and then will come over at 3:00. Is that a good time?"

"Good, I want to hear all about how things are going at the college."

Peter walked back to the cottage and began fixing a light supper. He threw some bacon on the fryer and made a bacon, lettuce and tomato sandwich, which he ate as he sat grading papers. Around 9:00 he stopped and stepped outside into the deepening darkness of the fall night. The cool country air felt wonderful. He walked over to the little pond where six small brown ducks sat in the still water. They observed him without moving. He tossed some breadcrumbs into the water and watched them scramble for the floating snack. Their sudden splashing echoed in the silent night air, setting off the barking of a distant dog. After a few more minutes of duck watching he went back into the cottage and turned on the television. By 10:00 he had fallen asleep with the evening news still on. The week of teaching had tired him out.

CHAPTER EIGHT

Peter woke up at 9:30 Saturday morning. He had slept almost 12 hours. The morning sun streamed through the front window of the cottage. After a breakfast of cereal and toast he went outside to wash his car. Everything was quiet. Mrs. Ashdown was not outside yet. He backed the MGB up to the faucet at the barn side of the cottage and attached a long, green garden hose. He then went back into the cottage and came out a few minutes later with a steaming bucket of soapy water that he placed by the garden hose. Screwing on a new nozzle he had bought at Simpson's Hardware store in Pinehurst he rinsed the entire car off with a steady stream of water. He then applied a generous amount of soap that brought out the vibrant British racing green color. After drying the car off he stood back and admired his work. At 112,000 miles the little car sure looked good, he thought. He loved the freedom of Saturday mornings when he could work outside. He felt invigorated.

At 3:00 that afternoon he had tea with Mrs. Ashdown. He filled her in on how his classes were going and the Board of Trustees faculty dinner the previous Friday night. She listened intently. He had fun describing Randolph Bolles. She was amused.

"Randolph Bolles takes himself far too seriously," she said. "He has always been that way. We went to school together, from kindergarten through to high school. He was always giving his opinion whether he had been asked or not. He also didn't like it when I got better grades, something I did on a regular basis. He couldn't understand how a woman could be smarter than him. It wasn't too hard," she said with a sly smile.

"Have you met Walton Trent?" she asked, her eyes narrowing.

"No, not yet," he replied. "Some of the faculty seem wary of him," Peter volunteered, recalling the conversation with Melissa and Ted at the board dinner.

"Well, I don't know what the hell James Cannon was thinking when he hired that man. He's always pestering me to meet with him and talk about leaving some of my money to Kingston when I die. I just don't trust those small beady eyes of his. Pardon my language, Peter."

"He is peculiar looking," said Peter. "He seems terribly intense. I wouldn't want to get on his bad side."

At 5:00 Peter glanced at his watch and stood up to leave. "Well, I better get going.

Mrs. Ashdown smiled.

"You don't want to be late for dinner at the Phillips's, do you," she said with amusement in her eyes. "Now go and have a wonderful time."

Peter thanked her and walked back to the cottage where he shaved and showered. He was excited to see Sarah Phillips again.

CHAPTER NINE

At 6:15 Peter drove his sparkling clean MGB out of the Ashdown place and turned right on Green River Road. About one
quarter of a mile west he came upon a rusty and crooked sign
that said Canterbury Lane. He took the sharp left and drove
along a bumpy and dusty narrow road with deep woods on
both sides. The old road was deserted. At one point tree limbs
reached out almost touching the other side. He felt like he was
driving through a forbidden land. The road curved sharply to
the left before finally coming to a black-top highway with a
sign that said Old Vermont Road. Remembering Sarah's directions, he turned left. Less than a minute later he saw the stone
wall she had described the day before. He slowed down and
turned left into the driveway. Beyond the stone wall stood an
elegant three-story home, painted white with black shutters
and sporting a huge wraparound country porch. A beautifully manicured lawn lay in front of the magnificent house.
Maple trees with their vibrant colors lined both sides of the
long driveway. A horse pasture and red barn were beyond the
house. Peter whistled to himself. Parking his car in the cir-
cular driveway he had hardly gotten out when a red Golden

Retriever came bounding up to him tail wagging vigorously. He
knelt down and was fluffing the dog's ears when he heard the
front door open. He looked up and there stood Sarah dressed
in blue jeans, a buttondown pink shirt and a pony tail. She
looked great, he thought.

"I see you've met Jamie," she grinned. "Jamie loves it when
people fluff her ears. You must like dogs. My goodness, look
at how transfixed she is." The dog stood quietly while Peter
played with her.

"Actually, I love dogs," he said. "I haven't been able to have
one since I left home in Nanuet to go to college. Boy, she is a
nice dog. She could sit here all day and have me pet her. How
long have you had her?"

"Just since this summer. I moved in with Grandmother in
June and decided it was time to get a dog. We have lots of
room here. I found her out at a farm near Lynwood. Her name
is Jamie. Jamie, this is Peter," she said formally. Jamie's lifted
her warm brown eyes to Peter's face.

"Well, please come in. Grandmother is looking forward to
seeing you again."

All three walked up the stairs and onto the big porch.
Peter held the red front door open for Sarah and Jamie quickly
ran in, followed by Sarah and Peter. A long winding staircase
leading to a second-floor balcony was Peter's first impression.
The spacious foyer with its pine hardwood floor led off in several directions. Jamie hustled off to the kitchen while Peter and
Sarah strolled into a huge living room where a fire blazed in
an old stone fireplace. Peter was immediately struck with how
comfortable and relaxed everything seemed. They sat down on
a couch facing the fireplace. The heat made Peter's face warm.
A moment later a woman in a maid's uniform entered.

"Peter, this is Nellie. She is the world's best cook. She has
been with us for over 20 years."

"Nice to meet you," said Peter.

"Can I get you anything to drink, Mr. Kramer?" Peter winced. He hated being called Mr. Kramer.

"Actually, I'd love a ginger ale, if you have one."

"A ginger ale," she repeated. "Of course we have some ginger ale. And you, Sarah?"

"Oh, I'm fine for now, Nellie. Thanks."

Nellie left Peter and Sarah alone. A moment of awkward silence before Sarah asked Peter, "Well, how do you like working at Kingston?"

"So far so good," he responded. "My classes are going well, at least from my perspective. Students seem to be engaged. I haven't gotten to know too many people yet. I like Dean Rutherford. She has been encouraging. Ted Wilson and Melissa Crane in my department have been great. I have only briefly met President Cannon and Randolph Bolles."

Before he could continue, Martha Phillips walked into the living room. Peter stood up.

"Mr. Kramer, so good of you to accept our invitation to dinner. I am so pleased to have you in my home. Please sit down." She was accustomed to having people stand up for her. She sat down on a blue wingback chair across from the two of them. "Are you enjoying living in our small town?" She looked at him waiting for an answer.

"Actually, I am, Mrs. Phillips. I was just telling Sarah that while I haven't met many people, those that I have met have been helpful. I like living in Mrs. Ashdown's cottage. It's nice to be out in the country a bit. I love teaching at the college. Pinehurst seems like a real nice town. My father wanted me to go into investment banking with him in New York City and so was disappointed when I decided to go into college teaching. My parents live in Nanuet, New York, and Dad takes the commuter train into the city every morning at 6:15. He's worked for Solomon Brothers for 25 years. I think he envisioned me doing the same. I couldn't see myself in that routine. While I was at Wharton earning my MBA I taught a seminar for first-year students and discovered I loved teaching. After that I was hooked."

"What do you think of the college?" She seemed to be after something.

"I've purposely kept my head low to the ground. I want to do well in my first year. I'm anxious to see how my teaching evaluations turn out after fall semester. The other faculty has been supportive. I like Dean Rutherford but haven't had much exposure to President Cannon or other administrators."

Martha Phillips nodded silently. Suddenly switching gears she suggested they go to the dinning room. Nellie came in with Peter's ginger ale and handed it to him. He thanked her and held it in his hand as they headed to dinner.

The dinning room was across the foyer and towards the back of the house, directly off the kitchen. An expensive cherry dining table had been set for three. Six flickering yellow candles cast an intermittent light over the tastefully decorated table. Martha Phillips sat at the head while she invited Sarah and Peter to sit on her left and right. Nellie came in with an appetizer of fresh fruit. At the door to the kitchen Sarah's dog Jamie lay quietly. Her eyes were closed peacefully.

Over a dinner of New England clam chowder, green salad and roast lamb, the three conversed. Martha Phillips continued to ask Peter questions. She had an unquenchable thirst for information about people, thought Peter. Sarah listened in interest to Peter as he responded. At one point Sarah stopped her grandmother and suggested she tell Peter about herself. He nodded in appreciation, his mouth full of tasty lamb and mint jelly. Sarah laughed at this.

"I'm sorry Mr. Kramer," Martha apologized. "Sarah is

always telling me I ask too many questions. I just like to know what's going on. Ever since Sarah's grandfather died so unexpectedly last Thanksgiving it seems like I've been left out of the loop. He was such a vital person. Every night at dinner he would tell me all the latest gossip from the college and the town. I'm a person who likes to know what's going on, you know." She looked at Sarah. It was hard to go on.

"Grandfather's death was a shock," continued Sarah. "He was only 77 and had never been sick. Oh, he had the usual colds and flu but nothing serious. Then early last Thanksgiving morning he suddenly died in his sleep. We never saw it coming. Dr. Glenn came to the house immediately after Grandmother found him lying so still in his bed and simply said he had died of natural causes. He attributed it to old age. The ambulance people took him away and the funeral was three days later. It happened so fast. We still aren't over it, I'm afraid. We were completely unprepared."

Peter listened wordlessly. This was no time to talk. He put down his fork. He looked at both women with a directness that impressed both of them.

"My husband was a wonderful man. He took over Phillips Textiles and made it what it is today. He treated his people well and never gave his competitors an inch. John had a great mind for business and a personality that never took no for an answer."

She paused and smiled.

"Sarah is just like her grandfather," she said proudly. "I'm so glad she moved back to Pinehurst from Boston.

Peter looked at Sarah who was blushing slightly.

"What were you doing in Boston?" he asked.

"After earning my MBA from Boston University I took a job with New England Bank in their finance division. I lived and worked in Boston for five years. New England Bank is an old bank with little tolerance for women who want to move up the ladder. Oh, they say the right things but after being passed up for two promotions that went to younger, less experienced men I decided that New Hampshire and particularly Kingston College looked pretty good. So when Dan Miller called I was ready to make a move back. I think I'm a little like you in the sense that I don't need the big city lights to make me happy. Anyway, I could never have a dog in the city," she said, glancing at the sleeping Jamie still at her place between the kitchen and dining room. "So I moved back to Pinehurst and took the job at Kingston. When Grandfather died it seemed natural for me to move in with Grandmother."

"And I'm so happy she did. It has been a blessing having Sarah here again. John and I raised her after her parents died in 1978 in that horrible plane crash on Mount Washington. We lost our son Thomas and daughter-in-law, Alice. Sarah lost two wonderful parents. She has become like our own daughter."

The Phillips had their share of tragedy, thought Peter. But here he was tonight with the most beautiful young woman he had ever met and her dignified grandmother. He never dreamed he would meet someone like Sarah in Pinehurst.

After dinner and a delicious dessert of homemade apple pie and ice cream, the three retired to the living room where the fire continued to blaze. There they stayed until 9:30 when Martha excused herself to go upstairs. Peter stood up and thanked her. She smiled warmly, shook his hand and made him promise to come back soon. Peter knew she meant it. Martha hugged Sarah and left the room.

"She's a wonderful person," said Sarah. "She will never get over Grandfather's death, I'm afraid. The shock still haunts her. She had no time or opportunity to prepare for his death."

"I know it's none of my business," said Peter, "but doesn't it seem strange to you that the actual cause of his death is unknown? I mean if he hadn't been sick and just suddenly died, shouldn't there be an explanation?"

"Well," she said sadly, "Dr. Glenn said it was just old age and that his heart simply gave out. It can't be that strange, can it? People die of old age all of the time, don't they?"

"Of course they do, but usually there is an illness leading up to it, I would imagine. Did Dr. Glenn examine your grandfather?"

"Not really, he just listened to his heart and pronounced him gone. It was really fast."

Peter hesitated, "I'm sorry, Sarah, my Mother says I am the suspicious type and see a conspiracy behind every door. I'm sure your grandfather died naturally, and in his sleep just they way you describe."

"Morris Glenn has been our doctor for a long time. Grandfather trusted him. Why he even came out in a terrible snowstorm to deliver me! Dr. Glenn may be old but he is trustworthy. Everybody loves him." She tried not to sound defensive.

Their conversation turned to other topics. Peter really enjoyed talking with Sarah. She was so unpretentious and genuine. She gave direct answers to his questions and did not try to impress him. He could tell she was smart and yet had a certain style to her. She was interested in her work but not consumed by it. She seemed a person content with herself and her life. He found her easy to be with.

He glanced at his watch and saw it was almost 11:00. "Hey, I better be going," he said. "I have a mountain of papers to grade."

Sarah stood up and looked directly at Peter. "I enjoyed tonight. Thank you for coming to dinner."

Sarah and Jamie walked Peter to the front door and accompanied him out into the cold fall night. As Sarah and Peter said their good-byes the dog ran around the front lawn looking for the perfect spot to go the bathroom. She sniffed the air and circled and circled before coming to a stop. Sarah and Peter watched her in amusement.

Sarah watched the little green MGB drive off into the dark night. She liked a lot of things about Peter Kramer. He was bright, very handsome, gentle and seemed to possess an inner confidence she found incredibly attractive. He was not unlike her grandfather in this way, she mused. It was ironic that he had come to Pinehurst. Boston was full of eligible men, a number of whom she had dated. After a while she had become bored with the shallowness of the whole dating scene. Sure she had met bright and capable men but most had been more interested in their careers and themselves than in a genuine relationship. She never would have thought she would meet someone like Peter Kramer back home in central New Hampshire. The crisp fall air, merging with her thoughts of Peter, made her feel alive and hopeful. "Jamie," she called, "let's go in." The dog came running up to her and together they reentered the big house.

CHAPTER TEN

The hit-and-run death of Leslie Patton absolutely shocked the town of Pinehurst and Kingston College. Her death was bad enough, but the brutality of the accident and failure of the driver to stay at the scene angered people. Sarah Phillips was at her desk Monday morning when she first heard the news. She and Leslie were good friends and Sarah couldn't help but thinking Leslie was coming out to see her late Saturday night. Why else would she have been on that road? Leslie lived east of town in the opposite direction and had no business being on Old Vermont Road. Dan Miller came into her office and gently asked if she was ok. Boy, he sure could surprise her. Just when she thought he had no people skills he could come and say more in fewer words than almost anyone she knew. Over coffee they talked about Leslie's death. It made Sarah feel better.

Later that day James Cannon issued a general campus statement about Leslie's death and said the police had no leads yet as to the driver. He praised her work and said she would be missed. The memorial service would be at 2:00 on Wednesday at the First Methodist Church of Pinehurst.

Later, in what turned out to be a hectic day, Sarah finally got to checking her e-mail. Among the myriad of campus messages, she was startled to find one from Leslie Patton. Sarah quickly checked the history for the date and time. She was shocked to see it had been written on Friday night at 9:00, less than one hour before she had died. The message was strange.

"Please call me when you get a chance. I have some very interesting information to discuss with you."

Sarah sat at her desk contemplating Leslie's message. What did it mean? All she could think about was Leslie lying in Trellis's Funeral Home. She and Leslie had grown up together in Pinehurst. They both attended Pinehurst High School and were reunited when Sarah came back to town to live. While Sarah was slim, graceful and beautiful, Leslie was short, and a little on the heavy side. She always reminded Sarah of Rosie O'Donnell. Leslie was acerbic, but in a funny way. She could always get Sarah to laugh. They shared a deep friendship. Sarah began to cry softly. After a few minutes she dried her face. She decided to go home early. Packing some papers into her carry bag she said good night to Bea Carter and Dan Miller and walked out to her car in the parking lot. She drove off campus and out along Old Vermont Road passing the accident scene. Two state police cars were parked along the side of the road. A state policewoman was writing on a pad while another was measuring something on the road. Sarah slowed as she passed and nodded to the policewoman. Suddenly, Sarah stopped her car and parked it along the side, got out and approached the policewoman.

"Hi," she said tentatively. "My name is Sarah Phillips and I was a good friend of Leslie Patton. I was wondering if there was any new information.

"I'm Corporal Bissert," one of the officers said. "We are still trying to figure out what happened. I'm a member of the accident investigation unit of the New Hampshire State Police. We gather data from the scene and reconstruct the accident from scratch. Usually we are called in if there is a fatality that might involve a crime. In the case of a hit-and-run fatality it's an automatic investigation. I'm very sorry about your friend. If it helps, we believe she was unconscious almost immediately after being struck and suffered very little. I know this isn't much. It looks like she was hit near the center of the road. We will know more in about 48 hours. We aren't finding any skid marks, which is unusual. But it is too early to draw any conclusions."

"Thank you very much," said Sarah. "I just appreciate any information at this point." Corporal Bissert smiled, reached out and gently touched Sarah's arm and then went back to writing.

Sarah slowly walked back to her car and drove home. It was almost unbelievable to think that Leslie had died less than a mile from the Phillips home. It hurt to picture her there lying on the road all alone, so terribly injured. As she turned into the driveway, Jamie, recognizing the rhythm of the BMW engine, came running down to greet her. The sight of the happy Golden Retriever was comforting. Parking her car she opened the door and Jamie pushed her cold wet nose into Sarah's outstretched hand. She fluffed Jamie's ears and the two of them walked up the porch steps. Inside she found her grandmother reading in the living room.

"Hi, Grandmother," she said.

"Oh Sarah, how are you? I heard about Leslie Patton from Anne Ashdown. She called late this morning. I am so sad and sorry for the Patton family and for you. You and Leslie were such good friends."

"I just can't believe it Grandmother. I only saw Leslie last Friday afternoon at the college soccer game."

"Sarah, I know. I don't know what to say. I'm so sorry!"

Sarah was silent. She stood at the entrance to the living room scratching Jamie, but looking off in the distance, as if in a trance.

"Oh, by the way, Peter Kramer called. He would like you to call him back."

"Peter called?" Sarah asked in surprise, her head turning towards her grandmother.

"Yes, just after 4:30."

Martha Phillips stood up and came over and gave Sarah a long hug. Words were not necessary.

Sarah slowly walked upstairs to her bedroom overlooking the back woods and pond. She felt excited that Peter had called. She dialed his number, which was answered on the second ring.

"Peter, this is Sarah."

"Sarah, thanks for calling back. Mrs. Ashdown told me that Leslie Patton was a good friend of yours. I just wanted to see if there was anything I could do. I don't mean to be intrusive but if you need to have someone to talk to I would be happy to come over. Or we could go into town and have something to eat."

"Peter, that would be wonderful. I mean it. I would like you to come over."

They agreed he would come over in about an hour.

Sarah went back downstairs and told her grandmother that Peter was coming over to see her. This brought a smile to her grandmother's face.

"I think that's a good idea, Sarah," she said. "He will cheer you up."

At 6:30 the MGB turned into the driveway and Peter

hopped out. He was wearing jeans and a striped blue dress shirt. Jamie was the first to greet him. Sarah came out in blue jeans and a green sweater over a white collared shirt and watched with pleasure as Peter knelt on one knee and warmly scratched Jamie. She liked that about him. He looked up at her with a smile on his face that made her heart jump.

"Hi," she said. "I'm glad you called."

He stood up and looked right at Sarah. "Me too," he replied. "I am very sorry about your friend."

Sarah shooed Jamie back to the front porch and into the house before climbing into Peter's car.

"Wow, this car sure is low to the ground," she said. She watched as he shifted the car into first and zoomed out of the driveway heading east back towards Pinehurst. A near full moon illuminated the dark New Hampshire countryside. Sarah pointed out the scene of the accident. They drove in silence lost in separate thoughts. As they neared town Sarah perked up and suggested they eat at the Old Country Kitchen, a local eatery. The parking lot was almost full as they drove up.

Inside the smell of good food and a noisy crowd served as a pleasant distraction. They were ushered to a table near a blazing fireplace. The waiter came up and took their drink orders. They both ordered a local microbrew at Sarah's recommendation.

"It is nice to be with you, Peter," she said. "It's been a strange day."

He smiled.

Peter sat and listened as Sarah talked about Leslie. He nodded occasionally but mainly listened. He hadn't known Leslie but nevertheless wanted to hear about her because Sarah needed to talk. He learned a lot about Leslie, but even more so about Sarah. After about 20 minutes Sarah suddenly stopped, realizing she had been talking nonstop and Peter had been patiently listening. She was amazed that he had been such a good listener. Most of the men she had gone out with wanted to talk only about themselves.

"You know, I've been doing all of the talking," she said.

"Hey, I called and asked if there was anything I could do. I meant it. You needed to talk."

"Peter, thank you. It's just that I haven't come to expect this from too many men."

"Well I come by it naturally. My mother is a wonderful listener. She tried to teach me the value of sitting and listening. You can learn a lot about someone when you listen."

"Sometime I'd like to hear all about you," she responded. How did this guy ever stay unmarried, she asked herself?

Over a dinner of delicious Yankee pot roast and garlic mashed potatoes, they talked about Peter, the college and their jobs. They both agreed that Kingston was a good environment in which to work. Later, Sarah asked Peter if he wanted to go with her to Leslie's funeral on Wednesday. He immediately responded "yes," which made her feel terrific inside.

CHAPTER ELEVEN

Wednesday dawned with a warm wind blowing from the south. It would be a hazy New England fall day. The inside of the 200-year old white clapboard church was full. Leslie's family occupied the front three rows. Her father, one of the town's three dentists, sat with his head in his hands the entire service. Sarah later told Peter that Kenneth Patton was devastated by his only daughter's death. After the service Peter and Sarah walked out of the old church into the late afternoon sunshine. They were grateful to be out in the fresh air. The inside of the church had been stifling hot. In the parking lot Sarah heard her name being called and turned to see President Cannon and Walton Trent coming up from behind.

"Sarah, it's nice to see you," said Cannon. He glanced at Peter; momentarily not recognizing him nor realizing he and Sarah were together. Catching himself, he smiled and greeted Peter.

"Dr. Kramer," he said, "I didn't realize the two of you knew each other."

Peter chose not to answer Cannon. He just nodded. Sarah immediately noticed this. She liked it. It was none of Cannon's business whether they were together. This was precisely what Peter was telling Cannon with his silence.

Trent, standing to Cannon's left, was looking directly at Peter as if he were studying him. He was dressed in an expensive gray suit with a starched white shirt and red and blue striped tie. Trent was shorter than Cannon but solidly built with dark bushy eyebrows atop an impassive heavy face featuring deep black eyes that seemed to penetrate into Peter's inner core. Peter felt a coldness in spite of the warm afternoon sun.

Cannon and Sarah saw Trent looking at Peter, who was returning his stare with equal directness.

"Dr. Kramer, this is Walton Trent, our Vice President for Advancement," said Cannon, somewhat quickly.

Smart but calculating was how some people described Trent. Others described him as intimidating and unapproachable.

"A pleasure to meet you, Dr. Kramer," said Trent.

Peter politely nodded. He wasn't going to give an inch to Walton Trent thought Sarah.

"So, Sarah," injected Cannon, "How is your grandmother? I haven't seen her since your grandfather passed away last November."

This guy has no class, thought Peter.

"Oh, she's fine," replied Sarah. That's all she said. The reference to her grandfather's funeral bothered her.

"Well, we must be going. Please give her my greetings," said Cannon. They said their good-byes and hastened off to the parking lot. Peter and Sarah stood transfixed and watched Cannon and Trent climb into a long, dark blue Lincoln Continental and drive off.

"What was that all about?" asked Peter. He suddenly recalled the conversation between Melissa Crane and Ted Wilson about Walton Trent at the board of trustees dinner. So this was the man they had been talking about.

"You've just met the campus mystery man," said Sarah. "Walton Trent!"

"The guy is weird," said Peter. "Did you see the way he just stared at me?"

"I liked the way you stared back," she replied. "You don't tolerate people like that very well, do you?" It was a compliment and Peter knew it.

"Is he that way with everybody?"

"Actually yes, he is a very intense man. He's been at Kingston for almost four years now and has raised some significant money. I think Cannon hired him because he hates raising money and wants Trent to take the pressure off. My Grandfather didn't like Cannon and liked Walton Trent even less. Grandfather only put the college into his will because I was a graduate and Kingston has been part of our family and the community for a long time. Grandfather also thought the world of Dan Miller. He trusted him like a son. He gave to the college for reasons far deeper than people like Cannon and Trent. Cannon and Trent are latecomers by comparison. Trent drew up the living will papers with Grandfather three years ago. I'll never forget that day because immediately after Trent left the house Grandfather washed his hands as if to rid himself of any of Trent's germs. It was amazing. He figured he was giving some of his money to Kingston and the college would certainly outlive Cannon and especially Walton Trent. Grandfather had an uncanny ability to see the big picture."

Peter continued gazing down the road at the dark blue Continental as it disappeared around a bend. "Well, the man is unsettling to say the least. I'm surprised he can establish any type of relationship with people, let alone get them to put Kingston into their wills."

Sarah nodded in silence. She was thinking about Peter and

how he had stood up to Walton Trent and James Cannon. She was beginning to really like this guy.

They walked out into the church parking lot and got into Peter's car. The waning fall sun cast soft shadows on the tall doors of the old church as they headed away. The cold clutch of winter wasn't far off.

CHAPTER TWELVE

DR. MORRIS GLENN

Everybody knew and loved Dr. Morris Glenn. If any man ever looked the part of the family doctor it was Morris Glenn. At a shade under six feet, he had dark brown hair, an open face with twinkling blue eyes and a kind and gentle personality. People immediately trusted Dr. Morris Glenn from the very moment they met him. He could do no wrong simply because there was not a mean bone in his body. His patients adored him. He had come to Pinehurst in 1954 as a young doctor fresh out of medical school at the University of Pennsylvania. He was the town's first full-time doctor. In 1953 the town selectmen had advertised for a doctor of family practice. Morris had seen the advertisement in the University of Pennsylvania career place-ment office. He and his wife Beth had come to visit Pinehurst and had fallen in love with the small town. Glenn's interview with the town selectmen went quite well and he was offered the job. In June of 1954, after completing his residency at a large city hospital in Philadelphia, he and Beth had packed their old 1947 Ford and made the 14-hour trip from Philadelphia to their new home in Pinehurst. Today, the trip would take only 10 hours. This was before the major highways had been built from Washington, DC, through to Boston and northward into Maine. The town selectmen had paved the way for a home loan from the Pinehurst Bank at a favorable interest rate. The Glenns bought a large home on College Avenue, which doubled as his doctor's office. The white two-story New England home with black shutters and an impressive front porch had been their home now for 47 years. Patients still made their way up the winding walk bordered by Beth Glenn's prizing wining roses. Every third year Morris had the home painted with a fresh coat of white paint. Over the years, Dr. Glenn had resisted the pressure to move his doctor's office to one of the new clinics opening around town. He loved the small-town feel of a doctor's office in his spacious home. He would never move.

Today at 76, Morris Glenn still maintained an active medical practice. For many years he was the only doctor in the area. He served patients in Pinehurst, Lynwood and west to the Vermont border. As a young doctor he grew in his profession and today was the trusted doctor for most of the people his age in Pinehurst and the surrounding towns – even after other doctors moved into the area and a hospital was established in Pinehurst in 1973. Long-time patients would call him at home and even in some cases ask if he would visit them in their wealthy vacation homes in the lake region in central New Hampshire. Morris Glenn loved medicine. He especially enjoyed his patients. The mutual trust was incredibly rewarding over the years.

Morris and Beth had one son, Mark, also a doctor, who practiced in Lexington, Massachusetts which was only two and half hours away by car. At 18 Mark Morris had decided to escape the small town atmosphere his parents loved so much and enrolled at Boston College in Brookline, Massachusetts, where he majored in biology. He eventually was accepted into Harvard Medical School and finished in 1978. He married and had two young daughters. Morris and Beth Glenn loved their grandchildren. They visited Lexington whenever they could. They had a wonderful relationship with Mark, his wife Jennifer and their children.

But sadly all was not well. Dr. Morris Glenn had a terrible secret. No one knew about it. At least not those close to him. Not even his wife. He had a gambling addiction. A severe one! Morris Glenn loved the horses. It had started innocently enough in 1962. He had been driving home from Boston where he had just attended a medical seminar on hypertension at Harvard, when on a whim he had turned off of Route 93 and drove into the racetrack, Rockingham Park. In the years since he wondered a thousand times where that whim had come from. Why had he had acted on it? His life had never been the same since.

He had tentatively entered the large racetrack looking around for someone who might recognize him. In 1962, family doctors were simply not seen at racetracks. If word got back to Pinehurst it would seriously jeopardize his reputation and practice. He carefully walked to the big glass windows and peered out across at the racetrack. He was stunned at the beauty. The inside of the two-mile oval track was a manicured green lawn rich with roses and other flowers in full bloom. He was not prepared for this. Brightly decorated jockeys astride sleek thoroughbred horses sprinted around the track in a closely packed group. The sheer power of the racing horses and the roar of the crowd were intoxicating. He watched two more races before picking up a racing program and studying the horses and their racing histories. He then warily walked to the betting windows and placed his first bet. He looked over his shoulder as he walked to the window. He had carefully scrutinized the racing form and placed two dollars on Lucky Lady to show. He didn't have the nerve to bet she would win or place. So he placed two dollars that she would show, which meant come in third. Hurrying back to the grandstand he took his place in the third row of seats where he had a grand view of the racetrack through the big glass windows. His pulse quickened as the bell signaled the betting windows were now closed. The race began and Morris was immediately caught up in the drama of the racing thoroughbreds as they leaped out of the gate and began their pursuit around the wide oval track. Lucky Lady began slow and at the first turn was near the back of the pack. At the halfway point she had moved forward and was in the middle of the pack. Morris's mouth went dry. He leaned forward with incredible anticipation. Three quarters of the way around the track, as the horses came down the stretch run, Lucky Lady was neck and neck with two other horses. Morris was breathing hard, small beads of sweat appearing on his forehead. Those sitting in the grandstand rose in unison as the horses reached the finish line. One final burst of energy and Lucky Lady broke the tape third. At first Morris couldn't tell who won but a moment later the win, place and show horses were flashed on the huge electronic scoreboard. His horse had placed third. At that instant Morris Glenn's life was changed forever. He went back to the betting windows and showed his winning ticket and was handed $24. He stayed for two more races before heading home.

This was in 1962. For the next 35 years Morris Glenn secretly drove to Rockingham Park in southern New Hampshire one afternoon a week. Thursday afternoons became his day off at the office. He scheduled no appointments with patients, telling Beth he was going fishing or golfing, or traveling to Boston on business. He left at 11:45 sharp, arriving at the park around 1:00. Morris gambled on as many races as he could before leaving promptly at 4:00 in order to arrive home for dinner at 5:30. His methodical personality would never let him deviate from this rigid schedule, which probably was the reason Beth never caught on. Morris was a decent man who felt terribly guilty for misleading his wife. The magnetic pull of those beautiful horses flying around the racetrack with his money riding on just one to finish first was irresistible. He was a faithful husband, loving father and well-respected member of the Pinehurst community. He just couldn't stay away from the horses. The primal urge was so strong it would even allow him to deceive Beth. He hated himself for doing this but was powerless to change.

Over the years Morris lost a lot of money. Since he handled the family finances he could hide his sad habit from his wife. Fortunately his medical practice was prosperous. He wisely set up good investments and a tax-sheltered retirement program but unknown to Beth contributed far less to it than he led her to believe. They lived comfortably, with Morris providing her with all she needed. But had she known the truth, they were living precariously on the edge. Gradually over the years their debts began to mount and threaten to overtake their assets. He began to liquidate some of his investments to generate cash for his gambling.

In 1998 Morris Glenn's gambling habit was abruptly discovered. He had always lived in fear of being recognized at the racetrack. He wore sunglasses and an old Boston Red Sox cap to avoid recognition among the crowd at the track. Ironically this was not where he was found out. In April of 1998, he decided to refinance his home on College Avenue. Interest rates were dropping and he wanted to try and consolidate some of his hidden debts at a lower interest rate. He innocently applied for a refinancing loan through Pinehurst Bank. The application required that he divulge his assets and liabilities. The bank conducted a routine credit check, which to the bank manager's shock revealed three notices from Rockingham Park for past due payments for credit extended at the track. The amounts were surprisingly substantial. Morris never imagined that these past-due notices would show up on a credit report. The credit report arrived on the bank manager's desk late one Thursday morning shortly before he was to have lunch with Thomas Lawton, a local attorney in Pinehurst. The bank manager was Phil Craft, a rather weak man who, while good with numbers, was essentially spineless. He had grown up in Pinehurst the only son of an equally timid accountant. While at Pinehurst High School Phil Craft had few friends but had excelled in math. He had worked at the bank virtually his whole adult life except for four years at the University of New Hampshire, where he had gone on a math scholarship.

Once a month he had lunch with attorney Thomas Lawton, but not out of friendship. Their lunches were a time for Thomas Lawton to extract information from Craft on unsuspecting citizens of Pinehurst. While he was subtle, it was clear to Craft what Lawton was doing. The activity was highly illegal and unethical but Phil Craft had too much to lose if he refused to help Lawton. In 1993, Lawton had accidentally learned that Craft had hit a young boy on a bicycle with his car over in Concord and never stopped. The police had never been able to identify the driver. The boy was not seriously hurt, save for a couple of scratches and a broken arm, but Craft had committed a serious crime by speeding away. Lawton had cleverly used this information to his advantage. For the last five years Thomas Lawton had quietly and quite effectively blackmailed Craft. The thin, bespectacled bank manager was in far too deep to ever do anything about it now. He hated Thomas Lawton but despised himself even more for his own cowardice.

Over lunch that Thursday Craft told Lawton about Morris

Glenn's credit report. Lawton's beady eyes narrowed with interest. "How much money does he owe?" asked Lawton.

"Well from the credit report it looks like $150,000," replied Craft. "Of course that's all we know about. It could be more," added Craft.

"Listen, I want you to keep this under your hat," Lawton instructed. Craft nodded a yes. He detested the situation he was in but didn't know what to do. After Lawton gathered a few more tidbits from Craft on several other Pinehurst citizens their lunch ended and they walked out of the restaurant and parted at the sidewalk. Lawton walked away with what he wanted and Phil Craft went back to the bank with that familiar empty feeling in the pit of his stomach. These lunches were horrible for him. He felt like a traitor with no courage to stand up and do what was right. Instead, he told Thomas Lawton the hidden secrets of some good people. It was that or jail.

CHAPTER THIRTEEN

Thomas Lawton was not one of Pinehurst's finest residents. Far from it! If Morris Glenn was a decent person, Thomas Lawton was not. He was tall but not in an impressive way. His sallow pimply face with its perpetual smirk rested on a thin frame that never saw exercise. Small, dark beady eyes gave off an aura of distrust. Thomas Lawton was born and raised in Pinehurst and attended Pinehurst High School, where he was one of those students always on the fringe. He was considered slick. He was not very good looking but could be quite persuasive. This skill usually got him out of trouble. He was not bashful about cheating in school. He was able to cover his tracks and was rarely caught. But above all, Thomas Lawton loved money. He would go to great lengths to get it. He considered money the one vehicle to power and prestige. In 1968, after graduating from Pinehurst High School, he was accepted at Franklin College, a small liberal arts school on the east side of the state. He did well enough in college and on his law school entrance exams to get accepted into the University of New Hampshire Law School. Thomas Lawton saw a law degree as the avenue to money, power and prestige. In 1975, after an undistinguished academic career, he graduated and immediately began preparing for the bar exam. Three months later in September he traveled to Concord and took his exam for entrance to the New Hampshire bar. He anxiously waited six weeks for the results. On Wednesday, October 15, he drove his Buick LeSabre to Concord, where the bar exam scores were posted on the wall at the State Building. His heart was pounding as he walked up the massive concrete steps to the 100-year-old state building. A large but deathly quiet group of students was straining to see if their names were posted. Only those who had passed were listed. The sweat was trickling down his arms as he peered at the list. He scanned the list, his anxiety mounting. Suddenly it was there. Thomas Lawton. He leaped for joy. He had passed. He was an attorney who had the authority to practice in the State of New Hampshire.

Thomas Lawton returned to Pinehurst, where he became a junior lawyer in the town's largest law firm, Bickford and Guilckson. Over the years he worked hard and eventually became a partner in 1990. Bickford, Guilckson and Lawton. The firm, which consisted of 12 attorneys, counted among their clients Kingston College and Phillips Industries. At about 50 years of age, Thomas Lawton was a successful lawyer in a good law firm. Some people in town wondered why such a good law firm had hired Thomas Lawton. Those closer to the truth knew better. Lawton brought more to the table than met the eye. He could and would do certain jobs for the firm that most lawyers refused. He was a necessary evil and more than brought in his share of clients.

CHAPTER FOURTEEN

Dan Miller quietly studied the quarterly fiscal report of Kingston College as he prepared for Thursday evening's meeting of the Executive Committee of the Board of Trustees. As Vice President for Financial Affairs at Kingston College he was responsible for balancing the $135 million annual budget. The Executive Committee met monthly and he was to report on the third quarter of the fiscal year. Miller had worked at Kingston for 25 years. Prior to that he had worked for Price-Waterhouse in New York. He had given up the smog, crowds and traffic to come back to Pinehurst where he had grown up and eventually graduated from Kingston. He was highly respected within and without the Kingston community. The New England Association of Colleges and Universities, the accreditation body for all colleges and universities in the Northeast, often called upon him to review the financial status of member institutions. Medium height with white-gray hair and 60 years of age, he was one who didn't mince his words. While some faculty and staff found him tough and unrelenting, he had played a vital role in keeping Kingston in good financial standing over the years. He didn't like surprises when it came to the budget. Miller had a habit of jingling the loose coins in his pocket when he was upset or under pressure. Jingling was a telltale sign to the astute observer. He and President Cannon were very different and seemed to get along, but there were times when Cannon clearly irritated Miller with his emphasis on institutional image over fiscal responsibility. No one doubted Dan Miller's ability to manage a complex budget. He just could be brusque and stubborn. He also was fair and straightforward.

Kingston College, like many private liberal arts colleges, relied heavily on student revenues. The college endowment was $85 million, a paltry amount when compared with other more prestigious institutions. Miller was constantly analyzing institutional expenditures with student tuition dollars and other sources of revenue income. When a negative trend developed he was quick to sound the alarm with the President and the administrative cabinet. Usually these were less than pleasant meetings.

The Board of Trustees trusted Miller's instincts. When he talked they listened. This day as Miller looked over the quarterly fiscal report ending September 30, 2002, he felt a familiar small alarm go off in his head. At the current rate, by the year's end, institutional expenditures were forecasted to exceed revenues including annual gift income by $200,000. Picking up the phone, he dialed Cannon's office. Twenty minutes later he was seated in the President's office.

"James, we are headed for trouble," an exasperated Miller said. "We're going to be $200,000 over budget at the rate we are going. I'm not sure we can balance the budget this year." Cannon felt that familiar inward pang of fear again...coupled with a deep frustration with Miller. Why couldn't Miller see the big picture? At every public function Cannon talked about the academic excellence of Kingston but also proudly reinforced the college's 20 years of a balanced budget. This simply couldn't end. Not during his tenure as President. The pressure to make Kingston a great college depended on the institution being sound financially. He certainly didn't want his Vice President for Financial Affairs publicly sounding the alarm.

"Don't worry, Dan," he said trying to placate his colleague. "We will not be over budget. We simply need to cut back on expenditures. We have no choice. We also have several grants and other development projects in the works. I expect we will see some big money soon."

Miller's face became red with anger. He came unglued. "Yes, but this is soft money," he almost yelled. "You know we need to balance the annual budget without depending on grants and foundation money. You know damn well that this kind of money is for capital campaign and building projects. We have to get the annual budget under control. We were fortunate to balance the budget for the last two years let alone finish the new Science Building and add to the endowment. We were just plain lucky that John Phillips and Elisabeth Ann Williams died. Where would we have been without the four million dollars from their bequests? Do we have to depend on people dying for money? The next thing you will want to do is take money from the endowment."

Cannon turned and looked out the window at the snowy New Hampshire landscape. He respected Miller's ability but despised his pessimistic approach. Today he was almost disrespectful. He wasn't going to let Miller goad him into a fight. Everything was a crisis with Miller. Miller never faced the pressure he did as President. Miller lived for balanced budgets and balance sheets that auditors and board members praised. Making Kingston College a great academic institution was not one of Miller's goals. He left that to the President and faculty.

Turning back to Miller he said that the cabinet would have to contend with the problem on Thursday morning. Taking this as a cue that the meeting was over, Miller grunted a short OK and stomped out. Cannon cursed him under his breath as he left.

A rather tall and thin man with a hawkish face, James Cannon loved the academic environment and would not tolerate mediocrity in either students or colleagues. Some described Cannon as scholarly and severe. Above all, Cannon possessed an unrelenting drive for academic excellence. He believed Kingston could and should become one of the finest colleges in New England and perhaps beyond. He was consumed by this notion. As a young Ph.D. student in history at Yale he had distinguished himself as a fine scholar. Colleagues and students respected Cannon more for his intellect and scholarship than anything else. While some were put off by his rigidity none could argue with his hopes and dreams for Kingston. It was perhaps this commitment to scholarship and vision for Kingston that faculty and board members saw and led to his eventual appointment as President. Cannon believed Kingston should be great. They believed he would make it happen.

Established in 1825, and named after Josiah Kingston, one of the original founders of the New Hampshire colony, Kingston College was considered a second tier Ivy League college. Unfortunately, Kingston lacked the significant endowment, immediate name recognition and sterling academic reputation of colleges such as Amherst, Williams, Cornell and others. Even though Kingston had a rich history, the glaring lack of a big endowment and name recognition resulted in continual financial pressure. Kingston was a tuition-driven institution. Seventy-four percent of the annual budget revenues came from student tuition dollars. Cannon despised this dependence on student admissions. He believed it to be a stranglehold on the college's ability to move forward.

James Cannon stared at the phone on his desk for a long time after Dan Miller stomped out of his office. After a while he picked it up and punched in four numbers. He said a few words and hung up. Exactly five minutes later Walton Trent walked briskly into the richly paneled President's office. The deep plush carpet and cherry wood furnishings never ceased to impress Trent. The blazing fire in the 18th-century stone fireplace cast a warm glow. His facial features gave off an intensity that people found intimidating. A cold massive face gave no ground to anyone searching for what he might be thinking.

"Miller is getting anxious again," said Cannon.

"So, let him," retorted Trent. "I don't give a tinker's dam what that glorified accountant thinks. This college's greatness won't be held back by some inward-thinking, fiscally conservative numbers guy. Listen, James. You brought me to Kingston for one purpose...to keep the money pressure off of you. Plain and simple! That's what I'm doing. You are the big President who gets up in front of the people and extols the virtues of a college education at good old Kingston College. Me, I'm the guy behind the scenes. The one who pushes the buttons to make this place and you look good. Just so we understand each other, no financial person is going to get in our way. James, we work together to make this a great college. Now, why you do it is for your own image or whatever. Me, I do it for the money. Let's not confuse the issue. We need each other."

Cannon nodded his head in agreement. He had hired Walton Trent four years ago to be his Vice President for Advancement. At most colleges this position required someone to work closely with the President, primarily in raising money. Trent had come from New York, where he had previously worked as an investment banker with Chemical Bank of New

York. Cannon had met Trent at a college fundraising dinner in Scarsdale at the home of one of Kingston's wealthy alumni. Ironically at the time Cannon was looking to fill the Vice President for Advancement position and Trent was under a cloud of suspicion at Chemical for investment irregularities with several clients. Trent needed a job and came across as smooth and persuasive to Cannon. Several months later the Securities and Exchange Commission quietly dropped the charges and Trent left Chemical with a lucrative retirement package. Cannon never clearly understood the situation. He was impressed with Trent's charisma and felt he could raise money and take the pressure of himself. At the time it looked like a good arrangement. He offered Trent salary of $150,000. Trent asked for a college car and $250,000 annuity. Cannon unwisely agreed over the strong opposition of Dan Miller. Cannon had been uncharacteristically impatient with regards to hiring Walton Trent. In the four years since coming to Kingston, Trent had successfully raised several million dollars. Cannon wasn't always sure of Trent's tactics but he was very pleased with the money he had raised. During this time the annual budget had been difficult to balance but they had always found a way to increase revenues and satisfy Dan Miller. The arrangement appeared to be working so James Cannon was reluctant to make any changes. If the truth were known, James Cannon didn't have the courage.

Cannon felt the presence of Walton Trent whenever there were financial problems. Powerless though Cannon was in these situations, he knew Trent would somehow resolve the problems.

Trent smiled at Cannon. "Don't worry," he said. "Everything will work out fine. You just work with Miller and the cabinet to get the expenditures a bit more under control," he almost ordered.

"I will," said Cannon in a loud voice, trying to gain some sense of control. He hated the position he was now in but didn't know how to change things. For the second time that day President Cannon watched one of his vice presidents walk out of his office. For the second time that day Cannon felt he was losing control of the college.

CHAPTER FIFTEEN

The next day James Cannon and Walter Trent traveled 100 miles south to Belmont, Massachusetts, to meet with Henry and Mary Townsend, 1950 graduates of Kingston College. Degree in hand, Henry Townsend went on to become a successful stockbroker and in 1962 invested heavily in a young startup company called Raytheon. Henry had seen the possibilities earlier than his colleagues and took an uncharacteristic plunge, investing most of his savings in the young company. The risk paid off. By 1975 Henry Townsend was a minority shareholder with one million shares with a market value of 85 million. Cannon and Trent were interested in some of the Townsends' money.

The Townsends lived in a wealthy Belmont neighborhood with huge homes, wide streets, long driveways and manicured front lawns. Tall Dutch elm trees lined the quiet streets. Cannon and Trent parked the blue Lincoln at the curb and walked up the red-brick front walk towards the impressive three-story home. The heavy front door was opened immediately by a butler in a black coat, white shirt and black tie who ushered them into a dark wood–paneled library with soft easy chairs facing a fireplace. Bookshelves lined three walls from floor to ceiling. A silver tea service sat on an old antique coffee table.

"Mr. Townsend will be with you in a few minutes," he said and then excused himself.

"Since I know Henry Townsend, I'll do the initial talking and you can explain the intricacies of the actual bequest if it gets to that. I've known Henry for 15 years and have nurtured the college's relationship with him for the four years I've been President. OK?" said Cannon looking at Trent.

"Sure, James," said Trent. "Just so long as we get this guy to send some money our way, I don't care who does what."

The door opened a few minutes later and there stood a slight diminutive man with thick glasses and a wisp of gray hair on the top of his head. "Hello, James," he said crisply. His voice strength belied his timid appearance.

"Henry, good to see you. I haven't seen you since the Kingston dinner in Cambridge last year. How have you been?"

"Fine, fine," he replied. He had no patience for such trivial questions but was polite about it. "Would you care for some tea?"

"Certainly," said Cannon. "Henry, I'd like you to meet Walton Trent, my Vice President for Advancement at the college. He's been with us for four years now."

Trent reached over and extended his hand to Townsend's.

"Mr. Townsend, I am very pleased to meet you," said Trent.

Townsend eyed Trent carefully, like one might look at a painting hanging on a wall. "Nice to make your acquaintance, Mr. Trent." His old eyes scanned Trent's face before turning back to Cannon.

"Please help yourselves to tea," said Townsend. "Now how are things at the college, James?"

Cannon loved this question. He could talk about Kingston all day.

"Things are going well, Henry. Our enrollment is now at

3000 students, up from last year. We have over 400 faculty and have been named once again by *U.S. News and World Report* as one of America's Best Colleges. We have some wonderful things happening with our faculty. The Carnegie Foundation just selected Susan Brian, an English literature professor, as one of the top teachers in the Northeast. We have several biologists conducting important research in the area of genetics. The new year is off to a great start."

The old man nodded. "So what brings you to Belmont?"

"One of the main reasons we are here is because of the capital campaign. As you know we are trying to raise $75 million for the new music and fine arts building, academic scholarship and the institutional endowment."

Townsend replied. "What's this academic scholarship piece?"

"We have a major faculty development program that will cost us almost $2 million. The money is intended to promote faculty research, lower faculty teaching loads and provide money for computer equipment and software."

"How much will the new music and fine arts building cost?"

Trent injected at this point, "The 200,000-square-foot building will include a 3000-seat auditorium and a state-of-the-art theater. Projected cost is 6.8 million."

The discussion continued on for several more minutes with Cannon finally asking Henry Townsend to consider how he could help the college. There were several moments of silence. Henry Townsend was not an impetuous man.

Becoming more specific at this point, Trent looked directly at Henry Townsend and asked him to consider a one-time gift of three million and to include the college in his will with a substantial bequest in the area of five million. Cannon almost fell off his chair. He was shocked at Walton Trent's numbers. Coming down in the car they had agreed to ask Townsend for a two million gift with the will amount open ended. He couldn't believe Trent's audacity. Cannon expected Townsend to tell them to get the hell out of his house.

"Well, Mr. Trent, you certainly get to the point, don't you? You must have done your homework on me. Are all college development vice presidents this bold?"

"Please forgive me, Mr. Townsend. I hope I haven't offended you. It's just that I believe so strongly in what we are doing at Kingston that I guess I am fearless when it comes to doing my part. Kingston is a wonderful place. We are turning out great students who are making an impact in society. My job is to raise money. Plain and simple! My commitment to the college is so deep that it sometimes gets the better of me."

Cannon looked at Trent. What a line, he thought.

Henry Townsend considered Walton Trent's short but impassioned speech.

"Listen, I will need to talk with Mary and my accountant. I want to help in some way. I will call you in a few days."

President Cannon knew it was time to go. He stood up and extended his hand to Henry Townsend. "Henry, thank you for hearing our pitch. We deeply appreciate your past generosity to Kingston. Thank you for considering us again."

In a few minutes Cannon and Trent were back in the Lincoln heading out on Route One towards New Hampshire.

"Trent, what under the sun were you doing back there? We had agreed on asking for a two million gift and to leave the will open ended." Cannon was irate. "That was downright stupid. These people don't respond to your kind of tactics."

Tent looked at Cannon before responding.

"James, the secret to raising money is to go in with brass balls. You can't be timid. They will smell your fear and consider you a lesser person and subsequently give less. You think Henry Townsend doesn't respect this kind of approach. Hell, he sees it all the time in his line of work. Why, if you saw him in action he'd behave just like me. Stop kidding yourself. These rich folks didn't get all their money by being nice."

Cannon was silent. He had to admit Trent had a point. He just wasn't comfortable with his approach.

Five days later Henry Townsend called James Cannon. After talking with his wife and accountant he had decided to give the college a one-time gift of two million and to include the college in his will with a yet to be determined amount. Townsend assured Cannon he would leave Kingston a substantial amount in his will but the details would need to be worked out.

Cannon was profuse in his thanks to Townsend. He asked if Henry would let the college name the new fine arts building after him. He declined but did ask to have the 3000-seat auditorium named after his wife Mary. Cannon readily said yes. They hung up with the promise that Walton Trent would coordinate the bequest paperwork as soon as the Townsends were ready. Henry would call Cannon in a few weeks.

True to his word, Henry Townsend called James Cannon six weeks later and invited him to come back to Belmont to finalize the bequest. The next day Cannon and Trent were back in the Lincoln driving the 100 miles to Belmont. They arrived by 10:00 A.M. Without preamble, Townsend handed Cannon a check for two million. Cannon shook Townsend's hand and thanked him. Henry told them he would leave the college five million upon his death. Trent was gracious in his appreciation. He suggested that that the will provision be kept confidential. Henry agreed and in fact wanted it confidential. All three signed the bequest papers and Trent put them in his briefcase, which he then locked. The two-million-dollar check was also placed in the briefcase.

On the way back to New Hampshire they stopped for lunch at a French restaurant in Lexington. Over delicious onion soup they discussed their success. It was moments like this when Cannon could relax. For the time being the pressure was off. Trent was equally happy and had two glasses of wine to celebrate.

Back in Pinehurst, Trent went directly to his office in Taylor Hall and told Susan Anthony about the gift and bequest from Henry Townsend. She was elated. Since Leslie Patton's death the development people had been pretty down. It was nice to have some good news. She asked about the amounts. He told her about the two million gift and that the bequest was supposed to be confidential. He asked her to bring in a new bequest file for the Townsends. He quickly filled it out with the provisions of the will including the amount. They signed the document in each other's presence but she appropriately averted her eyes from the actual amount. She sealed it and took it back to be put into the official file that was under lock and key in the outer office. He reminded her that the amount Henry Townsend was leaving the college was strictly confidential. The only people who were to know the amount were Trent and Cannon. She nodded her head in understanding.

After Susan left, Trent took out the two million dollar check and penned a brief note to Dan Miller. He then put the check and note into an envelope and asked one of the secretaries to hand deliver it to Dan Miller. The money would go directly to the capital campaign fund.

CHAPTER SIXTEEN

The fall semester seemed to be flying by for Peter. His classes were going well. If these first few weeks were any indication, he had chosen the right career. He loved teaching. Even the grading, while arduous, was at least showing him what students were learning. The colorful leaves were dropping off the trees in droves. They blanketed the campus and their crunching underfoot could be heard all over campus. Central New Hampshire was a beautiful place in the fall. He thoroughly enjoyed living in Mrs. Ashdown's cottage. They continued to have their Saturday afternoon tea, though she kept reminding him she now had competition. She loved to hear all about his classes and especially how things were going with Sarah. He was always reluctant to say much but once in a while she managed to extract a morsel of information from him. She was good at that. Once in a while he would help her with her flowers or run an errand for her. She would hand him a list of items and off he would drive into town and bring back a couple of bags of groceries. He liked to do this for her.

Peter and Sarah were spending a lot of time together. On Saturdays they would usually go to college soccer games or drive around the New Hampshire countryside whether it was going to antique furniture sales, stopping at apple stands, or hiking in the state parks. They would take Jamie hiking and she would run ahead on the trail barking and chasing every moving thing. She was a terrible hunter, barking first before giving chase. She never let Peter and Sarah out of her sight. Sarah collected giant leaves along the trail and would come back to the car with an armful. The car would always be loaded with old furniture, baskets of apples, leaves, and Jamie. It was a magical time for Sarah and Peter.

Peter was planning to go home for Thanksgiving until Sarah invited him to her grandmother's home. Martha Phillips also invited Anne Ashdown. He called home and explained to his mother, who while disappointed was happy for him She made him promise to come home for Christmas.

On the Friday before Thanksgiving, Peter attended the bimonthly faculty meeting. Faculty meetings were held in Taylor Hall in the Banning Lecture Hall that seated 400. Since only about seventy percent of the faculty usually attended there were plenty of seats. He walked in two minutes before it was to start and spotted an empty seat next to Melissa Crane. At precisely 3:00 Dean Rutherford stood up and opened the meeting. She asked for faculty approval of the minutes from the last meeting and then reviewed the agenda for the current meeting. Following approval of the minutes and review of the agenda she announced that President Cannon and Randolph Bolles were present to discuss faculty scholarship issues. A barely discernable murmur ran through the room. She turned to Cannon and invited him to come to the front. The slightly stooped and thin-looking President of Kingston moved to the podium.

"As you all know the college is engaged in a debate as to the meaning of scholarship for this community and its implications for faculty and students. I have invited the chairman of the Board of Trustees to come today and say a few words from the board perspective. When he is finished we can entertain questions. Would you please welcome Randolph Bolles."

The applause was light and scattered as the barrel-chested Bolles, dressed in a dark blue sport coat and white shirt tie, lumbered to the front.

"Thank you for allowing me to come today," he began. As if the faculty had any choice, thought Peter. "For a while now there has been considerable debate among faculty and the board regarding the place of scholarship at Kingston College. You need to know that the Board of Trustees has a deep and abiding interest in quality scholarship at this place. The board is not interested in Kingston being anything but a world-class academic institution. Our faculty should be engaged in ongoing research and scholarship of the highest caliber. The road to a world-class academic institution is through a faculty committed to and actively participating in scholarship and research within their discipline. Now, I am only relaying the message of the Board of Trustees. So please don't shoot the messenger."

Bolles' attempt at humor didn't work.

"Furthermore, the Academic Affairs Committee of the Board of Trustees will only consider faculty for tenure and promotion who show evidence of the scholarship and research we are looking for."

At this point Bolles abruptly stopped. "Are there any questions?" he asked.

The lecture hall was silent. Peter glanced over at Dean Rutherford, who was looking straight ahead. Her face was emotionless. What was she thinking, he wondered?

The silence continued. Peter felt angry. Why wasn't anyone asking questions?

Peter raised his hand.

"Yes," said Bolles. "Do you have a question?"

"My name is Peter Kramer and I realize I am very new here. But I do wonder where teaching is in this discussion? You have made a strong pitch for scholarship and research and yet not mentioned teaching. I specifically recall a definite emphasis on teaching during my interview. Yet, I have not even heard you refer to teaching today." Peter sat down. Melissa gave him a subtle smile.

"Well, of course, teaching is important," responded Bolles. "I would never imply anything else. I believe good research and scholarship inspires good teaching. Anyone can teach, but the best teachers are grounded in their research and scholarship."

Peter stiffened. "So are you saying that the best teachers are those who are actively engaged in research and scholarship activities? Furthermore, are you suggesting that good teaching is more a matter of knowledge than skill?"

Bolles stared at Peter. "No, I am not advocating that. I think teaching and scholarship go hand in hand."

"I don't mean to be argumentative but that was not the message I heard in your opening statement. I heard a definite ordering of research and scholarship and then teaching."

Bolles was getting angry and red faced. "Well you misheard me, young man."

Peter let it drop and took the plunge.

"Mr. Bolles, may I ask you a second question?"

Bolles grunted a stifled yes. Cannon moved uneasily in his seat. Dean Rutherford was listening intently. Her face was now far from emotionless.

"You have used the words scholarship and research quite freely in this meeting and in others where I have been in attendance. It seems to me that with so much riding on these words we need to have a clear working definition we all at least understand, if not agree with. How would you define scholarship and research within the context of this college?"

Bolles paused. "First let me ask you what you mean when you say, 'with so much riding on these words'?"

Peter stood up. "You have used two words, scholarship and research, that can significantly impact the lives of many of the people in this room. Earlier you mentioned them in the context of promotion and tenure. If there is confusion as to their meaning, and, if teaching is emphasized less, this most surely will have an adverse impact on faculty. Standards for performance and promotion must be clear. This college certainly can't be operating on several different meanings when it comes to faculty evaluation. Furthermore, the reason I came to Kingston was because of its emphasis on teaching. I would imagine a majority of the faculty in this room came for the same reason. Any shift in the academic mission will have an impact on faculty perceptions of this place."

Cannon made a move to the podium but hesitated. Dean Rutherford and the vast majority of the faculty were enjoying the debate immensely.

Bolles felt agitated and cornered.

"This place cannot become the world-class institution it is capable of becoming without top caliber research and scholarship. Every faculty member must be immersed in scholarship and research within his or her discipline."

Peter was still standing. "Yes, you have already said that but how do you define these two terms? How do you know it isn't already happening?"

Bolles became angrier. "The faculty must define it with the board's participation. All I know is it isn't happening as much as it needs to."

Peter held his ground. "Don't you think you need to be far more specific? I understand and appreciate the need for dialogue but can't you come up with anything more specific than 'it isn't happening'? Wouldn't you agree we shouldn't let faculty careers rest on such ambiguity?"

At this point Dean Rutherford went up to the front to rescue Bolles. "We are running out of time and have several more agenda items," she said. "This important dialogue will continue. Thank you, Mr. Bolles, for coming."

Bolles stalked back to his seat next to Cannon. He glared up at Peter before turning his granite-like head back to the front.

Peter, his heart beating rapidly, could have kicked himself. He had promised he would stay out of campus politics. So what does he do? He mixes it up with the board chair in one of his first faculty meetings.

At 4:30 the faculty meeting ended and Cannon and Bolles quickly made their way out of the room. They appeared in no mood to socialize with anyone. Peter and Melissa walked out together and met Ted Wilson in the lobby. Peter noticed a number of faculty looking at him.

Turning to Ted and Melissa, Peter held up his hands and said, "I know, I shouldn't have just done that in there."

"You said what a lot of faculty have been thinking for a long time," replied Ted.

"I can't believe I stood up and said all of that having only been on the faculty for two months. But this is the third time I have heard Bolles go off like that. The first time was in new faculty orientation, the second at the board dinner and now today. He's like a loose cannon. No pun intended!"

Ted and Melissa laughed and then Ted said, "Peter, believe me, we all know how exasperating Randolph Bolles is. This has been going on for a long time. Originally he came on the board as the chair of the Academic Affairs committee which was bad enough. He drove the former dean crazy. Always spouting off about academic quality. Three years ago he became chairman of the board and has continued his campaign."

Peter stared at the two of them. "Do you know that Bolles told the new faculty at orientation that the Kingston faculty is mediocre?"

"Doesn't surprise me," said Melissa.

"Kingston has a very good faculty," continued Ted. "They are tremendously committed to the college, their students, and their disciplines. Bolles either fails to recognize this or thinks they should be doing more. Right now the faculty are pretty discouraged. Morale is low and tension is high."

"What about the rest of the board? How about Cannon, where is he in all of this?"

"The board is generally unaware of the tension. It's hard to argue against Bolles because it appears we are against scholarship and research. Nothing could be further from the truth. This faculty is doing research and scholarship. In some ways Bolles is a lone wolf with no resistance. Cannon is very supportive of scholarship and thus is in agreement with Bolles. But even if he weren't, Cannon would not stand up to Bolles. Frankly, James Cannon is so concerned with leaving a legacy of greatness he will resort to almost anything. I know this sounds harsh but it is true. The two of them are somewhat dangerous for this college."

Peter sighed. "Well, I hope I didn't dig too deep a hole. I meant everything I said in there, but at what cost?"

Melissa said, "I wouldn't worry too much. As long as you do a good job in the classroom, stay current in your field and conduct good scholarship, such as giving papers at conferences or publishing, you will be fine."

CHAPTER SEVENTEEN

THANKSGIVING 2002

Peter woke up late on Thanksgiving morning. The sun poured through the curtains, warming the bedroom and making him want to stay in bed. He lay there for a few minutes, his conversation with Randolph Bolles at the previous Friday's faculty meeting running through his mind. He finally got up and after shaving and showering placed a call to his parents. His dad answered on the first ring as if he had been waiting for Peter to call. He probably was, thought Peter. He talked with his parents, brother Dave, and sister Julie, who questioned him at length about Sarah. Julie would then tell his Mother all about her later in the kitchen. He could just picture it.

Peter had promised to help Mrs. Ashdown pot some flowers in preparation for winter. She was always getting him to help her with her flowers. Deep down he knew she liked his company. At 2:00 they would drive over to the Phillips's place for Thanksgiving dinner.

The weather was turning cloudy and a cold wind was blowing from the north as Peter and Mrs. Ashdown got into his MGB. She loved riding in the little sports car. They turned right on Green River Road and then left on Canterbury Lane. The wind was stirring the low overhanging trees on the narrow road, making it seem like they were traveling through a moving tunnel. Soon they reached Old Vermont Road and turned left towards the Phillips's house. As usual Sarah's dog Jamie was the first to greet them. The MGB was becoming a familiar sound to her.

Dinner was served in the formal dining room. Martha Phillips insisted on a traditional turkey dinner with all of the fixings. Having been born and raised in New England, she loved the Thanksgiving holiday. It was a year to the day since she had found John Phillips dead upstairs in their bedroom. She missed him dearly but in her stoic way believed things should continue as before. Today would be no different. Tall cranberry candles graced the Thanksgiving table as Nellie served dinner. Peter sat next to Sarah.

Mrs. Phillips and Mrs. Ashdown were delighted that Peter and Sarah were together. They had decided early on that Peter and Sarah were good for each other. The very day that Peter had walked into Mrs. Ashdown's study to inquire about the cottage she had called Martha and told her about him. Her intuition told her Peter would be a wonderful person for Sarah. Throughout the fall they had watched the relationship develop.

"Well Peter, how is your teaching going?" asked Martha.

His mouth full of turkey and gravy, Peter waited a few seconds and said, "In some ways this has been a really hard semester with all of my classes being taught for the first time. I had to prepare new lectures for each class. Outside of this, it has been a terrific experience. I love teaching and enjoy being at Kingston." He paused as if he had more to say but stopped.

Martha and Anne looked at each other.

"Peter, is there a problem?" Anne asked in her usual blunt way.

Sarah looked at him and elbowed him to say more.

"Well, I had a run-in with Randolph Bolles at last Friday's faculty meeting. We kind of got into a public argument over the issue of scholarship. I think he overemphasizes research and scholarship to the detriment of good teaching. He says he supports teaching but his actions say otherwise. I didn't want to get involved in campus politics but…" His voice trailed off.

"Did you talk to him after?" asked Martha.

"No, he and President Cannon left too fast."

"That boy is a menace," said an agitated Mrs. Ashdown. "What does he know about running a college? He is a retired know-it-all who likes to stick his nose into everything. Why, he's like a flash flood sweeping everything and everybody in its wake."

Peter and Sarah laughed. They appreciated Mrs. Ashdown's wit and honesty.

Over dessert, the conversation shifted to Leslie Patton.

"This must be a terribly sad holiday for the Pattons," said Martha.

"Has the official police report come back?" asked Anne. "I mean how could that car have run into her? The road is straight where she was hit. It's not like there was a curve."

"I've been wondering why Leslie was on Old Vermont Road so late on a Saturday night to begin with," said Sarah. "She lives on the East Side of town."

"Maybe she was seeing a man on the sly," said Martha.

"I can't think that's the case, Grandmother. She would have told me."

"Let's assume she was coming to see you, Sarah," said Peter. "What might have been the reason? Could it have been a personal problem? Something at work?"

Sarah thought about Peter's questions for a few moments. Was there something going on Leslie wanted to talk about? Was she in trouble?

Sarah looked directly at Peter. "Are you suggesting she was murdered? Why, that would be incredible. These things don't happen in Pinehurst."

"I'm not suggesting anything. I just think you shouldn't discount anything at this point."

"Peter, this is scary."

"Listen, I'm not trying to scare you. It's just that right now nothing adds up."

"This sounds a bit exciting," said Anne.

"Let's not jump to any conclusions," said Peter. He wished he hadn't alarmed the three of them with his questions. "It's probably a terribly unfortunate accident and nothing else."

"I'm sure that's it," said Martha Phillips. It was clear she was uneasy with the discussion. Today was the one-year anniversary of her late husband's death, and his sudden passing was still fresh in her mind.

At 9:00 it was evident a tired Anne Ashdown was ready to go home so they prepared to leave. Peter didn't want to go so early but he and Sarah were going to Boston early the next morning to do some shopping and sightseeing, so after thanking Mrs. Phillips he helped Mrs. Ashdown down the front porch stairs to his car. Sarah and a frisky Jamie walked out with them. After getting Mrs. Ashdown settled in the front passenger seat, he walked around the back of his car with Sarah. She held his hand tightly as if she didn't want him to go.

"I'm sorry about making everyone uneasy with all that talk about Leslie's death," Peter told Sarah. "I should have kept my thoughts to myself and mouth shut."

"No," she said quickly. "Maybe keeping it from Grandmother and Mrs. Ashdown is good but not from me. I love to hear what you are thinking. You seem to see things from a different perspective. Maybe it's because you aren't from around here. Actually, I have been wondering a few things myself but just haven't said anything. Can we talk more on our trip to Boston?"

"Of course we can," he said.

Peter was aware of Mrs. Ashdown waiting in the front seat. He didn't want to give her too much ammunition. He said good night to Sarah with a quick but intense embrace before hopping into the car. She stood with Jamie in the cold night air and watched as he drove away into the New Hampshire night.

CHAPTER EIGHTEEN

The Friday after Thanksgiving began as a typical late fall day in central New Hampshire. Temperatures were in the low fifties under threatening gray clouds. Rain was in the air but had yet to start. Hundreds of white seagulls had taken refuge from bad weather at sea and were occupying the green grass of the college soccer field. The weather forecasters promised a heavy wind and rainstorm would move inland later that afternoon. Peter picked up Sarah at 8:00 A.M. and after discussing the weather, they made the decision to still go to Boston. The only change they made was to take Sarah's BMW because it had a hard top and a better heater. Peter left his MGB parked in the Phillips's four-car garage right next to John Phillips's old Chrysler New Yorker.

As Peter and Sarah drove through town and headed east toward Concord on the White Mountain Highway, a tired Dr. Morris Glenn sat with his head slumped on the worn oak roll top desk in his study at his old white clapboard house on College Avenue. Papers were strewn all over as if he had been frantically looking for something. In truth he had. He was supposed to have lunch with Thomas Lawton at 12:00 at the College

Inn. Somehow he had misplaced a two-thousand-dollar check he was to give to Lawton that day. Money he owed from a long-standing debt. A shiny sheen of sweat glazed his wrinkled forehead. His heart beat far too rapidly for a man his age. He detested Thomas Lawton. How had he ever gotten mixed up with him? It was a question that always had the same answer. Gambling! Somehow that weasel Lawton had found out he had a gambling problem and had come to him four years ago with an offer. Lawton promised never to reveal Morris's gambling problem if the doctor would do small favors for him from time to time. Lawton also promised to lend him money when he needed it. In a state of near panic, Morris agreed. At first the small favors were easy. Lawton wanted information on the medical condition of various people in Pinehurst. So Morris would tell him who he was treating for what illnesses or who came to him with such highly confidential conditions as unwanted pregnancies. Morris knew he was violating his patients' confidentiality by giving out such information but he was trapped. If his gambling and debt problems became public, he would be ruined. Lawton had him right where he wanted him. He fed his gambling with high interest loans and threatened to reveal his deep secret if he didn't cooperate on other matters. Gradually he had been drawn deeper into Lawton's web and turning back became impossible. Dr. Morris Glenn had unethically and illegally given away far too much patient information and was liable for serious civil action as well as the probable loss of his medial license. He disliked himself almost as much as he disliked Lawton.

Today Morris was expected to repay the two-thousand-dollar loan from Lawton that was months overdue. Slowly he picked up his head and continued rummaging through his untidy desk. A few minutes later, to his immense relief, he located the check under a stack of overdue bills. The bills could wait, he muttered to himself as he held the check tightly.

At exactly 12:00 Dr. Morris Glenn arrived at the College Inn. He was always punctual, something he had learned from his medical training. Ten minutes later Thomas Lawton strolled in wearing a shiny blue suit. He quickly located Morris and made his way through the maze of tables stopping at one or two to greet people. Morris hated being seen with Lawton. The man was not his type. What must people think, he wondered to himself?

"Afternoon, Morris," said Lawton smoothly.

"Hello," replied Morris.

"Do you have my money?" asked Lawton indelicately and a bit too loud.

Morris wordlessly handed over the check. He looked around to see if anyone was watching them.

Lawton carefully scrutinized the check before putting it in his pocket. He didn't even have the courtesy to say thank you, thought Morris disgustedly.

Over a lunch of shrimp and split pea soup, the two discussed business. Once again Lawton requested some sensitive information on one of Morris's patients. The old doctor was visibly reluctant. Lawton immediately observed his hesitation and fixed him with a hard stare. "Listen, Dr. Glenn," he said hotly, "don't fool around. One word from me and this entire town, as well as the New Hampshire State Medical Association, hears all about you. Are we clear?"

Morris nodded in resignation. "I'll have what you want by Wednesday."

The lunch meeting ended at 1:30. Morris Glenn sat at their table in the now near-empty restaurant long after Lawton left. He knew he was in an impossible situation. He was violating the law as well as his own deeply held convictions but the alternative was equally unacceptable. He couldn't face losing his reputation, his medical practice, and possibly his wife. Lawton confidently knew this. After a few minutes more Morris slowly trudged out to his old Buick, his heart heavy. As usual he had paid for both lunches.

Peter and Sarah reached Concord and headed south toward Massachusetts on Route 93. Traffic was light until they approached Boston. A light rain was beginning to fall. For almost the entire trip they had talked about Sarah. Peter was fascinated with Sarah's story of her parents' death in the small plane crash on Mount Washington and her life with John and Martha Phillips. She recalled very little except for her grandmother holding her on her lap and crying softly as the snowstorm raged outside. From that day on she lived with her grandparents and obviously never saw her parents again, not even at the funeral with its two closed caskets. She was too young and besides their bodies were too badly burned. She grew up in her grandparents' home with only pictures and stories of her mother and father. John Phillips was a tall and powerfully built man who adored Sarah. He would take her to Phillips Textiles headquarters and let her play with the adding machines. She loved numbers and calculations. During high school she worked part-time in the accounting and finance department of Phillips Textiles, quickly amazing everyone with her aptitude for math. Her grandfather would proudly poke his head in the office as he passed on his way to another of his innumerable meetings. John Phillips was widely known as a stubborn man who refused to let any obstacle get in his way. He was often described as a mixture of tenacity and generosity. Sarah loved this about him. He could act like a tough and relentless businessman one moment and help an employee with a family crisis the next. Sarah was just like him.

By 10:30 they were in the heart of a very crowded Boston

looking for a parking space near Boston Common. Peter suddenly spotted a Ford escort maneuvering to leave a tight parking space. He quickly drove up and, putting his blinker on, waited patiently. In a few minutes they were parked and walking along a noisy Commonwealth Avenue toward Macy's to do some Christmas shopping. The huge department store was packed with day after Thanksgiving shoppers. Sarah wanted to buy presents for her grandmother and Anne Ashdown while Peter looked for something for his parents. They took their time enjoying the sights and smells of the green and ivy Christmas decorations. Peter usually disliked shopping and the crowds that went with it but today was different. In his heart he knew Sarah made that difference. He could have shopped all day with her. About 1:30 they finished and, loaded with presents, went back to Sarah's car and placed them in the trunk. Peter filled the meter with quarters again and taking her hand they made their way through the rain-drenched Common in the direction of Park Street Congregational Church. Soon the old stately church loomed ahead. They came to the corner and headed east across busy Boylston Street to a small Italian restaurant. Inside Peter and Sarah ordered the best lasagna Peter had ever eaten. The red-checkered tables and small glowing candles created an inviting atmosphere.

"I used to come here a lot when I lived in Boston," said Sarah.

Peter looked at her rosy cheeks and blue eyes as he savored the good food. In a moment he said, "I'd rather be here with you this minute than anywhere else in the whole world."

She blushed and went silent. Peter was afraid he had said the wrong thing.

"It's ironic," she finally said, "but I lived in Boston for over four years and thought I'd meet a really great guy. I mean, look around, this city is full of eligible men. I met my share I guess but no one special. Then I decide to move back home to little old Pinehurst and lo and behold you come along. Peter Kramer from Nanuet, New York, who suddenly comes to live and work in Pinehurst. Meeting you was the very last thing I expected." She paused looking right at him. "I'm glad I came home."

Peter felt his face flush.

They finished lunch and holding hands walked out of the small restaurant. Outside the wind and rain had increased in intensity. Huddled together against the storm's onslaught they made their way along Boylston Street in the direction of Commonwealth Avenue and Sarah's car. They were almost in the front of the Bank of Boston entrance when Peter looked up just in time to see a vaguely familiar figure hurrying into the bank.

"Hey, isn't that Walton Trent?" he asked.

"I didn't see, my head was down," Sarah said.

"Shall we go in and see?" he asked.

Without waiting for an answer he almost pulled her through the massive entrance and into a huge and ornately decorated foyer with a shiny marble floor. Shaking off the dripping water from their coats they looked across and saw a bank of elevators. A group of men and women stood with their backs to Peter and Sarah waiting for an elevator to open. Soon a light went on at the same time a ping sounded and the group of strangers stepped into the empty elevator. As the door began to close, the group of riders turned as if choreographed and faced the foyer. There in the midst of the crowded elevator stood Walton Trent, immaculately dressed in a wool gray suit and a black overcoat looking across the way directly at Peter and Sarah. His face was devoid of expression. Peter felt a chill at the same moment he felt Sarah's hand gripping his tightly. The elevator doors closed smoothly and Trent's face, still staring at them both, disappeared. Wordlessly, Peter and Sarah exited the venerable old Boston bank.

Back on Boylston Street the wind and driving rain greeted them.

"I know he recognized us," Sarah said. "He was looking right at us. Now that was spooky. Why didn't he wave or smile?"

"I can't believe I did that," Peter said. "He was probably on college business. Does Kingston do any business with Bank of Boston?"

"No," replied Sarah. "We do our regular banking with New Hampshire Bank. We may work with other banks from time to time on personal gifts or bequests."

"Maybe it was that or he was there on personal business?" suggested Peter, looking for a plausible explanation.

"All dressed up like that?" she asked.

"I don't know what he was doing there but I sure hope he doesn't think we were spying on him."

They walked on in the rain toward Sarah's car. It was almost 4:00. Reaching her white BMW, Peter opened the door for Sarah and after hopping in quickly started the car so they could get warm. Originally they had planned to visit the Museum of Fine Arts but after a short discussion decided to head back to New Hampshire. It would be dark soon and the wind and rain were worsening.

Peter was lost in thought as they headed out on Storrow Drive along the Charles River The lights of Cambridge sparkled off of the dark river as they drove along its edge. Peter was mad at himself for so quickly giving in to his impulse to run into the bank and confirm if indeed the figure was Walton Trent. The guy had a legitimate right to be there and Peter had no business following him.

Sarah interrupted his thoughts. "Peter, do you remember last night at Grandmother's when I told you there was something I wanted to talk with you about?

"I remember, Sarah." He somehow knew it was about Leslie's death.

"Well, I hate to be suspicious but I think there is something funny going on at the college." She paused as if unsure whether to continue.

"Go on," he said keeping his eyes on the fast-moving traffic. He noticed they were passing Massachusetts General Hospital.

"I should have told you this earlier but was afraid to get you mixed up in whatever is happening." She took a deep breath.

"Leslie was killed late Saturday night. I didn't hear about it until I came to work Monday morning. Of course we were all in shock. I went over to her parents' house that morning and then came back to work after lunch. I had some work to do but was really looking for something to occupy my time so I logged onto my campus e-mail to check for messages and found one from Leslie. The date and time was 9:00 P.M. Saturday. She was writing me this message from her office shortly before her accident. The note was brief and mysterious, so I decided to print it off."

Sarah pulled a folded piece of paper from her coat pocket and read it aloud to Peter as he drove.

Sarah, I need to talk with you ASAP. Something is going on. Please call me as soon as you can. I better not say anymore on the network. NYNYNY. Leslie

Sarah continued talking. "Do you remember I told you I thought Leslie was coming to see me at Grandmother's that Saturday night? Well, I think she really was trying to see me. No matter how late it was. I believe she originally intended to wait until I read the e-mail message but changed her mind and decided to drive to Grandmother's that very night."

"Yeah, but that doesn't prove it wasn't an accident," said Peter.

"I know, but there is one more thing. On Tuesday morning I logged on to my e-mail again to reread the message and it was gone. Somebody had deleted Leslie's message to me. I know I didn't. Something like that has never happened before. Why would anyone want to delete her message?'

"Can't e-mail messages disappear by electronic accident?" Peter asked, trying to play devil's advocate.

"Sure, it's possible, but unlikely."

Peter didn't let her see the concern on his face. Looking straight ahead he asked, "What do you think is going on, Sarah?"

"It's puzzling. I haven't any idea. Leslie wasn't the type to get into trouble. She lived a pretty tame life. This is all very peculiar."

By 6:00 Peter and Sarah had arrived back in Pinehurst. During their trip back the winds had increased and were blowing branches and some small trees down. The pounding rain had made visibility very difficult. As they drove into town they noticed street lights swaying in the driving wind and minor flooding along some streets. They continued on to the Phillips's home where a relieved Martha Phillips met them at the door. Peter dropped Sarah off and drove home to check on Anne Ashdown. He would see Sarah later that night for dinner. Driving down Canterbury Lane he found several small trees blocking the road and about a foot of standing water that had spilled out of the creek. He had to get out and struggle with the trees before continuing on. He finally arrived home and immediately went to check on Mrs. Ashdown. Like Martha Phillips she was greatly relieved to see Peter. He was soaked but grateful to be home. He jumped into a hot shower.

CHAPTER NINETEEN

On Sunday afternoon and evening after the long Thanksgiving weekend students began streaming back into Pinehurst. The side streets and college residence hall parking lots began filling up with cars and the quiet town was transformed once again. The men's and women's soccer teams had both lost in the semifinals of the New England small college championships, wiping out any chance for them to go the nationals. The women's volleyball team did win the New England championships and were scheduled to fly out on Friday to the national championships in Oklahoma City. The basketball season was about to begin, with a men's and a women's game on Friday at home in Phillips Fieldhouse. Basketball season was very popular in Pinehurst. The competitive men's and women's programs helped make the long New England winter tolerable. The college theater department's fall production of *Our Town* was scheduled to begin its first of six performances on Thursday evening. On Sunday, December 5, the annual Christmas Festival of Music and Lights would be held in the Fieldhouse. This was one of the music department's major productions of the year.

At 7:00 Monday morning Peter was elbow deep in student

tests and papers that needed grading. He had done very little grading over the Thanksgiving weekend. He and Sarah had spent most of the time together. He reflected on the weekend with a smile. They were thoroughly enjoying each other's company. He was anxious for his parents to meet her. Glancing up at the clock he realized he had only a few minutes before his 8:00 class. He turned his attention back to the work at hand.

Sarah arrived at work promptly at 8:00. Walking into the office she almost bumped into Dan Miller, who was waiting impatiently for something to come out of the fax machine. He looked up and said, "You're just the person I want to see. Can you come down to my office in a minute?"

"Sure," she said. "Give me a minute to get settled in my office."

Five minutes later she was in Miller's office. He motioned for her to sit down. He was still holding the fax in his left hand.

"Sarah, I've got something in my hand that is none of my business." He waved the fax in the air. "It has to do with Leslie Patton's death. Do you want me to continue or shall I take it straight to James Cannon? In other words, do you want to get involved? I know you and Leslie were good friends."

Sarah didn't move. "What is it, Dan?" she asked.

"Captain Donald Parker of the New Hampshire State Police is a long-time friend. We grew up together. The Accident Investigation Unit is under his command. Last week I ran into him and he asked me what I knew about Leslie Patton. I asked him why and he told me that the investigation of her death was drawing to a close with some interesting results. Naturally curious, I asked him what he meant. He promised to fax me a summary of the findings. That's what is in my hand." He waved the paper again.

Sarah swallowed hard. She remembered her conversation with Corporal Bisset at the scene of the accident. What had she found?

Dan handed her the fax and sat back in his chair while she read the report summary. He watched her carefully.

Five minutes later she put the fax down and sat there with her eyes closed. The State Police had concluded that Leslie Patton had been the victim of an intentional hit-and-run driver. Finding no skid marks or evidence that the vehicle had taken evasive action to avoid hitting Leslie, and due to the fact that the precise place she was hit was on a straight stretch of the road, the report 's conclusion was clear. Leslie Patton had been intentionally run down and killed.

"Sarah, are you all right?" Dan asked.

She nodded silently. She wasn't all right. Suddenly she felt cold and very scared.

"I'm going to have to give this to James Cannon. The State Police are now actively investigating her death. The President needs to know."

"Of course, you'd better tell him," she said. She wanted to leave and go see Peter.

Dan Miller stood up and walked around his desk. "I'm sorry about Leslie. Let's hope the police catch the killer."

Sarah left Miller's office in a daze.

Sarah and Peter met for lunch in the student union café. The popular eating place was packed with students and faculty. They found a table by the window overlooking the campus. The trees had lost almost all of their colorful leaves, giving the grounds a bleak, cold appearance. Peter recalled his interview in the spring when he had first eaten in the café. Sarah filled him in on her conversation with Dan Miller and particularly the State Police findings.

"Well, this certainly puts a different slant on things," he said. "Up to this point I hoped her death was an accident. This changes everything."

"What do you mean by that?"

"Sarah, your friend was murdered less than two miles from your home. She probably was trying to see you that night. She had something very important to tell you. Her e-mail message probably confirms that. At the very least it suggests the possibility. Her death means someone didn't want her talking."

Sarah bit her lip in deep thought. She tasted the warm blood on her tongue. She looked hard at Peter.

"Let me tell you what I think you aren't saying. If Leslie was coming to see me, then I may be in some danger? Is that what you are concerned about? You have worry all over your face."

Peter's eyes surveyed the café before returning to meet her look.

"I don't know what's going on here. Let's look at what we do know. Leslie was murdered. She wrote a mysterious e-mail message to you deleted by someone a few days later. Your friend knew something, was afraid of that knowledge, and was killed. This we do know."

"What about my relationship with Leslie? Obviously the mystery person who deleted her message to me knows I read her message. He can simply check the history and see the date and time that I read her message. This person knows I know she was trying to get information to me and that she died two miles from my house shortly after sending me the e-mail message. I can't help but think I'm in danger."

"I can understand your reasoning," responded Peter. "But you are basing your conclusion on the fact that Leslie's message alarmed you. Of course you and I know it did but that doesn't necessarily mean the person who deleted your message believes it alarmed you. And even if it did, Leslie died before she could talk to you. You don't know what she wanted and the people who killed her know she never reached you. They made sure of that."

"You make sense but I'm still nervous. My goodness, Leslie

Patton was killed and the last thing she was doing while alive was trying to see me."

Peter placed his hand on hers. "Listen, you have a right to be nervous. This is hitting too close to home. What we need to do now is keep our wits about us and figure out what in the hell is going on. I'm sure you are being watched. Me too. So we better behave as if everything is normal. Let's not give these people, whoever they are, any reason to be nervous. Leslie made them nervous and they killed her. We can't make the same mistake."

"You sound like James Bond," she grinned. "Do you really think we are being watched? This is Pinehurst, New Hampshire, and Kingston College for heaven's sake. The most exciting thing that ever happened here is when a farmer's barn burns. What you are suggesting happens in the big city."

"Sarah, I can't believe this any more than you. All I wanted to do was come to this college and begin my teaching career. I've got enough on my mind with four classes and 150 students. I'm certainly not looking for adventure. But the reality is we have stumbled upon a mystery and it involves someone's death. To some degree we both have become involved."

Sarah's eyes roamed the still crowded café as if looking for clues. Maybe they were being watched now.

"What do we do next?" she asked.

"I've been thinking about that," said Peter. "Let the police investigate Leslie's death and see what they come up with."

"What about the e-mail message? Should I give it to the police? Do I tell them I think she was coming to see me that night?"

Peter paused. "I don't know. Let's give that some more thought."

CHAPTER TWENTY

The next day the President's Cabinet met for their usual weekly meeting. James Cannon was in an upbeat mood. He reported on the substantial gift from Henry Townsend: two million towards the capital campaign and a significant amount in a bequest to the college. Cannon told the other vice presidents that Henry Townsend wanted the amount he was leaving the college in his will kept confidential. He also told them he and Trent would be working hard to raise money in the next five months.

Elisabeth Rutherford told the cabinet of a recent meeting she had with Randolph Bolles concerning the quality of academic scholarship at the college.

"This man continues to be almost obsessive about scholarship at this place," she said exasperated. "I wish he would look around and see what our faculty is doing. We have a strong faculty engaged in some very good scholarship. This is getting to be a serious matter. Faculty morale is low."

At this point Cannon interrupted her. "Elisabeth, Randolph Bolles and I share the same concern. We have the potential to be one of the finest liberal arts colleges in New England

and along the eastern seaboard. We must elevate the level of faculty scholarship in order to achieve this dream."

"James, if this is the board's intention, then it is going to change the kind of institution we have been for over 100 years. Historically we have been a very fine liberal arts college with a primary emphasis on teaching. Our institutional mission is one that emphasizes teaching and scholarship. The shift you and Bolles are talking about is primarily scholarship. Oh, he won't admit it but in truth teaching is a lower priority. Do you have any idea how much this will change the face of his college?"

Cannon bristled. "Elisabeth, you are wrong. Randolph Bolles and I both place a high priority on teaching."

She fought on. "Let me give you an example of how things are changing. At our last Board of Trustees meeting the Academic Affairs office presented for promotion several faculty members. Now as you know, faculty promotion recommendations must first go through the Academic Affairs committee of the board. The pattern is becoming clear. The board is extremely reluctant to approve faculty with strong teaching evaluations unless a publication record accompanies them. During this last board meeting we had a particular faculty member who is heavily involved in research. Unfortunately this teacher's classroom teaching is mediocre at best. Do you know what happened at the committee meeting? Each committee member is sent a file on each faculty promotion recommendation, which includes a summary of their teaching evaluations. This particular faculty member's promotion was approved with no mention of her teaching. The board was so focused on the faculty member's scholarship that they promoted a mediocre teacher. Now, we have a teacher in the classroom who is not cutting it. Whether you like it or not, or are willing to admit it, this institution's academic mission is shifting.

"Furthermore, the college is going to have to take a long

hard look at faculty teaching loads if we are going to raise expectations for scholarship. Increased resources for research will be necessary. A case in point is the new faculty development program. We must fund this if we are going to expect to grow and develop our faculty."

Cannon's face reddened from the exchange. He wanted Kingston to be a college with a great reputation. It frustrated him when Elisabeth Rutherford and others like her stood in his way.

"Let's talk about this later, shall we?" he said to her, cutting her off.

The meeting continued for several more hours. Dan Miller reported that the institutional budget was current with virtually no overruns up to this point in the fiscal year. This was good news. Miller continued talking.

"Now the faculty development program is not anywhere in the regular budget since it is part of the capital campaign. I agree with Elisabeth on the merits of the program but at present there is no provision in the faculty development program for lowering annual faculty teaching loads. If we were to lower a regular teaching load from the fixed 24-hour load to let's say 21 teaching hours, the impact on the regular budget would be an increase in adjunct teaching costs of approximately $500,000. Our budget simply can't absorb this extra cost. Where is this money going to come from?" Miller asked.

This was exactly the kind of pressure James Cannon detested. He hated being asked thorny money questions without easy answers. He would do almost anything to avoid these complex questions.

"Walton and I realize the importance of this issue. We will continue to raise money for Kingston including non-designated funds for such needs as lowering faculty loads."

Walton Trent seemed to come alive. "That's if we think

lowering faculty loads is an appropriate goal," he said with an obvious edge to his voice. "Who determined this to be an institutional goal? I don't remember any discussion let alone a decision. We have enough financial needs at this place without trying to soften the workloads of a faculty already underworked."

Elisabeth tensed. "What do you know about the appropriate workload of a faculty member? How dare you presume that our faculty are underworked?" She glared at Trent.

"I know enough when I see faculty leaving the campus at 3:00 or when some faculty don't even come in on certain days of the week." He looked at Elisabeth smugly.

Elisabeth was livid. "You simply don't know what you are talking about. You've never taught in college and can't possibly know the time it takes to prepare for the academic classroom. You speak out of ignorance!" She cast Trent a withering look.

"Folks, folks, let's not let this get out of hand. We all have enough pressure to go around. We must support one another. Elisabeth, you may believe Walton speaks from inexperience but you must admit you do too. Honestly, do you have any idea what it is like to raise money? The pressure is enormous."

"Let me be brief and to the point, James. This college cannot continue to have such high scholarship expectations of its faculty and at the same time increase class sizes given the current 24-hour teaching load."

It was clear the debate would go nowhere. Cannon realized this and asked everyone to try and understand each other. He had no solution to the vexing problems presented by his vice presidents. The meeting concluded with a brief update from Cassandra Butler on the drinking party in one of the fraternities in which the police had to be called to break up a brawl. Several students were being suspended and the fraternity had been placed on probation for a year. Kingsford had a zero tolerance policy on drinking and fighting. Students were immediately suspended when this occurred.

At 11:30 the cabinet meeting ended. Cannon lingered around to try and smooth things over with Elisabeth. Trent left immediately.

CHAPTER TWENTY-ONE

Thursday afternoon of the same week Dr. Morris Glenn was urgently called to the home of Jack and Phyllis Allen, patients of his for over 22 years. Phyllis was the daughter of old Samuel Stone, a wealthy businessman from Concord. She had married Jack Allen in 1955, over her father's strong objections. Jack was a local who was employed by the City of Pinehurst. Stone and his daughter had never reconciled and in 1964 he had died a bitter old man. Much to Phyllis's surprise her father left her his entire estate valued at slightly over $8 million. She had wisely reinvested the money and by 1997 her net worth was over $17 million. In 1999, James Cannon and Walton Trent had persuaded Phyllis Allen to include the college in her will. She had two daughters who graduated from Kingston, one of whom returned to work as a reference librarian in the college library. After several years of nurturing Phyllis Allen, Trent and Cannon were delighted to see her declare Kingston in her will. The actual bequest amount was kept confidential, as was the college's practice.

Morris pulled his old Buick into the driveway of the Allens' modest home. He wasn't surprised to see a Pinehurst fire rescue truck. He had received a frantic call from Jack Allen 10 minutes earlier.

"Phyllis isn't breathing," he screamed into the phone. "I was supposed to wake her from her afternoon nap but I can't." He sobbed into the phone.

Morris immediately called 911 and had the rescue truck respond before running to his car and hurrying to the Allen place. He also called Thomas Lawton, the family attorney, and told him to go over to the Allen home. Lawton was there before Morris Glenn arrived.

Inside he found two emergency medical technicians from the Pinehurst fire department furiously working on Phyllis Allen. Jack was sitting in a chair across the room, shaking with fright. In contrast, Phyllis's face was gray and peaceful looking. The medical personnel could not find a pulse and were readying her for the trip to Pinehurst Hospital. Morris knew that it was too late. Phyllis Allen had a history of degenerative heart trouble. He could tell just by looking at her face that she was gone. Realizing he could be of no help to the emergency personnel he went over to comfort Jack. He helped him stand up and drove him to the hospital behind the rescue truck. Once at the hospital Jack called their one daughter at the college, who came over immediately. Morris went into the emergency room and assisted the emergency room doctor with Phyllis. She had earlier that year requested no heroic measure be taken if quality of life couldn't be sustained. After 10 minutes of hard work Dr. Cary Wilson pronounced her dead. The highly trained medical staff knew their work was done. Nothing more could be humanly done for Phyllis Allen.

Out in the waiting room Morris and Dr. Wilson quietly told a weeping Jack Allen and his composed but grief-stricken daughter Cindy. They requested to see the body and followed Morris back into the emergency room.

CHAPTER TWENTY-TWO

Dan Miller was in his office three days later when he received a call from Thomas Lawton. As attorney for the Allen family, he was filling Dan in on Phyllis Allen's will and the money she had left the college. Dan was surprised at the amount of money she had bequeathed to the college. He was also pleased to hear it was undesignated and thus could be used for anything the college deemed necessary. He hung up the phone and called Sarah Phillips.

She came down to his office in a few minutes and Dan told her about Phyllis Allen's will. Sarah was also surprised at the amount which Dan asked she keep confidential at the family's request. He then asked her to set up the account and legal documentation for receiving the money, which he anticipated in about four weeks.

"The actual check will be coming from the Bank of Boston," said Miller.

"How does that work?" she asked. The Bank of Boston reference had startled her.

"What do you mean?" asked Miller. He looked up at Sarah.

"Well, I didn't think we used the Bank of Boston. I guess I'm also surprised this was the Allens' bank."

"Of course we use the Bank of New Hampshire to do regular college banking but with bequests and wills we use the Bank of Boston. It's simple really. Walton Trent and James Cannon want to funnel all major gifts and requests through the Bank of Boston. When a bequest comes through we ask the family attorneys to route the paperwork through the Bank of Boston. They don't care where it goes first, just that it gets to the college. Trent tells me that with such large amounts of money sitting in one spot for any length of time we can accrue a decent amount of interest. I have the paperwork to show he's right. I hate to admit he's right however."

"So, the Allens don't normally use the Bank of Boston." said Sarah. "We will just have their attorney send the money to the Bank of Boston, which will in turn send it to the college."

"That's right. I think they use the First National Bank of Concord."

"I guess I still don't understand why it's done this way outside of the interest earned."

"Well, the amount of interest can be substantial. I'm always willing to wait a few weeks or even months for a large sum of money if it is earning interest elsewhere."

"Yes, but why not immediately take the money and put it into our college investment portfolio? Wouldn't this earn a greater return? Especially given the large principal we are working with?"

Miller paused. "Actually that's technically correct. But the paperwork and transaction costs mitigate against doing this. It's almost easier to keep it in the Bank of Boston for the short term. Of course, once we decide where the money is going, it is then diverted to our portfolio account if that's the intention. Anyway, Cannon and Trent think using the Bank of

Boston as the central clearinghouse for these sums of money is more efficient. They would rather have one bank handle all of the bequests that came to Kingston. Trent knows all the right people at Bank of Boston to make the necessary transactions quickly and without a lot of red tape. Actually I can understand and appreciate that. I hate dealing with bank people I hardly know. I like to be able to be free to call the same person at the bank."

Sarah decided not to ask Dan any more questions. His answers seemed logical. She walked back to her office and wrote herself a note to begin creating the documentation for Phyllis Allen's bequest. She couldn't wait to see Peter.

CHAPTER TWENTY-THREE

The first basketball game of the season was Friday night at 7:00. Kingston was playing Colby College from Maine. Peter picked Sarah up at 6:30. Leaving the MG running he went in and chatted with Martha and fluffed Jamie's soft red ears as he ate a chocolate chip cookie fresh out of Nellie's oven. Saying their good-byes they went out into the cold evening. The little car was warm and cozy as they zipped along Old Vermont Road towards the Kingston campus. The men's team was coming off a 20-win season from last year and with three new freshmen recruits they looked even stronger this year. Peter was especially excited to see two of his students play.

Peter pulled up to the almost full Phillips Fieldhouse parking lot at 6:40 and found a parking space for compacts far from the entrance. They showed their employee ID cards at the door and walked into the brightly-lit fieldhouse. Peter was struck with the immense size of the gymnasium and the crowd of people already in their seats. The student section was full and incredibly noisy and the game hadn't even started. A band was playing but the main attraction was a thin, frizzy-haired drummer who was playing with great energy and facial contortions that matched the beat of his drum. Students were dancing in the aisles and down on the floor. Peter estimated the gym held 5,000 people. A reserved seating section with cushioned seats was situated in the middle. The student section was just to the right of the reserved section and all along the north end of the gym. To the visiting basketball team, the student section was indeed imposing. The Kingston team in their striking green and white uniforms was lined up doing lay-ups. A number of the players would dunk the ball, each time bringing a roar from the crowd, especially the students. The atmosphere was festive.

Peter and Sarah chose to sit between the students and reserved seating section. They were six rows up from the floor right behind the Kingston team bench. Shortly before the game started Peter happened to look over into the reserved seats and saw James Cannon, dressed in a red cardigan sweater, and Walton Trent in a black turtleneck pullover talking animatedly. They seemed oblivious to the noise all around them. He turned back to Sarah and quietly motioned her to look in their direction.

"I wonder what those two are so engrossed in," he said to Sarah.

"Who knows, it seems like they are always together," she replied.

Soon the public address announcer welcomed people to the game and then introduced a heavyset young woman dressed in a blue-gray suit who sang the national anthem. The crowd rose in unison and immediately quieted as she confidently held the mike and began singing. Her strong voice impressed Peter as she sang with poise and incredible energy. As she ended, the crowd, especially the students yelled and applauded their appreciation.

The game began with Kingston taking a 10-point lead just

minutes into the game. The students were wild in their enthusiasm. Kingston had a six foot four guard who took six shots, making all but one. Colby had trouble stopping him. Kingston passed the ball with precision and as a result got a lot of easy shots. Their defense was stifling. Colby College was good but no match for the quicker and more athletic Kingston players. Peter was surprised at the quality of basketball. At halftime Kingston led Colby by 22 points.

The players ran off the floor to their locker rooms while the band played and students screamed at the opposing players. Peter and Sarah left their seats and stood in line at the concession stand for a Coke. Drinks in hand they walked to the other end of the crowded lobby where Sarah told Peter about her conversation earlier that day with Dan Miller.

"You mean to say Trent probably was on college business at the Bank of Boston when we saw him?" asked Peter.

"It looks like it," she replied.

"Miller told me that Cannon and Trent think it is more efficient to funnel all of the money from bequests and wills through one bank. Miller loves the interest the college earns on these substantial sums of money so he's happy to oblige."

"How does it work?"

"Easy! The college asks the family attorney to have the money sent directly to the Bank of Boston rather than the college. The family doesn't care. The Bank of Boston holds onto the money until the college needs it. Miller doesn't think it's worth reinvesting the money into the college portfolio account until it has been decided exactly what to do with the money."

Peter thought about her explanation. It did make sense. Walton Trent certainly had a purpose for being at the bank that day.

"Of course that doesn't explain Trent's unfriendly glare,"

she said. "That look still bothers me. It was as if he didn't like us seeing him."

"That's a bit of a stretch, don't you think? Maybe he was embarrassed or deep in thought," Peter said. "Shouldn't we give him the benefit of the doubt?"

Sarah was hesitant. "One thing I know for sure. My friend Leslie was murdered. She was frightened of something and was at her office right before she died. I'm not so willing to give Walton Trent the benefit of the doubt. At least not yet."

Peter was surprised at her intensity. It was incredible to even speculate that someone at the college murdered Leslie Patton. Why would someone at Kingston kill her? It just didn't make sense. This is a college in a small town. These things just don't happen. Peter had to admit that the circumstances were strange. Of course maybe being at her office was entirely unrelated to her murder.

They walked back into the loud and raucous gymnasium for the second half. Cannon and Trent were still in their seats. The game resumed with Kingston continuing to dominate. Midway through the second half, Kingston had built its lead to 35 points and the coach was sending in his second team to try to avoid running up the score. With about nine minutes left Peter saw James Cannon and Walton Trent stand up preparing to leave. Peter was surprised and curious. It seemed a little inappropriate for the college president to leave a basketball game before it was over. Peter wondered where they were going.

"Let's follow them," he whispered to Sarah.

Her eyes lit up. "OK, but we better be really careful."

They waited and watched as the two men worked their way down the stands to the main floor. The noise continued to be deafening as Cannon and Trent walked out. Thirty seconds later Peter and Sarah also left the gym. Once in the lobby they spotted them leaving through the main doors to the parking lot. Peter slowed down and took Sarah's hand continuing in the same direction. Out in the dark cold night they saw Cannon and Trent getting into a blue Lincoln Continental. Peter quickly memorized the license plate as it headed out of the parking lot towards town. Peter and Sarah sprinted to the outer end of the parking lot and jumped into the MG.

"LL 656," he repeated three times to her. "That's the license plate. Write it down."

Peter pushed the small gas pedal to the floor and headed to town.

"They went towards the center of town, but where do you think they are going?" he asked her. Meanwhile he kept his eyes riveted on the road ahead.

"I don't know. They might be going to the College Inn for a late dinner or to the New Hampshire House, a restaurant and bar. It's the most exclusive eating place we have in Pinehurst."

"We'll check both," said Peter his eyes staring straight ahead. "You know I'm not sure why we are doing this but my gut tells me something isn't right at Kingston College. Call it a hunch! Things don't add up. Walton Trent doesn't seem like the typical Kingston employee. He's slick and intimidating. James Cannon is driven by whatever demons, and Randolph Bolles has an unrealistic view of things and uses his position as chairman of the board to exert an inordinate amount of pressure. Is this all related or are they just off doing their own thing?"

Pinehurst was very quiet as they circled the brightly lit town commons and headed towards the College Inn. Slowly driving by the Inn, Peter and Sarah's eyes scanned the parking lot for the big Lincoln. It was nowhere in sight. Sarah instructed Peter to head back to the commons and go a half-mile south on a tree-lined street to the New Hampshire House. They came upon a beautiful white three-story clapboard home with bright candles in every window.

"This is the old Josiah Kingston home, built in 1746. Josiah was an original founder of the New Hampshire Colony. Kingston College is named after him. In the mid 1930s the house was restored and turned into an eating establishment. This is the finest place to eat in central New Hampshire. My grandparents and I used to eat here every Sunday for dinner. We would always have the Yankee pot roast. Anne Ashdown likes to come here too. You should bring her here sometime. She would love it."

Cars were parked along the street and at the back. It was obvious the place was busy. The Lincoln was not on the street but could have been at the back. A skinny-looking valet in a neatly pressed red jacket and black tie with white shirt stood at the curb entrance to the back lot. Peter and Sarah didn't want to be to be too obvious so they continued on down the street.

"Their car could be at the back," she said.

"Yes, but how can we find out without being seen?"

Peter parked the MG along one of the side streets facing the New Hampshire House, trying to figure out what do to when they noticed the valet disappear and a few minutes later the blue Lincoln came down the driveway and stopped with its lights on and motor running. Suddenly Cannon and Trent emerged from the front entrance and walked down the front porch stairs followed by two men in dark clothes. The four got into the Lincoln and drove off in the direction of town. Peter slipped his little car into gear and began following them.

"Who are those other guys?" he asked.

"I couldn't see them both. One was Dr. Morris Glenn, a long-time doctor here in town."

Sarah was puzzled. Why would Morris Glenn be meeting with James Cannon and Walton Trent? And who was the other man?

They followed them back to the Kingston campus. When the Lincoln got to Taylor Hall it stopped and James Cannon got out. He walked towards the main entrance and opening the door went in, presumably to his office. The Lincoln drove off into the night.

Peter and Sarah did not hesitate. They continued to tail the Lincoln as it left town and headed north on Old Mountain Road. Sarah explained that the road paralleled a defunct railroad that used to carry logs down from the White Mountains to timber mills in the south. Twenty miles north were the foothills of the White Mountains. A few farms dotted the countryside but otherwise it was dark forest.

Peter was worried Trent and Cannon would see his lights since the road was so deserted. He kept far back. He turned off his car lights and used the light of a half moon to illuminate their way up the increasingly dark road. They had gone 10 miles up the steadily ascending two-lane road when Sarah saw the red taillights of the Lincoln suddenly blink. She grabbed Peter's arm in warning. He braked hard as they saw the Lincoln literally disappear in the forest. Peter slowly continued along until they came upon a narrow dirt road where the Lincoln had turned down. They could barely make out the fading red lights of the car as it traveled deeper into the New Hampshire forest.

Sarah's heart was beating fast. "Peter, I'm getting scared. Where are they going? Why would Trent, Morris Glenn and some guy we don't know be going into these woods so late at night?"

Peter made up his mind. He took a deep breath. "Sarah, I want you to take the MG a little further up Old Mountain road, turn it around facing south and park it there with the lights off but close enough so you can still see this old dirt road. I'm going in on foot."

She froze. "You can't go in there! It's too dark. You could get lost or it might even be dangerous." She couldn't believe he would venture into the unfamiliar woods so late at night.

"I've got a flashlight in the glove compartment. I'll be fine. You just keep the car running, lights off, and doors locked. If you see the Lincoln come back just wait for me. Don't follow it. If it happens to turn in your direction, quickly put it into gear and drive down the road as casually as possible."

"What if you get lost?" she asked trying to stall him with hope of changing his mind.

"I won't! I'll stay to the side of the road and just follow it in. Listen, back at the game you said you didn't want to give Walton Trent the benefit of the doubt. Well, that's what this is. We are going to find out what in the heck is going on."

She admired his tenacity and courage. "OK, but hurry back and don't take any chances."

Grabbing his yellow heavy-duty flashlight from the glove compartment he reached over, squeezed her arm, and gave her a quick smile, then was off into the darkness. In a moment he was swallowed by the inky black night.

Sarah climbed into the driver's seat and drove up the road for about 300 yards and turning around faced the narrow dirt road where the Lincoln and Peter had gone. She kept the motor running and locked the doors. The quiet rumbling of the English car's engine was the only noise in the silent night.

Peter kept his flashlight on low beam and pointed it directly at the ground in front of him. He didn't want it to be seen from anyone ahead. He walked along the rough rut-filled road with leafy trees and branches encroaching on both sides. He felt claustrophobic as the old road narrowed the farther along he went. The night air was getting colder. He could hear his breathing in the silent woods. He rounded a bend and came upon a steep hill. At the top he heard voices. Jumping into bushes along the side of the road he held his breath. A door slammed and the voices went silent. Quietly he crawled out of the prickly undergrowth and inched down the steep slope in the direction of the voices. Lights from a cabin abruptly came into view. He stopped. The Lincoln was parked in a clearing in front of a small cabin. Peter could hear the bubbling flow of a stream nearby. He saw people moving in the yellow glow of the light. He pondered what his next move should be. There was only one car so he decided that the cabin held the three men from the Lincoln. Checking to make sure his flashlight was off he crept closer to the cabin. As he got closer the voices became louder. He edged around the big blue car and then sprinted the open distance between the car and the cabin. He reached the cabin wall and held his breath. He listened for voices yelling in alarm. Nothing. He plotted an escape route if discovered. Back pressed against the wall, he slowly craned his neck and head in a position to peer into the cabin.

Inside he saw Walton Trent sitting at an old wooden table smoking a cigar. A little man with a wisp of gray white hair on the top of his head was standing at a counter with what looked like medical supplies. A thin man with an unattractive face sat across from Trent smoking a cigarette. The three were engaged in conversation. The little man who Peter decided was Dr. Morris Glenn was gesticulating angrily at the two men at the table who appeared indifferent to his arm waving. Suddenly the thin man stood up, grabbed the doctor's arm, and pushed him into the wall. The little man was stunned. His expression instantly changed from anger to fright. Peter strained to hear their voices. He caught bits of phrases and words. Trent then stood up and walked over to the doctor and put his arm around him and led him to a third chair by the table. The three continued their animated conversation but without the earlier wild emotion. Gradually Dr. Glenn relaxed but still stole glances at the tall thin man from time to time. Peter wondered what time it was. Abruptly Trent and the thin man stood up and putting on their coats moved to the door. The doctor did the same. Peter ducked down and hugged the outside wall. It was too late to run into the woods and hide. He prayed they wouldn't see him. The men came out and headed straight to the car. The cabin went dark. Peter heard Trent say "Thomas" and then couldn't hear anything else as the car doors opening and slamming muffled their conversation. He watched the car slowly drive up the steep hill and disappear over the top. He let out a deep breath. He hoped Sarah was ready when the Lincoln came to the main road.

Peter looked around the area. He knew he should get back to Sarah but before he did he wanted a look inside the cabin. He ran to the back and jimmied a window open. He pried the screen off and lifted up the window and climbed in. The cabin was dark but its warmth felt good to Peter. Using his yellow flashlight he looked around the cabin. Fishing poles were stacked in one corner next to an axe and a stack of wood. A large stone fireplace dominated the living room. A small kitchen and bathroom and two bedrooms down the hall completed the cabin. Peter looked at the counter where the doctor had been standing and saw several bottles and beakers. He had no idea what these were for. Everything else looked normal. This was a simple hunting and fishing cabin in the woods of New Hampshire. Tonight it had been the scene for something else.

Peter decided he had better get back to Sarah. He went out the same back window and carefully left everything as he had found it. He hurried up the steep hill and back to Old Mountain Road. The woods were silent and dark. He felt like he was a million miles from nowhere. Soon he came to the main road. He looked left and right. No cars in sight. Where was Sarah? He looked up the road to where he had told Sarah to wait. Soon he saw yellow car lights flick on and Sarah drove down to meet him. He quickly hopped into the passenger side.

Sarah hugged him tightly. Her face was warm.

"They came out a few minutes ago and sped off back towards town. I was so afraid they had you in the car but that was irrational. What took you so long? What's down there?"

Peter warmed his cold hands on the vent. He recounted what he saw.

"Do you know who a tall thin man named Thomas is?" he asked her.

"That sounds like Thomas Lawton, an attorney in town. Was he kind of," she hesitated, "kind of unattractive?"

He laughed. "Well, there aren't too many men that I do find attractive."

"You know what I mean." She punched him playfully on the arm.

"Yes, he is unattractive," he said seriously. "His behavior is also unattractive."

She raised her eyebrows. "What do you mean?"

Peter told her how Lawton had shoved the elderly Morris Glenn against the wall.

She shuddered. "Lawton is the college attorney. I have never trusted him. Morris Glenn is a kind man who should never be treated that way. He delivered me during a snowstorm by coming out to our home on a snowmobile when the roads were impassable. I've known him all my life. Morris and Thomas Lawton are as different as night and day. More to the point, what are these guys doing meeting in a cabin deep in the woods late at night?"

"That's the big question," said Peter. "This is just more evidence that something is going on."

They drove south towards Pinehurst. By 11:30 P.M. they rolled into town. Driving by Taylor Hall they were surprised to see the blue Lincoln out front, its engine idling and exhaust trailing into the night air. Sarah slowed down and parked behind the Business and Economics building. Shortly thereafter James

121

Cannon came out and got into the car. They followed at a distance and watched as the Lincoln dropped Morris Glenn off at his home and then proceeded back to the New Hampshire House where Thomas Lawton got out and went to his gray Oldsmobile. Trent, who was driving, then took James Cannon back to his house on the outskirts of campus and after dropping him off went home.

Peter and Sarah slowly drove back to the Phillips's home. They were exhausted. Jamie enthusiastically greeted them as they came up the driveway.

Over a cup of hot chocolate in the kitchen they quietly discussed the night's events. They first agreed to keep all they knew secret. If Martha Phillips knew what they had done she would be frightened. Anne Ashdown on the other hand would love to know.

Something was amiss. Was it connected to the college? Probably, since Trent and Cannon were involved. But what was Dr. Morris Glenn's role? Thomas Lawton was the least surprise, thought Sarah. He could easily be involved in shady stuff. Was this about Leslie's death? Peter and Sarah decided there were too many questions needing answers. Tomorrow they would meet and develop a strategy to try and get answers.

They kissed good night and Peter went home. He fell into bed and soon was fast asleep. Sarah had more trouble getting to sleep. Something was nagging her but she couldn't place it.

CHAPTER TWENTY-FOUR

It suddenly came to Sarah very late that night. She sat upright in her bed. The nagging thought crystallized for her like a clear and flawless diamond under a jeweler's lamp. That dreadful morning of her grandfather's death flashed in her mind. Holding her grandmother and the two of them crying softly, a few feet away from his bed as he lay still, in death. A scene from that morning, which at the time had no significance, now suddenly shocked her with its prominence. It was the moment after Dr. Glenn, feeling for Grandfather's pulse, had looked up at Grandmother and said he was sorry, indicating Grandfather had passed away. He then glanced at Thomas Lawton and nodded his head. That was all, a slight subtle nod.

Sarah climbed out of bed and walked over to her bedroom window that overlooked the dark woods and flat still pond at the back of the house. Why did Morris Glenn nod at Thomas Lawton? She remembered something else. Lawton left and made a telephone call. He had used his cell phone just outside the bedroom. Whom did he call? Why was Thomas Lawton there to begin with? Did family attorneys usually come when a client died? Maybe in the Mafia, but not in Pinehurst,

New Hampshire. Sarah stood in her nightgown, nose pressed against the cold glass, pondering the events of the evening and her grandfather's death a year ago. She felt terribly uneasy.

CHAPTER TWENTY-FIVE

Sarah arrived at work Monday morning at 7:30. She had spent Sunday at Peter's cottage reading and watching television while he graded papers. It had rained all day so they decided to stay put in front of a roaring fire in the cottage. Peter was grateful for the time to grade and yet still be with Sarah. At one point during the afternoon they had a long discussion about what happened Friday night and Sarah's suspicion of Thomas Lawton's behavior at the time of her grandfather's death. They decided to keep their observations quiet while continuing trying to uncover answers to their multitude of questions.

Dan Miller was in a great mood that morning. Usually he worked quietly in his office but this morning he came in to see Sarah. She soon realized the root of his happiness was the recent $2 million bequest from Phyllis Allen's will. Dan didn't respond well to financial pressure and so a sudden and undesignated $2 million was incredible news. The cabinet would decide how the money would be spent but it certainly would help the cash flow situation, though he hated to depend on money outside the budget. Dan was a stickler for staying within the budget and would probably stash away a small portion of the money for end-of-the-year surprise expenses. He would use that money to balance the institutional budget at the end of the fiscal year.

Dan's exuberance was in sharp contrast to Sarah's worry about Leslie's death and the strange behavior of Trent, Cannon, Lawton, and Morris Glenn on Friday night. She had promised Peter to keep things quiet and so felt frustrated that she couldn't talk to Dan. He seemed so happy and yet so unaware that she wanted to shake him into the reality she and Peter knew.

CHAPTER TWENTY-SIX

At the same time Sarah and Dan were talking, Peter was down the hall in the Academic Affairs office in a meeting with Dean Rutherford. Peter had received a message in his campus mailbox early last week asking him to meet with her on Monday morning.

"Thank you for coming, Peter," Elisabeth said. "I know you are busy and have a class at 9:00. I just wanted to touch base with you on several items. First of all, I hope you are enjoying it here at Kingston. I am hearing very good things about your classes. How are things going from your perspective?"

"Things are going well. Since this is my first full-time teaching position I am realizing how much work goes into teaching. I have developed a new appreciation for faculty."

Elisabeth laughed. "I wish some of my administrative colleagues had the same appreciation. I can't seem to convince them that college teaching is demanding work."

She looked wistfully out the window as if she had someone in mind.

Peter continued. "I do like it here. My students are working hard and care about their learning. Kingston seems to be a good environment for students and faculty. The faculty in my department have been especially supportive and encouraging. All in all my first semester is going well."

Elisabeth smiled broadly. She was pleased to hear Peter say this. She had high hopes for his success at Kingston.

"I am happy to hear this," she said. "I want you to know that we have high expectations for you. May I ask you another unrelated question?" she asked.

"Of course," replied Peter. His intuition suggested she had something else on her mind. He shifted a bit uneasily in his chair.

She hesitated as if unsure where to begin.

"Ah...how did you feel after our last faculty meeting?"

Peter paused. His stomach lurched. Was he in trouble?

"To be honest I wish I had kept my big mouth shut."

"Why do you say that?" she asked in surprise. Her dark green eyes seemed to zero in on Peter.

"I promised myself I would not get involved in campus politics, this first year especially. My dad has always cautioned me that first-year employees should do much more listening than talking. You can't get into trouble by what you don't say, he always preaches. I didn't take his advice this time."

"What made you stray from his advice this time? You strike me as a careful and deliberate young man."

Peter wondered two things: what she was after and how much he should say.

"When I interviewed for the position I clearly remember you saying that Kingston College was primarily a teaching college. I believe these were your exact words. This was what motivated me to seriously consider Kingston. Three times this fall, the first at the new faculty orientation, second at the board-faculty dinner, and finally at the last faculty meeting, I have heard the board chairman say something very different.

128

Randolph Bolles stresses scholarship and research over teaching. I don't think he truly understands and appreciates teaching as it relates historically to the core values of a liberal arts college such as Kingston. I came to this place because of the emphasis on classroom teaching. Now I am hearing something quite different. With all due respect, I imagine the board chair has more influence on the institutional mission than the dean does. So I guess after having heard Bolles spout off three times, I reached my limit. I apologize if I in some way hurt you or the college."

Elisabeth was impressed with Peter's analysis. She weighed her response.

"I don't wish to involve you in Kingston politics. You have wonderful potential and if you stay at Kingston you can be one of our best faculty members. I would hate to see these issues sidetrack you."

She paused, uncomfortable about saying much more.

"I'll be frank with you, Peter. I've got some real concerns with both Randolph Bolles and James Cannon. I shouldn't be expressing these concerns, especially to a young new faculty member like you. For some strange reason my good friend Anne Ashdown strongly urged me to. Can you think why she would encourage me so?"

Peter was reluctant to respond. Evidently Mrs. Ashdown had mixed up the death of Leslie Patton with Cannon and Bolles. He remembered their Thanksgiving conversation at Martha Phillips's home. This confirmed his fear that he shouldn't have talked so openly in front of Anne and Martha Phillips. Now at least one of them was confusing things. He couldn't figure why Mrs. Ashdown would want Dean Rutherford to talk to him.

"I can't really explain why she would," said Peter.

Dean Rutherford sat straight in her wing back chair and continued talking.

"I meant what I said in our interview about Kingston College being primarily a teaching college. Randolph Bolles on the other hand is strongly committed to the research-scholarship model and wants Kingston to move pointedly in that direction. His intensity and drive is going to change the face of this institution. Randolph Bolles is almost obsessive with faculty scholarship and research. He sees it as the ticket to stardom for the college. I believe, like you, that in his haste he is altering the very fabric and mission of the college. One day people are suddenly going to look around and ask what happened?" Her aristocratic face was flushed. Peter could almost feel her intensity.

She shifted in her chair then switched to talking about James Cannon.

"Cannon has always been a fine scholar. Something Bolles isn't, though he labors under the illusion that he is. Cannon was a good dean. Oh, sure he can be cold and aloof at times but he truly loves scholarship and the classroom. He understands what it is like to be a college professor. Today, however, James Cannon is also consumed by a deep drive to put Kingston College on the map. He is terribly concerned with Kingston's image and reputation. The odd thing is he didn't used to be this way. Somewhere along the way he changed. He has lost his way. He would have fought Bolles tooth and nail over this research and scholarship issue when he was dean. He believed in a healthy balance between teaching and scholarship back then. His priorities have gradually changed to where reputation and visibility takes precedence over our original mission. He doesn't even react when Bolles goes off like he does. I believe Bolles and one or two other board members are exerting tremendous pressure on Cannon to move in this direction. All of this makes for one determined college president who will do anything to achieve his goal of increased visibility and prominence for Kingston."

She stopped, almost out of breath.

Peter sat in his stiff chair, stunned. He was suddenly conscious that his mouth was open. He tried to subtly close it. Elisabeth Rutherford didn't even notice this obvious attempt so absorbed was she in her passion. She gulped a fresh batch of air and forged on.

"The philosophical combination of a Randolph Bolles and James Cannon will profoundly alter the institutional mission of Kingston College. If we aren't vigilant we will be doing things we shouldn't and become something we ought not to become."

She stopped again and fixed a steady gaze at Peter. Several moments passed in silence.

"Well, have I said too much?" she asked.

Peter bit his lower lip trying to fashion an answer.

"Frankly, while I'm somewhat surprised you have shared these views with me, I'm equally not surprised you hold them."

Elisabeth Rutherford nodded silently, a slight grin giving away a competitive side to her personality.

"Anne Ashdown told me you were a perceptive one."

Peter said, "I watched your face when Bolles was speaking at the new faculty orientation and then again at the last faculty meeting. Your face was expressionless. Not the slightest nod or affirmation of what he was saying. It was almost more interesting watching you than Bolles."

He returned her grin with one of his own.

Up to now the two of them had been like boxers early in the fight throwing light jabs and feints in order to assess how much the other knew. Now the sparring was over. It was if an invisible curtain had lifted and they could be utterly frank with one another.

Peter didn't hesitate. He plunged forward.

"Dean Rutherford, I don't know very much about campus politics at Kingston. I agree with you that Randolph Bolles is obsessed with this college becoming something different than a good liberal arts college with a strong teaching emphasis. In truth, I bet the majority of the Board of Trustees doesn't really know what he is up to. I also sense a definite unease among the faculty. They seem to feel a sense of powerlessness. Cannon though, strikes me as someone who is simply out of his element, almost like one floating out of control in a swiftly moving river current. I have been sitting here trying to make sense out of what you are saying and how it fits or doesn't fit with our experiences these last two weeks. We have seen James Cannon, Walton Trent, and two other people from town, Dr. Morris Glenn and Thomas Lawton, acting very strangely. Finally, there is Leslie Patton's death. We now know that the car that killed her never swerved or attempted to miss her. Did the driver fall asleep or intentionally run her down? Are all of these simply isolated incidents or part of a larger puzzle? I don't know if there is a connection but my instincts tell me there is a relationship."

He paused, letting his words sink in.

Elisabeth Rutherford suddenly stood up and walked over to the big window overlooking the inner campus. Peter watched her, remembering his first interview when the snow had been falling so steadily and beautifully outside this same window. She stared out at something Peter couldn't see. Her profile reminded him of a painting. She had an elegant bearing about her. After a few moments of silence, as if she were digesting Peter's words, she slowly turned and faced him. She spoke carefully.

"I have been waiting a long time for a conversation of this magnitude. There is one person who concerns me, perhaps the most."

"Walton Trent," said Peter suddenly.

Rutherford blanched. She was completely taken off guard. How had this new young faculty member learned so much so soon?

"Yes," she acknowledged. "Walton Trent is the most ill-mannered man I have ever met. Besides being boorish and rude, he is a complete misfit in this college and town. Why James Cannon ever hired him is a mystery. Certainly he has raised money for the college but it's a wonder how, what with his overbearing and intimidating style. In the President's cabinet he sticks close to Cannon and rarely engages with the other vice presidents. He has attached himself to Cannon like a leech. The cabinet should function like a team but Walton Trent is not a team player. He is a maverick. Cannon either is blind or intentionally chooses to let him operate this way. Rather than a spirit of camaraderie among the cabinet, an air of mystery and divided loyalties exists. Trent almost seems to control Cannon. Walton Trent has an agenda much different than the rest of us. I don't know what it is but it threatens this institution. Dan Miller and I simply do not trust Trent."

Her bright green eyes pleaded with Peter.

"We need to unearth whatever is happening at this place. We need your help."

Peter felt butterflies stirring in his stomach. His pulse quickened. What was he getting into? He felt drawn into a confusing web of strange events that made no sense up to this point.

"I should tell you what Sarah and I saw over Thanksgiving and last Friday night."

Her eyes widened in anticipation.

He recounted running into Walton Trent at the Bank of

Boston and how they had wordlessly stared at each other across the spacious ornate foyer as the elevator doors closed. Peter still felt a chill as he once again saw in his mind those black bushy eyebrows sitting like two small hills atop a fierce face. He described Trent's cold and impassive face.

He continued, detailing the Friday night spying on Trent, Cannon, Dr. Glenn, and Thomas Lawton. Peter saw Elisabeth Rutherford's anxiety rise when he told her about the cabin incident deep in the woods on Old Mountain Road.

"The four of them are up to something," said Peter. "Sarah and I probably shouldn't have followed them but the impulse was too strong. Coming on the heels of the other unexplained events we were naturally curious. After Friday night we are even more curious."

"What do you think they were doing at the cabin so late at night?" she asked.

Peter could see she was uneasy.

Peter shrugged his broad shoulders.

"I could only hear muffled voices. Their movements were animated as if arguing. I saw some medical bottles or something like that. Maybe someone got a cut. They didn't stay long. I barely had time to hide around the back when they came out of the cabin to go home."

"You shouldn't have put yourself in that kind of danger," Rutherford said.

"Intellectually I know you are right but my gut tells me something weird is going on at this college. I gave in to my impulse to find out more."

Rutherford sat in her chair pondering this latest information. She looked up at Peter.

"Why was Trent at the Bank of Boston?"

"Well, Sarah tells me the college funnels all of its will and bequest money through that bank. It's more efficient for some reason. This is what Dan Miller tells her anyway."

Suddenly Elisabeth Rutherford bolted up in her wing back chair. Her face lit up.

"My father is semi-retired from the Bank of Boston. He goes into work two days a week to consult on their long-term investments. They like him to handle the accounts of people who have been with the bank for a long time. He calls it the old timer's accounts. He has all of the rights and privileges accorded a regular full-time employee. He's been with them for almost 35 years. Maybe he can help us now."

Peter was intrigued by this latest information. Maybe Dean Rutherford's father could find out why Trent was at the bank. He could have a perfectly legitimate reason. It was worth checking out.

Their meeting ended so that Elisabeth would have time to prepare for a meeting with several department heads. They pledged to keep their discussion confidential. Dean Rutherford would call her father in Boston.

CHAPTER TWENTY-SEVEN

Sarah and Peter met for lunch in the student union café at 12:30. As usual, the place was crowded with students, faculty, and staff. Over a steaming bowl of New England clam chowder Peter told Sarah about his remarkable conversation with Elisabeth Rutherford. Sarah listened intently, occasionally nodding ever so silently.

"Wow, I had no idea Elisabeth Rutherford had such deep concerns," said Sarah after Peter had finished. "How does all this add up?"

Peter sighed. "That's just it, it's all so complicated and seemingly unconnected. I mean we have a board chair and college president trying to influence serious institutional change, a Vice President for Development acting mysteriously, a town doctor and attorney meeting with Cannon and Trent deep in the New Hampshire woods in the middle of the night, and the unexplained and violent death of the Assistant Director of Development. It simply doesn't come together."

"I'm still bothered by Thomas Lawton's presence at my grandfather's home on the morning he died," she persisted.

"That's another funny thing," said Peter. "I can see Dr. Morris being there but the college's attorney?"

They ate their lunch in silence for a couple of minutes.

Abruptly Peter said, "Look, we are going to drive ourselves crazy. Either we forget the whole thing and decide these are just a weird series of isolated and benign events or we begin to take it seriously and jump in with both feet."

He searched her face looking for a reaction.

Sarah's face darkened in intensity. "I don't want to just forget it. There is something going on at this college. If you had asked me this question before your meeting with Elisabeth Rutherford I wouldn't have been as sure. Now I can't ignore what she says, what we have seen, and what my instincts tell me. No, not me! I'm not about to look the other way."

Peter knew this would be her answer. He smiled affectionately.

"I figured you would say that. I haven't known you long but you're not one to back down. OK, so where do we go from here?"

"I think we should do several things. First, let's talk to Grandmother about Grandfather's bequest to the college. Second we need to go see Morris Glenn."

"Why this strategy?" he asked her.

"We have identified a number of strange things going on. I think we have to look at each one independently. We know Leslie was probably murdered. We have questions about Walton Trent and since he raises money and was seen at the Bank of Boston, maybe it has something to do with wills and bequests. My Grandfather left Kingston $1.7 million. Let's see what Grandmother says about this. Then we look into the life of Dr. Morris Glenn. He is the kindest and weakest of the four. We should start with him. Then we move on to Walton Trent and Thomas Lawton and act on whatever information we dig up. How's that sound?"

Peter liked her decisiveness. "How about we not see Dr. Glenn just yet? We don't want to alert any of the others we are on to something. I suggest we try find out more about Glenn but do it quietly."

"Sounds like a good plan." They finished lunch and agreed to meet for dinner and begin planning their strategy.

CHAPTER TWENTY-EIGHT

Tuesday night Peter drove over to the Philips home for dinner with Sarah and her grandmother. Sparkling Christmas lights lit up the small farms along the dark county road. The noisy MGB engine echoed in the cold December night. As if in response, the lonely wail of a barking dog pierced the still night. Peter couldn't decide whether early winter in New Hampshire was beautiful or lonely. Maybe both, he thought. Turning left on Canterbury Lane he gunned the small but powerful engine and raced towards Old Vermont Road, where he turned left again. Five minutes later he came upon the warm bright lights of the Phillips's house. Jamie came running out to greet Peter, her tail wagging with delight. She now recognized the MGB even before Peter turned into the Phillips's driveway.

Peter and Sarah had prearranged to ask Martha Phillips about her husband's bequest to the college. They would do so without giving too much information so as not to alarm her. They were well into a delicious dinner of Yankee pot roast when Sarah posed the first question.

"Grandmother, can you tell me about Grandfather's bequest to the college?" she asked gently.

Martha Phillips looked up from her dinner with a quizzical expression. "Why are you interested in that?" she asked.

Sarah glanced sideways at Peter and replied in a measured tone, "I was checking the gifting records in the office today and wanted to verify the amount Grandfather left Kingston. It's just good accounting practice."

"But wouldn't the college have the amount in their records?"

Sarah fidgeted slightly in her seat. "Of course we do, but I want to make sure the amounts match."

Martha Phillips wasn't convinced by Sarah's argument but decided not to pry.

"Well, I'd have to check in John's office. He rarely told me much about our finances. I'll be right back." She got up from the cherry dining table and went to the office across the hallway to her late husband's office.

"She seems suspicious," said Peter.

"I can't put much by her," said Sarah. "I think she suspects something is up but is afraid to learn more."

A few minutes later Martha reentered the dinning room gripping a weathered leather satchel bulging with papers and documents.

"This is John's old satchel containing all of his important papers. He once told me if the house was on fire to make sure I got this old thing out of the office safe before anything else. I hope he meant after I got myself out," she said with a sly grin.

She sat down and with both hands pressed the worn leather pouch on her lap. She was reluctant to part with it. Sarah knew it made her think of Grandfather. The familiar smell was overpowering. It was like he was still in the room seated at the head of the table. A sense of sadness pervaded the room.

Martha looked resolutely at Sarah and Peter. "I don't know what you two are up to, but please be careful. I know it has something to do with the college. My husband left some of his money to the college, not Trent or Cannon. He steadfastly made that distinction to me in private. I remember the night the two of them came out to meet with us. John had already given several million for the new fieldhouse the college named in his honor. This time they wanted him to consider leaving the college in his will. Cannon stumbled over his words, but that man Trent was far more smooth and direct. John always liked direct people but I could tell he was irritated with Trent. John had enough money to give the college 10 times what he eventually left in his will but he didn't like the way they conducted business."

She paused to look down at some documents in the pouch. "Ah," she said. "Here it is."

She adjusted her glasses and peered down at one document. It was sealed so she carefully opened it and slid out an official looking letter. She slowly read the content to herself. "He left the college 3.7 million," she announced. "I didn't know it was that much. I only knew he left a fairly substantial sum. But like I said, he had a lot more. He left the majority to me. She stopped and looked at Sarah and Peter.

Sarah thought she had heard wrong. Her face went white. "Did you say 3.7 million?" she asked.

"Yes, Sarah. Look here." Martha Phillips showed her the official looking document that had been notarized at the bottom. The word confidential had been stamped in bold black letters several times across the body of the letter and at the top and bottom. Sarah reached over and gently took the document from her grandmother. She sat back and read the contents.

Sure enough, the paper read that John Phillips bequeathed to Kingston College upon his death the actual sum of $3.7 million. The document ended with an agreement to maintain the confidentiality of the bequest and would not be revealed by either the benefactor or college. At the bottom were the signed signatures of Walton Trent, James Cannon, and John Phillips.

Peter and Sarah were shocked. Nothing was said for a few moments. They both knew the college had received $1.7 million upon John's death. Where had the other two million disappeared?

Sarah made the decision not to reveal the discrepancy. She and Peter needed to talk first.

Sarah maintained her composure and asked her grandmother, "so Grandfather left Kingston $3.7 million upon his death and wanted it kept confidential?"

Martha Phillips nodded a silent yes.

"Why did he want to keep it quiet?" asked Peter.

"Well, I don't think he cared one way or another. He said President Cannon and Walton Trent suggested it be confidential. They told him making large gifts and bequests public sometimes adversely impacts the potential for additional giving from other people. John told me he didn't know much about college fundraising and so he agreed with their suggestion."

Peter and Sarah exchanged looks.

"Mrs. Phillips, how was the actual bequest handled?"

"What do you mean, Peter?"

He leaned toward Martha. "Who handled his will and financial affairs and how would the money have been distributed from your husband's estate to the college?" Peter answered tenderly.

Martha Phillips anxiously twisted a brightly colored Japanese handkerchief in her hands. Sarah placed her hand on her grandmother's for reassurance. This seemed to help.

"Bickford and Guilckson have been our family's attorneys for years. John went to high school with William Bickford, and until his stroke four years ago, William was John's primary legal counsel. Somehow Thomas Lawton took over that role. John was convinced that William Bickford wanted it this way so he relented even though he couldn't stand Lawton. He has always struck me as a sleazy character. Lawton was our attorney when Cannon and Trent persuaded John to leave the college all that money. The three of them set up the bequest. It really wasn't too complicated. They came back another night and had John sign the bequest papers that included the agreement letter to keep it confidential. When John died last Thanksgiving, Thomas Lawton activated the bequest documents. I just assumed that the money John left to the college was automatically withdrawn from the Bank of New Hampshire and sent to the college bank."

"Do you know for certain that the deposit from your husband's bank to the college bank was $3.7 million?" asked Peter.

"Well, I thought so since that's what the bequest document says," she replied looking at the paper she was holding in her trembling hands.

"We can easily find out," said Sarah. "Grandmother can simply call her bank and see how much money was withdrawn."

"Sarah, I would rather you place the call. All of this business is making me nervous. I don't know what is going on, but the implications of what we are discussing here are terribly serious."

Peter nodded in agreement. "That makes sense."

After dinner Martha Phillips retired to her upstairs bedroom, leaving Peter and Sarah alone downstairs.

"Sarah, we need to find out how much money was withdrawn from your Grandfather's account. The amount will answer some major questions."

"I'll get the bank numbers from Grandmother and call first thing in the morning."

CHAPTER TWENTY-NINE

The next morning Peter found two voicemail messages on his phone at work. The first message told him Dean Rutherford wanted to see him immediately. The second message warned him to mind his own business and stop asking question about Leslie Patton or the same thing would happen to him. A few minutes later he was sitting in the dean's office.

"Why does Cannon want to fire me?" asked Peter. He was stunned.

"Obviously he is getting some real pressure from Trent," Dean Rutherford said. "This just confirms your suspicion that some people are getting very nervous. Cannon couldn't come up with any credible reason. I expect that Trent told him to get rid of you. He's trying to do that but its clear his heart isn't in it."

Peter sat back amazed at this latest turn of events.

Dean Rutherford looked at him. "Don't worry. This is simply not going to happen. I told Cannon I would not fire you and neither could he. I am just irate that he even let it get this far. The faculty Manual of Operations is very clear on procedural due process for faculty. Certainly you have not violated any college regulations. Trent is unfamiliar with how we do things here. He's probably used to firing people at will."

"What happens next?" he asked.

"Nothing. I will take care of this. I just wanted you to be aware of this latest turn of events."

Peter walked out of the Dean's Office and went straight to Sarah's office to tell her the latest news.

"Are you sure you want to hang around with me?" he asked looking at Sarah.

"Of course I do, since you came to Pinehurst things have become much more exciting."

"I think things are about to become much more exciting. It's time to go on the offensive," he said.

"What do you mean?" She asked.

"Well, we agreed last week not to ignore our suspicions. We need to follow through and truly find out what's going on. We have to talk with Dr. Glenn, go to the Bank of Boston, using Dean Rutherford's father to get us access and then take a peek at Walton Trent's records in his office. I would also like to find out more about Thomas Lawton. Whatever is going on he is sure to be involved."

"Peter, what do we do? We can't just ignore it. Shouldn't we go to the police?"

"What can they do? I have no proof. I say we gather more hard evidence and then go to the police."

Sarah's uncertainty was almost palatable, yet she didn't know what else to do. Peter's suggestion seemed to make the most sense. Yet it scared her too.

CHAPTER THIRTY

Three nights later on a late Friday night Peter picked up Sarah at her home and the two traveled into town. Dressed in dark clothing, they didn't say much as they drove along Old Vermont Road heading into town. The town and campus were quiet as Peter turned his car into the Taylor Hall parking lot. Their plan was simple. They would walk into the building as if they were going to Sarah's office. Once there they would make sure the building was empty and with Sarah acting as lookout, Peter would break into the Development Office and then into Trent's office.

Peter parked the MGB in a regular parking space as close to the front as possible and the two made their way up the red-brick walkway. They attempted to act as normally as possible. After Sarah unlocked the heavy main doors they quietly entered the darkened building. The silence of the empty main hall with its high ceiling was disquieting. They made their way along the first floor to the stairs and quietly walked up the wide stairway to the second floor where Sarah's office was. They felt like someone might pop out of a dark corner at any moment. Sarah opened the door to the finance office area and went in and opened her inner office, leaving the lights off. They didn't want to attract security. Sarah stood lookout at the entrance while Peter made his way further down the dark hall to the Development Offices. He paused at the door and looked back at Sarah, who waved an all-clear signal. Reaching into his pocket he grasped a small lock pick and thrust it into the door lock. A moment later he heard the lock click. He held the doorknob tightly as he carefully turned it and pushed open the heavy door. Sliding his body around the partially open door he entered the office and once in quickly closed the door behind him. A trickle of sweat rolled down the bridge of his nose. He tasted the salty drop as it continued its journey across his upper lip and made its way into his mouth. Quickly he made his way across the thickly carpeted outer office down the hallway to Trent's office at the end of the complex. Using the lock pick once more he soon found himself in Trent's office. Bending low to avoid casting off any shadows he half crawled to the huge cherry desk across the spacious room next to the window facing the inner campus. Keeping his head low as he reached the window he kneeled down and facing the desk began to search through Trent's file drawers. Ten minutes later he had come up empty-handed. He clicked off the small pen light flashlight and turned his attention to the sixteen inch computer on Trent's desk. His hand touched the mouse and the screen immediately came to life. A menu of files instantly replaced the starry night screen saver. His eyes scrolled the files and landed on one labeled bequests. Double clicking the file a request for a password flashed across the screen. His heart sank. Suddenly the shrill ring of a telephone shattered the quietness. His heart almost leaped out of his chest. Peter stared at the intrusion. The phone rang a second time. He picked up the black phone and put it to his ear. He heard a whispered voice calling his name.

"Peter, this is Sarah, campus security is in the building and making their way up the stairs. Hide quickly." The phone clicked dead.

Peter quickly looked to see if he had left anything out and ducking under Trent's desk pulled the chair towards him, squeezing his body between the chair and the inside front of the desk. A few minutes later he heard the main door to the office complex open and voices talking. He held his breath as footsteps approached Trent's office. The door rattled and then all was quiet. The voices soon faded. Peter stayed in his hiding place for five more minutes and then slowly extricated himself. He debated what to do next. Suddenly the phone rang again. He picked it up and heard Sarah's voice.

"What's happening?" he asked.

"Security came by just to check the doors and now I can see them heading over to the Student Union. I hid in my office until they left. I didn't want anyone to know I had been here in case Trent discovers someone was in his office."

"I'm at Trent's computer but can't get into the bequests file without the password."

"Wait," said Sarah. "Let me look at Leslie Patton's e-mail again. Maybe she left a clue."

A few minutes Sarah came back on the line. "Try NYNYNY," she said excitedly.

Peter typed in the letters and was amazed to gain access. "That's it," he said. "Give me a few more minutes and I'll meet you at the top of the stairs."

He opened the folder and easily found the John Phillips file. It was marked confidential at the top. Opening the file Peter found copies of the bequest agreement and other supporting documents. Everything looked in order until he came to the actual amount of the bequest. He rubbed his eyes in disbelief. The figure was 1.7 million. Trent's records showed the

John Phillips's bequest to Kingston College to be 1.7 million. Peter looked around for a printer and found one on a small table at the back of Trent's desk. He punched in the print key and once it started printing he closed out the file and began looking for the Phyllis Allen file. Opening her file he found an agreement that stated she had left the college $800,000. Once again $2 million was missing. Peter printed this document too. Once it was printed he decided to leave. He checked to see if everything was in place and walked to the front office and stepped into the hall. He found Sarah at the doorway to her office. Clutching the printed documents he hugged her and they quickly went down the stairs and out the main floor entrance into the cold December night. It was 11:45. They jumped into the MGB and drove off. They never noticed the dark blue Lincoln Continental with its engine running quietly idling in the shadows of the side driveway of Taylor Hall.

Jamie came running out to greet Peter and Sarah as they drove into the Phillips's driveway. Seated in the living room they read and reread the Phillips and Allen documents. The information was irrefutable. Somewhere along the line $4 million had disappeared.

"We have to track where this money went," said Peter. "Somehow this money vanished and no one knows it. Your Grandfather and Phyllis Allen were led to believe it was one amount and the college a much lesser amount. So as long as the Allen family and Phillips family maintain confidentiality no one would ever suspect anything. Everyone remains in the dark while a very subtle theft of millions of dollars takes place. These people are extremely bold yet it is a very simple system. Just keep the families thinking it was one amount; record the lesser amount in forged college documents and the bad guys pocket the difference. They have to have an attorney helping them alter the documents. Why even when the college's annual auditors come around they won't suspect anything because all the paperwork is in order. It just has to be Thomas Lawton. That's also why Phil Craft was so rattled when you came to see him about your Grandmother's account. For the first time one of the families began asking questions. This is their worst nightmare come true. Their simple but dangerous plan is starting to unravel. We're into this deep, Sarah, and they aren't going to let it go. They suspect we know too much. We need to move on this fast. I am going to Boston and try to figure out how the Bank of Boston is involved. Dean Rutherford's father will help us there."

"How do we do this without showing our hand?" she asked.

"I really don't know yet," he replied. "I'll have to talk with Mr. Rutherford first and figure out a plan. I'm sure he will have some ideas. After all, we do know that the money from both the Concord Bank and Pinehurst Bank was transferred to the Bank of Boston. We just need to trace its path once it arrived at the Bank of Boston."

"Peter, this is sounding very scary."

"I'm sorry, Sarah, to have gotten you into this."

"No, it's not your fault. This directly involves my family and me. You just happen to be the one who stumbled upon the conspiracy. I'm grateful but just getting nervous. At the same time I want to nail the people who stole Grandfather's money."

Three days later on a Tuesday morning, Peter and Elisabeth Rutherford met in the parking lot of Taylor Hall to drive down to Boston so Peter could meet with Elisabeth's father. Two and one half hours later the three of them were sitting in the formal living room of Bill and Mary Rutherford in their three-story red-brick home in Boston's fashionable Beacon Hill. The 300-year-old home overlooked a leafless Boston Common.

Bill Rutherford was tall like his daughter and possessed

an elegant bearing. Peter could see a remarkable resemblance between father and daughter.

"So Elisabeth tells me something odd is going on at the college," began Rutherford.

Peter recounted the discrepancies between the college and the Phillips and Allen wills. Peter stuck to the facts as he told his story, including the Bank of Boston connection. Bill Rutherford peered intently at Peter as he talked. For a few moments Rutherford said nothing.

"So you think my old bank is up to something," he asked a puzzled look on his refined face.

"Well sir, I don't really know. I was hoping you could help me trace where the money went once it got to the Bank here in Boston. A large amount of money has vanished somewhere along the line. The last place it was seen was on its way to Boston." Peter paused to let this last statement sink in.

"Suppose we do find an irregularity. What then? Do I turn in my own bank?"

"Well, that will have to be your decision, Mr. Rutherford. I'm just interested in tracking down some missing money and its possible connection to the college."

"Fair enough, young man. I just wanted to see if you would stick to your guns. Of course, I will help you. After all my daughter told me, I'd better," he said smiling at Elisabeth. "Now what do you propose?"

Peter considered the question.

"If we can tap into the computer system undetected we could track when the money came in and where it was distributed. That's the big question, where did it go? I assume all transactions are maintained on the central computer."

"Yes, certainly they are. Actually I have access to the system so it shouldn't be any problem. I can have you accompany me as if you are a client and we can sit in my office and do a search. How does that sound, Mr. Kramer?"

Two hours later Peter was seated in Bill Rutherford's small but elegant office on the thirty-fifth floor of the John Hancock Building. The office was just off a busy hallway and separated by a floor-to-ceiling glass wall. People constantly walked back and forth in the hallway, some glancing in, others looking straight ahead oblivious to the two of them sitting there.

Rutherford busily typed in his password and a series of other numbers and letters and then sat waiting for a few moments his back to Peter. Soon the screen came alive with data.

"This security system is pretty sophisticated. Luckily I have senior executive status. Any entries are only reflected as simply a hit on the account and that's all. My name does not appear on the screen."

"Why is that?" asked Peter. "Wouldn't they want to know who is accessing accounts? Sounds a bit like a security leak."

"Of course that makes sense," said Rutherford, "but at the same time we are dealing with major investors and most want their names kept confidential. Rather than asking for their permission we simply allow only a select few bank officials access."

"Ah, there it is," said Rutherford, staring intently at the computer screen. Glancing briefly over his right shoulder at Peter he said, "I've just called up the Kingston College Portfolio. Tell me again the name you are looking for."

Peter leaned forward on the edge of his seat in anticipation. "Phillips, John and Martha, Pinehurst Bank."

Several moments passed in silence as Rutherford studied the screen before him. Peter heard the quiet hum of the computer. More people passed by in the hallway.

"OK, here it is. On December 17, 2001, the Pinehurst Bank transferred $1.7 million from the account of John and Martha Phillips to the Bank of Boston and the Kingston College portfolio account. It looks like it was a straight cash transfer. Probably the bank in New Hampshire liquidated some of the Phillips's assets. This is a fairly routine transaction. I see these all the time."

Peter's disappointment was visible on his handsome face. His eyes squinted in thought. "Isn't there anything else"? he inquired in desperation already knowing the answer.

"I'm sorry, Peter, but the screen tells the story."

A sudden thought came to Peter.

"What about the Phyllis Allen account? Can you access that one?"

"Sure, wait just a moment."

Several agonizing minutes later Rutherford located the Allen account. Leaning back in his chair he stared at the screen. Peter sat in his chair anxiously waiting.

"OK, on February 15, 2003, the Bank of New Hampshire transferred $800,000 to the Bank of Boston, Kingston College account, from Phyllis Allen, Pinehurst, New Hampshire." Rutherford turned around in his chair and looked at Peter.

Peter wasn't surprised. Nothing about the entire affair surprised him anymore. He glanced down at the piece of paper Sarah had given him.

"Mr. Rutherford, may we try one more time?"

"Certainly, who is it?"

"Elisabeth Ann Williams, from Lake Winnipesauke, New Hampshire."

Rutherford punched several keys again and waited. He tapped his fingers gently on the desk.

"Here we go. The Bank of Wolfeboro, New Hampshire, transferred $2,3 million from the account of Elisabeth Ann Williams on September 5, 2002, to the Bank of Boston and the account of Kingston College."

Peter stood up and walked to the window and looked

thirty-five floors down to Boylston Street where people scurried about their business. He turned back to Rutherford.

"A lot of money is missing. Where do you think it went? I mean, we know Phillips, Allen, and Williams all bequeathed a lot more money than you have there on your computer screen."

Rutherford shrugged his shoulders. "I really can't answer that."

"Wait a minute! OK, $2 million of the John Phillips estate disappeared. Can you check and see if $2 million came into this bank around the dates in question?"

"Peter, we have millions and millions of dollars transferring in and out of this bank on a daily basis. This isn't the Bank of Pinehurst."

"Can you at least check the $2 million transactions on December 17, 2002?"

Rutherford turned back to his computer and typed in an extensive series of numbers. At one point he pulled out his desk drawer and consulted a piece of paper taped to one side. The screen lit up and he looked at it closely before punching the print key. In a moment a clicking sound emanated from the Hewlett-Packard 560 laser printer. Twenty seconds later a single sheet of paper emerged.

Grasping the paper, Rutherford turned to Peter. "OK, Peter, this is highly confidential."

"On December 17, 2002, the Bank of Boston conducted seven transactions, each over several millions of dollars and two at exactly $2 million. The first $2 million dollar transaction was a transfer of funds to the Boston Naval Shipyard. We do lots of government contract business with the Navy. No surprise there! The second was a $2 million transfer from the Bank of Boston to Empire Insurance Company of New York."

Peter was perplexed.

"Are there any names on the transactions?"

Rutherford hesitated. He scanned the computer screen.

"Justin Nichols, our Vice President for Domestic Investments, consummated the New York transaction. He probably received the request from Empire Insurance and routinely transferred the funds from their account to New York."

Peter bit his lower lip in concentration. "Does Empire Insurance have an account here?"

"Yes, they do, according to the records."

"Could any of the missing money have been diverted to Empire Insurance?"

Rutherford paused. "I really can't answer that."

"Do you know much about Nichols?" asked Peter.

"Well, he has only been here three or four years. He came to us from Chemical Bank in New York. He seems friendly enough. We don't have much contact. He tends to keep to himself."

"Peter, it seems highly unlikely something this irregular is going on. Most likely the missing money was never sent to our bank in the first place. What if it is being embezzled by the other banks or someone familiar with these peoples' estates, like their attorney or a family member? The possibilities are almost endless."

CHAPTER THIRTY-ONE

Walton Trent stabbed at a sizzling chunk of top sirloin steak and after artfully cutting it hungrily placed it in his mouth. Seated across the white linen table were Thomas Lawton and James Cannon. The Pinehurst Inn was almost empty at 5:30. Most people came for dinner around 6:30 or 7:00. They had chosen this time for privacy. Cannon unenthusiastically picked at a crab salad while Lawton wolfed down his Yankee pot roast.

Trent looked at Cannon and Lawton after wiping his mouth with the heavy white dinner napkin with the Pinehurst Inn emblem embroidered on the corner.

"You two are quiet tonight. Worried about something?"

Neither ventured an answer.

Trent continued on. "So what's the problem?"

"Kramer went to Boston today," said Lawton gloomily.

Trent glared at him. "You think I don't know that. Of course he did. He's too smart not to. Why he just has to satisfy that curious professor mind of his. Listen he's not going to find a damn thing. Everything has been fixed. The only thing he will find is that John Phillips and Phyllis Allen left the college exactly what is recorded in both the college and Bank of Boston files. Not a cent more. We have covered our tracks."

Cannon looked up from his salad. He had hardly touched it. "Walton, things are beginning to worry me. I've got a professor asking questions and actually doing some investigating."

"James, if you really want something to worry about, if we all want something serious to worry about, then we start to open our mouths about what's been going on." Trent turned his dark bushy eyebrows towards Cannon and fixed a threatening stare at the college president.

The message was clear. They were in too deep to get out now.

Walton Trent knew that Thomas Lawton would not be the problem. It was James Cannon who was beginning to worry him. He was starting to lose his nerve. Trent would talk with him privately.

"Listen you two, this entire operation is completely under control. Peter Kramer and Sarah Phillips have not uncovered a thing that can link us to the missing money. All of the records at Kingston and the Bank of Boston are in perfect order. That's the beauty of this thing. Furthermore the college is in the clear. Nothing can remotely connect the college to any wrongdoing."

"I see your point, Walton," said Cannon, "it's just that I'm not used to this sort of business."

"Well get used to it, James, because it's not going to go away. The best thing for you to do is stay cool. Go with the program and continue being the wonderful college president everyone thinks you are."

Cannon nodded silently. He kept his embarrassment to himself.

"Now, just so we are all on the same page, we continue with business as usual. I'll take care of Kramer and Phillips. Since you didn't have the courage to fire Kramer, I will just have to figure a way to neutralize him. Don't worry, he won't get hurt."

Shortly after 6:30 the three walked out of the Pinehurst Inn dining room as it began filling up with people from the town and college.

Near a candlelit window in one corner of the room Anne Ashdown and Martha Phillips had just been seated for dinner. They saw the three men exit.

"Wonder what they have been talking about," mused Mrs. Ashdown.

"They sure don't look very happy," responded Martha.

"Well President Cannon looks downright depressed," said Mrs. Ashdown. "He hardly looked past his two big feet as he walked out," She chuckled. She made a mental note to tell Peter the next time she saw him.

Peter and Elisabeth were arriving in Pinehurst after their long day in Boston. Peter let Elisabeth off next to her car in the parking lot of Taylor Hall and after agreeing to stay in close contact, they parted. He waited until she got her car started before driving off towards the Phillips estate. After a few minutes he pulled the small MGB into the driveway. Jamie and Sarah came running out the front door. The red Golden Retriever reached Peter first. Peter gave her a quick pat on the head before turning towards Sarah, who wrapped her arms around him. The greeting felt good after such a long day.

"Tell me about your day," an expectant Sarah asked Peter.

He paused on the brick walkway. "I'm not sure we have that much new information, but my gut feeling has never been stronger."

"What do you mean?" She felt a mix of disappointment and excitement.

Peter carefully told her about his entire trip, paying close attention to his time in Bill Rutherford's office in the Bank of Boston.

Sarah listened quietly.

"Have you stopped to consider that Empire Insurance Company might not be a legitimate business?"

Peter scratched his chin. He hadn't thought of that one.

Sarah continued. "I remember in one of my bank training workshops the instructor warning us never to assume that every business is on the up and up. That warning always stuck with me."

"So maybe Empire Insurance is a front, is that what you mean?"

"I don't know. All I know is a ton of money has disappeared and someone took it. Maybe this company is involved."

"Bill Rutherford couldn't confirm anything other than Empire Insurance has an account with the Bank of Boston and they did in fact transfer two million dollars from their Boston account to their New York account at Chemical Bank."

Sarah chewed her lower lip in deep thought. Suddenly she said, "Let's go to New York and check out Empire Insurance."

"What, you mean just fly down there and walk into their main headquarters. What do we do when we get there?"

"Peter, we need to establish their existence. We know Boston Naval Shipyard is legitimate. We now need to turn our attention to other possibilities. What else do we have to go on?"

"OK, that makes sense, but it may be a waste of time and money."

"Well, it's a risk worth taking. Who knows what we will find."

CHAPTER THIRTY-TWO

The following Tuesday, Peter and Sarah drove to Boston and boarded the 9:00 A.M. shuttle from Logan to LaGuardia, arriving in New York at 9:50. They deplaned and walked through the busy terminal to the Avis Car Rental where they picked up a small Toyota compact. Peter had called Bill Rutherford, who found the address for Empire Insurance. At a dirty Texaco Station they got directions to 1500 West 150th. Traveling north on Amsterdam Avenue they fought the daytime traffic finally arriving at 150th. Peter turned left and headed toward the 1500 block. The tall sky skyscrapers seemed to shrink in size in their rear view window as they drove farther and farther away from the city center. Brownstone apartments dominated both sides of the street but these also faded and were replaced by a mix of old dilapidated homes and dirty brown buildings. Peter began to wonder if they were lost. He rechecked the directions and was satisfied they were right. He and Sarah exchanged anxious glances. They came to the intersection of West 150 and 1500. On their immediate right was a four-story building with dirty windows and filthy streaks of brown running down the front. The sign said Macintosh Building. Peter stopped and pulled over to the curb so Sarah could jump out and read the small lettering under the Macintosh sign. A moment later she came back and reported that Empire Insurance was on the fourth floor. Two blocks farther Peter found a small parking place and squeezed in the Toyota. After locking the car they walked hand in hand down the narrow sidewalk past a bar and several old men out front who leered at Sarah in obvious drunken states. They hurried on, crossing at the intersection and approaching the Macintosh Building on their left.

They entered a dark and dank lobby. A number of old stuffed chairs and yellow-lighted lamps dotted the small lobby. The carpet was thin and worn. A dirty-looking elevator awaited them at the far end of the lobby next to a stairway. They glanced at the elevator and opted for the stairs. They quickly began ascending the well-worn stairwell until they reached the fourth floor. Opening the door to the hallway they cautiously entered a wide hall with offices on either side. Passing a door with the name State Loan and Mortgage, they came to Empire Insurance Company. Peter tried the door but it was locked. He knocked but got no answer. Several minutes went by and finally a shadow appeared at the inside of the office door followed by the door being slowly opened. A young woman in a tight skirt with far too much makeup on her face peered around the corner. She was tall and thin with a face that once been attractive.

"Can I help you?" she asked.

"We are looking for Empire Insurance," answered Peter, all the while trying to get a look at the inside of the office.

The young woman appeared nervous.

"I'm sorry but all of our agents are out right now".

"When will they be back?" asked Sarah.

The woman stared at Sarah. "I really couldn't tell you."

"May we come in and wait?" asked Peter.

"No, but I can take your name and number and I'm sure one of our agents will call you."

Peter made slight eye contact with Sarah mouthing the word "no" before turning back to the young woman.

"No, that's all right. We will come back another time."

Peter and Sarah turned and began walking back towards the stairway.

They glanced back and saw the young woman still looking at them. They bounded down the stairs as fast as they could anxious to reach the lobby. Once out into the street they slowed down and began walking to their car.

Back on the fourth floor of the Macintosh Building the young woman checked the locked door before picking up the black telephone on the old scarred wooden desk. She dialed nine digits and while waiting for an answer pulled two large pictures of Peter and Sarah out of a locked drawer. She studied their faces. They made a good-looking couple, she thought to herself. Suddenly a smooth voice on the other end interrupted her thoughts.

"This is Mr. Nichols."

"Mr. Nichols, this is Gloria at Empire Insurance. You told me to call you when our two clients came to visit. Well they were just here a few minutes ago and left. I told them there were no agents available just like you told me."

She paused listening to the voice at the other end.

"Yes, I am very sure that was them. I have their pictures right here in front of me."

"Thank you Gloria, you did fine. Please stay in the office until 4:00, then you can go home."

"Thank you Mr. Nichols. Should I come back tomorrow?"

"Yes, come to work at 8:30 like you have been doing. Either I or Mr. Trent will call you."

"I will. Thank you. Mr. Nichols."

She hung up the phone and reached for her makeup bag. Soon she was engrossed in manicuring her nails. The loud smacking of her gum was audible in the hallway.

Peter and Sarah drove back to the airport, hoping to catch the 3:00 shuttle to Logan. They were stunned to have learned that Empire Insurance was nothing more than an office in a dirty brick building in a decaying neighborhood in east New York. The scary part was now they had a solid lead. The question was what now.

"I think I'd better go back to Bill Rutherford. He needs to know about Empire Insurance. All signs point to the Bank of Boston and Empire Insurance in this together."

Sarah nodded in agreement. "But what do we ask him? What does he look for?"

"He has to access the computer system and dig up as much information on Empire as possible. Hopefully we can trace the stolen money and identify who is behind this conspiracy."

They arrived at LaGuardia at 2:35 and after dropping off the rented Toyota literally ran through the crowded concourse, reaching gate 65 just as the doors were closing. They were allowed to board and soon were in their seats for the 55-minute flight to Boston.

They were back in Pinehurst by 7:30 that same evening. It was decided that Peter would call Bill Rutherford in the morning right after his 9:00 class. They were seated in the living room when Jamie began barking. Peter looked up to see the yellow lights of a car turn into the driveway. He stood up and walked to the big bay window and saw Martha Phillips's blue Mercedes coming up the drive. A few minutes later she came into the living room from the rear of the house.

"Well, hello you two," she said affectionately. She liked the idea of Peter and Sarah together. Sarah knew this because Martha Phillips had point blank told her so last week.

"Hi, Grandmother. We just arrived back a little while ago," said Sarah, anticipating her question.

"Tell me, how was your trip to New York. I'm almost afraid to ask."

They both hesitated before Sarah plunged ahead.

"We discovered something very interesting." Sarah told her about Empire Insurance Company and its seedy location.

"My goodness, Sarah, this is getting stranger and stranger. I'm also getting really worried about you both."

"Don't worry, Grandmother. Peter and I are being very careful."

Martha Phillips crossed the spacious living room and took Sarah's hand. "I just don't want to see you get hurt. I'd better be going off to bed." She smiled at Peter and lightly kissed Sarah's cheek before turning and walking slowly up the grand staircase.

Peter and Sarah watched her.

"She misses Grandfather, Peter. I can tell. I still don't think she understands how he could have passed away so suddenly."

Peter stayed for a few more minutes before heading home. He had to prepare some class notes for his 9:00 Introduction to Business class the next morning.

CHAPTER THIRTY-THREE

Peter reached Bill Rutherford by telephone the next morning and filled him in about his trip to New York.

Rutherford was incredulous. "You mean to tell me that Empire Insurance doesn't exist."

"No, well, I'm not really sure. The place is in a run-down old brick four-story dive in a bad part of town. I expected a nice building with decent furniture and a lobby with a receptionist who would smile and direct us to the right people. So, no, I don't think Empire Insurance is a legitimate business. It has to be a front."

"Sounds pretty suspicious to me," said Rutherford. "Look, let me do some more checking and I'll get back to you, OK?"

Peter could sense he was taken by surprise and seemed anxious to dig deeper.

"That would be great, Bill. I'll be up here at the college."

Bill Rutherford hung up the phone and sat back in his soft leather chair. Up to this precise moment he had not really put much stock in Peter Kramer's assertions that such large amounts of money had been actually stolen and certainly not by someone in the Bank of Boston. Now, with this odd news about Empire Insurance his curiosity was piqued. He wasn't anxious to get into the corporate accounts section files but unfortunately that was where Empire Insurance was located. Should he risk an entry into the file system? Should he call Justin Nichols? He weighed the alternatives and decided against alerting Justin Nichols. He didn't know him well enough. If Bill Rutherford entered the corporate accounts file he knew it would be undetected but still since this was not in his domain he nevertheless felt uneasy. After 10 minutes of deliberation his curiosity got the best of him.

At 11:25 am Bill typed in his password and gained entry into corporate accounts. The screen displayed an immense menu, which he scrolled down to domestic accounts where he found Empire Insurance. He typed in a second password and immediately was granted access to the firm's file. The account was a straight corporate blue chip which meant that Empire was given full banking services including premium interest rates as long as there was a minimum of $1 million in the account at any given time. Bill studied the electronic ledger. It appeared that Empire kept an account in Boston as a means of transferring substantial amounts of money to its New York Bank, Chemical Bank. Bill noted a series of significant deposits and almost immediate same-day or next-day transfers to Chemical. He reasoned that if Empire was fraudulent then the source of money it deposited in the Bank of Boston could be the stolen money. His next step was to trace the deposits. Where were they coming from and who was authorizing them. Peter Kramer had suggested that the $2 million deposited on December 17, 2001, into Empire's account was actually John Phillips's money diverted from the college to Empire. So this was where Rutherford started.

Bill Rutherford was a seasoned bank executive. He had seen his share of people and companies trying to steal money.

But always without fail the key ingredient was the knowledge that money was missing. In this case no one apart from Peter and maybe a few others believed anything had been stolen. There was simply no evidence of any money being stolen. Either no money was missing or the thieves had covered their tracks extremely well. In any case Bill Rutherford was going to have to establish an illegal diversion of stolen money into the Empire Insurance Company account, money intended for Kingston College. The Bank of Boston was highly regarded. A theft of this magnitude would have serious public relations repercussions. At 76 years of age and financially able to retire at any time he had little worry for his own job security. The bank, however, was his life and if anyone was doing something to harm its reputation he would do all he could to expose them.

"OK," he said to himself. Time to get to work. He consulted a piece of paper on his desk that held the names, dates and amounts of the three bequests to Kingston College. He decided to check all three again against the deposits made to the Empire account. The John Phillips bequest transfer was made on December 17, 2001, and in the amount of $1,7 million. Peter said the amount should have been $3.7 million,. On that same date $2 million had been deposited into the Empire account. The second bequest was a Phyllis Allen, who had died and left the college $800,000. According to Peter's notes the actual amount Phyllis Allen left to the college was $2.8 million. Another $2 million had disappeared. Rutherford scanned the Empire deposit ledger on his screen and found a $2 million dollar deposit entry on December 9, 2002, the same day the $800,000 from Phyllis Allen's bank, Bank of New Hampshire, transferred to the Bank of Boston and Kingston College's portfolio. Rutherford began to feel his excitement rising. He grasped the piece of paper and looked at the third and final bequest. On September 5, 2002 Elisabeth Ann Williams died and left the college $1 million. The computer screen told him that The Bank of Wolfeboro, in Wolfeboro, New Hampshire, transferred the $1 million to the Bank of Boston on September 5, 2002. He turned to the Empire Insurance accounts ledger on his computer screen and found a $1,300,000 deposit entry to Empire on the same day.

Rutherford slumped back in his chair and stared out at the Boston skyline. He felt sick. He now had information that Empire Insurance was probably fraudulent and that three separate entries had been made to Empire on precisely the same days three bequests had been transferred to the college, all of which were less than their Peter Kramer and Sarah Phillips believed them to be. Were these deposits to Empire from these three bequests? If so, who was behind this? He pondered these questions for a long time as he sat in his chair on the 35th floor. Suddenly he knew what he had to do next.

At 11:45 A.M. Bill Rutherford made his way down the hallway to the bank of elevators. As he waited for the bell to ping, Justin Nichols suddenly appeared beside him. Dressed in a gray banker's suit, his 280 pounds on a 5"11' frame presented an imposing presence. He reminded Bill of a bull with his dark protruding eyebrows and penetrating eyes.

"Hello, Bill, how are you?"

"Fine and you, Justin?" he asked.

"Oh, I 'm doing well. Where are you headed?"

The elevator arrived before Bill could answer. They both stepped in. Bill pushed the lobby button instead of the tenth floor where the management information systems department was located.

"I'm headed out to lunch," lied Bill. He was startled by Justin's presence.

"Me too," replied Justin.

They rode down in silence, arriving in the spacious lobby a few moments later.

"Have a nice lunch, Bill," said Justin as he strode across the lobby in the direction of the main entrance.

Bill watched him leave and after waiting a few minutes headed back to the elevators. Outside across Boylston Street, Justin Nichols waited on the sidewalk watching the main entrance for Bill Rutherford to emerge. He stood there for ten minutes, finally deciding that he wasn't coming. Bill Rutherford had lied to him. Nichols wasn't surprised. At 11:25 this morning while he was working on his computer the soft beep had sounded, signaling that someone was accessing the Empire Insurance account. When Nichols had first set up the account he had installed a warning beep program to detect unauthorized entries. No one in the bank or for that matter in the Information Systems Department knew of the program's existence. Immediately upon hearing the beep he had punched a six-code number that identified who the unauthorized entry was. This was another secret program he had installed. Bill Rutherford's name instantly popped onto the screen. Justin didn't like this latest turn of events. Bill Rutherford was getting a bit too close.

Rutherford rode the elevator back up to the tenth floor and got off. He quickly walked down the hallway to Jeff Peters' office. He opened the door and found the gangly six-foot computer wizard hunched over a 16-inch computer monitor eating a peanut butter and jam sandwich. A skateboard and fishing pole leaned against the wall in the corner. Jeff turned, his mouth full, and grunted a hello to Bill. The two were unlikely friends but when Jeff had first come to work at the bank he had been assigned to help Bill learn the bank's new network system. Bill immediately liked Jeff's unpretentious manner. He found it refreshing after working all day with stuffy bank people. The two struck up a friendship. Bill would often visit him in his small cramped office just to get away from the corporate politics.

"Jeff, I need your help."

"Sure Bill, what's up?

"Jeff, this is a bit unusual but I need you to gear up that computer brain of yours and help me unravel a mystery. What I'm about to ask you could be a bit on the edge. If you aren't comfortable, we can just drop it."

Jeff swiveled in his chair. "Hey, now this sounds interesting. You're not asking me to break any laws, are you?"

"No, of course not, but I am asking you to violate bank policy."

Jeff stopped eating his sandwich.

"Bill, if you are asking me to do this, there has to be a darn good reason."

Rutherford nodded. "There is, Jeff. Let's start with a few hypothetical questions."

Jeff wiped his mouth and took a swig of his lemon-lime Gatorade, never taking his eyes off Bill.

"OK," said Bill, "if someone at this bank wanted to intercept an incoming transfer of money and secretly divert a portion of it to another account, could they do it and do so undetected?"

Jeff considered the question. He reached over and took another drink from his Gatorade bottle.

"Well, all transfers are done electronically. The transferring bank sends it electronically and a tape is then kept for documentation purposes. It's all done on the tenth floor here. Our information systems people have it set up so all the suits upstairs have to do is punch in a few coded numbers and then hit the magical initiate key. The sending bank initiates a fund transfer request, which is then authorized at this end. I'm sure you know that. We trained everyone on how to operate the system. But that's not the question you are asking." The young man paused.

"What you're asking is highly technical, not to mention very illegal."

Rutherford nodded and remained silent, waiting for Peters to continue.

"If someone wanted to do what you're suggesting, they would have to set up a rogue program that would intercept the transfer the instant it was sent to our bank. You see once the electronic transfer is complete, the computer automatically files the transaction and immediately asks for a tape for documentation. This is completed within seconds so no one at the receiving end can have opportunity to screw around with the funds. Makes sense, doesn't it? It's all part of our bank's security system. But a rogue program could insert itself into the electronic transfer a few milliseconds ahead of the tape documentation and technically divert funds to another source. A second tape is created documenting funds to the diverted account. The remaining funds would then proceed as usual with the sending bank not knowing anything illegal occurred. They just know the money got sent.

"Do you remember the story of that Mafia guy in the sixties who set up a system where he knew the outcome of horse races and would telephone bookie places across the company in different time zones with the results and people would place huge amounts of money on the winner? He had only a few seconds to communicate the results but it bought the Mafia just enough time to place bets. They got caught but not until after a lot of money was stolen. This is the same type of thing."

Rutherford leaned forward in his chair. Things were starting to take shape. He took a wrinkled piece of paper out of his tweed sport coat.

"Jeff, can you document the exact times of these transactions?" he asked, waving them in the air. "I also need you to compare them with deposits made to a company called Empire Insurance. This is where it gets a bit dicey. I'll have to give you authority but you need to know it is not in my domain. I will take full responsibility."

"Sure, Bill." He turned to his monitor. Bill gave him the names of John Phillips, Phyllis Allen, and Ann Elisabeth Williams along with the code for Empire Insurance. Jeff Peters skillfully manipulated the keyboard so fast Rutherford could hardly follow. After 10 minutes of working the computer keys like a magician, he was finished.

"Holy smokes," he said. "Look at this."

Bill moved closer and looked over Jeff's right shoulder at the screen. He had brought up the three bequest transactions and cross compared them with the three deposit entries at Empire Insurance. On December 17, 2001, the Bank of Pinehurst electronically transferred the $1.7 million into the Kingston College account at 9:47.30 A.M. The $2 million transfer into the Empire Insurance account was completed at exactly 9:47.35 A.M. Less than a tenth of a second separated the Allen transfer and Empire deposit and less than three tenths of a second the Williams transfer and the third Empire deposit.

Bill went back to his chair and sat with his head in his hands.

"Jeff, is there a rogue program operating in this bank?" he asked, looking up. He already knew the answer to his question.

"This is clear evidence that one is at work. One could say it is a coincidence, but I wouldn't believe them for a second. Look, you have three transactions all followed by instantaneous deposits to this place called Empire Insurance. Too close for comfort by my standards. Is Empire reputable? If they aren't, that would really sound the alarms for me."

"Jeff can you get me evidence that there is a rogue program at work?"

"I don't know if I can, Bill. The fact that it is done so quickly and resembles the thousands of other legal transactions completed in this bank makes it tough to distinguish. That's the beauty of a rogue program. The creators have taken great pains to make it quick, simple, and extremely similar to routine transactions. But let me give it go. I'll do my best."

"Listen, Jeff, I may have placed you in a difficult position. Quite honestly I believe there may be illegal activity going on at the bank and now I have involved you. I must ask you to keep this completely confidential."

"Hey, this is kind of exciting, but I know this is serious business, Mr. Rutherford. You can count on me being quiet."

"Please just try and get me some evidence on his rogue program and only tell me, OK?"

"You got it. I'll get right to work on it." He was already at work on his computer as Rutherford shut the outer office door on his way out.

Justin Nichols ate a hearty lunch of steak, salad, and two glasses of red wine. He came back to his office at 1:30 and immediately logged onto this computer. A flashing red arrow indicated he had electronic mail or someone had accessed the Empire Insurance account again. He swore under his breath. He hoped it was his mail. Quickly he typed in his password and found the second entry into the Empire Insurance account that day. Who is Jeff Peters, he wondered? He called his secretary and asked her to find out. A few minutes later she told him he worked in the management systems department. He swore again. Bill Rutherford must have gotten to him.

Justin Nichols's professional resume said he had been in the banking business for over 25 years. According to his resume, at 24 years of age, freshly graduated from Cornell, he had taken a position with City Bank of New York. He stayed 10 years before moving on to Chemical Bank as an investment banker. Gradually over the years his tastes in fine things had grown as had his weight. He now lived in an elegant 3000-square-foot uptown co-op that he had paid off several years ago. He ate dinner out every night. His wife had divorced him five years ago after becoming tired of competing with his love of power, money, and food. He bought his clothes from the finest establishments. His love of rich food and vintage wines was almost legendary. But it was his quick anger and reputation for tenacity that were his trademark. At 280 pounds, Justin Nichols posed a massive physical presence wherever he went. He would move through the bank like a force five tornado. His bulldog face with its small beady eyes would seek out its prey and lock on like a heat-seeking missile. One moment he could be savvy and charming with a client and the next moment reduce a harmless assistant or secretary to tears. He was someone people loved to hate but almost always bowed to like a king to when they encountered him in the hallway. Like a seasoned ballet dancer he could walk that fine line between right and wrong. He came close several times but never got caught. In reality, Justin Nichols crossed the line a number of times. The big man could hide his tracks well.

He picked up the telephone with his meaty right hand. His white starched shirt and diamond cuff links stretched back to reveal a Rolex watch. Aggressively punching in 10 numbers he leaned back in his big leather chair and considered the situation with Bill Rutherford. The man was getting too close for his own good.

A voice suddenly came on the other end.

"This is Walton Trent."

"Trent, Justin here. Listen, Bill Rutherford got into the Empire Account today. He's getting close. We need to do something."

Back in New Hampshire, Walton Trent swore under his breath before getting up to shut his office door.

"OK, let's not panic. How much do you think he knows?"

"What a stupid question," responded Nichols angrily. "Once he gets into the account he will see the Empire deposits match the exact dates of the Kingston bequest transfers. You told me Peter Kramer had those dates in his hand and gave them to Rutherford. He's too smart not to put two and two together."

Trent cringed, waiting for Justin's quick temper. Justin Nichols was one of the few people who could intimidate him.

"Do you think he's discovered the rogue program?" asked Trent. He waited for another outburst.

"I don't know," said Nichols. "He did meet with one of our information systems staff during lunch. I do know that person also logged onto the Empire account too."

This time Trent swore more loudly. Rutherford was getting way too close.

"We have to get a handle on this," said Justin. "The boys aren't going to be happy."

"I know, I know," said Trent. "Listen, you take care of your computer guy and I'll handle Rutherford."

"OK, but cover your tracks well. Use the same people, and for goodness sakes, make it look accidental."

CHAPTER THIRTY-FOUR

President James Cannon sat in his usual place next to Randolph Bolles at the Board of Trustees meeting for Kingston College. The rest of the President's Cabinet sat at the back of the conference room, while the 28-member board sat around the cherry table. Bolles was speaking to the board about the need to improve the scholarship among the faculty. A recurring theme!

"Most of our faculty are mediocre when it comes to scholarship. Kingston can't become a first-class institution unless we raise the bar and really get our faculty conducting first-rate scholarship."

His passion was evident. The board sat silently as he continued to ramble on. A few heads nodded in affirmation but most thought the college had a good faculty and in fact were doing scholarship. They all had heard this speech before. The cabinet sat in the back equally bored. Elisabeth Rutherford listened to every word but maintained an impassive face. She was getting tired of Bolles's tirades. Worst of all, the faculty was becoming demoralized.

Cannon's thoughts were a million miles away. Long ago he had been inspired and held great hope for Kingston College.

He too, wanted to put the college on the map. But somewhere along the line things had gotten very confused. He knew it had first started with Bolles's constant pressure to improve scholarship and move the college forward. But the real trouble had begun when he hired Walton Trent. He glanced at Trent sitting in the back in his dark gray $800 suit and white starched shirt and red and blue tie. Walton Trent had become the vehicle to take the pressure off him that Bolles so steadfastly exerted. But Trent had taken it a lot further. James Cannon was now deeply immersed in a scheme he never dreamed possible. At first he believed the two of them could help the other. Gradually he saw that Trent was only in it for the money and would tolerate Cannon as long as it served his purposes.

Bolles soon finished to everyone's relief and Dan Miller walked to the podium to give his financial report. The board members shifted in their seats with evident interest. Miller was someone they could more easily understand. Miller shuffled his papers and after adjusting his glasses he reported that the college was about to balance its books for the 24th straight year. He knew they would like this news. He presented the statement of income and expenditures for the third quarter of the fiscal year. Several board members had questions at the end but clearly they trusted Miller and his numbers.

Walton Trent stood up next and walking confidently to the front delivered his fundraising report. He told them about the eight $800,000 Phyllis Allen bequest. The money would go the college endowment and capital campaign. He next reported on the Henry Townsend $1 million gift for the new fine arts center. He did not mention much about Townsend's will except to say that Kingston was to be included. Trent's report was upbeat and certainly encouraging to the board. He sat down a few minutes later to light applause.

The meeting ended at 2:00 in the afternoon. The conference

room quickly emptied except for the cabinet, who lingered behind. Rutherford and Miller expected Cannon to want a debriefing for a few minutes but were surprised to see him and Trent engaged in deep conversation. After a few minutes of fruitless waiting, she and Miller left the room and walked out of the building.

"I thought James would want to debrief a bit," said Elisabeth.

"He seems distracted," replied Miller. "Yesterday he in came into my office and wanted information on the last three bequests left to the college. He left with hardly a word of thanks, let alone any conversation."

They walked across campus to Taylor Hall and entered the old administration building. Elisabeth glanced back and saw Cannon and Trent get into Trent's Buick and drive off. She wondered where they were off to.

CHAPTER THIRTY-FIVE

Jeff Peters had graduated from Boston University in 1993 with a degree in Computer Science. He came to work for the Bank of Boston six months later. He knew computers better than anyone at the bank. He also couldn't have cared less about corporate politics, which is why he continued to work in the information systems department as a systems analyst. Fishing and computers filled his life. He didn't ask for more. Single and unattached, he still lived with his parents in South Boston in their 80-year-old two-story white clapboard home. During his nine years at the bank he had become known as a technical genius with few social skills. His performance evaluations were consistently outstanding simply because he was great at what he did. But there was also an adventurous side to Jeff Peters which few if any people saw. He was drawn to the lure of conspiracy and intrigue especially when it came to the computer world. So when Bill Rutherford came to see him he could barely hide his excitement.

For two days he used every spare minute to search the vast Bank of Boston computer network. As a systems analyst he had fairly wide access to most of the computer network system. He was careful not to log on to the Empire Insurance account too much. No use drawing unwanted attention. He started from the premise that there were eyes and ears on the system. He also knew how to cover his tracks as he moved through the system. He was a maestro at work. His was a rare gift and he reasoned correctly that not many people had his ability. Most people on the network left evidence behind. Jeff Peters could figure out who had been where and when on the network at almost any time. He could pinpoint the computer tracks of people with amazing accuracy. If there indeed was a rogue program, he would find it and identify its creator.

The first day he simply eliminated all of the obvious possibilities. He figured the creator would be good but it didn't hurt to search for the easiest solutions first. By 5:30 P.M. he had come up empty handed. Throughout the day he ran a program search on user activity surrounding the time period of the three bequests. He studied the screen and could find no irregularities. He was well acquainted with all system users and easily identified their password and activity logs. The creator was no doubt far more sophisticated and would devise a program to cover his or her tracks. He now knew he had to dig far deeper into the system if he hoped to discover a rogue program. He yawned and stretched his lanky legs out as far as he could. Time to go home. He left the seventh floor and rode the elevator down to the main lobby. Tomorrow he would resume his search.

The next morning he came into work at 7:00 and after tossing his bag lunch on one corner of his messy desk sat down to work. He worked the keyboard rapidly. At 9:45 he finally found something interesting. For the last hour he had been running a scan on the activity log of all persons associated with insurance company accounts. He conducted his search under the guise of a maintenance program to detect any viruses. He hoped this would not draw attention and yet allow him to investigate the activity of users in the Empire Insurance account. He noticed a small programming code called DET X. He immediately knew this as an alert code. A programmer could install this code into a specific account on the system. A red flag would appear on a designated monitor when someone was accessing the account. All of this, of course, would be unknown to the user. The DET X code was often used for security purposes, but Jeff knew it was not authorized for use at the Bank of Boston. Whenever someone accessed Empire Insurance Company's account, the red flag would pop up on a computer somewhere in the bank along with the user's name. Jeff's heart raced. He began working the keys furiously trying to identify the person who programmed the code. Thirty-five minutes later he had the name. The DET X code was attached to the computer of Justin Nichols. Jeff sat back in his chair and chewed on a piece of red licorice. Why would Justin Nichols be so interested in placing a red flag alert on Empire Insurance? Usually this was the activity of the security department, not a vice president. And in fact, the Bank of Boston did not use DET X codes. A second thought hit him. Both he and Bill Rutherford had accessed the account and didn't know that Justin Nichols knew they had. Not until now.

Turning back to the computer he continued to work. Something was going on. He had to be careful now. Whoever had installed the DET X code was sophisticated and could be monitoring activity on the account beyond simply seeing a red flag alert. He searched almost all morning to no avail. Every transaction looked routine. Nothing odd stood out. The activity logs for Kingston College and Empire Insurance held no surprises. The deposit codes for both were ordinary and met bank standards. At 11:45 he decided to start tracing backwards to the initial original transaction from the Bank of Pinehurst. On that day the bank engaged in thousands of transactions from all over New England, across the country, and even internationally. Jeff tediously scanned down the first several thousand before his eyes became tired. Every entry and its movement into the inner workings of the bank looked normal. If there was a rogue program, it was a good one. He heard the outer office door open. He quickly punched a key that closed the screen and brought up the screensaver. Suddenly, Jeff heard the soft footsteps of someone approaching. He had no time to react. Looking up, he was relieved to see Bill Rutherford poke his head around the corner of his cubicle.

"Sorry if I startled you," apologized Rutherford.

"Actually, you did," admitted Jeff.

Rutherford entered the cubicle and sat down.

"Found anything yet?"

Jeff told him about the red flag alert on Justin Nichols's computer. Rutherford's patrician face went pale.

"You mean he set this up so he would know who is accessing the account?"

Jeff nodded his head and then asked Rutherford.

"This isn't normal bank practice, is it?"

"No, some banks do it but not here."

Jeff paused before continuing. "Mr. Rutherford, are you aware that Justin Nichols knows you were accessing the Empire account, aren't you?"

"Yes, I'm afraid I know. Listen Jeff, can you speed things up and try to find this rogue program?" Jeff noticed the urgency in Rutherford's voice.

"Sure, Mr. Rutherford. I'll keep working on this." He hesitated for a moment.

"Mr. Rutherford, I'd suggest you not access the Empire Insurance account anymore. It might not be safe."

"No, I won't. Thanks Jeff. Just get me the information as soon as possible."

After Rutherford left, Jeff decided to step up his search by creating his own program to search for any irregularities in the transactions during the time period in question. He spent 30 minutes creating a search vehicle that would spot even the subtlest changes in the thousands of transactions. At 2:00 he finished and started running the makeshift program. He hit the start key and sat back in his chair. At 3:00 he hit pay dirt. He stared at his screen in awe and appreciation. He had discovered the rogue program. A very good rogue program. It was incredibly difficult to pick up by even the best programmer. A coded number and time and date next to the number identified every bank transaction. The key was that the time numbers were six digits long and consecutive. A regular number would read 10:20.50 that meant 20 minutes past 10 and 50 seconds. This was the exact time of the transaction. Thousands and thousands of these transactions filled the screen. Many were almost at the exact time. Next to the number was the transaction amount. Since there were so many duplicate transactions at close to the same time the bank computer system allowed the time digits to extend beyond six and move to hundredths of a second, which allowed for every transaction to have its own time of entry. This would not show up on any screen except for recordkeeping in the information systems department. Next to the Bank of Pinehurst transaction number and time was 9:47.30.68. Immediately following this transaction was an entry into the Empire Insurance account with a log entry time of 9:47.30.70. He knew that in this briefest of mini seconds a deposit transaction could take place. It happened all the time. This was what the rogue program was counting on. The creators had installed the program to capture the split moment and divert the money from one account into the

Empire Insurance account. In that moment the system would obey the rogue program's instructions. The Bank of Pinehurst would never know the difference. They believed the transaction was normal. The rogue program was brilliant except for one small but crucial detail. The computer system maintained a backup of all transactions. This was common knowledge. Certainly the rogue program creators knew this. What most people didn't know was that the history of bank activity was not only contained on computer screens. Of course, the computer screen was what everybody looked at and used the data to make decisions. Jeff knew the computer held one last secret. For just one instant every original transaction flashed on the screen back to the original date of entry. To recapture the transaction required someone with extensive computer knowledge. Even though the rogue program had diverted a portion of the actual amount into Empire Insurance and the new records showed this, the original deposit from the Bank of Pinehurst, an amount that existed in the Bank of Boston for only a few hundredths of a second, had not entirely disappeared. Jeff excitedly typed in a series of numbers. Suddenly there it was. A flashing number retrieved from deep in the mind of the computer system showed the original Phillips deposit of $3,700,000. No one in the bank but Jeff Peters knew this flashing number existed. He had outsmarted the rogue program. He felt a shiver of exhilaration and fear.

He quickly began documenting his findings and after printing what he needed placed the materials in his backpack. He also decided to e-mail a duplicate file to his home just in case. He got up to go see Bill Rutherford.

Fifteen minutes later he was finished explaining to Bill Rutherford what he had found. He handed Rutherford the documentation before leaving.

"Jeff, I can't thank you enough. You also understand this is very confidential?"

"Of course, Mr. Rutherford. I won't breathe a word of it. If you need more help, just give me a call. This is fun stuff."

Rutherford stopped Jeff before he walked out the door. He hastily scrawled Peter Kramer's name on a piece of paper. "Hang onto this name. He is a faculty member at Kingston College where my daughter is the dean. If anything goes wrong, call him immediately. He will help you."

After Jeff Peters left his office Rutherford wondered what to do next. He had no idea how far this conspiracy extended within the bank. Who could he trust? He decided to call Peter Kramer first.

Peter was in his office grading papers when Bill Rutherford called. He listened intently as Rutherford told him what Jeff Peters had discovered. Peter felt his pulse quicken. At long last something tangible, some real evidence of a massive wrongdoing. Rutherford agreed to express mail the documentation to Peter immediately. As their conversation came to a close, Peter urged him to be careful and promised they would stay in contact.

Peter hung up the phone and walking out of his building made his way across campus to Taylor Hall to see Sarah. She was busily working away in her office when he walked in.

"Hey," he said with obvious affection in his voice.

She looked up and smiled. "Peter, you know something, it's written all over your face."

He quickly recounted his phone conversation with Bill Rutherford.

"I knew it," she said excitedly.

He nodded. "We've finally got some of that evidence we were looking for."

"What do we do next?"

"I don't know yet. Bill Rutherford is sending me the documentation but we have to figure how to effectively use it."

"Why can't we go to the police?"

"Not yet, I'm afraid we might lose the big players if we go too fast. Let's wait and see what he sends us. After that we plan our next step."

"Come by for dinner tonight," she said.

"See you then."

CHAPTER THIRTY-SIX

Bill Rutherford was born in Boston in 1925. Now at 76 years of age he was about ready to close out a distinguished career in banking primarily with the Bank of Boston. He was well respected by his colleagues at the bank as well as the Boston banking community. He had graduated from Harvard with a degree in finance in 1951. His college career had been interrupted in 1943 by World War II, when he was drafted as an 18-year-old straight out of Brookline High School. He served four years in Europe before returning home and enrolling at Harvard in 1947. In 1953 after two years with State Street Bank, he took a position with the Bank of Boston and had worked there ever since. He was in his 48th and final year with the bank. In two months he would officially retire to spend his time traveling and sailing on the family sailboat out of Marblehead. Bill Rutherford had an ability to relate to all people, young and old alike. He and Jeff Peters, though so far apart in age, had established a good friendship. While extremely proper and always dressed in the traditional banker's suit and tie, Bill Rutherford was as friendly and down to earth as one's next door neighbor. Completely trustworthy, Bill Rutherford was a most honest person. He believed there was no substitute for hard work. Shortcuts did not exist in his world. His fierce loyalty to the bank, coupled with his honesty and strong work ethic, motivated Bill Rutherford. The question of illegality at his beloved bank did not sit well with him this day. He was quietly very angry.

At 3:30 on the afternoon Jeff Peters had passed along the dramatic information to him, Bill Rutherford walked through the ornate lobby of the venerable bank. He held the materials from Jeff tightly under his left arm. No one would have ever guessed the distinguished white-haired gentleman immaculately dressed in the gray suit held a secret that would certainly rock the banking world and beyond. A number of people greeted Rutherford, including old Benjamin Brady, the long-time bank doorman, in his red and blue uniform. The two had been at the bank together for over 35 years. They held each other in mutual respect and esteem. Ben saluted Bill as he walked out the door. Rutherford tipped his hat in obvious respect. They didn't have to say much to each other. It was understood. Benjamin watched his old friend walk out of the bank never dreaming it would be the last time he would ever see him alive.

The heavy bank doors closed behind Bill Rutherford for the final time. He disappeared into the crowded sidewalk on Boylston Street. The steaming heat from the underground heating vents swallowed Bill Rutherford from sight.

He made his way down the old Boston street clutching the package. At the corner of Commonwealth Avenue and Arlington Street he waited patiently for the light to turn and the orange walk sign to flash. The crowd soon surged across the wide street towards Boston Common. On the other side most people turned right or left and continued their way along the cold concrete sidewalks. He decided to escape the crowds by walking through the forest-like commons. Mothers and their children were skating on the iced-over ponds. He stopped for a moment and watched the winter scene, thinking back to the days when he had taken his own daughter to play on these very same ponds. He trudged up a short incline, the woods becoming thicker and the noises of the children and traffic fading in the distance. Bill Rutherford was headed towards Park Street and the United Parcel Service depot. He would never get there. The air was noticeably cooler and cleaner as he walked deeper into the huge city park. He was looking forward to getting to spend more time on his sailboat upon his retirement. He and Mary would have time to drive up to New Hampshire to see Elisabeth. Life would be full in retirement. He came to a narrow part of the walkway with a steep slope. He noticed a yellow Park Department construction tape extending across the walkway at the top. Nobody was in sight. The path was empty. He was completely alone. Puzzled, he continued up the steep walkway. Birds chattered nosily on either side of the path. He instinctively tightened his hold on the package. Halfway up the slope it happened. Rutherford sensed a movement from his left immediately followed by a lightning-like unrecognizable blur. Everything happened so fast that his brain did not have the time to interpret, let alone react to, what was coming. He felt an unbelievably hard impact on his face followed by his falling and rolling down the steep wooded slope away from the path deeper into the cold woods. He landed face down, his nose and mouth ground into freezing cold dirt and leaves. Coughing and holding the left side of his face, he desperately struggled to sit up. Blood streamed down his face, dripping into the palm of his left hand. He stared in amazement at the pool of bright red blood collecting in his hand. He had risen shakily to one knee when the second blow came. Once more he sensed the blur of movement and turning his face in the direction of the approaching force caught it full in the face. He vaguely heard the crunching of nose ligaments as the sharp searing pain tore through his senses like a hot poker. The third and final blow was administered to the back of his head, shattering his skull and causing massive internal bleeding and brain damage. He landed on his back, his unseeing eyes staring up at the lonely leafless branches of a New England Dutch Elm tree. Several muscles twitched in final response to the violence perpetrated upon his body before he lay dead, hidden in the wild cold clutches of the city park. A hand roughly grabbed the package Rutherford still clutched in his left hand. The man tugged at the package that even in death Bill Rutherford refused to give up. The man then rifled through Rutherford's pockets taking his wallet, watch, and jewelry. A moment later the man, stuffing the yellow park construction tape into his pocket, was casually walking down the park path in the direction of Boylston Street and the waiting black Lincoln Continental. He disappeared into the car, which was soon lost in the busy afternoon traffic. The birds shortly resumed their chatter. A family of ants made their way to the pooling blood around Bill Rutherford's head.

Bill Rutherford was reported missing by his wife Mary that evening at 7:00. She called the Boston Police and her daughter Elisabeth. He was a creature of remarkable habit having arrived at home precisely at 6:00 each evening for the last 48 years. By 6:55 Mary knew something was wrong. The beefy Irish patrolman came to the house because his desk sergeant told him to. Normally a person had to be missing for a lot longer period of time and in fact the Boston Police were too busy to send out a patrolman on a missing person report. Truth was, residents on Beacon Hill got better treatment probably because they were wealthy. He dutifully took down a physical description and some other information before leaving to go back to the station. He promised Mary Rutherford the Boston Police would get right on this case when in reality he would file the report with the duty officer and the police would simply wait for a call or body to appear. He knew people liked to hear the police would get right on it. But there simply wasn't the manpower to conduct a search. Not even for the people on Beacon Hill.

By 9:00 the next morning Bill Rutherford had not been located. Word passed through the bank quickly. People stopped in the plush corridors and talked and speculated what had happened. One employee didn't stop to speculate. Jeff Peters left the bank immediately when he heard the news. After overhearing two secretaries talking about his missing friend he hurried to his office and grabbing a few of his things, left the bank. Moments later he had disappeared into the city.

For two days, no news. The Boston television and radio stations briefly carried the story before turning to other news. The bank hired a private investigator. Elisabeth Rutherford traveled down from New Hampshire to be with her mother. The waiting was exhausting. Mary Rutherford was simply not used to having her husband gone. She and her daughter hoped for the best but were deeply worried. On the third day the waiting ended. Two young boys stumbled upon Bill Rutherford's decaying body while chasing their dog, which was in turn chasing a squirrel in the wooded area off the steep path where Rutherford had been attacked. The little boys ran screaming out of the woods in horror and revulsion. A park policeman heard their screams and upon investigation called the Boston Police immediately. The area was soon cordoned off with yellow police tape. News crews arrived almost as fast as the police investigators. The coroner was summoned and three days later issued a report stating that Bill Rutherford died from blunt trauma to the head and face. In layman's terms, a heavy object crushed his head in. Fortunately, death came fairly quickly. The police investigation concluded Bill Rutherford died from a particularly vicious mugging. His missing wallet and watch was all the evidence they needed to reach their conclusion. The police interviewed several officials at the bank who confirmed nothing was amiss at the bank with regards to Bill Rutherford.

Peter and Sarah came down for Bill Rutherford's funeral in Boston. The church was full with friends, family members, and bank colleagues. The sat near the back of the 200-year-old Episcopal Church. They watched Elisabeth Rutherford escort her mother down the aisle to the front pew. Sarah held Peter's hand tightly throughout the service. Her anxiety was apparent. Peter felt enormous guilt. He had gotten Bill Rutherford involved in the Kingston College mess and now he was dead. Sarah knew he felt awful and tried to reassure him that it wasn't his fault. He had spoken to Elisabeth Rutherford, who had also reassured him. Her grief, while heavy, did not attach blame. She wasn't that kind of person. She was bright enough to know that Peter was helping the college and that her father was probably the victim of a mugging unrelated to what was going on at the college. Peter was far less certain. As the minister spoke, Peter wondered what his next step should be. Anything Bill Rutherford had discovered had gone to the grave with him. He felt frustrated. It seemed he was thwarted at every turn. The service ended with just the family going to the graveside. Elisabeth came over to Peter and Sarah outside the front door of the church and thanked them for coming. Sarah gave her a hug. She asked them both to call her when she got back to Pinehurst.

Peter and Sarah got into Sarah's white BMW and headed towards Route 93. They stopped at a small wayside burger and fries place and hungrily ate tasty cheeseburgers and greasy fries before continuing on to New Hampshire. Two hours later they arrived in Pinehurst. Peter dropped a sleepy Sarah off at her home, picked up his MGB, and continued on to the Ashdown place. He was exhausted. The long drive home along with the difficult funeral had sapped his energy.

The red blinking light on his answering machine pierced the darkness as he entered his cottage. His eyes were drawn to the pulsating flicker. Punching the button he walked over to the refrigerator and took out a can of Pepsi as he listened to the message. A man's voice spoke.

"Mr. Kramer, my name is Jeff Peters. Bill Rutherford gave me your name and told me to call you immediately if anything went wrong. Well Mr. Kramer, something has gone wrong. Something terrible has happened. Bill Rutherford is dead and I don't think it was an accident or a mugging like the newspaper says. I also believe I too may be in a lot of trouble. I don't have time to say more and frankly I don't know who to turn to. Bill said you were a good guy so that's why I'm calling you."

Peter could almost feel the desperation in the man's voice.

The message continued. "I hope you get this message soon. I'll call back tomorrow morning at 9:00. Please be there."

The phone message machine clicked off.

Peter was now wide awake. His mind raced back through the events of the past week. Who was Jeff Peters and how was he involved with Bill Rutherford? What did he want? Why did he sound so scared?

He finished the rest of his Pepsi and after setting his old alarm clock for 8:30 the next morning climbed wearily into bed. The soft mattress felt soothing to his tired and aching body. The cold winter air drifted in through his partially open window. The night sounds of chattering insects at home in their pond at the back of the cottage comforted Peter. The peaceful New Hampshire countryside seemed so incongruous with the mystery that he felt drawn into at Kingston College. Despite his extreme fatigue he couldn't sleep. Something awful was going on at the college. People were dying because of it. His thoughts raced like a speeding train in the night darkness towards an unknown destination. Finally at 1:30 A.M. he drifted off into a restless sleep.

Seven hours later Peter was shaving the creamy white Gillette lather from his lean face. He wanted to be fresh and alert for the phone call from Jeff Peters. He hoped the man would call.

At exactly 9:01 the phone rang. Peter still jumped, even though he was fully expecting it to ring. He carefully picked up the receiver. He noticed his hands were moist. The phone felt slippery in his right hand.

"Hello," he said.

"Mr. Kramer, this is Jeff Peters. I called last night. I assume you got my message."

"Yes I did," replied Peter. "Can you tell me what this is all about?"

The voice on the other end faltered. Peter feared the man would hang up. His fear and confusion was almost palatable.

There was a long silence. Finally the man began talking.

"I work with," he began and quickly changed it to, "I worked with Bill Rutherford at the Bank of Boston. I'm in the information systems department. Well, Bill came to see me a couple of weeks ago with a strange request. I trusted Bill so I got the information he requested. Problem is what I discovered in that information is really scary. He told me to call you if anything happened to him. He gave me your number at home. I'm sure you know he's dead. I don't know who to turn to. I'm afraid to go back to the bank and I can't go home."

"Why not?" asked Peter.

"I still live at home and last night was turning down the street to my parents' house when I saw two men in suits at the front door talking to my mom. We never have men in suits come to our house. Not in our neighborhood. Hell, they stuck out like neon lights. I knew something wasn't right so I kept going and drove right past the house. Fortunately they didn't see me. A dark blue Lincoln Town Car was parked out front. We don't get many of those cars on our street either. If we do, people mind their own business and look the other way. There are some things you just don't want to know about. Especially down where I live. I haven't been home since. I called my folks and they told me two men were looking for me. Mom said they weren't very nice. She described them as rude and abrasive. Listen, Mr. Kramer, I'm sure this has something to do with the bank and Bill's death. I can't go home or to work and some pretty mean looking bad guys want to talk to me. This can't be good at all! I don't know what to do. That's why I called you."

Peter bit his lower lip in intense concentration. He instinctively knew Jeff Peters was a gold mine of possible information. He was also spooked out of his mind. The young man's life possibly hinged on Peter's response and subsequent actions.

"Jeff, you did the right thing to call me," he said with as much conviction as he could muster. "I don't think we should talk more on the phone. Can we meet somewhere?"

"Yeah, I can do that. Trouble, is where do we meet? I think my house is being watched." He seemed to fixate on the fact that he couldn't go home.

Peter thought for a moment and then replied, "OK, that may be true about your house being watched. Can you get safely out of the city and come up here to New Hampshire?"

The frightened young man considered Peter's suggestion. "Well, what choice do I have? Sure I can come up there. Bill told me I could trust you, Mr. Kramer, so that's what I'll do. I'll just need directions."

Peter gave him detailed directions to Pinehurst and then to Mrs. Ashdown's place.

"It will take you about two to three hours to get up here. Don't leave Boston until tonight when it's dark. I suggest you fill up the car with gas, get some food, including coffee to keep you awake. I'll wait up for you. Just drive straight back to the small cottage at the back of the property. The lights will be on. OK?"

"Sure, Mr. Kramer."

"Jeff, it's important that you tell no one you are coming here. Don't even let anyone see you leaving the city. Remember hang out in Boston till it gets dark. Then hop in the car and drive straight to my place. I will look for you around 10:00 or 11:00 tonight."

"That sound fine, Mr. Kramer. I will see you later tonight." The line went dead.

Peter sat back in his old chair and pondered his conversation with Jeff Peters. He wondered what the man would tell him tonight.

He called Sarah at 11:00 and went over for lunch at her place. Jamie ran out to greet him at the end of the driveway and happily followed Peter's little sports car up the long drive. Mrs. Phillips greeted him warmly at the front door. She was happy to see him. Sarah was just coming down the stairs casually dressed in a faded work shirt and blue jeans. She looked tired but was excited to see him. Once they were alone, he told her about the telephone call from Jeff Peters.

"Wow, what do you think he has to tell you?"

Peter considered her question.

"I've been trying to figure that out since he called. All I am sure of is that it has something to do with what Bill

Rutherford was looking into for us. It just may be the missing link. We've uncovered bits and pieces of some kind of shady business and maybe, just maybe, this new information will tie it all together."

They talked some more and decided that Peter would meet Jeff alone first. Peter would then share whatever he heard with Sarah. They wanted to be cautious since they really didn't know who Jeff Peters really was.

Later that day at around 11:00 in the evening Peter was alone in his cottage reading student research papers. He and Sarah had spent the day together before Peter dropped her off at home at 9:00. He had visited briefly with Anne Ashdown before settling to wait for Jeff Peters' arrival from Boston. Mrs. Ashdown had told him about seeing an unhappy-looking James Cannon in the Pinehurst Inn earlier in the week eating dinner with Walton Trent. Peter filled her in on the funeral of Elisabeth Rutherford's father. She listened intently, soaking up every word. Her vibrant eyes sparkled with deep interest. She knew something suspicious was going on at the college and did her best to get Peter to reveal what he knew. He resisted in part to protect her. He told her a friend would be arriving from Boston later that evening and so not to worry if she saw car lights coming up the driveway at a late hour. She seemed content to hear this much.

At 12:15 A.M. Jeff Peters had yet to arrive. Peter began to worry he might never come. His eyes felt heavy from lack of sleep and exhaustion. It had been a long week. He began to nod off. Suddenly he saw the yellow glare of car lights bouncing off the huge Dutch Elm trees lining the long driveway. He glanced at the Seth Thomas clock on the mantel above the fireplace. It was almost 1:00 A.M. He quickly jumped up and made for the door. Opening it slightly, he saw a battered old yellow Volkswagen Bus slowly approaching the cottage. He felt immediate relief. Somehow an old VW Bus didn't seem too scary. The engine sputtered to a stop and out stepped a lanky young man of about 30 years of age, wearing jeans, tennis shoes, an old polo shirt, and a faded Boston Red Sox cap. He appeared tentative and wary. He glanced uneasily around the grounds of the estate.

Peter approached him, holding his hand out in greeting. He sensed the man's anxiety and sought to reassure him.

"Hi, I'm Peter Kramer."

The man looked directly at Peter and offered a cautious smile in response.

"I'm Jeff Peters."

They went inside where Peter fixed him a late-night breakfast of bacon, eggs, toast, and a glass of cold milk. He wolfed down the food in a matter of minutes. Peter watched him eat. He appeared ravenous and didn't utter a word while he ate. In truth, Jeff Peters was discreetly observing Peter and the cottage, gauging how safe he would be with this stranger. Soon he pushed back his empty plate and looking right at Peter thanked him for the meal. He had made up his mind. He had no one to turn to but Peter Kramer. Abruptly he began speaking.

"Mr. Kramer, I gotta tell you this whole thing makes me really scared. My friend Bill Rutherford is dead, people are watching me, I can't go back to my job at the bank and my house is being watched. I feel like I'm in a James Bond movie, only it isn't too much fun."

Peter shifted in his seat in anticipation.

"First, please call me Peter. Putting the word Mr. in front of my name makes me feel old, OK?"

Jeff nodded, a slight smile spreading slowly across his thin face.

"Bill Rutherford was helping me," Peter began. "His daughter Elisabeth is the dean of Kingsford College. Several months ago

I accidentally discovered what may be some kind of financial wrongdoing at the college but I have been unable to find any solid evidence. I went to the dean, who put me in touch with her father at the bank. We had reason to believe the Bank of Boston was somehow involved. So, a couple of weeks ago I drove to Boston and met Bill in his office at the bank. He was skeptical at first. His loyalty to the bank runs deep. I'm sorry, ran deep. I think he had a difficult time believing such a venerable institution could be involved in shady financial dealings. He ran some computer checks and came up with nothing. That seemingly was the end of it."

"What kind of computer checks?"

Peter paused momentarily to catch his breath.

"Kingston College raises money from people by asking them to leave the college in their will. This is common practice for colleges and universities. The institution cultivates people who believe in its mission and eventually decide that leaving the college a portion of their assets is a worthy thing to do. Sometimes these people are alumni. Evidently Kingston runs all of its major gifts and annuity transactions through the Bank of Boston. I asked Bill to check and see if the money was truly getting to the bank or if it was being diverted elsewhere. He established that indeed the money was getting to the bank and that all of the records were in place. Nothing was amiss. Now, I knew that significant amounts of money were missing, but according to the bank records everything was fine. So, where was the money going? Then I asked Bill to check all single internal transactions of over a million dollars during the days in question. I thought possibly we could track the missing money that way. Only two possibilities emerged. The Boston Naval Shipyard and a firm called Empire Insurance out of New York. To make a long story short, I flew to New York and visited Empire Insurance. It doesn't exist except for a seedy fourth-floor office in a decrepit building with a rather suspicious secretary wearing far too much makeup, chewing gum, and no role other than to answer the door and offer to take a message. I called Bill and told him what I'd found. He was shocked and suddenly was very interested. He promised to dig deeper. That was the last time I would ever talk with him. I only wish I knew what he found."

"I think I can answer that."

Peter didn't take his tired eyes off his young visitor. He felt his pulse quicken.

"What did he find?"

"What he found is what got him killed. I'm sure of it. It's the same reason they are after me."

Peter waited for the answer. The angular computer wizard seemed to hesitate. He then plunged ahead.

"The police report is wrong. Bill Rutherford didn't get mugged. It was just made to look like a mugging so the Boston Police wouldn't suspect an intentional killing. Sure his wallet and watch were missing but that was to throw the police off. I mean how many people get creamed the way Bill did in a simple mugging. My gosh, his head was almost caved in according to the Boston Globe. Some might argue that he was the victim of a real vicious mugging or a thrill killing, but let me tell you why it was murder. Bill Rutherford knew something real bad was going on at the bank and accidentally tipped off the wrong people. He knew because I discovered what was going on and told him. It is no accident that I uncovered a rogue computer program that is funneling money to the wrong account, tell Bill, and within 24 hours he's dead. Then I'm followed and strange men in expensive suits come looking for me at my parents' house."

Peter winced. He couldn't tell if Jeff was angry, scared, or felt guilty about Bill Rutherford. Maybe a little of all three, he wondered. He instinctively knew Jeff Peters held the key to who was involved at the bank's end of things. The guy also was all alone without anybody to turn to. They could help each other, that was certain, but Peter felt a deeper obligation than mutually helping each other. Bill Rutherford, a decent human being by everyone's account, was dead. Jeff Peters, also a decent person and friend of Bill, was in serious jeopardy simply because he innocently tried to help Bill. Somehow maybe he was responsible for Jeff Peters because he had gotten Bill Rutherford mixed up in this mess.

He turned to Jeff

"Listen Jeff, let's think this thing out. I know you are in trouble. I'm not going to kid you. Some really bad people are afraid of what you and I may know. They aren't going to stop until they silence us just like they did with Bill. We've got to take the offensive and get them before they get us."

The thin man looked warily at Peter. "What does all this mean?"

Peter paused. "Well you've got to show me the evidence. I need solid proof that the Bank of Boston is involved in wrongdoing. It sounds like you have something, but do you have names to go along with it?"

"I can give you what I have. I'm pretty sure who one of the guys is."

"So where is the information?" asked Peter.

"That's just it. I printed off copies for Mr. Rutherford and e-mailed myself a copy. The trouble is I can't access my e-mail. Someone canceled my account at work and at home. Mr. Rutherford had the other copies."

Peter stood up and looked down at an exhausted Jeff Peters. "How about I show you where you can sleep. You're really tired. We can talk more in the morning."

"Thanks, that's a good idea. Hey, I appreciate all you are doing for me. I really didn't know who to turn to."

Peter showed him the made-up bed in the corner of the living room. A few minutes later he was sound asleep.

The next morning Peter rose early while Jeff was still sleeping. Leaving a note telling him he would be back by 9:00, he drove over to Sarah's where he filled her in on his late night conversation with Jeff. Peter could see the tension in her face as he told her about Jeff's belief that Bill Rutherford had been murdered.

"Sarah, Jeff and I have to go back down to the Bank of Boston and get into their computer system and find hard solid evidence. We are going to go this morning."

"Peter, are you sure? What if you get caught? I'm really scared for you."

"We'll be careful. Listen, we have to go now. I'll stay in touch with you throughout the day."

She stood up and watched him walk out of the room and drive away in his little sports car.

CHAPTER THIRTY-SEVEN

They traveled southwest on Route 123 in the direction of Amherst, Massachusetts. Their destination was the University of Massachusetts and its huge library. Kingston College had a reciprocal agreement with the University that allowed Kingston faculty library privileges. The rolling New England countryside was dotted with small farms between quaint towns that required them to slow their speed as they drove through. Shortly before 11:00 they entered the charming university town. Peter planned to have Jeff access the Bank of Boston's network system via the internet. They wanted to make sure it wouldn't be traced back to New Hampshire and Kingston College. The University of Massachusetts library system would serve as a good cover.

A few minutes later the two entered the ivy-covered central library. Peter showed his Pinehurst faculty ID card to a sleepy-looking dark-haired young woman who looked like she had just gotten out of bed. Her tired, red eyes glanced at Peter's card. She barely nodded her head for them to pass through the computerized gate. He marveled at the power of a plastic card. They entered the vast white marbled foyer, their footsteps echoing throughout the empty chamber. Peter spotted the directory in the center and moved quickly in its direction. Running his hand down the alphabetized listing he found the computer network lab. "It's on the third floor," he whispered to Jeff, while at the same time wondering why he was whispering. They found a bank of elevators and soon were on the third floor. They had to pass a second computerized access point. Once again Peter's Kingston College card ushered them in. Peter cautiously looked around the computer room. It was empty. They found a cubicle at the back that afforded them a view of the entrance. Peter wasn't going to take any chances. Peter logged on and then stood up motioning Jeff to take over.

"OK, now, you take it from here," he said to Jeff. "Show me what is going on at this wonderful bank of yours."

Jeff grunted, "Not so wonderful, and I'm sure I don't work there anymore." He turned his full attention to the screen. Expertly typing a series of numbers, he soon had logged into the Bank of Boston's internal and highly confidential financial transactions. A maze of complex numbers and letters filled the screen. Looking over at Peter who had drawn up a chair beside the screen Jeff said, "This will get me fired and arrested if I get caught. I'm not supposed to be anywhere near this client information. But I figured out a long time ago how to get into the program. It's not hard if you know what you are doing. Right now though, I don't give a tinker's damn. Not after what happened to Mr. Rutherford. OK, now, look closely at the top right-hand column."

Jeff showed Peter the Bank of Pinehurst transactions and the deposit into the Kingston College account at the Bank of Boston. Peter saw the John Phillips transfer deposit of $1.7 million going to Kingston College. Jeff then pointed out the Allen and Williams transfers. Everything looked in order. All the amounts matched college records. Nothing appeared amiss.

Jeff then punched in more series of complicated numbers, which took him a good 10 minutes. His intensity at the screen was fascinating. Suddenly, a new bank of figures appeared with flashing numbers alongside several names. "Here, look at this!" commanded Jeff. Peter saw the John Phillips account. He felt an exhilaration as the number 3.7 million flashed for a few brief seconds and then disappeared. He watched in disbelief as 3.7 million indeed was transferred from the Bank of Pinehurst to Bank of Boston, but almost instantly was split with 1.7 million deposited into the Kingston college account and 2 million deposited into the Empire Insurance account less than a tenth of a second later. The rogue program had done its job perfectly. The two of them then checked the accounts of Phyllis Allen and Elisabeth Williams. Sure enough, it was an identical scenario.

Peter sat back in his chair, his heart beating rapidly. He felt the sweat trickling down his arms. He now had evidence that Sarah's grandfather's money had been stolen, disappearing without a trace until now. He looked at Jeff. "Can this information at the bank be deleted or somehow disappear?"

Jeff pondered the question. "Possibly but not without a lot of work and risk."

"Can our entry today be traced?"

"Maybe. I used Bill Rutherford's password and it could only be traced to this library, but it can't be linked with us."

"Yes, but they probably will figure it was us," said Peter.

"So, what do we do now?" asked Jeff. "I mean, they are looking for me and probably you. Hell, they killed Mr. Rutherford and won't hesitate to silence me and you!"

CHAPTER THIRTY-EIGHT

Walton Trent was in a black mood. He walked out of President Cannon's office heading back to his office. For the last 90 minutes he had listened to Cannon fret over the fear of the exposure of Trent's grand scheme to raise money for the college. Trent knew Cannon didn't know everything but he knew enough. A panicky James Cannon could jeopardize years of planning. Trent wasn't about to let that happen. Arriving at his office, he told his secretary to hold his calls. He had some thinking to do. He shut his door and taking off his suit coat sat at his desk overlooking the center of campus. He watched the students making their way to classes. How peaceful they looked. Their smiling faces suggested not a care in the world. He on the other hand had a real problem. Peter Kramer! Oh, he could handle James Cannon and the others simply because they were in too deep and besides, they were all scared to death of him. Peter Kramer on the other hand was dangerous. He was both smart and curious, a deadly combination. He recalled earlier in the fall trying to get Kramer fired. It would have worked if Elisabeth Rutherford hadn't stood up to Cannon. Now it would look too suspicious if he tried to get him fired. He had to think of a more subtle way. But this was exactly the kind of maneuvering Walton Trent was so good at. A behind-the-scenes guy all the way. The less visible the better. His power came from setting up situations and using the weak-minded people who were in power to do his dirty work. A perfect arrangement! Back in his early days with the investment firm, he could work magic. He used the number one and two human weaknesses, greed and power, and worked them beautifully to his advantage. Charles Stover came to his mind. A senior partner with Chemical Bank, Stover craved money. He could never get enough. Early on Trent figured this out and quietly forged a relationship with Stover, helping him craft his personal investment portfolio. Soon Stover came to almost depend on Trent in an almost hypnotic way. Casually Trent persuaded Stover to use one of the bank's clients to obtain insider information on a yet-to-be-made-public merger, resulting in a significant financial windfall for Stover and Trent. From that time forward, Trent owned Stover and for five years used him for his own financial gain. The arrangement ended when Stover was instantly killed in a horrific accident on the Brooklyn Bridge. Witnesses reported his black Lincoln Town Car driving at a high rate of speed had suddenly veered and crashed through the guardrail and hurtled airborne into the cold murky black waters below. The police investigated and concluded suicide, no skid marks, or indication of sudden slamming brakes. It appeared Stover intentionally took his life. Walton Trent knew better.

Trent turned back to the matter at hand. He was getting some pressure from the clients at Empire Insurance. The message had come earlier that morning. Do not in any way jeopardize the arrangement. He knew exactly what this meant. The clients, as he referred to them, were not patient people. He felt a cold fear. He stared out the window for a few more minutes as a plan slowly began formulating in his fertile mind.

As Trent sat in his college office, Peter's green MGB sped

along the Massachusetts Turnpike heading to Boston. Two hours after leaving the University of Massachusetts library and sleepy Amherst, they stopped at a McDonalds for breakfast in Southbridge, just off the Massachusetts Turnpike. While Jeff hungrily ate an Egg McMuffin, Peter called Sarah from his cell phone. He filled her in on what he had learned through Jeff Kramer's breaking into the Bank of Boston computer network system. Sarah wanted Peter to come home.

"Please come home and we can go to the police here in Pinehurst," she urged. "It's safer here."

Peter bit his lip. The way she said home made him really miss her. He was tempted to heed her advice. He missed her a great deal. Jeff's description of the way Bill Rutherford died suddenly flashed through his mind and he knew he couldn't go back to Pinehurst no matter how much his heart hurt to see Sarah. Not yet! It wasn't safe. He had to uncover solid evidence. He didn't know how yet, but he desperately needed proof to back up his suspicions.

"Sarah, as much as I want to come home and see you, I just can't yet. There is too much at stake for me to stop trying to uncover what is happening at Kingston." He did not tell her about how violently Bill Rutherford died. He didn't want to scare her anymore than necessary. He heard the sadness in her voice.

"I understand, Peter. It's just that I miss you...a lot! On top of that I'm beginning to get really frightened. I don't want anything to happen to you."

Peter's heart almost leaped out of his chest.

"Sarah, I miss you very much. I will get back there as soon as possible. I promise."

"OK," she conceded, "but please come home soon."

Peter mulled over their conversation as he and Jeff headed east towards Boston. Coming to Kingston College had brought far more than he could ever have imagined. He loved his job for sure. But that was almost to be expected. Stumbling upon this mystery and meeting Sarah was another story. He knew he was falling in love. Sarah Phillips was someone special. She was bright, beautiful, and strong. She possessed a resiliency that Peter knew came from her grandfather, John Phillips, and a gracefulness from her grandmother. She could have risen to the top in the Boston financial industry. Instead, she had spurned all of that for the peaceful life of small-town New Hampshire. Sarah Phillips had a sense of balance to her life that made her incredibly attractive. She could be at home in jeans and tennis shoes playing with her dog. She didn't require the bright lights of Boston's financial world to define her identity. Sarah loved to ride around the New Hampshire countryside stopping at farms hoping to find an antique for her house. In a world that said success requires moving up the ladder at all cost, to family, friends, and coworkers, Sarah Phillips had taken her stand and said, no. That was it! No further argument. She possessed a sense of self unlike any woman Peter had ever met. He thought back to the numerous talks with his own father and the disappointment in his father's eyes when Peter told him he wanted to become a college teacher instead of an investment banker. He loved his family and even now missed them. But he couldn't deny the strong pull he felt towards Sarah and Pinehurst. He felt a surge of energy and anxiety course through his tired body.

The heavy gray clouds of the late fall sky loomed ahead as the little MGB headed east towards Boston. Cold wintry air seeped noisily around the creases of the convertible top and into the passenger compartment. Peter turned the old heater on full blast to counter the unwelcome frigid air. He wondered if he would have to buy a second car for the New England winter...maybe a Jeep. They passed the turnpike exit to Route

128, the highway that circled Boston from the south to the north. Since they were approaching Boston from the west they continued on the turnpike until they reached the end where it became the Southeast Expressway. Exiting the turnpike Peter slowed as they approached the last turnpike ticket booth. Peter handed the young woman a $20 bill and received a smile and loose change in exchange. He thanked her and continued on down the ramp and turned left onto the expressway. They headed north towards the heart of Boston. Almost immediately a light snow began falling.

CHAPTER THIRTY-NINE

Dr. Morris Glenn was listening intently to the heart of Phyllis Grogan when his nurse quietly stepped into the examining room. He glanced at her with minor irritation and resumed his examination. He detected a slight murmur as he pressed the instrument to his patient's frail chest. He moved the stethoscope around listening to her heart. Always that pesky murmur greeted his old ears. His nurse gently touched his arm almost like it was a hot poker. He grunted and looked up at her.

"What is it, Fran?"

"Sorry to bother you, Dr. Glenn, but Thomas Lawton is on the phone and says it is urgent."

"Mrs. Grogan, would you please excuse me for a moment. I apologize for the interruption. I'll be back in a moment." Dr. Glenn exited the room immediately behind Nurse Fran. The old doctor walked down the hall to his office and entering it slowly made his way to the old roll top desk. Morris Glenn was from the old school. He detested being interrupted when he was with a patient. He picked up the phone in as much haste to silence the offending blinking light as to talk to Thomas Lawton.

"What is it, Lawton," he asked without preamble. He

could visualize the slick attorney sitting in his leather chair behind that shiny desk.

"Dr. Glenn, I wanted to let you know we have a meeting scheduled for tonight."

A chill coursed through the slight doctor. Suddenly he felt sick to his stomach.

"Same time?" asked Glenn.

"Yeah and don't be late," ordered Lawton.

Dr. Glenn hung up without another word. He slowly made his way back to the exam room where Phyllis Grogan patiently waited.

At that moment, as Dr. Glenn reentered the exam room, Peter and Jeff sped along Boston's Southeast Expressway entering the city from the south. Shortly after 3:30 they arrived in downtown Boston. Jeff directed Peter to a small grimy parking garage off of Boylston Street just three blocks down from the Bank of Boston building. Peter entered the old red-brick building and drove up to the second floor. The structure built in 1948 housed a taxi service on the first floor with parking on the second and third levels.

"This is where Bill Rutherford parked his car when he drove to work," said Jeff. "It's safe here because all the bank executives park in the fancy garage on the north side of the bank. Bill hated to park there because it was only for the big boys. He didn't like the fact that staffers like me couldn't park there. So in his unique way he protested. I think that's what I liked about him. He always had time for people like me. No one from the bank knew he used this garage. He liked to keep it a secret. So I think it's safe to leave your car here. You can park anywhere on the second level. The attendant will walk by and check to see if each car has a pass displayed on the dash."

Jeff grinned as he pulled out a green parking pass out of his pocket. "Here, just put it on the dash."

Peter reached for the pass and after glancing at it placed it on the black dash of the MGB. He paused for a second after turning off the little sports car. For three hours he had been pondering what they would do once they reached the bank.

"Jeff, we need to talk about what we do next."

"Yeah, I've been wondering about that. I'm afraid I already know. Frankly I'm getting a little nervous. I mean the last time I was here some pretty nasty guys were looking for me."

Peter looked him in the eye. "Jeff, we need proof. We have to get into the bank and actually get documented evidence of criminal wrongdoing. We have to do it without tipping our hand. Can you get us in?"

Jeff bit his lower lip in concentration. "It's going to get real dicey. Security is tight. They have cameras and guards constantly patrolling the building. But if we can just get into the information systems I would need only a couple of hours."

"What floor?" asked Peter.

"The seventh. There is the mail express elevator and also the employee-only elevator. I still have my code number for that one. Maybe we could sneak in and access the seventh floor that way?"

Peter shook his head. "I bet they have security alerted watching to see if your code number is activated. They'd be on to us in a flash. They aren't dumb, just crooked."

Jeff didn't reply. He wasn't very good at this kind of thing.

Peter thought for a moment. He glanced at his watch. "Listen it's getting close to 4:00. We need to get in today. Let's wait until about 4:55 and as most people are leaving for the day we simply walk in and carefully blend into the crowd. We walk straight into the lobby, take the main elevator and go to the seventh floor.

When we are done we just come back the same way we came in. I'm sure there will be people working late."

Jeff nodded. "Actually there is an afternoon shift made up of staffers and also maintenance people. The bank is usually busy up until 9:00."

"Good," replied Peter. "We just have to watch where the cameras are and avoid them. Can we do that? They might not expect the obvious. We walk in the front door like we belong. Maybe they aren't even expecting us. They could be that confident."

"I think so, but we have to watch out for the guards and any employees working late. Hey, what if someone recognizes me?"

"I don't think the whole bank knows you are no longer working there. The bad guys aren't about to broadcast why you left. The most important thing is to be cool and not panic. OK?"

They climbed out of the little British roadster and started walking down the old concrete ramp to the first level. Their footsteps echoed loudly, bouncing off the old walls. They passed a number of parked cars but saw no people. Soon they rounded the curved wall bringing them to the first floor and a taxi garage. Here they heard voices and came upon six yellow taxi cabs being worked on by mechanics and with what appeared to drivers standing around smoking and talking. No one paid them any attention. It was evident that the taxi company employees were used to people walking through their work area. The scene reminded Peter of the old television show "Taxi." They passed the last taxi and emerged onto Boylston Street and the late afternoon traffic and pedestrian rush.

Snow was falling steadily as they made their way up Boylston in the direction of the Bank of Boston. The sidewalk was crowded with people getting an early start on their commute home. No smiles or eye contact in this crowd, thought Peter. Yet he felt safe in the anonymity of the sea of nameless faces. The smell of car exhaust permeated the air in spite of the freshly falling snow. The invention of the automobile was clearly winning this epic battle of man and nature. No wonder Sarah had moved back to New Hampshire. He turned his head away from the busy street in a futile effort to avoid inhaling the annoying fumes. Jeff walked very closely to Peter afraid he might lose him in the crowd. As they approached the bank Peter slowed his pace. He glanced across the popular street at the snow-covered trees and ponds of Boston Common. The idyllic winter scene contrasted sharply with Peter's memory of Bill Rutherford's recent violent death. Rutherford's life had ended so abruptly as he innocently entered the park that fateful day. Peter's mind worked itself back to the present. He began to feel warm even in the cold snow. A trickle of sweat made its way down the inside of his left arm. He forced himself to remain calm. A lot depended on staying unruffled, especially the nervous young man beside him.

The time was 4:50. People were indeed pouring out of the bank's massive entrance just as predicted. For a brief irrational second he wondered if someone had pulled a fire alarm. Most had their heads down as they engaged the falling snow head on. Not a bad distraction, thought Peter. They were too busy with the surprise of the snow and just trying to navigate their way home to take notice of people walking into the bank. Peter struggled against the mass of humanity surging towards him and Jeff. He turned sideways in an effort to more easily edge his way into the bank lobby. A moment later they emerged into the ornate lobby. The flow of people continued and Peter could hear the steady ping of elevator doors opening, depositing more home goers into the already jammed lobby. The old bank guard in his blue uniform sat in his elevated booth virtually powerless to monitor the comings and goings of so many people during rush hour. Truly the man's largely ceremonious job was a throwback to earlier days at the bank. Peter cast a sideways glance at the security cameras mounted discreetly in the upper corners of the lobby. These were the real security measures. I guess every bank needs security in the lobby to reassure the customers, he thought to himself.

With Jeff right at his heels Peter walked briskly across the lobby to the bank of elevators. They stepped aside as the door to one of the elevators opened, disgorging another batch of people. A slim young woman in a dark blue dress was the last rider to disembark. She smiled at Peter as he stepped into the empty elevator. Jeff hurried in behind him. Peter paused to look across the lobby for signs of trouble and then looking at the panel of buttons punched the seventh floor. The light came on but it seemed like an eternity before the doors began slowly closing. He held his breath hoping no one else wanted to ride up with them. Finally the heavy doors closed. He exhaled a deep sigh and then looked at Jeff.

"So far, so good," he muttered to the terrified young man.

"Yeah, that walk across the lobby about did me in. I've crossed that place a thousand times. I never believed it could be so frightening."

"You do look a bit pale but listen, we made through the place where you stand the greatest chance of being recognized. We're doing fine. OK?"

He nodded slightly as if he only partially believed Peter.

Peter knew Jeff was really upset and frightened. How could one not be in his position? The elevator quietly ascended humming soothingly as it carried them to the seventh floor. Peter lifted his eyes to the control panel of lights. He held his breath as they silently swept past floor after floor. He didn't want them to land on another floor and have to encounter any riders. His heart dropped as the soft ping coincided with the flashing panel light and the sudden loss of vertical movement.

They had arrived. The elevator doors opened gracefully concluding with the gentle stopping of the elevator. Peter stepped aside and motioned for Jeff to lead. He peeked out the door followed by a firm shove from Peter. No time to look timid now, thought Peter.

"Look like you belong here," whispered Peter. "Walk straight to where we are going and look confident." He hoped they could pull this thing off.

Offices lined the wide hallway. Most were shut but there were a couple open with people inside hunched over their computers. No one even looked up as they passed along. Further down they heard voices and a door suddenly opened and a man and woman came out of an office laughing at something the man had just said. Peter and Jeff were almost upon the couple. The woman shot a surprised look of recognition at Jeff.

"Hey, Jeff, what are you doing here?" she asked. "I thought you quit the bank. What brings you back?" The woman's companion just stared at Jeff and then Peter.

"Hi Molly, how are you doing? Where did you hear that?"

She looked puzzled. "Well, Tom Brady announced it to the information systems group a few days ago."

Jeff shifted nervously from his left to right foot. "Well actually, that's true. I took a job over at Mass General in their information systems group. More money, you know. I just came here to pick up a few of my things. This is my security escort," he said motioning to Peter. "He's escorting me to my old office."

Molly's face showed understanding and to Peter's relief, acceptance. She replied.

"Oh, well, your leaving was so sudden. It's nice to get to say good-bye." She looked him straight in the eye and turning away wished him well over her shoulder. Her eyes lingered on Peter for a few seconds before she turned her attention back to her companion. A moment later they rounded a corner and disappeared.

"Nice recovery," Peter said to Jeff.

"I learned that in an old movie. I can't even remember the name. I figured she probably knew I wasn't working here any more, so I came up with the story of Mass General."

"Do you think our friend Molly suspected anything?" asked Peter, keeping his eyes on the remaining office doors.

"Maybe, but Molly's cool. Even if she doesn't buy my story she won't say anything."

A moment later they came to the main doors of the information systems department. Jeff cautiously opened them and cautiously peered inside. Once again Peter all but shoved him into the room to avoid suspicion. The lights were still on. Peter saw a few people working at computer screens in their cubicles. No one even noticed them enter the area. There were probably 50 work cubicles, each with a computer hooked up to the bank's mainframe computer system. Jeff strode over to a small cubicle in the back corner next to a window. No name was on the cubicle. Peter somehow knew this was Jeff's old workspace. Glancing around Jeff quickly sat down and immediately began working at the keyboard. Peter sat in a spare chair and watched. He felt better now that their heads were hidden from view. He looked at his watch. The time was 5:15. Jeff worked the keyboard furiously. The man was a magician, thought Peter. Peter also knew Jeff wanted to get out of the bank as soon as possible. Who could blame him? Me too, he muttered to himself, but not before they got what they came for. Peter looked for cameras while Jeff worked his magic. Incredibly there were none in the room or at least ones he could see. Time moved slowly as Jeff worked and Peter sat. The hum of the computer room was almost soothing. A couple of times Jeff stopped, nervously chewed on his lower lip, and then continued. Ninety long minutes later he sat up straight and stretched his neck. He reached down and inserted a disk into the hard drive waiting for the computer to generate a copy. He did this two more times before stuffing all three disks into his pocket.

"Let's get the hell out of here," he whispered to Peter. The bad guys probably have installed a red flag alerts on some of these accounts. If they are being continuously monitored, security will be down here pronto. I'll tell you what I did once we are out of the building." The screen went blank.

They quietly began walking across the vast computer room in the direction of the main doors. This time Peter led the way. Peter opened the door and stepped into the hallway. It was empty. They retraced their steps back down the hallway to the bank of elevators where Peter reached out and hit the down button. The wait for the elevator seemed like an eternity. Jeff kept looking back over his shoulder, fear etched across his thin face. Peter looked up at the panel of light indicators and saw the elevator would soon be at their floor. He breathed in deeply, forcing himself to remain calm. The familiar ping signaled the elevator's arrival, quickly followed by the silent opening of the massive doors. The elevator was empty. They hurriedly entered the car with Peter punching the buttons on his way in to close the doors as fast as possible. The hum of the elevator as it descended to the first floor added to the tension. At the third floor it suddenly came to a halt and the doors opened. Peter placed his hand on Jeff's arm to help keep him calm. Peter almost gasped as a tall, heavily built security guard entered. The beefy man had a red complexion and looked as if he had been running. He looked at Peter and then Jeff. Peter forced a smile of greeting. Jeff looked like he was ready to pass out. The guard nodded ever so briefly before turning his huge neck back to the front where he hit the already lighted lobby button. Peter felt a single drop of sweat trickle down his hot neck. The three men descended in silence. Peter had never felt so vulnerable in his life. His hands were wet from the tension. The elevator reached the lobby. The doors opened and the guard surprisingly stepped aside and held the doors open, beckoning Peter and Jeff to exit first. Peter thought it might be a trap but he had no choice. Any other move would raise the guard's suspicion. He nodded a thanks and strode out into the now nearly empty lobby with as much confidence as he could muster. Jeff was literally right on his heels. The gangly computer genius was so close he almost fell over Peter. The near empty lobby increased Peter's sense of vulnerability. The main doors to the street and safety seemed miles across the huge lobby. As they made their way across the lobby Peter glanced at a colossal mirror on the wall. His heart skipped a beat as he saw the beefy bank guard watching them. He forced himself not to panic. Every fiber in his body screamed for him to run like the wind out of the bank and into the freedom of the early evening Boston traffic. He felt Jeff's presence almost like a cloak draped around him. Half expecting a shout for them to stop, Peter willed himself to slow his pace. Their steps echoed loudly in the deserted lobby. Suddenly the crackle of a walkie-talkie shattered the quiet. In the mirror Peter saw the guard reach for something on his belt. Peter froze. Was the man reaching for his gun? He saw the guard lift his walkie-talkie and speak into it. A split second later the man jerked his head up and started at Peter and Jeff. Peter then saw him reach for his gun.

"Let's get out of here quick," muttered Peter at Jeff. They sprinted the remainder of the way to the huge doors and burst out of the bank onto Boylston Street. They heard shouting behind them. Afraid to look back, they darted across the street dodging cars and made their way towards the safety and darkness of Boston Common. Soon they were deep into the city park and eventually swallowed up by the overwhelming darkness. The men chasing them stopped at the edge of the park.

Back in Pinehurst, Walton Trent picked up the ringing phone. The smooth voice of Justin Nichols was on the other end.

"Walton, what's the latest?" he asked.

"Things are fine Justin," Trent reassured him. "Our problem at the bank has been taken care as you know."

"What about that teacher, what's his name, Kramer?"

"I'm not worried about him," lied Trent.

"Well, maybe you better. He's asking a whole lot of questions and we think may have been snooping around the bank tonight. What are you going to do about him?"

Trent absently began plucking his bushy eyebrows. He was getting angry.

"He can snoop all he wants but he won't find anything. He came up empty at Empire Insurance and we have possession of Rutherford's package. The picture of the blood soaked package Rutherford intended to send to Kramer came to his mind. His men had retrieved it from the park and delivered it directly to Trent in New Hampshire that very night.

"So you don't think he can get close to us?" asked Nichols.

"What's he going to find out? We've covered our tracks really well."

"Listen, Walton, we have a lot invested in this. We are also in pretty deep. There is a lot riding on this one."

"I know, Justin, I know! We've just got several more to do and it's over. The boys aren't going to let us back out until every last portfolio is finished. You know that. Speaking of finished, what's with the computer guy at the bank? He gave Rutherford all the data. Your job was to take care of him."

There was a slight hesitation at the other end of the phone. "Yeah, well the little computer geek slipped out of our grasp.

Don't you worry, we'll get him. He's disappeared. We can't locate him anywhere. We have his house and parents under watch." Nichols decided not to tell Trent bank security had spotted him at the bank that night along with Peter Kramer.

Walton sucked in his breath and exhaled slowly.

"Justin, this guy has some pretty damaging information. We need to get this taken care of fast."

"Don't worry, we'll find him," he responded irritably.

"OK, let me know when you do."

"I will," promised Nichols. "Now where are we with the Townsend portfolio?"

"Tuesday night," replied Trent.

"Good, stay in touch," said Nichols and then hung up.

Trent put his phone back in its place and sat back in his plush leather chair. He swiveled the expensive chair and looked out over the darkened campus. The lights along the campus pathways seemed to serve as beacons. They reminded him of flying into Logan at night and seeing the brightly lit runways guiding the huge aircraft home. Tonight he felt like there were no lights for him. No signal pointing him in a safe direction. He was in very deep now. No where to go but to stay the course. A dangerous one it was. He thought about Peter Kramer. The young professor was getting in way over his head. The kid had no idea who he was up against. He would be dead in a matter of weeks if he didn't stop. The trouble was he wasn't alone. Sarah Phillips was involved too. She made things more complicated with her connection to old John Phillips and his wife and that nosy Anne Ashford. Everything had been going so smoothly up until this fall when Kramer came to Pinehurst. No one suspected a thing. Now people were starting to take notice. Well, Walton Trent wasn't going to just sit by and let it all be ruined. Too much was on the line. He picked up the phone. It was time to move the Townsend portfolio forward.

Time also to put a little pressure on some people. He picked up the phone.

Sarah was worried about Peter. She hadn't heard from him since that morning as he drove from Amherst to Boston. It was now 9:00 and darkness had set in. She missed him a great deal. Without acknowledging it aloud, Sarah Phillips knew for a fact she was in love with Peter Kramer. If she could trace it back it would be the time he approached her as she sat in her car after the Board of Trustees dinner. His relaxed yet straightforward manner had caught her off guard. His dark eyes and handsome face simply took her breath away. The irony of finding someone to fall in love with in Pinehurst, the very town she grew up in, was not lost on her. Now, tonight the person she was in love with was in Boston and maybe in trouble. She stared at the phone almost willing it to ring. She determined to wait up all night if she had to.

At that moment Peter and Jeff were deep in the cold darkness of Boston Common. Peter could hear their labored breathing as they continued their flight. A few minutes later he stopped, motioning Jeff to do the same. The woods were quiet.

"I think we are safe here," said Peter. They strained their ears to hear if someone was in pursuit. Quietness greeted their inquiry. Blessed quietness.

"What now?" asked Jeff, bending over to catch his breath. He clutched the backpack with the software inside.

"We make sure no one is behind us and then try to get back to the car. Now, are you sure the car is in a safe location?"

"Yeah, like I told you, no one from the bank uses that garage except for Bill Rutherford. The big dogs use the fancy new one up the street."

"OK, then let's head back to the garage. How do we get there without going back in the same direction? You know this park better than I do."

"We can go through the park and come out on the north end by the state building and then work our way along the edges till we come to the garage. We'd better get going. I don't want to be here any longer than I have to. It's getting colder by the minute. This is no place to be at night."

Peter knew what Jeff was referring to. Somewhere in these same woods Bill Rutherford had been killed. He felt a chill run up his back. This whole thing was getting far too real.

"OK, you lead the way. Just be on the lookout for flashlights and voices. Oh, and make sure you hang on to that backpack."

Jeff looked at Peter. "Don't worry. No one is going to take this from me."

They trudged up the desolate snow-covered path. No one was out on a night like this. The lights and sounds of traffic on Boylston faded. It became darker and colder as they headed north. The darkness was almost overwhelming. The cold seemed to penetrate to their very core. The exertion of the last few minutes had kept them warm. Now the cold worked to take over. Peter kept glancing over his shoulder but all was still. Ten minutes later they reached the crest of a small rise and came upon a deserted fountain with benches. They sat down for a moment to rest. No words were spoken. They were tired and determined to conserve their strength. A few minutes later Peter silently motioned to Jeff and they continued on their journey. Not long after their stop at the fountain, Peter first heard the sounds of cars and then saw the shinning lights of the state capitol's dome looming like a giant beacon through the darkness. Moments later they came to a moderately busy Park Street. Venerable Park Street Church was down the street on the left. Directly ahead the state capital. They headed south back in the direction of the old parking garage where Peter's MGB was parked.

"Keep your eyes peeled now," instructed Peter. "We're in the open. They may still be looking for us."

Fifteen long minutes later they approached the red-brick garage. Normal traffic and a few pedestrians greeted their watchful eyes. Nothing suspicious or out of the ordinary. They walked into the garage and up the several flights of concrete stairs. The little green MGB sat all alone in the corner right where they had left it. Peter wondered if there might be a car bomb under the hood. I've been watching too many Harrison Ford movies, he muttered to himself.

They jumped into the roadster. Peter pulled out the manual choke and turned the key. The electronic pump began its usual clicking sound moving the fuel from the gas tank to the carburetor. A moment later he turned the ignition key and the engine sputtered and then came to life. He revved the engine and shifted into reverse. He backed out quickly and stopped and put it into first and proceeded down the curved ramps to the first floor. They exited the garage and entered Boylston Street where Peter took a left rather that going south past the bank.

Jeff still clutched the backpack containing the data he had retrieved from the bank.

"Where to now?" he asked.

"First I call Sarah and then we head back to New Hampshire."

"I figured that, but what happens next? For me! Heck, I'm out of a job, I can't go home and some really nasty people are looking for me. I don't mean to whine but I don't know what to do next with my life. I can't go back to the bank. I kinda feel lost."

"I'm sorry, Jeff. It's got to be tough for you. I won't pretend to understand, because I don't. We got you into something pretty big. Sometimes I wish I had never called Bill Rutherford and opened up this bad can of worms."

Peter stared straight ahead as they drove north. They were both silent.

"Listen," said Jeff. "I hope you don't think I am blaming you for my troubles or even Bill's death."

"No, I don't think that at all. These people, whoever they are, are responsible. I just think I stumbled upon something going on at Pinehurst College that is connected to the Bank of Boston. In a sense we are all victims, you, Bill, others, and me. I will not subscribe to the notion that we have done anything wrong. It is terribly unfortunate that Bill died and what is happening to you, but this is not my doing. Anyway, I am in deep enough to see this thing through. Do I have a choice?"

Jeff nodded. "Peter, first, we are in this thing," he responded putting an emphasis on the we. "And secondly, I am in this with you to the end."

Peter grinned. "That sounds good to me."

He reached down, picked up his cell phone, and dialed Sarah's number.

One hundred forty miles away to the north Sarah sat in her grandmother's formal living room with its magnificent picture window overlooking the sloping front lawn now covered in several inches of fresh snow. Dressed in jeans and an old baggy sweater, she sat cross-legged in one of the overstuffed chairs pensively sipping from a steaming mug of herbal tea. Jamie sat sleeping at her feet. Her grandmother was upstairs in bed. All evening Sarah had kept a vigil. Even Jamie had sensed her anxiety and responded by sticking close to her and dragging herself up and following Sarah whenever she went into the kitchen. Sarah sat thinking about Peter and all that had transpired since he came to Pinehurst. The sudden ringing of the telephone jolted her back to the present. She leaped out her chair, jumping over the dozing Jamie, and almost reached the phone before it finished the first ring.

"Hello," she said. "Peter, is that you? Are you all right? Where are you? Are you on the way home?" The questions came pouring out in a torrent.

"Sarah, Sarah, slow down. Yes it's me and we are on our way home. I'm fine."

"Oh Peter," she cried. "I'm so relieved." Her pent-up emotions spilled out. "I've been waiting all day to hear from you. When you didn't call I thought something dreadful had happened to you. All I could think about was Dean Rutherford's father." She paused to catch her breath.

"Sarah, Jeff and I are here heading north to New Hampshire. We should get in about midnight. Don't worry, I will come straight to the house."

"Peter, please drive carefully. It's been snowing and the roads are slippery. Just get here safely."

She drew in a breath and forged on. "Peter, I love you. I can't wait to see you."

Back in the MGB Peter was stunned. A tremendous sense of exhilaration enveloped him. He wasn't sure how to respond, especially with Jeff in the car.

"Sarah, I can't wait to see you either. I will see you in a couple of hours. I'll keep my cell phone on."

He hit the end button and placed the phone on the console.

Peter and Jeff continued on in silence. Both were lost in their own thoughts. The snow was falling more rapidly and was beginning to stick on the road. The little British sports car motored through the snow bravely. Peter had the heater turned on full blast. The three little windshield wipers worked furiously to keep pace. To their relief the highway was well plowed with little traffic. Peter knew the farther north they went the more difficult the roads might be, and he was glad he had snow tires.

"Let's talk about what you did in the computer room back

at the bank," said Peter. He was anxious to hear what Jeff had done.

"Well, like we found out last week, they created that rogue software program that automatically and secretly transfers a portion of the designated money to the college into another account. We now know that other account is Empire Insurance. The rogue program is almost instantaneous in its transfer, thus creating no suspicion. In reality the originally designated amount of money to the college is illegally changed at the college's end and also at the bank. The only parties who know the true amount are the donors and that knowledge goes with them to their death. The bank and college hopes that the members of the families don't know otherwise. Even if they suspected something, the records at the college and bank refute their suspicions. It's almost foolproof! If nobody asks questions, like let's say the family attorney or family members, then the bad guys get away with a lot of money."

Peter thought back to his and Sarah's conversation with Martha Phillips when they had told her about the discrepancy between the amount of money John Phillips had designated to Kingston College and the actual amount recorded at the bank. She had been shocked. More importantly, she would never have discovered the discrepancy on her own. That's exactly what these people were banking on.

Jeff interrupted his thoughts.

"So I took a picture."

"What do you mean you took a picture?"

He reached into his backpack and took out a small orange colored computer disk. Grinning he held it up and showed Peter.

"This is the picture! I created a program that searched back into the bank's computer archives and was able to find the three illegal transactions created by their rogue program. You see, they thought the program was so quick that it wouldn't show up anywhere. Of course it was an instantaneous transaction but even those leave a trace. I just got a copy of the trace and copied it on to the disk. Pretty nifty huh?"

"So you are telling me that this computer disk shows the true amount John Phillips left to the college and then the actual amount the college received? And the Elisabeth Williams and Phyllis Allen estates as well?"

"That's exactly what I am saying."

"And it shows the illegal transfer of funds to Empire Insurance?"

Jeff just grinned at Peter in affirmation.

Peter continued looking ahead at the snowy road as he pondered what Jeff was saying.

"Are you sure about the Empire Insurance account?"

"You betcha! I copied the trace transfer from the family estates to the bank and the subsequent diversion to Empire Insurance. It's all on this little disk."

They continued driving on in silence.

"I'll bet the bad guys would kill for this disk," said Jeff.

"They already have" replied Peter.

"Yes. I know," Jeff responded soberly." They were both thinking of Bill Rutherford.

The snow was thickening on Route 93 as they drove on in silence. The implications of what Jeff had on the disk were beginning to sink in. They passed the state line and crossed into New Hampshire. Just south of Manchester they stopped for gas in the small town of Londonderry. After filling the small tank and purchasing some candy bars, chips, and soft drinks, they continued on their journey. Soon they reached Concord and began heading west towards Pinehurst. The dark woods seemed to press in on them from both sides. The snow was relentless. By 11:45 they had reached Pinehurst. The snow-covered town was dark and silent as they drove through and headed out towards the Phillips estate.

Jamie was the first to hear the now familiar low rumble of Peter's MGB. Her ears perked up and using her nose she nudged Sarah, who was dozing in the big soft chair. She awoke with a start. The lights of the little car moved over the large picture window, briefly lighting up the room. Sarah ran to the door and opened it, snow blowing in. Jamie edged past her and ran out onto the porch and down the snow-covered steps to the little car. Sarah was close behind. The dog greeted Peter as he worked his way out of the small car and stood stretching his tired muscles, the snow falling heavily around him. Sarah reached Peter and, throwing her arms around him, hugged him tightly.

"I'm so glad you're safe. I've been worried all day. It's so good to have you home." She then realized Jeff was standing in the snow watching. A little embarrassed she looked over at him and smiled. "I'm glad you're both safe. Come on into the house."

Once in the house she fixed them steaming hot chocolate. It was very late and they were all tired but wanted to stay up and talk about the events of the day. Peter filled Sarah in on what had happened at the bank. He didn't leave anything out. She listened intently and showed some emotion when he described their hasty retreat from the bank. She glanced at the backpack Jeff was still clutching.

"You mean you have the actual documentation that implicates the college and bank in the theft of Grandfather's money"? Jeff nodded in affirmation. Peter looked at Sarah waiting for the reality of this revelation to sink in.

"These people must be stopped," she exclaimed! "Now we have the proof."

"I don't think so, not just yet" cautioned Peter.

"What do you mean?" she asked. She looked over at Jeff's backpack as if to prove she was right.

Peter paused. "Well we have proof that the transfer of money occurred. A large sum of money was illegally transferred from its intended designation, the college, to Empire Insurance. That much we do know. And it's a lot of money. Your grandfather's money is just one of at least three donor-designated bequests that were illegally tampered with. The total sum could be well into the millions. The incredible thing is it is virtually undetectable. First, the families have no clue that all of their money never reached the college. That's because the original sum was usually confidential and known only by the donors, their attorney, and the college. Now we know why the college or more specifically the development office encouraged the donor to keep the actual sum a secret. The thing is these type of people are usually quiet about their money to begin with, so this played right into the college's hands."

Sarah was listening intently. "So that's why Grandmother had to look up the actual designated gift amount Grandfather bequeathed to Kingston. Grandfather never told her."

"Exactly. The only reason she ever found out was because of our prodding. Think of it. She could be unaware today, just like the other two families."

Sarah bit her lip trying to let it all sink in.

"So these murderers get innocent people to bequeath money to the college and then wait for them to die. In the meantime they alter the college and bank records and steal a good portion of their money. Money intended for the college."

She looked at Peter who appeared lost in thought.

He looked up. "The problem is we have proof of wrongdoing but can't really pin it on anyone. Sure we have what they call circumstantial evidence. Like when we saw Walton Trent at the bank that one day. And the Boston Police have officially declared Bill Rutherford's death a mugging. Who knows what Trent, Cannon, Morris Glenn, and Thomas Lawton were doing at the cabin that night? But we don't have any hard evidence to go to the police with. If we go with what we have, they will investigate and give Trent time to cover his tracks. Jeff's computer disk tells a story but without characters. We have to fill in the story with real characters. That's the only way we are going to get to the bottom of this whole mess."

Jeff, who had been silent up to this point, chimed in.

"Peter, I don't think I can handle any more sneaking around at the bank to get more data. I feel like I'm living on borrowed time as it is. These people whoever they are know I have something that will possibly hurt them."

"I understand," Peter replied. "Actually, I don't think we need to go back to the bank. First of all, we mustn't let them connect you and me together. You can stay here in Pinehurst, where you should be safe. Listen, we all need to get some rest. I have been doing some thinking about what our next step might be. We can talk about this in the morning. Jeff you can stay with me. In the meanwhile, we need to act as if there is nothing wrong. Sarah, you and I will go to work on Monday as usual. Nothing we do should raise their suspicions. I have been thinking of a plan to bring these people out into the open. Let's get to bed now."

He got up and went over to Sarah and gave her a hug and kiss good night. The snow was falling heavily as Peter and Jeff walked out the front door.

CHAPTER FORTY

Early the next morning the old blue Ford pickup slowly made its way down the deserted road outside the Phillips home. The time was 4:00 A.M. The snow-covered countryside made it seem much later. The driver wore an old navy pea jacket. His bushy unkempt hair spilled out from under a dirty Boston Red Sox baseball cap. The exhaust left a trail of smoke 20 feet behind the old truck. Lights turned off, the truck slowed to a crawl as it approached. Upon reaching the driveway, the driver stopped and, leaving the engine running, got out and walked up towards the house a little ways, where he tossed an object out into the middle of the snow-covered lawn. Wiping his hands on his dirty blue farmer's overalls, he proceeded back to the truck and drove off in the direction of town.

Early the next morning Peter took Jeff over to Mrs. Ashdown's house. He wanted them to meet and to let her know he would be staying for a while. He knocked on the back kitchen door. A moment later she appeared at the door.

"Why, Peter, good morning."

"Hello Mrs. Ashdown. How are you? Do you have a minute

for us to come in and talk?" The directness of his request was not lost on her.

"Of course, please come in."

Once in the large country kitchen, Peter turned to Mrs. Ashdown and introduced her to Jeff.

"Mrs. Ashdown, Jeff is a friend of mine from Boston. If it is all right with you, I would like him to stay with me for awhile."

She shook Jeff's hand firmly and looked him in the eye. "Pleased to meet you, young man."

Peter was unsure how much to tell her about the situation. He knew she had her suspicions already but was reluctant to draw her in much more. Yet he knew he might need her help.

"Mrs. Ashdown, Jeff worked at the Bank of Boston. He knew Dean Rutherford's father at the bank. Unfortunately he doesn't work there anymore." He paused.

Her response was immediate.

"Peter, you don't have to tell me any more. I see where this may be going. This all has to do with those strange things occurring at the college, doesn't it?"

Peter nodded silently.

She winked at them both. "Well, don't you worry. I can keep my mouth shut. Frankly, this is all kind of exciting. I just know this has something to do with that slippery creature Walton Trent and probably that buffoon Randolph Bolles. President Cannon is probably mixed up in this too."

Peter wasn't surprised at how in touch she was with things. He also found her frankness refreshing.

"Well I have to get to the college. I have an 8:00 class. Jeff will be at the cottage all day. Please call me if anything unusual happens, OK?"

Mrs. Ashdown turned to Jeff. "Why don't you come over for lunch? We can get better acquainted."

"That would be great. Thank you." Jeff had already picked up that one didn't say no to Anne Ashdown.

"Now, Peter, you be careful today. You take care of Sarah, too!"

"I will, Mrs. Ashdown."

The campus was busy with cars pulling into the main parking lots and students and faculty walking to their classes. Peter parked the MGB in his usual spot and began walking to the Business and Economics building. He looked for Sarah's red BMW but didn't see it. Once in his office he gathered his notes for his Introduction to Business class. It was difficult to refocus back on his teaching after such a busy and strange few days. He felt weary. This morning the topic was ethics in business. Ironic, he thought. At 7:50 he left his office and began walking across campus to class. The snow-covered walkways were crowded with students. He glanced over at the main parking lot and again did not see Sarah's car. This surprised him. She usually was at her office by now. Fifty minutes later Peter's class ended. Walking back across campus to his office he noticed Sarah's car still was not in its usual place. Once in his office he saw the blinking red light on his phone indicating a message. He dialed in his code and heard a frantic Sarah on the other end.

"Peter call me as soon as you can. Something has happened to Jamie." Alarmed, he grabbed the phone and dialed the Phillips home. A moment later Martha Phillips came on the line.

"Mrs. Phillips, this is Peter. Sarah called about Jamie."

Peter heard the urgency in voice. "Oh, Peter, I'm so glad you called. Sarah found Jamie out at the end of the driveway. She couldn't get up and just lay there. Sarah put her in the car and drove over to Carl Wilson. He's our local veterinarian. His office is two blocks south of campus on Hancock Street."

"Thanks, Mrs. Phillips. I'll go directly there. We will call you when we know more." He picked up his backpack and ran out the door to his car.

Three minutes later he was parking next to Sarah's BMW. He entered the small building and found the lobby empty. A slight woman sitting behind the receptionist's counter looked up and asked if he needed help.

"Yes, I'm here to see Sarah Phillips."

"Oh. She's in with the doctor. They are working on Jamie. You can wait here in the lobby."

"I'd rather go in and if that's all right."

She hesitated. "Well I don't know."

"It's important that I go in. What room are they in?"

Giving in, she motioned for Peter to follow her.

They entered a small room where Peter found Sarah staring intently at Jamie, who lay sprawled out on a table with the doctor working furiously over her. He was injecting the dog with a vial of fluid while a nurse administered oxygen.

Sarah saw Peter and came over to him. Her eyes were red from crying. He couldn't take his eyes off of Jamie on the table.

"What happened?" he asked as he tried to take in the scene.

"We don't know. I let her out for her morning run and went back in for breakfast. Usually she comes and sits by the back kitchen door waiting to come in. Halfway through breakfast it dawned on me she wasn't there. So I went out looking for her and saw her in a heap at the end of the driveway. I ran down and tried to get her up but she wouldn't move. She was so still I feared she was dead but I could detect a slight heartbeat. I brought her over to Carl's as fast as possible."

Finished with the injection, Carl Wilson turned and Sarah introduced him to Peter. He was a tall angular man of about 55 with thinning black hair. He had kind eyes. Peter could tell immediately he loved animals.

"Nice to meet you."

He turned to address them both. "I can't tell you exactly what is wrong with Jamie. Right now she is stabilized. She came in here with an incredibly slow heartbeat so I gave her an injection of adrenaline to get her heart working faster. It's a good thing you got her here so fast. She probably would have died if you hadn't. The oxygen is intended to substitute for a clear lack of heart activity. We just need to monitor her for a while. I plan to take some blood to run tests. It will take some time before we know the results. I don't think she had a heart attack or stroke. Frankly, I'm a bit puzzled. I believe she will make it but I think we need to keep her here for a few more hours."

"Thanks so much, Carl," said Sarah.

"Do you think she could have ingested something that caused her heart to slow down so considerably," asked Peter?

Carl Wilson considered Peter's question. "Sure, it's possible, but the kind of drugs that manage someone's heartbeat are traditionally injected directly by syringe. Even then they are intended for human beings. Once in a great while they are used for animals. Zoos use them as tranquilizers when they are transporting animals. If any such drug is in Jamie's bloodstream the tests will pick it up. I would be surprised. I mean how would such a drug get into Jamie?"

They left the room. Jamie was sleeping and her breathing was almost back to normal.

Peter followed Sarah in her car back to campus. It was almost 11:30 so they decided to have an early lunch at the college's student union. They ordered soup and grilled cheese sandwiches and sat by the window overlooking the snow-covered campus.

"Well, what do you think?" asked Sarah.

Peter looked directly at Sarah. "Someone is sending us a message."

Her expression froze as she put down her grilled cheese

sandwich. "What do you mean? You think someone poisoned Jamie. Are you serious?"

"Think about it, Sarah. One minute Jamie is healthy and frolicking in the snow and the next minute she is near death. What's interesting is she was out of your sight. So something had to happen in the span of a few minutes. Finally, and most interesting, is where you found her. Down by the road." He stopped talking and let his words register with Sarah.

"You mean like someone from the road? Why would someone try to harm Jamie? What do you mean a message?"

Peter just looked at her without saying a word.

Her eyes widened. "They are telling us to back off this whole conspiracy thing."

"That's exactly what they are telling us. They are trying to scare us off by hurting Jamie. We are getting a little too close and it is worrying them."

Sarah's blue eyes flashed in anger. Her brow furrowed in resolve. "This makes me more determined, you know."

Peter smiled. "I thought you would say that. It's one of your most attractive features."

She reddened in obvious pleasure. "So you think you know me pretty well?"

"Well, what I do know, I really like. A lot!"

She just looked at him.

Peter became serious. "I believe I am falling in love with you, Sarah Phillips."

"It's ironic that I left Boston with all its opportunities and came home to Pinehurst to fall in love."

"And who said you can't go home," said Peter.

They laughed and talked for a few more minutes before it was time for them to get back to work. They would have to figure out what to do about this latest threat later.

At that moment across campus Walton Trent and Thomas

Lawton sat in President Cannon's office. The three had been embroiled in a heated conversation for well over an hour.

"Listen, Cannon, we have had this conversation too many damn times for me to remember," said an exasperated Trent. We still have several portfolios to complete before my work is done here. I am not going to let you get cold feet and back out before we have finished what we came here to do. Besides we don't have a choice. There are other more powerful people involved."

President Cannon, dressed in a gray suit and expensive white shirt and blue and red tie, sat still in his leather chair, a worried look creasing his face. He felt sick to his stomach.

"But Walton," he stammered, "things are getting out of hand. Peter Kramer and Sarah Phillips are asking questions and they probably have Martha Phillips and Anne Ashdown involved. All we have to do is have one family start digging and this whole thing could unravel. This is the first time we have had any family members asking questions about their desig-nated gift after the donor dies."

"So what! What can they find? The college and bank records are in sync. We have erased all evidence of the original transactions and replaced them with the new amounts. The paperwork reflects the new lesser amount. It's documented and all quite legal. We also made sure that John Phillips, Elisa-beth Williams, and Phyllis Allen kept their original gift amount confidential. Now you see why it made sense for Thomas to be their attorney. He has access to all of their financial dealings. James, this is foolproof. There is no way anyone can discover what is going on. There is simply no paper trail. You need to relax and let us handle things."

Cannon's face seemed to sag. He knew he was in deep, far too deep to get out. Walton Trent's assurances did make sense. But he still worried.

"What about Leslie Patton? We are responsible for her death. I had no idea it would ever come to this."

"James, Leslie's death was unfortunate. She discovered our operation and had to be stopped. She shouldn't have been snooping around in my office."

"I can't believe this happened to one of our employees."

Trent stood up and walked over to stand in front of Cannon, who remained seated behind his desk.

"James, you came to me complaining about the financial pressures here at Kingston. Randolph Bolles was all over you to change this place into an academically elite college. Whatever the hell that means! So I help get you some real money for new buildings and programs. You didn't complain then and you better stop complaining now. The only thing that is going to blow the lid off is if you panic. Do you understand?"

Trent's implication was clear. His small beady eyes submerged deep under his bushy eyebrows bored into Cannon.

Cannon nodded in understanding. Tiny beads of sweat appeared on his forehead. Trent noticed them with satisfaction. He smiled and walked back to his chair.

"OK then, we have work to do." He motioned to Thomas Lawton and the two walked out of President James Cannon's office. Looking over his shoulder, he told Cannon he would call him later that afternoon. Cannon knew that meant be available.

Back in Walton Trent's office, Lawton and Trent continued the conversation.

"Listen, Lawton, I want you to keep an eye on Cannon. I don't think he will do anything. He doesn't have the courage and besides he knows what will happen if he opens his mouth. But still be watchful. Now, what about Peter Kramer and Sarah Phillips? I am most worried about these two."

Thomas Lawton replied. "Well I sent them a warning this morning. I had someone give Sarah Phillips's dog a nice treat early this morning. They are now over at the veterinarians." A nasty smile crossed his sallow pimply face.

"Let's hope that scares them off, but I rather doubt it. That Peter Kramer is a persistent one. I just don't think they have much to go on. They can't have connected any of us to the bank transactions. But nevertheless, I want you to keep a very close eye on Kramer."

"I will, Walton. I have several friends who will help with that." Again the smile.

Trent turned his attention to some papers on his desk.

"We have two more portfolios to complete. The Townsend one is ready to go. We just have to initiate the action. Are you ready to do that?"

"Yes we are. I have all of the people lined up as usual. We are just waiting for the go-ahead from you."

"OK, you have the green light. Be extra careful. We are getting down to the wire. I don't want any slip-ups."

"You got it."

Now we have one more portfolio on out target list. Unfortunately, this is by far the most dangerous and also the most lucrative. Anne Ashdown."

Lawton hesitated.

"But what about the problem with Peter Kramer and Sarah Phillips. Aren't they kinda close to Anne Ashdown? We could be walking right into a hornet's nest with this one. Isn't there someone else less risky?"

Trent shook his head. "Lawton, I came here to do a job. Anne Ashdown is the final person on a carefully developed list. She is one of the richest people in the state. The people in New York are not going to let me walk away from this one. Besides, this one could be the most fun. I would like nothing better than to stick it to Kramer right under his nose."

"How are we going to pull it off?"

"You let me handle that. You have two jobs to do now. Initiate the action on Townsend and keep an eye on Cannon and Kramer."

CHAPTER FORTY-ONE

At 5:00 in the afternoon that same day Peter followed Sarah as she drove over to Carl Wilson's clinic, where they picked up Jamie to take her home. A different dog greeted them when they arrived. She was almost back to her old self.

"She's bounced back remarkably," said Carl Wilson. "We did some more tests this afternoon and also pumped out her stomach. We found remnants of spoiled meat that I can't believe you would feed her. Is there any chance she got into some bad meat?"

Sarah glanced ever so briefly at Peter and responded.

"Yes, she may have gotten into some back at the barn. Who knows?"

"Well, I am still waiting for the test results. I will call you. She is doing fine now. You can take her home."

"Carl, thanks so much. You saved her life," said a grateful Sarah.

He smiled. "If you hadn't brought her in so fast she would have died."

They left the clinic and after putting Jamie into the back of Sarah's car, they headed out to the Phillips home.

That night after dinner Peter, Jeff, and Sarah met in Peter's cottage. The college semester would be coming to a close in a few days. Soon the campus would be empty of most students for Christmas break. Now seemed like the best time to enact the plan Peter had been thinking of for several weeks. It was this plan that he began sharing with Sarah and Jeff.

The three sat in the great room next to a blazing fire in the old fireplace.

"It's now time to start putting the pieces of this puzzle together," he began. "For the last two months we have noticed several unexplained events related to Kingston College and the Bank of Boston. First we had Leslie Patton's death. Then came the discrepancies in Sarah's grandfather's gift to the college followed by our discovery of irregularities in Elisabeth Williams and Phyllis Allen's gifts. Then Bill Rutherford dies after his own investigation into the bank. Then there is Empire Insurance. Then Jeff gets threatened and fired. Lastly we now have hard data from the bank that show illegal financial transactions. So how does all of this fit? Is there a pattern here?"

He paused and looked at Sarah and Jeff and then continued.

"What we don't have is actual proof of who is behind all of this. Like I said before we have the wrongdoing but not the characters. Sure we know Walton Trent is involved but how much and to what extent? That's what we need to discover next. I have some ideas but we need proof."

"Peter, why don't we go to the police with what we have?"

"Sarah, what we have is pieces and conjecture. More importantly we don't want to tip off Walton Trent and whoever else is involved. I think we can get more evidence ourselves. We can do some things the police can't do."

"Uh-oh, I don't like the sound of that," said Jeff.

"Makes me nervous too," responded Sarah.

"Listen, hear me out. We have the data Jeff copied from

the bank archives. Now we need to connect this with Trent and the others."

"So how do we do that?" asked Sarah.

"This will take several steps. First, is Anne Ashdown. My gut tells me she is next on their list."

Sarah's eyes widened. "Oh, my goodness, is she in danger?"

"I don't know. Trent specifically and probably President Cannon are going to approach her about leaving the college a gift. Probably a big one."

"So basically you want to use Mrs. Ashdown as bait?"

"Only if she is willing. My guess is she will jump at the chance. Remember that she doesn't care too much for Cannon or Trent. She certainly is feisty enough."

Jeff asked, "What's the next step after Mrs. Ashdown?"

Peter looked at Sarah. "We need to go back to the cabin in the woods."

Sarah grimaced. "Oh no, not that place! Why there?"

"Well, I don't really know, but they were up to something in that cabin that night. I want to have a real thorough look around. I figure you and Jeff can help me."

"And the third step," asked Sarah.

"Dr. Morris Glenn. Sarah, I think you and I need to talk with him. He may be the key, but honestly I don't know to what. Remember he was at that cabin that night too. He simply doesn't strike me as someone who would be involved in all of this. Maybe we can get him to talk."

"You sure have been doing some thinking," said Sarah. "Like I told you, I've known Dr. Morris all my life. He is an old family friend. I think he will talk to us."

"OK then. Tonight we talk with Mrs. Ashdown and tomorrow night we go the cabin."

Twenty minutes later the three of them were seated in Anne

Ashdown's living room in the main house. She was delighted to have them there.

"Mrs. Ashdown," began Peter. "We have something very important to discuss with you."

She looked intently at Peter, her blue eyes sparkling. He could see her deep interest and excitement.

"Sarah and I believe that the college is involved in some illegal activity. I know you have some concerns too but this may be more serious than we all originally believed."

"I knew it," she responded. "That old blowhard Randolph Bolles and insipid James Cannon are up to something. And as for Walton Trent, I just don't trust the man. He doesn't belong in this town or at the college. He just doesn't fit."

For the next 10 minutes Peter outlined for Mrs. Ashdown most of what he knew. He left out the possible murders of Bill Rutherford and Leslie Patton.

"Mrs. Ashdown, this is pretty serious. We have to be careful what we do from this point on. I mean it. These are not nice people. You mustn't say anything about this. To anyone!" His pale blue eyes pleaded with her.

Her face tightened. Narrowing her now steely blue eyes she looked directly at Peter and said, "Mr. Kramer, I've lived in these parts for a very long time. I love this town and the college. I'm not about to let anyone, especially outsiders, come and hurt what we have here. I understand the need for confidentiality. Don't you worry about me." She continued her fixed gaze at Peter.

"Thank you, Mrs. Ashdown. We just needed to make sure that we don't reveal our hand too early. You see we have a plan that involves you."

"I want to help in any way possible. What do you want me to do?"

"OK, as I just told you we believe people at the college and the bank are conspiring to fraudulently change the amount of donor gifts to a lower amount and then divert the difference to another account. No one knows about the change except the bad guys. The deceased donor certainly never knows nor do his survivors ever think to ask any questions. Why should they, they have no reason to suspect any wrongdoing. That is up until now. Sarah and I accidentally stumbled into this and began asking some questions. We discovered that John Phillips's original gift was one amount and the actual amount of money the college received was a lesser amount. What we don't know is exactly who is doing this. The college is not guilty but certain people at the college are involved. We think it may be Walton Trent and possibly James Canon. Randolph Bolles we are less certain of. The Bank of Boston is also a player but again we are uncertain what people are mixed up in this."

Peter paused to take a breath. He considered his next words.

"Mrs. Ashdown, while we have strong suspicions and some hard evidence we have up to this point failed to connect anyone to the wrongdoing. We need proof that Trent and others are doing this. That's where you come in. We believe you are on their short list for a major financial gift. I know you have resisted their initial overtures and with good reason. But now we would like you to listen to them when they come asking for a gift. Why? Because we want to use you to get at them."

Anne Ashdown's aged face went white for the briefest of seconds.

"You mean use me like bait?"

Peter smiled at her honesty.

"Yes, that is precisely what we mean. We want to set up Walton Trent and James Cannon. You can help us do this."

Sarah interjected. "Mrs. Ashdown, we really need your help. Like Peter said, we think they are coming to you next. This is a great opportunity to catch them."

Anne Ashdown pondered their words.

"Well, I'm an old lady without much excitement in my life. That is until Peter came along this fall. Now you all have uncovered a real mystery. Sarah, you know how much I love controversy. So, why not some more. OK, what do I do?" Her eyes sparkled in anticipation.

"We believe Cannon and Trent will call on you in the next few weeks or even less. This time we want you to invite them to your home to listen to their pitch. Be open and gracious but don't be too much different than normal." They all laughed at this. Peter paused.

Sarah jumped in. "What Peter means is, up to this point you have been cool to President Cannon and Walton Trent. They may suspect something if you suddenly are all warm and fuzzy with them."

This time Anne Ashdown laughed. "Oh, don't you worry. I can smell people a mile away who want my money. And these two sure smell bad! It would be impossible for me to be all warm and fuzzy. I'd rather die first."

Peter was satisfied.

"OK, so here is what we want you to do. Once you have set up the appointment, call Sarah or me immediately. Oh, and make sure it is in the evening. We will explain the next step after the appointment is set. OK? Remember, we think they will call you first. Please don't call them. That might tip our hand."

As they got up to leave Anne Ashdown took Sarah's hand and winked at her. Sarah smiled and gave her a gentle hug and quietly said to her, "Don't worry everything will be fine."

Walking back to the cottage, Peter turned to Jeff and asked, "How much do you know about electronics?"

Jeff laughed. "I think I know where you are headed with this. Actually I know a fair amount. I was one of those nerds in high school who was always fiddling with sound systems and audiovisual stuff."

"That's what I thought."

"Oh, thanks," replied Jeff.

Peter and Sarah laughed. "I don't think Peter meant it that way," she said. Grinning, she looked at Peter. "You didn't, did you?" They all laughed this time.

"I just figured if Jeff is so good with computers he might be good in electronics too."

"So what's up?" asked Jeff.

"I want to get Mrs. Ashdown's meeting with Cannon and Trent on camera. Pictures and voices don't lie."

"What a great idea," said Sarah.

"Of course," said Jeff, suddenly realizing Peter's thinking. "The camera will capture the actual amount of money Mrs. Ashdown decides to will to the college. So when Cannon and Trent change the amount, we got them."

Peter nodded. "So tomorrow we get the equipment and also make plans to visit the cabin. We still have to find out what that creepy place in the woods has to do with all of this."

Peter gave Sarah a ride home. He stopped at the house to say hi to Martha Phillips and see how Jamie was. He didn't have to wait long. She came out to greet him as usual. After a few minutes Peter kissed Sarah good night and drove home. She held on to him tightly and whispered in his ear to be careful. "I don't want anything happening to you." Peter felt a rush and hugged her back.

The next day was Tuesday. In mid-afternoon Peter drove back to his cottage and after picking up Jeff drove back to the college. Jeff stayed in the car just in case while Peter went to get Sarah from her office. The three of them drove 70 miles away to Concord, the state capital, to a large retail electronics store. Jeff led the way throughout the store selecting tiny video cameras, remote controls, assorted wires, and a 13-inch television monitor. Peter was impressed with how quickly Jeff picked out the necessary equipment. He obviously knew what he was doing. They packed the equipment into the trunk of the car and headed back to Pinehurst. Back at the cottage Jeff set up the television monitor in a corner of the great room and then they went over to Mrs. Ashdown's house and began work in the main living room. There they carefully set up one of the cameras where it would be hidden from view behind a vase of flowers high on the fireplace mantel. Jeff very carefully placed the small camera so that it was not visible from the large high-backed couch. The second miniature camera was hidden above the door to the living room. The plan was to maneuver Cannon and Trent so they both sat on the couch. By the time they were finished it was close to 9:00. They decided it was too late to go to the cabin in the woods.

CHAPTER FORTY-TWO

Susan Turner was five foot eight inches tall, with long brown hair and dark hazel eyes. She had worked at Kingston College for three years. A graduate of the University of New Hampshire where she had majored in finance, she had come to Kingston as an assistant to the Director of Planned Giving, Todd Collins. Her role at Kingston required her to assist the director with university donors and manage all of the delicate issues surrounding people's gifts to the college. Part of her job was to cultivate relationships and in essence make sure those who gave money to the college were well taken care of. One slip or even the most minor of mistakes could result in a donor giving their money elsewhere. Susan Turner was good at her job. She could detect even the subtlest peculiarities in human nature. This gift was essential in her line of work. She also was privy to the amount people gave to the college. Early on the morning of December 16, the first day of Finals week, she received a telephone call from an attorney named Kevin O'Donnell. He had asked for her boss, Todd Collins, but the call had been transferred to her. O'Donnell identified himself as an attorney with the law firm of Giles, Melvin, and Simpson.

Susan immediately recognized the firm. They were located in Brookline, Massachusetts, and represented Henry Townsend. She knew the Townsends well. Todd Collins had put her in charge of the Townsends' bequest to the college. Even Walton Trent was interested in the Townsend bequest. He was always stopping by her office to check up on the Townsend bequest. She remembered his intense and persistent manner whenever he came by. He had made her nervous.

"This is Susan Turner," she said into the phone.

"Yes, Ms. Turner, this is Kevin O'Donnell. My firm represents Henry Townsend. I am trying to reach a Todd Collins. Is he available?"

"I'm sorry but he is out of town for several days. Is there something I can help you with?"

She detected a pause on the other end. "Well, we have instructions to notify the college with any status change regarding our client Mr. Townsend."

Susan bit her lip. "Well, Mr. O'Donnell, you can certainly inform me. I am Mr. Collins's associate."

Another pause. "Well OK, then. Please make sure he gets this message as soon as possible."

Susan was irritated but kept it to herself. "Of course, Mr. O'Donnell," she replied in her most helpful tone. It worked every time.

The attorney continued. "Please inform Mr. Collins that Henry Townsend died last night."

Susan felt her heart jump. "Yes, I will inform him right away. Is there anything else?"

"Obviously the college will want to know since he left a substantial amount of money in his will to the college. We are under legal obligation to notify the college in the event of his passing."

Susan wasn't sure what to say next. "Thank you, Mr.

O'Donnell. I will make sure Todd, I mean Mr. Collins, hears of this immediately."

The attorney muttered a thank you and hung up, leaving Susan staring at the receiver in her right hand. Todd was on a trip to California to visit his ailing parents in San Francisco. She should call him, though it might be better to let Walton Trent know right away. She was reluctant to even go down the hallway to his office, but after weighing the pros and cons, decided it might be wise to tell him straightaway about Henry Townsend. She walked down the carpeted hallway of the Advancement Suite and approached Sylvia Conrad, Walton Trent's secretary.

"Good morning, Sylvia, is Mr. Trent available?"

Sylvia, an affable woman of 40, warmly greeted Susan. They both shared a common dislike for Walton Trent.

"Hi Susan, he's in. Go on in."

Something passed between them, unspoken but nevertheless Susan caught the message. Be careful, he is in one of those moods. Susan smiled a thanks and knocked on the door; hearing the grunt of an answer, she opened it and walked through. The richness of Walton Trent's oak-paneled office never ceased to amaze her. He looked up from his papers and asked her what she wanted. Walton Trent's rudeness also never ceased to amaze her.

"Mr. Trent, an attorney representing the Henry Townsend family called Todd this morning, but since he is on his way to California the call was transferred to me." Trent looked up with immediate interest. Susan feared she had said the wrong thing.

"Go on," he implored. His dark bushy eyebrows seemed to penetrate her soul. She felt a coldness in the air.

"Well," she began a bit shakily. "A Kevin O'Donnell called and said his firm was required to notify the college of Mr.

Townsend's death. That was the purpose of his call. Since Todd wasn't in I thought you should know as soon as possible."

Walton Trent stood up, walked from behind his huge desk, and approached Susan. A thin smile washed across his face. "Yes, you did the right thing. We need to know these things right away. Henry Townsend left the college, as you know, a substantial sum of money. We will need to attend to his family and write a press release thanking the Townsend family for their generous gift." He shook Susan's hand and then turned back to his desk. She was being dismissed and immediately knew it. She pivoted and walked through the open door glancing back at Walton Trent. She saw him reaching for his phone. She felt forgotten and insignificant.

Walton waited for the door to fully close before completing his call. A moment later Justin Nichols answered. Trent filled him in on Townsend's death. The call was short. Trent nodded and said he would stay in touch. Walton Trent then called Thomas Lawton, the college attorney, and upon finishing, left his office and walked down the hall to President Cannon's office. There he spent about 10 minutes.

CHAPTER FORTY-THREE

On that same December morning Peter was up by 6:30. He had to do some grading of student research papers. Jumping into the MGB he huddled in the small confines of the old car waiting for the electronic fuel pump to generate enough gas to the carburetor. After about 15 seconds, he turned the key and the little English roadster sputtered and noisily coughed into life. He waited for a few more seconds before putting the car into gear and slowly drove down the long driveway and out onto the main road to Pinehurst. The surrounding hills were graced with a touch of snow. Winter had arrived in central New Hampshire. By the time the inside of the car had warmed he had reached a very quiet college campus. He headed straight for the Business and Economics building and his office. By 11:45 he was making great progress. He figured he had a few more hours to finish. The sudden ringing of his phone startled him. Grabbing it before it could ring a second time he answered hello, expecting Sarah.

"Is this Peter Kramer?" asked a tired voice.

"Yes, it is," Peter responded cautiously. "Who is this?" he asked. He felt a tinge of fear. An extraordinary feeling indeed.

"I'm sorry to bother you, but this is Dr. Morris Glenn. We met earlier this fall. I am a friend of Sarah Phillips and her family. Do you remember me?"

Peter was surprised to realize who was on the phone. "Why yes, of course I remember you."

"Mr. Kramer, I need to talk with you very urgently." Peter detected genuine fear in the old man's voice.

"What is it you want to talk about?"

"I can't talk over the phone. Listen, Mr. Kramer, I don't know who to turn to. I don't even know if I can trust you, but frankly you are my only option. Sarah Phillips I know. You I don't! But she seems to know and trust you. My instincts say you are the one I should turn to."

Peter was struck with the doctor's reasoning. He sounded rational yet scared.

"OK, Dr. Morris. I will meet with you. Where and when?"

A long pause. "I really don't know where it is safe. This town is so small I'm sure someone will see us."

Peter was stunned. Dr. Morris Glenn, a long-time resident, if not a fixture in Pinehurst, was afraid in his own town. What was happening? He thought for a moment.

"Dr. Glenn, how about we meet out at Anne Ashdown's estate? It's safe there."

"OK, that seems like a good place. When can you meet?"

Peter sensed the urgency in his question.

."Can you come by at 5:30 this afternoon?"

"I can come out there right after my I see my last patient at 4:30."

"Good," replied Peter. "Come directly to the little cottage at the back."

"Thanks, Mr. Kramer. I will see you at 5:30." Dr. Glenn hung up.

Peter quickly dialed Sarah's extension and told her about

the call from Dr. Glenn. They decided to meet for a quick lunch where they discussed what the old doctor might have on his mind. Sarah insisted on being at the meeting. Actually Peter wanted her there. She knew the doctor well and her presence would encourage him.

The afternoon went by quickly. Peter failed to get all of his grading completed but made good headway. His thoughts kept drifting to his earlier conversation with Dr. Glenn. What would he have to tell them that evening? At 4:45 he stopped working and grabbed his coat to leave. The building was quiet and completely empty. He slung his backpack over his left shoulder and made his way down the empty dark hallway and walked out the front door to his car. He had arranged to meet Sarah at the cottage at 5:00.

As Peter made his way slowly out of campus to head home, Dr. Glenn was just about finished seeing his last patient. After writing a prescription for Jean Thompson who had come down with the flu, he bade her good-bye in his well-loved kindly manner. He put a few of his medical instruments away, washed his hands thoroughly, and closed his office door. The front waiting room was empty. He turned off the lights and went out the front door to his car. The penetrating cold of the New England winter evening almost took his breath away. He was really starting to feel his age. He slowly climbed into his old Plymouth and backed out the driveway onto Summer Street and headed west towards Anne Ashdown's place. He passed the old Mobil gas station at the end of Summer and headed west on Green River Road. He began to pick up speed on the dark road when suddenly a voice from the back seat asked him, "So where are you headed, Dr. Glenn?"

The white haired doctor almost passed out from the shock. He slammed on the brakes and swerved to the side of the road. Turning around he asked in a frightened voice, "Who are you?"

The old doctor's heart was beating rapidly from sheer fright.

The strange voice was suddenly reassuring.

"Don't worry Dr. Glenn, I won't hurt you. I just want to talk with you, that's all. You've been so busy today with all of your patients that this is the first time I have been able to see you."

Dr. Glenn turned off the car's motor and, turning, looked straight into the small beady eyes of Thomas Lawton, dressed in a black leather coat.

"What in the name of heaven are you doing in my car?" he almost yelled at the attorney.

The pimply-faced lawyer grinned at the doctor and replied, "Oh I just need to talk with you for a couple of minutes."

"About what?"

"Well, first of all, where are you headed on this dark evening?"

"None of your damn business," said Glenn.

The attorney smiled and looking him right in the eye responded, "Oh, I think this is very much my business."

Dr. Glenn felt a sudden coldness sweep over his fragile body.

"What do you mean?"

"Let's cut the games, old man. I know exactly where you were headed. You're headed out to see Peter Kramer."

The doctor was visibly shaken. How did Thomas Lawton know that was where he was going?

"Well, so. What if I am? I don't know what business it is of yours."

The smile on Lawton's face vanished.

"I think we better be frank with one another, Dr. Glenn. What happened the other night in Belmont is our secret. You weren't planning on telling Kramer, were you?"

Glenn stammered for a brief moment. "No, of course not, I wasn't planning any such thing," he lied.

Lawton suddenly and quickly jumped into the front seat of the car. Glenn edged closer to the driver's side door.

"Dr. Glenn, let's go for a ride to the cabin. There are some people who want to see you."

Glenn didn't hesitate. "I am not going anywhere with you, you shallow ingrate."

Lawton's face reddened at the insult. "Look, calling me names will do us no good here. Just turn around your car and head back to the cabin."

"And what if I don't," challenged the doctor.

Lawton had had enough. He pulled out a small revolver and pointed it at the doctor's stomach.

Glenn's eyes widened. Good Lord, the man was pointing a gun right at him. His mouth felt dry from the fear.

"Is this enough to convince you?" asked Lawton. He enjoyed seeing the fear sweep across the doctor's face.

Morris Glenn couldn't believe this was happening to him. He slowly turned the old Plymouth around and began heading back to town and in the direction of the cabin. The cabin was a place he had grown to detest. Yet, he could have driven to it blindfolded. They passed the college campus and drove directly through town and came to Old Mountain Road. Neither said a word as the old Plymouth made its way north up the winding road into the White Mountains. Thirty minutes they came to the very familiar but equally obscure road that led deeper in the silent mountain forest. Dr. Glenn slowed the car and turned left, carefully heading down the narrow rutted road that descended deeper into the woods. Minutes later the old cabin, a yellow glow in the dark forest, came into their view. Glenn stopped his car next to a Buick LeSabre. He looked at

Thomas Lawton as if for permission for what to do next. He looked for the gun. It was nowhere in sight.

"OK, Dr. Glenn, what do you say we go inside and talk with our friends?"

Glenn despised the man's inane sense of humor. But what could he do? He opened the car door and got out. Lawton followed closely behind.

They walked into the brightly lit cabin. Dr. Glenn was not surprised to see Walton Trent. There was another man in the room whom he had never seen before. The giant man was dressed in faded dirty denim overalls, a frayed red plaid shirt, and scuffed boots. He sported a long black beard flecked with gray hairs. An odd pair indeed! The strange man greeted Dr. Glenn with a cold stare.

"Well, good evening, Dr. Glenn," greeted Walton Trent. "Thank you for joining us. I was beginning to think you didn't like us."

Dr. Glenn glared at Trent. "I don't like you." His anger permeated the small cabin's front room where all four men stood.

Trent's face suddenly lost its smug smile. "Oh, is that how you feel about us now? After all we have been through? Come on! Can't you be more grateful than that?"

"Listen Trent, I am done with you and your evil. No more! It's all over."

Trent gave Glenn a hard look. "Oh really, so you think it's over when you want it to be over? Wrong, pal! It's over when I tell you it's over." Trent's beady eyes bored into Morris Glenn. This time Trent's anger showed.

Morris Glenn suddenly stopped. He was beginning to realize just how foolish he had been. Here he was deep in the woods of the White Mountains, surrounded by three men, one who was a total stranger and other two he both despised and feared, and here he was babbling like he was going to go to the police.

"Why were you going to meet with Peter Kramer?"

The old doctor felt a chill. How did they know?

He attempted to bluff his way out. "You idiots, I was on my way to see Anne Ashdown."

"Nice try, Doc," said Thomas Lawton. "We know who you were really going out there to see."

Trent took several steps and looked directly down at Morris Glenn. His voice softened. "Come on, Dr. Glenn, we know who you were really going to see. It is no use lying. Just tell us what you told the professor."

Morris Glenn looked up at Trent's penetrating gaze. He felt fear. His legs stared to wobble.

"I have told the young man nothing. How could I? Your goon here intercepted me before I even got out of town."

Trent replied, "This we know Doctor, but what have you told him in the past or possibly on the phone today?"

"Nothing. I have told him nothing," the doctor insisted. How ironic he thought, he really hadn't told Peter Kramer anything, yet he knew they would never believe him.

Trent was not satisfied. "Does the professor or Sarah Phillips know anything?"

"If they do, it didn't come from me."

Trent looked long and hard at the doctor. He studied the old man as if he was attempting to read his thoughts. Suddenly, as if he had made up his mind, he straightened up and, nodding ever so subtly to Thomas Lawton, he silently slipped on his coat and walked out the front door without so much as a glance at Dr. Glenn. Everyone in the room remained in their places. No one said a word. The room was silent except for the persistent ticking of an old Seth Thomas clock hanging on the south wall. The sound of a car starting followed by the spinning tires disturbing loose gravel broke the quietness. As if on cue, Thomas Lawton stood up and made his way to the door. He opened the cabin door and cast a final quick look at Morris Glenn standing in the center of the cabin. Just as quickly he was gone out the door too. Dr. Glenn was left alone with the strange man. He looked over at the man. A cruel grin greeted him. The doctor looked away. Unbelievably it all became crystal clear. The old doctor abruptly thought of his wife back home in the old white house they had occupied for so many years. She would be sitting in her favorite stuffed chair knitting or maybe writing a letter to one of their children. He pictured her there contentedly waiting for him to return home. He imagined her checking the clock from time to time. The doctor was suddenly startled by the cold metallic presence of a gun painfully pressing into the back of his neck. The meaning and cruelty of the moment stunned him.

"Get moving, old man," commanded the bearded bully.

Morris didn't know where he meant. "Moving where?" he asked.

"Just move yourself straight out the back door onto the porch. Oh, and don't try to make a run for it. You ain't got no car and you're frigging out here in the middle of nowhere."

Morris did as he was instructed. He opened the cabin door and walked out onto the back porch. The December sky was a vibrant deep blue highlighted by the twinkling of thousands of stars. How ironic, he thought, the sky had never looked more beautiful. He thought of his wife once more and wished they could be seeing this colorful early winter sky together. This was the last thought Dr. Morris Glenn ever had. A loud explosion filled his ears quickly and was mercifully followed by darkness. Forever darkness.

The bearded bully knelt down to where Morris Glenn had crumpled onto the snow-covered grass and lifted his limp wrist searching for a pulse. He felt nothing. He easily hoisted the dead man onto his broad shoulders and began swiftly walking into the woods. He traveled deeper and deeper into the snowy woods and was soon swallowed up by the penetrating darkness. Even the twinkling stars of that beautiful starry night failed to illuminate the man walking in the woods carrying the lifeless body of the man he had just killed. Thirty minutes later the man reached a small clearing that fronted a small stream. Next to the stream was an old shack. He kicked open the door with his right foot and walked in. A small mining shaft greeted both men. The bully peered down into the inky blackness of the hole and then dropped Morris Glenn into the shaft, without feeling. He heard the body plummet down the 60-foot shaft followed by a muted splash. Grabbing a few old boards he knelt down on one knee and placed them back in their original position. Wiping his dirty hands on his filthy denim coveralls he backed out of the small shack and made his way back through the woods to his old truck hidden in the woods near the cabin, where he had so callously ended the life of Dr. Morris Glenn. He would be paid well for his work. He had to get home for supper.

Peter looked at the clock again. It was six minutes after 6:00. Where was Dr. Glenn?

Sarah took another bite of her ravioli. She glanced at Peter. He had hardly touched his dinner. She sensed his anxiety. By 7:00 they knew Dr. Glenn wasn't coming. They debated what do so. All at once Peter's phone rang. He leaped out of his chair and grabbed the phone. Sarah watched intently. He listened to the voice on the other end. His eyes widened then he quickly slammed down the phone.

"Who was that?" asked Sarah. She clutched her fork in right hand frozen in mid air.

"That was a warning. Some guy told me that I'd better

mind my own business or else what happened to Dr. Glenn would happen to me too."

"Oh no," cried Sarah softly.

Peter stood up and went to Sarah. He held her. He could feel her heart beating wildly. She was really frightened.

"Someone must have intercepted Dr. Glenn on his way out to see us. I feel so guilty. What have they done to him?"

Sarah stepped away from Peter. "Well we just can't sit here and do nothing. We had better call Mrs. Glenn and see where he is." She dreaded the answer to her own question.

"You're right. We're going to see her right now. First I am going to call Elisabeth Rutherford and keep her informed. We need someone to always know where things are with this whole sordid affair." He picked up the phone and dialed her number. After several minutes he was finished. He looked at Sarah.

"OK, she's been brought up to speed. She will be our contact person and will call the police tomorrow if we don't check in with her by 9:00 A.M."

Sarah felt relief wash over her. It felt assuring to know someone else knew what was really happening at the college.

"What about our plan with Mrs. Ashdown? Is it still on?"

"More than ever," replied Peter. "We just have to be incredibly careful."

They decided to drive to Dr. Glenn's house. A few minutes later they were headed to town. At 7:30 they arrived at his old white two-story house. The yellow glow of the porch light greeted them. Peter pushed the weathered doorbell and heard the old-fashioned ring echo in the huge hallway. A moment later the door opened and a kind-looking white-haired women in her late seventies faced them.

"Oh, Sarah, it's so good to see you," Mrs. Glenn said. A broad smile accompanied her greeting.

"Hello, Mrs. Glenn. This is Peter Kramer, a friend of mine and a new faculty member at the college."

She looked up at Peter and immediately thrust out her hand and acknowledged Peter.

"Nice to meet you, young man."

"Mrs. Glenn, may we come in. We need to talk with Dr. Glenn. Is he in?"

Confusion swept over her face. "Why I thought he was going out to see you and Anne Ashdown tonight. He said he would be back by 8:00. Did he not come by?"

Sarah bit her lip. This was not going to be easy. "No, he didn't come by. We were expecting him but he never showed. We hoped he would be here."

The confusion was giving way to worry. "Well where could he be? He's never late like this."

Peter stepped closer to Mrs. Glenn. "Mrs. Glenn, do you have any idea why he was coming out to see Sarah?"

"No, he just said that he had to talk to Anne, you Sarah, and your friend" She looked directly at Peter. "I presume he meant you, Mr. Kramer."

"Mrs. Morris, has your husband been worried about anything lately?"

She rubbed her left eyebrow in concentration. "I don't think so. He always has something on his mind so it wouldn't be unusual if he seemed preoccupied."

Peter persisted gently. "Did you notice anything out of character for your husband? Maybe a change of habit or routine?"

She thought for a moment. "Well, I have wondered about one thing. Usually after work he will always sit by the fire in the living room where we spend the evening. It is our time together. We've done this for almost 40 years. But lately, maybe in the last few months he has started to spend time in the little study off the bedroom. He often works there on occasion late at night when I am in bed. But recently he has been spending more time up there, during the evenings. I'm not sure what he is doing but I think he's just doing some writing."

Sarah cast a knowing glance at Peter.

"Mrs. Glenn, would you mind if Peter and I took a look in Dr. Glenn's office up there?"

Now she looked really worried. Peter and Sarah could see it in her sad eyes. She knew something was up. Her resolve strengthened. "What possible connection could there be between what's up there and my husband's missing his appointment with you?" It was clear she didn't want to be worried any further about the situation.

Sarah continued gently. "Mrs. Glenn, there probably is nothing, but we do need to find out where Dr. Glenn is."

"Shouldn't we call the police? I mean, they can help find him better than you two can."

Peter cleared his throat. "Do you want us to call the police?"

She hesitated. Calling the police would be an acknowledgement that something was terribly amiss. She wasn't ready to take that next step just yet.

She relented. "OK, both of you can go on upstairs. The office is just off the bedroom to the right. If you don't mind, I'd like to stay down here."

Sarah and Peter walked up the carpeted stairway passing walls with pictures of the Glenns' son and daughter-in-law with smiling grandchildren. At the top of the stairs they paused, feeling like intruders. Pressing on, they entered the master bedroom and quickly found the little office. Not knowing what to look for they started going through papers and other documents, careful not to disturb anything unrelated to the matter at hand. The old desk was cluttered with legal papers and articles from medical journals. They searched deeper into the drawers and under piles of papers. After a few minutes they had found nothing. Exasperated, Peter stood up and closed his eyes as if willing some form of evidence to appear. Suddenly, Sarah gasped. Pulling a sheaf of old yellow legal paper from the bottom drawer of an old filing cabinet she held it high for Peter to see. All he could make out was scribbled handwriting.

"Look," she exclaimed. This may be something. Upon closer inspection Peter saw columns of dates followed by numbers after each date. The dates stretched back almost 10 years.

"This is a ledger of losses at the racetrack," she said excitedly. "Rockingham Park in Salem! It looks like Dr. Glenn has a gambling problem." She was shocked.

Peter still didn't get it. "So, what's the connection?"

"Don't you see? Morris is being blackmailed. His connection to this whole mess at the college is because someone is blackmailing him."

Peter was stunned. "So, Dr. Glenn is the victim of a blackmailer. Why?"

Sarah's response was immediate. "Think about it, Peter. People are blackmailed because they have something the blackmailer wants. So if we can figure out what that is we are that much closer to the bad guys."

"What does a kindly old country doctor have that Walton Trent and whoever is working with him wants?"

"Well it must be medical in nature, wouldn't you think?"

Peter looked intently at the old ledger. "Whose initials are TL?" he asked.

"What do you mean?" asked Sarah. She peered over his shoulder.

A faded but still distinct tiny initial was at the bottom of the yellow paper. Next to the initials was a short sentence: *No more, I'm tired of this and am going to put a stop to it.*

"What does that mean?" asked Sarah.

A tired old voice startled them. "The initials stand for Thomas Lawton."

They both whirled around in shock.

Mrs. Glenn was quietly standing at the entrance to the little office, a light blue cloth handkerchief clutched in her hand. Her eyes were red from crying.

"My husband is a wonderful man. You must believe that! But he has maintained a terrible secret for over 10 years. No one knows. He even thinks I don't know but I do. I discovered it three years ago. I haven't had the courage to confront him about it."

Peter and Sarah stood quietly, waiting for her to continue. They could see how difficult it was for the doctor's wife.

"My husband has a gambling problem. He simply can't stay away from that wretched racetrack in Salem. He goes there every week on Thursday afternoons. You see, Thursdays are his afternoon off. He tells me he is going fishing, golfing, or to Boston on medical business. After a few years I was struck with how routine this had become. Never once did he invite me to go with him. So, one Thursday I decided to follow him. I borrowed Betty Clarendon's car and followed him. I'm ashamed to tell you this. What kind of wife resorts to following her husband around? So I waited for him to leave and then took Betty's car, she lives next door, and followed my own husband." She dabbed at her eyes with the handkerchief.

"I thought he would go the lake or maybe the golf club. That's what I hoped. Then I could turn around and come home and everything would be all right. Just as before. But no, he had to head straight out of town and east towards Concord where he then took Route 93 south to Salem and that dreadful racetrack. At first, I couldn't believe it. I parked the car and stayed well behind him as he went into the betting area. He had on that old Boston Red Sox cap so no one would notice him. I've never before felt so ashamed for both what I was doing and what he was doing. I watched him go the betting window and then as he watched the race. He got so excited and looked so happy. That made me sadder than anything else. How could a damn racetrack give my husband more pleasure than I could? I ran out of that place of evil and drove home crying the whole way.

Peter and Sarah were terribly embarrassed. They didn't know what to do next. Sarah walked over and put her arm around Beth Glenn. "I'm so sorry, Mrs. Glenn."

She dried her tears and looked up at Sarah. "Please find my Morris. I'm so afraid something bad has happened to him."

"We will do our best, Mrs. Glenn. We will also keep his secret to ourselves. You can count on that."

They walked along the upstairs hallway and then down the carpeted stairway past the family pictures to the first floor.

Sarah gave Beth Glenn one more hug and she and Peter walked out into the cold December night. The silence of the New Hampshire night was punctuated by the squeaking of their shoes on the rapidly freezing snow. Neither said a word until they were inside Sarah's BMW. She started the engine, adjusted the temperature to warm, and slowly backed out of the driveway.

"So what do we do now?" asked Sarah as she drove in the direction of the college. She looked over at a silent Peter. He was lost deep in thought and didn't answer for a moment.

"There is nothing we can do about Dr. Glenn for the moment. I mean what do we tell the police? No police agency, let alone the district attorney, will act on speculation. These guys have done a great job of covering their tracks. The only tangible evidence is the disk with the supposed bank irregularities. But we need more."

The campus lights came into view. "So what next?" persisted Sarah. Her heart ached for Beth Glenn.

"You're not going to like this but it's time to go back to the cabin in the woods."

Sarah groaned. "Oh no, that place gives me the creeps."

"I know, it scares me too. But I really think there is something there that can help us."

"Peter Kramer, you are going to be the death of me, of us," she sighed.

He reached over and held her hand. "Hey we have to finish what we've started here, don't we?"

She nodded silently and continued driving. His hand felt warm and reassuring.

She headed the BMW straight through town and turned north on Old Mountain Road. The night sky sparkled with a thousand stars illuminating their way towards the deep and dark place in the woods that had swallowed up Dr. Morris Glenn earlier that evening. Both were lost in their own thoughts. Sarah followed the winding road as it climbed higher and higher into the rural mountain region. Her car lights cut a path of yellow light through the inky darkness. Twenty minutes later they approached the obscure turnoff. Sarah slowed the car and carefully turned left and gently steered her car down the dark narrow dirt road. She felt frightened. Peter prayed there were no people at the cabin. Sarah came to the little hill that took them down to the cabin. She paused and looked at Peter, who nodded. She gripped the steering wheel tightly and moved forward. Soon the cabin came into view. It was completely dark. Peter breathed a sigh of relief. Moments later they stepped out of the car and stood quietly at the bottom of the front steps listening for anything out of the ordinary. The woods were as quiet as they were black. The night quiet was fragile, almost waiting to be shattered. Sarah looked behind her several times as if waiting for someone to leap out of the darkness and wrestle her to the hard cold ground. Peter's boots crunched on the snow as he made his way up the rickety stairs. Sarah clutched his coat from behind. He tested the front door and found it locked. They went around to the back door. They both noticed footprints in the snow surrounding an area on the ground where it had been packed down somewhat. The footprints led away from the cabin into the woods. Peter was surprised to find the back door unlocked. He cautiously entered the silent dark cabin. It was empty. He quickly turned on the lights.

"What are we looking for?" asked Sarah.

"I don't know," said Peter. "Let's look around."

They searched the cabin thoroughly for thirty minutes. There wasn't really much to search. A table with four chairs next to a small kitchen with an old stove and refrigerator. The living room contained several easy chairs and one sofa, all facing a stone fireplace. An old Seth Thomas clock hung on one wall. A tiny bathroom was off to the left of the living room adjacent to a small bedroom with one double bed and an old dresser. Everything looked the same as the first time Peter had been there. Sarah was intently searching through drawers in the kitchen, her head down in front of the small kitchen window when she happened to look up and found two dark eyes staring at her through the window. She screamed in shock and dropped the knives she was holding in her left hand. She backed away from the window just as Peter reached her.

"What is it?" he almost screamed.

"A man's face, outside the kitchen window," she gasped. All the color had drained from her face.

Peter reached down and, grabbing one of the knives, started for the door. The back cabin door exploded in a blinding burst of splintered wood and the doorframe shattered into a hundred pieces. Peter fell back in surprise, still clutching the knife in his left hand. He looked up in utter fear as a huge man with a long, scruffy black beard dressed in a faded red plaid coat descended upon him. Sarah screamed again. The giant stranger lunged for Peter, an absolutely wild look in his eyes. Peter had no doubt in his mind the wild man intended to kill him with his with his bare hands. Suddenly the man slipped on a small throw rug and lost his balance and began falling out of control towards Peter. Peter could smell alcohol and garlic on the man's breath. He was that close to Peter's face. Still grasping the nine-inch kitchen knife in his left hand he quickly brought it around to his front and holding it as tightly as he could inclined the blade at an angle. The wild man's eyes grew wide with fear as all at once he saw the extended knife but was unable to avoid falling on it. Time seemed to stand still. The sharp blade penetrated his chest, fatally piercing the man's heart. The man emitted a slight hissing sound as the weapon found its mark. He fell heavily on Peter without a sound, his face resting directly on Peter's in a bizarre scene that looked like two people kissing one another. For a moment all was silent and then blood began seeping around Peter's chest and midsection soaking him through and through. Suddenly Sarah was pulling the dead man off Peter, tears streaming down her face. She thought Peter was dead. She yelled his name hysterically frantically looking for some sign of life. There they lay, the wild mountain man, his sightless eyes open staring at the floor with the knife protruding from his chest. Next to him lay a stunned Peter, who looked like a raging bull had gored him. All of a sudden he opened his eyes and looked at Sarah, who just as abruptly realized he wasn't dead. Relief flooded her face as she hugged Peter, crying and spilling hot tears onto his face. She helped him to the sofa where they tried to gather their composure. The massive man lay dead on the floor. They both sat there shaking for several minutes.

"I just killed a man," said Peter.

"He was going to kill you. You had no choice."

"I think I'm going to be sick." He scrambled for the bathroom and barely made it. Several minutes later he came out his face damp and wet.

"Are you all right?" asked Sarah.

"I feel kinda of shaky but I'm OK."

She glanced at the dead body and asked the inevitable question. "So what do we do now?"

Peter looked at the still body. "Well let's first find out who he is and then get the heck out of here."

They went through his pockets and retrieved a dirty brown wallet and a yellow piece of lined notebook paper with several names, addresses, and phone numbers written on it. Peter quickly tucked the wallet back into the dead man's pocket. The driver's license identified the dead man as Harold Bozeman from Clearville. Sarah told Peter Clearville was a tiny rural village tucked in the foothills. She said it was a poor farming community of about 200 people. They debated what to do with the body. Should they tell the police? If they did, how would they explain their own presence at the cabin? Would they be accused of murder? What would happen with their careers? What about Trent and the conspiracy at the college and the Bank of Boston? Was the dead man related to Trent? In the end they decided to leave the body at the cabin and place a call to the Pinehurst Police once they got back to town. They quickly cleaned up any evidence that would tie them to the cabin. They jumped into Sarah's car and headed out of the woods back to town. They passed an old pickup truck half-hidden in the woods, a hundred feet from the cabin, in the direction of the highway. They knew whose truck it was. He must have been there all along. How had they missed seeing it when they drove in earlier? A confederate flag hung inside the window of the cab just above a gun rack.

CHAPTER FORTY-FOUR

Walton Trent and Thomas Lawton sat in Trent's office at the college as Peter and Sarah made their way back to Pinehurst. They were discussing the events of the night. Lawton was nervous. At his worst he was a common criminal who used people to his advantage. How had he gotten mixed up in murder? He felt badly about Dr. Glenn. He had known the doctor for over twenty years. Glenn had delivered his two children. He knew he was in so far he would never get out. Even if he tried, Walton Trent would have him killed too. He wished he had never met Trent. Lawton was glad to leave the cabin and let Harold Bozeman do the dirty work. He had known Bozeman since high school. Bozeman was a New Hampshire hillbilly. He was a bully who loved to fight and hurt people. He should never have put Trent in touch with Bozeman. The two were made for each other. Both were violent men. One was urbane and literate while the other was boorish and ignorant.

Lawton waited for Trent to get off the phone. After 10 long minutes Trent put down the receiver and looked directly at Thomas.

"That was one of the big boys in New York. He wants us

to begin wrapping up the operation. They think the locals are getting a bit too close for comfort. Specifically they mean Professor Kramer and Sarah Phillips. They don't like the fact that we had to kill so many people outside the plan. So they want us to complete one more project, tie up any loose ends, and close it down. That sounds just fine to me. I'm getting pretty tired of this backwoods town and all its eccentric people."

Lawton bit his lip. "So what happens to me?"

Trent laughed. "Why nothing at all, my country lawyer friend. Once I'm out of here you just go back to your little law practice and lie low for a while." He gave Lawton a steady look. "That means you don't spend all of your money so that it attracts attention. Got that?"

He breathed a silent sigh of relief.

"Of course, Walton. I can keep quiet."

"You damn well better, Lawton. We always know where you and your family live." The threat was clear.

Trent continued. "Now President Cannon and I are going to meet with Anne Ashford sometime in the next week. You know what that means. It will be a bit difficult with Dr. Glenn no longer helping us but we will manage just fine. You go home now and call me at 10:00 tomorrow morning."

Lawton nodded a yes. He was most anxious to get out of Trent's office. A few minutes later he was in his car driving home. He always did what Walton Trent said. He had no choice.

CHAPTER FORTY-FIVE

Peter and Sarah drove back to the cottage on the Ashdown estate. They were tired and scared. The lights were on in the cottage. Jeff opened the door, a look of apprehension on his face turning to shock, when he saw the blood on Peter and Sarah's clothes. Peter recited the events of the evening leaving nothing out. Sarah grabbed some eggs and bacon from the refrigerator and hastily made them all something to eat. Over their meal they tried to piece together all the information they had gathered. Everything made sense but Dr. Glenn's involvement. They were certain that Walton Trent, Thomas Lawton, and possibly James Cannon were illegally diverting money intended for the college to their own private accounts. It was outright fraud. They were also convinced that people associated with the fraud had killed Bill Rutherford, Leslie Patton, and Morris Glenn. What they couldn't figure out was what Morris Glenn's involvement was. They only knew he had frequented the cabin in the woods and had a secret gambling problem. What was his connection? Peter was greatly bothered by the death of the man at the cabin. They debated whether to call the police. His body was still lying back at the cabin. In the end they decided that Peter, Sarah, and Elisabeth Rutherford would go the police that night. Peter called Dean Rutherford and agreed to meet her at the Pinehurst Police Station as soon as they could get there. In the meantime Jeff would stay at the cabin continuing to work on the plan to videotape the upcoming meeting between President Cannon, Walton Trent, and Anne Ashdown. While they felt right about going to the police, they wanted to continue to try to get more incriminating evidence on Trent and Cannon and the others.

Sarah said, "We'd better tell the police that Dr. Glenn is missing. I'll call Mrs. Glenn and see if she has heard anything. If not, I'll tell her we are going to the police."

"Wow, this is getting pretty complicated," sighed Jeff. "I feel like I've been dropped into a deepening mystery that will never get sorted out."

Peter put his hand on Jeff's shoulder. "I know this is scary. We need you to help us solve this mystery. We'll be back as soon as we can. You just continue to lie low here."

Peter and Sarah put on their coats and headed out into the late winter night. The time was 10:30 P.M.

The Pinehurst police station was located in a two-story red-brick building in the center of town directly across from the town commons. The building was built in 1949 soon after World War II. Two tall white pillars graced the entrance located at the top of a set of concrete steps. The view gave one the impression of standing at the top of the steps looking out for the safety of the Pinehurst citizenry. Inside, the station housed three small cells, four offices, and a large reception area. On the second floor were the district attorney's offices and a rather large and somewhat ornate courtroom. The imposing building was a fixture in Pinehurst.

Peter and Sarah parked their car along the curb adjacent to the building and walked up the steps and into the building.

They found Dean Rutherford sitting in the reception area waiting for them. She rose to her feet with a reassuring smile. She gave them both a firm hug.

"I've already talked with Detective Connors. I wanted to give him a little background. He is back in his office waiting for us." She grabbed Peter's arm. "Listen Peter, Cary Connors is a good person. Sarah knows him too. He may surprise you with what he already knows. So just tell him everything. OK?"

Peter felt nervous as heck. How had he gotten mixed up in this whole affair? He had actually killed a man today. He tried to relax as he walked into the detective's office. It was impossible.

Cary Connors stood five foot six and weighed almost 250 pounds. He had a full head of dark wavy hair and a startlingly handsome face for someone so short and heavy. He was hunched over a computer staring intently at the screen. He didn't even notice their presence until Elisabeth Rutherford cleared her throat. He looked around in surprise and immediately jumped to his feet.

"Sorry," he apologized. "Hello, Sarah, how have you been?" He extended a large meaty hand.

"Hi Cary, nice to see you again," replied Sarah. "Truthfully, things have been better," she answered.

Sarah turned to Peter and introduced him to Cary Connors. "Cary, this is Peter Kramer."

Peter shook the detective's hand.

The detective looked him directly in the eye. "Well, Mr. Kramer, what can I do for you? It's pretty late for business. Elisabeth called me and said whatever you have to tell me is important."

Peter hesitated. Where to begin, he thought?

"There is a small secluded cabin in the woods off of Old

Mountain Road, maybe 20 miles north of Pinehurst, with a dead body. I know this because I killed the man earlier this evening."

Cary Connors arched his dark eyebrows but said nothing.

Sarah thought to herself. Leave it to Peter to be incredibly direct and not try to sugarcoat the issue. Wow! This was one of the things she loved about him.

"Sarah and I were at the cabin around 7:00 this evening when this man burst into the cabin through the back door and began attacking me. I was convinced he would kill me with his bare hands. Clutching a kitchen knife, I retreated backwards as he came at me when suddenly he slipped on a small rug and fell into the knife I had extended out in front of me. He landed heavily on me, and as he did, the knife plunged into him. He died right there in front of us."

The detective looked at Sarah. "Is that how it happened, Sarah?"

"Yes, Cary, that is exactly what happened. I was in the kitchen when this man looked through the window and about scared me to death. He then ran around to the back and exploded his way through the door and began attacking Peter. I thought he was going to kill him. Peter had no choice but to defend himself."

"Why were you two out there?"

They looked at each other. At that moment Elisabeth interjected.

"Cary, there are some things going on at the college that are quite suspicious. Presently we have a plethora of strange events but nothing to really connect them together. Peter and Sarah were out at this cabin trying to find some more information."

"Like what, Elisabeth? What's with this cabin?"

Peter replied, "Mr. Connors, I'm afraid I started this whole thing when I began questioning the amount of money John

Phillips left the college. It seems there are two different amounts. The publicly announced amount is considerably lower than the actual amount. We have been trying to determine where the missing money went. It didn't go to the college and may in fact have gone to a phony account in New York City."

"Now hold on there, Mr. Kramer. You're beginning to lose me. First we have a dead body at some cabin in the woods, someone you say you killed. Now we have Kingston College involved in some criminal conspiracy to steal money from John Phillips, who died over a year ago. This is all a bit farfetched, isn't it? How does this all tie together?"

Peter paused to gather his thoughts. He had to slow down and start sounding more coherent.

"Mr. Connors, let me go back to the beginning. This last summer I took a position on the faculty at Kingston College. Dean Rutherford hired me out of Michigan State University, where I completed my doctorate last spring. I came to Pinehurst and found a place to live in a cottage on Anne Ashdown's estate. I was minding my own business as a new faculty member and things were going well. I met Sarah shortly after I came to the college and began spending time with her. Sarah works in the college's business office, as you may know. One evening we were having dinner at Sarah's grandmother's home and the subject of John Phillips's gift to the college came up. We were shocked to learn that the amount of the gift reported by the college was substantially lower than the actual gift as recorded in John Phillip's personal papers."

"What was the difference?" asked Connors.

Sarah answered his question. "My grandfather left Kingston College $1.7 million according to the college's records and the bank records. My grandmother tells me he left the college $3.7 million. We have no idea where the other 2 million is."

Connors whistled. "Wow, that is a bundle of missing money." He looked skeptical.

"So, maybe Martha Phillips made a mistake. Maybe it was only 1.7 million."

Connors was a good detective and as good detectives looked for the most logical answer to a mystery.

Peter anticipated the question. He, too, would be skeptical.

"Mr. Connors, we wondered the very same thing. So Sarah and I did some checking. We actually saw the bequest documents from Mr. Phillips's office. The amount was indeed $3.7 million. This leads us to the next event we want to tell you about. Actually two events. I'm sure you remember the hit-and-run death of Leslie Patton."

At this point Connors raised his beefy right hand for Peter to stop. "Now, Mr. Kramer," he asked Peter. "Please don't tell me that the Leslie Patton death is somehow related to this college conspiracy and the body in the cabin in the woods."

"Mr. Connors, I know this sounds ridiculous but we believe there is a connection."

Dean Rutherford interrupted. "Cary, you'd better listen. I think the young man and lady are really onto something."

The detective relented. "OK, I'm listening."

Peter persisted.

"The night Leslie died she sent a rather cryptic e-mail to Sarah saying she needed to talk to Sarah. Sarah didn't get the message until the following Monday after Leslie's death. Leslie told her she had some interesting information that she needed to share with Sarah. Unfortunately less than an hour after she wrote the e-mail she died."

Sarah continued. "Cary, Leslie worked in the Development Office of the college. This is the department that handles the gifts bequeathed to the college. We think there is a connection between what happened to Leslie and the missing money."

Cary Connors was too smart of a detective to quickly dismiss this connection. He held up his hand, motioning them to stop. Standing up he went over to a gray three-drawer file and rifled it through the top drawer for a moment. Extracting a blue folder, he returned to his seat. He looked at the paperwork in the file for several seconds and then looked up.

"Leslie Patton was intentionally hit and run over. The State Police Crime Team determined it was no accident. We have exhausted all of our leads. We are at a dead end." He paused as if trying to decide if he should tell them more.

"We talked with people at the college where Leslie worked to see if there was anything going on that would tie in her death. We came up with nothing. As of now we are nowhere." Peter could tell the man didn't enjoy admitting this. It had to be frustrating.

Sarah spoke up. "Cary, after I read and printed the cryptic e-mail Leslie sent me just hours before her death, I discovered it had been deleted from the college's network."

Peter picked up where Sarah left off. "We also discovered several other interesting pieces of information. In November, I met with Bill Rutherford, a senior level officer with the Bank of Boston." He paused and glanced at Elisabeth Rutherford. She nodded for him to continue. Connors saw the exchange but said nothing. "Bill Rutherford is, I'm sorry was, Dean Rutherford's father. Unfortunately he was killed in a mugging on the Boston Common. I had asked him to check the bank records on the amounts of money actually delivered electronically from the John Phillips Estate to the Bank of Boston and from there to Kingston College. He discovered that indeed $3.7 million came to the bank, but that only $1.7 went to Kingston College while the remaining $2 million was wired to the Empire Insurance Company in New York. I know this because I had another friend at the bank run a special software program to determine how the transfer was made. It is a slick operation. The money is transferred almost instantly to both accounts. No one ever sees the diversion. Luckily the backup software program picked it up. Sarah and I then traveled to New York and found the Empire Insurance Company to be an office in an old brick building, in an seedy part of the city, with one secretary. The place had phony written all over it. It was obvious it was a front."

At this point Sarah decided it was time to tell Cary about Dr. Glenn.

When Sarah was done the detective responded. "Whoa there! This is getting pretty complicated. I must admit you've got my interest. Let's put all of this aside and get back to the dead body in the cabin. We need to check that out tonight. I want to take a few of my officers and go to the cabin. You three can ride with me. OK?"

"Certainly, Cary, we will take you up there," said Sarah. "It's just a bit scary, that's all."

"I understand, Sarah. But we have to go there and begin our investigation."

Connors picked up the phone and issued a few instructions. A few moments later three Pinehurst Police officers crowded the doorway to the small office. They listened to further instructions from Connors and then immediately left. Picking up his hat and coat, the burly detective stood up and motioned for Peter, Sarah, and Elisabeth to follow him. They walked through the police station and out a side door to the parking lot for police vehicles. The three officers were waiting by a police cruiser. Connors jumped into an unmarked police car with Peter, Sarah, and Elisabeth. Both cars proceeded out of the police parking lot eventually heading north up the Old Mountain Road. Peter was in the front seat giving Connors directions. It felt strange but also comforting to have the police with them this time. The dark highway loomed ahead. It was almost 11:30. No one would be out on the road at this time of the night. Twenty-five minutes later they approached the turnoff to the narrow road that led to the cabin. Both cars slowly made the turn with Connors leading the way carefully down the bumpy dirt road. The darkness was almost suffocating. It was hard to imagine coming up here alone with Sarah, Peter thought to himself. What had he been thinking?

The reached the top of the steep grade and began the ascent to the bottom and the dark cabin. The police cruiser's lights illuminated the small cabin, casting a yellow glow that flickered like a bolt of lightning before extinguishing. The darkness settled in around them as they all got out of the cars and walked to the front.

Connors spoke. "Well, we believe a crime of some sort has occurred, which gives us reason to enter the premises." One of the policemen tried the front door and found it locked. Another went around to the back and soon the front door opened. "The back door was all bashed in," he said to Connors. "There is a body in the kitchen."

"OK, everyone stay out here," ordered Connors. "I don't want us disturbing the crime scene." He entered the cabin alone. Soon a light came on. Everyone tried to peer in through the open door and window. A few moments he came out. "Well you two were right. There is a dead body with a knife sticking out of his chest just like you said." He paused. "OK, Charlie," he said to one of the officers. "Call it in to the station. Tell them to notify the District Attorney, the Coroner's Office, and the State Police Crime Lab. We are going to do this by the book. Everyone stay out of the cabin. Hey, Tommy," he said to another of the officers, "you take the cruiser search light and have a look around outside the cabin. Be real meticulous. It's getting cold so you three," he said motioning to Peter, Sarah, and Elisabeth, "can sit in my car to stay warm. Oh, we will need the clothes you were wearing, so we can match up any blood on your clothes with the dead guy's blood."

They watched from Connors's car as the police went about their business. The bright lights of the police searchlight played on the tall pine trees and the grounds surrounding the cabin. Soon a yellow crime scene tape circled the cabin. Thirty minutes later the narrow road was descended upon by red and blue flashing police lights as several police vehicles slowly made their way down the steep slope and into the yard. A police dog and his handler climbed out of one of the cars. Cary Connors was busy giving instructions and managing the crime scene. Peter was impressed with how organized and efficient the detective appeared. Forty-five minutes later Connors came to the car where Peter, Sarah, and Elisabeth sat. He rested his elbows on the car window panel and reported on what they had come up with so far. He held the dirty old brown wallet and yellow piece of paper.

"The dead man's name is Harold Bozeman. He comes from the next town over from Pinehurst. Small place called Clearville. Bozeman was someone familiar to the police. He was a local boy who got in his share of bar fights and petty crimes. He had a violent side to him. I'm not surprised he ended up this way, but at the same time I'm perplexed as to why he would try to attack you. It doesn't make sense. Except," he paused, looking directly at Peter and Sarah, "both of your names are on this paper."

Cary was interrupted by one of his police officers. He stepped away from the car for a few moments, listening to the young officer. It was the one with the searchlight. Their conversation ended and Connors returned to the car. His face was grim.

"I'm sorry, but I've got some bad news. We found some

footprints out back and decided to follow them into the woods. The search dog picked up a scent and dragged the two officers deep into the woods to a small shack about a half-mile from the cabin. The dog got real excited around some old boards covering an old mining shaft. The officers stuck the searchlight down the shaft and saw what looked like a body at the bottom. They used rope and grappling hooks and pulled up Morris Glenn. He was dead."

Sarah gasped, holding her hand to her mouth. She began crying softly.

"Listen," said Connors. "I'm going to send an officer to tell Mrs. Glenn." He looked at Sarah. "I sure could use some help, Sarah. This is going to be a tough one."

Sarah quickly dried her eyes. "Of course, Cary. I'll help."

Cary then looked at Peter. "Mr. Kramer," and stopped suddenly as Peter interrupted him.

"Detective Connors, please call me Peter. You are beginning to make me nervous when you keep calling me Mr."

Connors stood back and hung his head slightly. "I'm sorry. I really don't think you are a suspect at all. It's just that we Yankees can be a bit reserved. I mean I just met you a couple of hours ago."

"Thanks," replied Peter. "Honestly, that makes me feel a lot better."

He looked at all three and said, "Listen, folks, this is getting to be a pretty big case. First we have one body and then two; Dr. Glenn was the town doc. Everybody loved him. People in Pinehurst are going to be pretty upset about this. If it is somehow connected to the college, that's going to make people even more mad."

Elisabeth spoke up. "Cary, I can't help but think this is related to the college. I believe my father was killed because of what he discovered at the Bank of Boston."

The detective chewed on his lip in concentration. Everything was coming at him at once.

"Detective," said Peter. "I have in my possession the copy of a disk from the bank that may help explain where the money went. It's like I told you earlier. So far we have bits and pieces of a crime but with no one implicated yet. We have our suspicions but that's all. I have a plan in mind that I think may help us."

"Listen, everyone, this case is getting complicated. Why don't you all go home? I'll be here with the crime scene for most of the night. We can talk later about Peter's plan. I'll have one of my officers take you back to Pinehurst." The detective turned and walked back towards the cabin.

The three were driven back to Pinehurst. At the station, Elisabeth gave Sarah and Peter a hug and told them to be careful and to call her the next day. Peter could tell she wanted to find her father's killers in the worst way. Sarah and Peter accompanied the police officer over to Mrs. Glenn's house. It was midnight.

There were lights on in the living room. The porch lights blazed as if in anticipation of Dr. Glenn's return. Sarah was struck by the sense of hope the lights gave. She dreaded the next few minutes. The police officer gently knocked on the door. Peter and Sarah stayed slightly behind, their breathing giving off white clouds of cold air. Their hearts were heavy. Suddenly the door creaked open and Mrs. Glenn, clutching her robe, looked out expectantly. Her eyes dropped in surprise and fear as she realized Morris Glenn wasn't with them. She knew by the looks on their faces. Her eyes filled with wet tears. Sarah stepped around the police officer and, putting her arm around Mrs. Glenn, ushered her back into the house, away from the frigid New Hampshire night. Peter and the officer followed them inside.

"Mrs. Glenn, the police found your husband's body a short while ago. I'm so sorry."

Crying softly, she looked into Sarah's eyes and asked what had happened. "How could my Morris be dead? It doesn't make any sense."

The policeman offered his sympathy and explained in a general way where the doctor had been found, but purposely left out how he had died or who was responsible.

Sarah suggested they call Betty Clarendon, the Glenns' neighbor and good friend. A few minutes later she came over and immediately began taking charge. She brewed tea and started making telephone calls to the children. Peter, Sarah, and the officer left a little while later.

Peter took Sarah home to the Phillips estate. On the way they talked about the evening and what they should do next. They were glad the police were now involved but at the same time frustrated that Trent and the others might get away with whatever they were doing. They decided to continue with their plan even though the police were now involved. Peter walked Sarah up to the porch. They were dead tired. The events of the evening had exhausted them. He gave her a hug and after kissing her gently on the lips returned to his car for the drive back to his own place.

CHAPTER FORTY-SIX

The persistent ringing sounded so far off. Sarah thought it was the warning wail of a lighthouse telling ships to beware. All she could think about was sinking ships lost in the thick fog destined never to be seen again. She couldn't shake off the ringing. It would not stop. Suddenly the sound wasn't a lighthouse bell but the telephone next to her on the cherry night table. Sarah tried to rouse herself but felt so tired she imagined she had been drugged. She glanced at the clock telling her it was almost 10:00 A.M. She jumped up to grab the phone, not believing she had slept so long. The memories of last night began to take shape in her foggy mind. Slowly the horror came back to her. A frail voice at the other end asked for Sarah.

"This is Sarah."

"Oh, Sarah, this is Mrs. Glenn. I wanted to thank you for coming over to tell me about Morris. I know it must have been hard on you. You and Martha have been wonderful to Morris and me over the years."

"Mrs. Morris, I am just so sorry about Dr. Glenn. He was a dear friend of my family for so many years."

"Yes dear, I know. He loved all you." She paused, "Sarah,

there is something I need to show you. I found it early this morning hidden in some of Morris's papers. Evidently you and Peter missed it the other night. Can you come right over?"

"Of course I will. May I bring Peter over too?"

"Certainly, dear, certainly."

Sarah quickly dialed Peter's number and arranged for him to pick her up at 11:00. A few moments later she was standing under a hot shower enjoying the force of the water cascading over her tired shoulders and neck. Gradually her neck muscles began to loosen. By 10:30 she was down in the kitchen filling a stunned Martha Phillips in on the events of the previous evening. Her grandmother fixed bacon and eggs and put on a fresh pot of coffee as she listened to Sarah.

"I need to go over and see Mrs. Glenn this morning," said Sarah. "She called me and has something to show Peter and me."

"What do you suppose it is?" asked her grandmother.

Sarah pondered the question. "Well, it is something Peter and I missed the last time we were there. I can't imagine what it is."

"Please be careful, honey. I'm getting terribly worried about this whole sordid affair."

Sarah got up as she heard the doorbell ring and Jamie barking at the same time. "That must be Peter," she replied.

She walked quickly to the front door, slightly behind Jamie, whose wagging tail showed she somehow knew it was Peter. Opening the door, seeing a smiling Peter, Sarah suddenly felt a slight tingling sensation throughout her body. She ushered him in and gave him a huge hug. This feels so right, she murmured to herself.

"It sure does," responded Peter.

Sarah blushed. "I didn't think you heard that," she said.

"I sure did and I'm glad I did."

They jumped into Peter's MGB and drove over to Ms. Glenn's home. The driveway was full of cars. Tragedies brought out the best in small towns, Peter thought. Inside the crowded house they found family and friends and plenty of food filling the kitchen counters. Mrs. Glenn saw Peter and Sarah and excused herself from a tight circle of people in the living room. She approached them, her hands outstretched in welcome.

"Thank you for coming. Let's go upstairs to Morris's study." They trudged up the stairs and down the hallway to the main bedroom. She closed the door behind them.

"Here," she said, handing Peter a brown envelope bound by a thick elastic band. "I found this in the bottom drawer of Morris's dresser hidden under some of his sweaters. Actually it was taped to the side of the drawer. It's clear Morris didn't want me to find it. I was too afraid to open it, but thought you and Sarah might want to see what it is. It may have something to do with our safe deposit box." She hesitated. "Maybe you could wait and look at it after you leave. Would that be all right?"

Peter gently took the old envelope and tucked it into his coat pocket.

"Mrs. Glenn, you have enough on your mind," Peter replied. "We will just take off now and see if what is in the envelope is helpful. Thank you for calling us."

Mrs. Glenn turned and walked down the hallway and stairs back to the people whom she had been talking to when Peter and Sarah had first arrived.

Back in the little sports car Sarah carefully opened the brown envelope while Peter drove to his cottage. Attached to some yellow almost faded papers was a handwritten note from Morris to his wife. He apologized for misleading her on his gambling problem. The note also told her to use the enclosed safety deposit key and look in the box for more information. The papers in the envelope were a dated list of all of his gambling losses. One glance at the amounts was staggering. Morris

Glenn had lost a pile of money over the years. Peter and Sarah felt embarrassed for the doctor.

"Let's go straight to the bank and look in the safe deposit box," suggested Peter.

"We are going to need Mrs. Morris to go with us," said Sarah.

"Hey, isn't this the same bank where that guy, what's his name, is the manager."

"That's right, Phil Craft is the manager."

"Let's get Mrs. Morris to call him to let us come in without her."

"That's a great idea." Peter turned the car around and they headed back to the Glenn home. Mrs. Glenn quickly agreed to their request and placed a call to Craft. It was 12:00 so they had plenty of time to get to the bank before it closed. Craft told her to write a letter authorizing them to use her key.

By 12:15 Peter and Sarah were at the bank. Craft met them at the entrance to the vault, examined the letter, and then allowed them inside once Sarah had signed them in. Craft looked nervous, thought Peter. He ushered them to the safe deposit box area, inserted the bank's duplicate key and then quickly left them alone in the room. Apart from a weak hello, the thin bank manager said nothing else.

Peter opened the box and was astounded to find three bundles of $100 bills. He did a quick tally and figured each bundle contained about $25,000 each. The contents they discovered in a sealed envelope proved to be the most interesting. A letter from Morris Glenn addressed to the police in the event of his death startled both Peter and Sarah.

"Upon my untimely death, please ask Phil Craft, Thomas Lawton, and Walter Trent questions. They will know what has happened to me. Phil Craft has blackmailed me for years, at Thomas Lawton's request, and all because of the worst man

I have ever met, Walter Trent. I am so sorry for the pain and distress I have caused. Please forgive me."

Included in the sealed envelope was a list of names with their attached obituaries from the newspaper. The names included John Phillips, Elisabeth Williams, Phyllis Townsend, and Henry Townsend.

"Wow," said Peter. "What do you think all of this means?"

Sarah's face was livid. "I don't really know, but Phil Craft does. Let's go talk to him right now."

They put the money back in the box and wisely kept Dr. Glenn's letter before exiting the small chamber.

Phil Craft was sitting in his office staring out the window. It was as if he expected them.

"Phil, what is heaven's name is going on?" Sarah showed him the note.

He read the note, a rigid fixed stare on his emaciated face. He looked ill. Abruptly he made up his mind. It was the first courageous action he had taken in a very long time. Suddenly years of fear and anger came pouring out, as if a dam, holding back the water for years, had broken.

"Thomas Lawton has been blackmailing me for 15 years now. Somehow Lawton learned I hit a kid on a bicycle over in Concord and fled the scene. The boy lived, but I committed felony hit and run. I would have gone to jail. So rather than own up to it, I let him blackmail me all these years. You have to understand I had a wife and family. What would they have done?"

"What was he blackmailing you for?" asked Peter.

"Any dirt I could dig up on people in Pinehurst. Stuff like debts, bad credit, illegalities, anything he could use to his own evil advantage."

"What about Morris Glenn?"

Craft put his head in his hands, too embarrassed to look up. "One day I discovered Morris had some pretty big gambling debts from the racetrack in Salem. He does his banking here. I was shocked. So at our regular monthly tell-all-lunch I told Lawton about Dr. Glenn."

"What was Glenn doing for Lawton?" persisted Peter.

"That's just it. I don't know. I could never figure out why Lawton was blackmailing Morris. It didn't make sense."

"How about Phillips, Townsend, Williams, and Allen. What do these names mean to you?"

"I don't know, honest."

"Listen, Phil, you can't tell Lawton we know any of this. Is that clear? When this all gets to the police you will be a lot better off if you stay on our side. This is a lot bigger than you."

"Trust me, I won't say anything. Please understand I just want to do what's right. I'm so tired of living this lie."

They left a shaking Phil Craft alone in his office and drove back to Peter's cottage where they tried to sort out all they had learned.

Over dinner with Jeff, they decided to proceed with Peter's plan. It was risky to say the least, but they needed hard evidence. Anne Ashdown was the key. Peter outlined the plan. They would arrange for Anne Ashdown to accept the inevitable call from President Cannon for a meeting to discuss a major gift of her money to the college. The meeting would take place at her home. Jeff would electronically tape record the entire meeting. Hopefully the discrepancy between Anne's pledge and the actual amount recorded at the bank would reveal the conspiracy. They met with Anne later in the evening and explained the plan. She readily agreed.

"Listen," she said, "I have always planned to leave the college $3 million. I just haven't told Cannon, Walton Trent, and Randolph Bolles. I wanted to wait until they were no longer associated with the college." A coy smile crossed her stately face. "Now I've found a way."

Peter was impressed with the woman's intelligence.

They decided to go and see Cary Connors to get his blessing. The burly detective was reluctant but also in the market for hard evidence. He agreed, with the stipulation that Peter would keep him informed all along the way. Before Peter left the police station, Connors ran upstairs to the judge's chambers where he obtained a warrant authorizing the electronic surveillance.

The next morning Jeff was busy at work in Anne Ashdown's living room installing additional cameras and audio equipment. He expertly placed another two miniature cameras in the room. Audio eavesdropping devices were placed in obscure locations virtually undetectable unless one knew they were there. He double-checked the connections and then walked back to Peter's cottage and set up more television monitors and recording equipment. He then asked Mrs. Ashdown to sit in her living room and quietly read the newspaper aloud. He had her do this in three different chairs. When she was finished he had her come back to the cottage and see herself on the tape. Not to his surprise, her voice and picture came through perfectly. That night Jeff showed Sarah and Peter the tape. The trap was set.

CHAPTER FORTY-SEVEN

Walton Trent sat in James Cannon's office, a hard stare on his face.

"James, this will be the last account. Once we get Anne Ashdown's bequest documented, I will clear out and you can get back to running your little college." His tone was derisive. Cannon hated Trent when he treated him this way. But as he had learned long ago, he had no choice.

"OK, I understand," replied Cannon. "I will call Anne and set up the appointment for this week."

"Great, that's all you have to do. Once we get her commitment you can relax."

Trent knew Cannon was terribly nervous so he tried to placate him so he wouldn't go to pieces. They were too close to the end.

"Call me when the meeting is set up. I'm free anytime." He got up and left.

Cannon sighed heavily. He was always glad to see Trent leave. In a few short weeks the man would be gone entirely. Then he would be free to run the college on his own terms. He could even handle the guilt. He had long ago rationalized the necessity. No one could understand the immense pressure from Bolles and the board.

Trent walked down the hall to his office, where he placed a call to Justin Nichols at the Bank of Boston.

"We are on schedule for this next week with the final account," said Trent.

"Good," said Nichols. "I'm getting some real pressure to wrap this thing up."

"I will, don't worry. Everything is fine."

"Just don't screw things up. The boys don't like mistakes."

"I'll call you as soon as we have the commitment." Trent hung up the phone and quietly swore to himself.

The meeting between Anne Ashdown, Cannon, and Trent was scheduled for the Thursday evening at 7:00 P.M. On that Thursday morning Peter and Sarah carefully reviewed with Anne what she should say and not say. She seemed ready. The glint in her eyes told them she was looking forward to the meeting. Above all, Peter urged caution. Jeff told Peter he would begin running the recording the minute he saw Trent and Cannon arrive at Anne's front door. Peter and Sarah would stay in the cottage and watch the television monitor. Peter would be ready to go to her aid if something bad happened.

At 7:00 P.M. Emma, Anne's long-time maid, announced the arrival of Trent and Cannon. She ushered them into the living room, where Anne was seated in a light blue antique chair. She had chosen this one specifically because it had been in her family for over 100 years. She liked the sense of history the chair gave her. What did Walton Trent and, for that matter, James Cannon truly understand about history?

She got up to greet both men in a very cool and measured tone. After offering them a place to sit she returned to her chair. Emma offered them coffee and an assortment of cookies. Neither man accepted. Rude, thought Anne.

"Well, what's on your mind, James?" began Anne. She wasn't about to make this easy for either man. Yet she knew she would play the part of generous benefactor to some degree. Not too much, she hoped.

"Anne," began Cannon. "Thank you for inviting us into your lovely home. You have been a wonderful supporter of the college for many years. You husband was also. The college deeply appreciates your generosity."

"Why thank you, James. I do believe Thomas's and my support has always been for good reason. We both believed in what Kingston College stood for and I still do."

Cannon breathed a silent sigh of relief. He liked her response. Maybe this wouldn't be so difficult after all.

"Thank you, Anne. That's encouraging."

Anne turned her attention to Trent. Her steely blue eyes sought to penetrate his hard exterior. "And what about you, Mr. Trent? Do you believe what Kingston College stands for? You must know I don't like to see my money wasted."

Trent returned her stare with one of his own. "Mrs. Ashdown, this college has a long and rich history. The product we deliver is one of outstanding graduates who leave Kingston and are remarkably successful in the world. Yes, I strongly believe in the product."

Her eyes twinkled. "Oh, Mr. Trent, I'll bet you say that to all of your potential donors."

"Well, as a matter of fact I do." There was no twinkle in his eyes.

She turned back to Cannon and asked him bluntly. "So James, how much do you want?"

He was taken back. "Well, Anne," he stammered, "we were hoping you could help us fund the new fine arts center. We are planning an $8 million fine arts building complete with a

3000-seat auditorium. We need an initial seed gift of three to four million."

Anne was surprised but kept a passive face. She had anticipated an outright request for a bequest that would go to the college upon her death. She did not plan on a request for an immediate gift.

Recovering her composure quickly, she responded. "Well, James, my money is not quite as liquid as you might think. It's tied up in several major investments that make it pretty difficult to liquefy. Besides, I'm not prepared to give you several million dollars at this time." She turned her head slightly and looked directly at Walton Trent as she said this last phrase. The meaning was not lost on either man.

Trent interrupted. "Mrs. Ashdown, would you be more comfortable leaving the college a major gift in your will?" He enjoyed asking her the question.

Anne looked at both men. What she wanted to say was, "Not a chance you two bastards. I won't leave the college a single penny as long as you two are in charge." But the plan didn't let her indulge in this wonderful fantasy. She had to stick to the game plan.

She forced herself to respond. "Yes, I would be willing to leave the college a major gift. Thomas and I always planned to leave Kingston College some of our money." She felt a bit sick to her stomach saying this to Cannon and Trent.

Cannon responded, "Anne, we really appreciate your commitment to the college."

She wanted to throw up. What a line she thought to herself. Cannon was so transparent. Suddenly she wanted to get this whole meeting over.

"I will talk with my accountant, but I am sure I can leave the college $3 million in my will. I'll see him in the morning and we can draw up the papers and have them sent over to the college. How does that sound?"

Cannon almost fell over himself in gratitude. Trent was his reserved self but offered a forced smile of thanks.

"That would be wonderful, Anne," said Cannon.

At this point Trent asked the crucial question.

"Mrs. Ashdown, how would you like the college to announce this news? Normally most people like to have us keep their gifts confidential. Actually, we like to maintain confidentiality too. Our reason is that publicly announced gifts of this magnitude tend to discourage other givers. They think well the college just got that big gift, they certainly don't need my money. We also find that most people simply value their privacy."

Anne smiled. "Why Mr. Trent, I hadn't thought of that. I certainly wouldn't like people to know I have all this money. Lord knows who might come calling on me next."

Trent couldn't tell if she was serious, but he had to play along.

"OK then, we will draw up the bequest contract as well as a document of confidentiality to be signed by both parties. I can have Thomas Lawton draw up the papers in the morning and have one of my associates bring them over for you to sign."

Anne Ashdown was clever. She raised her voice ever so slightly and imperceptibly tilted her head in the direction of one of the miniature cameras. "OK, then just so we are clear. I will plan to leave the college $3 million in my revised will. The college's attorney's law firm will draw up the papers. And at your recommendation I will agree to a document of confidentiality."

The three engaged in a few more minutes of obligatory conversation before ending their business. Emma escorted the two men to the front door while Anne sat back down in her favorite chair and, looking at one of the cameras, winked. She then rested her head against the high-backed chair. She didn't like to admit it but the meeting had left her exhausted.

Back in the cottage Peter, Sarah and Jeff were ecstatic. Everything had been recorded perfectly on the tape. The voices and pictures clearly showed the agreement between Anne Ashdown and Trent and Cannon. The agreed-upon $3 million came through loud and clear on the recording.

Ten minutes later they were seated in Anne's spacious country kitchen sipping hot cider. Anne sat quietly listening to every word, yet feeling very tired. The meeting with Trent and Cannon had proven to be more stressful than she thought. The mix of anger at what they were trying to do, coupled with her not wanting to reveal her true role, had taken its toll. They eventually agreed that Jeff would make five duplicate tapes of the meeting. One copy would go into Sarah's safe deposit box at her bank, a second would be lodged in Martha Phillips's wall safe, and the three remaining copies would go with Peter and Jeff, with one for Cary Connors. They bid Anne goodnight after thanking her profusely for her courageous help. Sarah and Peter gave her a warm hug before they went with Jeff back to Peter's cottage.

Jeff began making duplicates of the taped meeting while Peter explained the next step in their plan. Thus far they had the electronic tape of the illegal transfer of funds from the New Hampshire banks to the Bank of Boston to Empire Insurance. Now they had a tape of the meeting between Anne Ashdown and Trent and Cannon. The evidence was beginning to take shape but they still needed more physical evidence. Soon they would have enough to hand over to Cary Connors. But it was the next step that would be both difficult and dangerous. Sarah and Jeff listened intently as Peter outlined his plan. The next phase would begin in the morning. Unfortunately, Peter's plan would be suddenly interrupted by what Sarah would discover the next day.

The very next morning Sarah was in her office at the college when she received a telephone call from Cindy Allen.

"Sarah, this is Cindy. Are you free for lunch today? There is a matter of some urgency that I must discuss with you."

Sarah couldn't imagine what Cindy Allen wanted. She hadn't seen her since the funeral of her mother, Phyllis.

"Sure, Cindy, but I must admit you've got me curious."

"Well, I'd rather wait until lunch if that's OK?"

"Of course, shall we meet in the college union?"

"That will be fine. How about 11:45?"

"See you then."

Sarah sat back and wondered what that was all about. She knew Cindy to be taciturn and extremely proper. It was unlike her to initiate social contact. She returned to the financial spreadsheet on her computer screen. She would just have to wait.

At 11:40 Sarah headed across campus to the college union. The place was full of faculty and students eating lunch and studying. She bumped into several colleagues and students before she found Cindy sitting alone in a far corner. She was conservatively dressed in a black corduroy dress and a heavy white pullover sweater. Her hair was pulled straight back with a bun on top. My gosh, thought Sarah, if one ever looked the part of a college librarian, Cindy Allen did. Sarah approached the table, a warm smile spreading across her face. She was fond of Cindy because of her honest, straightforward approach to things.

"Hi, Cindy, let's order. I'm pretty hungry."

They left their coats and things on the table and went to the counter where Sarah ordered the soup and salad special, while Cindy got a salad and baked potato. Back at the table Cindy pulled out a piece of paper from her pocket. She stared at the paper as if trying to decide what to do. Clearly she was anxious to talk and wanted to do so before their food came.

"Sarah," began Cindy, "I have something to show you." She indicated the paper. "I have been trying to get a handle on things since my mom died. It's been really hard. Mom and I were such good friends. Dad, well he just isn't the same. He cries every night. I can hear him in their bedroom. He doesn't think I can hear him, but I can." She bit her lower lip as if she too was about to cry. She continued. "I know we've known each other since grade school. I've always admired you, Sarah." She was rambling a bit and Sarah wondered where she was going. "I believe I can trust you. You know I work in the college library. I am really good at research and finding information. I mean, that's the essence of my job. You send a college freshman my way and I will help him find anything. Well, a few weeks after my mother died, I started thinking about things. Like, why did she have to die so soon? Gradually my grief and anger turned into suspicion. Once I get into such a state I develop an unquenchable thirst for information. It all began when I remember you asking me questions about my mother's bank. At first I wondered why you were so intrigued with her financial affairs. Then it hit me. You were suspicious too. My mother left a lot of money. So I began a database search of every single thing associated with the college and my mother. It took weeks on end but gradually I realized it was a good way for me to deal with her death. A wonderful distraction that was almost therapeutic. At first nothing came up. I kept running into dead ends. Soon I began to believe there was nothing suspicious at all. It was just the tormented imagination of a grief-stricken daughter. Then last Saturday afternoon I discovered something that shocked the living daylights out of me."

Sarah noticed her hands were shaking and her face had gone pale.

"Are you all right, Cindy?" asked Sarah.

"Yes, fine, please let me finish. Please!"

Sarah nodded a silent yes.

"Well, when I do research on an unknown subject I use words or phrases to look for connections or themes. Last Saturday I discovered a connection. A common thread that raises serious questions about the college and some people in town. Do the names Henry Townsend and Elisabeth Williams sound familiar?"

Sarah silently drew in a breath. What could Cindy know about these two?

"Why yes, both died in the last year and left the college several million dollars. Why do you ask?"

"Sarah, Henry Townsend, Elisabeth Williams, Phyllis Allen, and," she paused, "John Phillips are all connected. They all had Dr. Glenn as their primary physician, all died rather suddenly, had Thomas Lawton as their attorney, and were asked by James Cannon and Walton Trent to include the college in their wills."

She paused to let this sink in.

Sarah just stared at Cindy. She waited for more.

"That's not all. I did some looking into my Mother's papers. The college says she left them $800,000. That's what's in the college's documents. I know this for a fact. Mother's personal papers say the actual gift was $2.8 million. So where is the other two million? Sarah, I bet if you checked your grandfather's papers as well as the Williams and Townsend gifts, you would find similar discrepancies."

Sarah was stunned. Her mouth felt dry. Cindy Allen, her obscure librarian friend, had uncovered even more than Peter and she had. The money was one thing, but the people connections. Were these similarities a simple coincidence? Hard to believe they were! She thought back to Morris Glenn's angst as Peter described it when he spied on Glenn, Lawton, Trent and, the man Peter had killed in the cabin that dreadful night. What about her own blackmail comment to Peter? She told him people are blackmailed because the blackmailers want something. What did Morris have? He was a medical doctor. Surely it wasn't money. Like a sudden bolt of jagged lightning across the hot summer evening sky, it came to Sarah. Dr. Morris Glenn had killed her grandfather and the other three. They had forced him to do it because of his wretched gambling addiction. Another shock assaulted Sarah's senses. The look that passed from Morris Glenn to Thomas Lawton the night her grandfather died. The knowing look! Suddenly she hated Thomas Lawton and Walton Trent. She looked wildly around the union dining room for Trent. She wanted to confront him and expose his evil to the whole world. Her heart was beating rapidly. Almost automatically her intelligence and cool began to win the battle over her emotions. Things began to slow as Sarah's rational side prevailed.

"Cindy, isn't that kind of a big leap to say Dr. Glenn killed my grandfather and the others?"

The plain young woman looked Sarah directly in the eyes. Her next words left no doubt in Sarah's mind. Suddenly the air in the crowded eatery felt chilly.

"Dr. Glenn told me three days ago that he killed my mother." Her eyes were void of emotion. She said it in such a detached way Sarah was startled.

"Oh my goodness, Cindy, what are you saying?"

"He told me that he did it and how he did it." Cindy's face was expressionless.

Sarah looked around the union dining room to make sure no one could hear their conversation. The college students and faculty were oblivious to the drama unfolding so close by.

Cindy continued almost as if Sarah wasn't even there.

305

"After my mother died I couldn't sleep for weeks. It all just didn't seem right. Something was nagging in my soul but I didn't know what it was. I kept playing over and over again the day she died. See she was doing so well. Her heart was doing pretty well and she was taking her medicine and watching her diet. Why she was even walking two miles every day. Mother was in good spirits and taking good care of herself. She shouldn't have died right then. But she did! Why the day before, she had seen Dr. Glenn and he said she was in really good shape. She came home in such a wonderful mood. She had so much to look forward too. So what happens? The next day she goes into cardiac arrest and dies at home before ever reaching the hospital. Dad is devastated and I'm in shock. So for several weeks we cry and just mope around the house. Mother was such a vital force in our lives and suddenly she's gone. We didn't know what to do. Gradually we begin to pick up the pieces and try to move forward. Dad still cries a lot but he is slowly beginning to come to terms with Mother's death. Then I'm lying in my bed during another sleepless night when all of a sudden it dawns on me. A simple obscure fact leaps out of the overwhelming darkness. It was so minor at the time I missed it. That night it came to me like a bolt of lightning."

"What was it?" asked Sarah. She already knew the answer to her question.

Cindy's face brightened. "Thomas Lawton. He was there shortly after the ambulance arrived. He's my family's attorney, but what was he doing there?" she continued.

"And then I recalled the oddest thing. Dr. Glenn was watching the ambulance people working on Mom and after a few moments he looked directly at Thomas Lawton. Something passed between them like a communication of some sort. I know it sounds odd but that's exactly what happened."

She stopped and looked to Sarah as if for an explanation. Sarah didn't respond immediately.

Her heart was pounding. She remembered the morning they found her grandfather. Morris Glenn had come soon after the ambulance. That made sense. What didn't make sense was Thomas Lawton. Just like with Cindy's Mother, so with her grandfather; both women had later recalled the look between Lawton and Glenn.

"What do you think the look meant?" asked Sarah.

The other woman looked at her directly. "Sarah, I think you already know the answer to your question."

Sarah nodded silently, lost in her own thoughts. How could a beloved family friend be responsible for her grandfather's death?

Sarah asked Cindy, "Would you mind coming with me? I think we need to go see Peter Kramer and have you tell him what you told me. We also need to hear a lot more of your conversation with Dr. Glenn three days ago."

"Sure, I'll talk with him. I know there is more to this than Morris Glenn. Anything to get whoever is behind all of this."

The two got up, leaving their food untouched, and left the crowded College Union and headed across campus to Peter's office in the Business and Economics building. Peter was sitting in his office grading papers. He looked up, a surprised look on his face as the two entered the office. He stood up. The grim looks on their faces told him the story.

"Hi, you two look like you have serious business on your minds." He stood up and closed his office door.

Sarah touched Peter lightly on his left arm. "Peter, we have to talk with you right now." She nodded to Cindy, who proceeded to tell Peter all of the information she had gathered on Morris Glenn and the others. Peter sat there taking it all in, unsuccessfully trying to hide his astonishment.

"After my mother died, I refused to accept her death. So I did all of this research and found some interesting things. Like I told Sarah over in the College Union, it suddenly dawned on me weeks later, in the middle of the night, that it was unusual for Thomas Lawton to suddenly appear at our home while Mother was having her attack. Then I remembered the look between Morris Glenn and Lawton. So that's why I went to see Morris Glenn a few days ago."

Peter interrupted her.

"Cindy, you didn't have anything to do with his death, did you?"

The thin woman's face went white. "No, of course not. I saw him three days ago at his office. He died two days later."

"I apologize, but I had to ask you that just to clear the air. I know you didn't kill him. What did you two talk about in his office?"

"Well, I made an appointment just so we could meet privately without raising any eyebrows. Plus, I wanted to catch him off guard."

Sarah smiled. She had underestimated her friend.

She continued.

"He sat behind his old oak roll-top desk and looked at me with the saddest eyes as I walked in. I'll never forget the scene. He looked so tired and worn out. His hair was a bit unkempt. Nothing mattered to him. Sarah, you remember how fatherly and kind he was. People were so important to him. You walked in his office and he made you feel like the most important person in the universe. Walk in depressed and you walk out alive again. Not this time. He looked defeated. I almost lost the courage to confront him. But I owed it to my mother and father. So I took out my notes and laid it all out for him. I told him I knew about the others who had died and the differences in reported estate gifts to the college. The poor man's face went white. He looks at me for a moment and then gets up and walks over to the office door and locks it. My first thought is he's going kill me. Then I realize there is a waiting room full of people. He comes back and sits in a chair next to me. His hands are shaking and tears are rolling down his old wrinkled face. He takes my hand in his and asks me to forgive him. I ask for what and he outright tells me."

"Cindy, I killed your mother."

"At first I want to scream, but he is so brutally honest without a trace of guile that I'm compelled to just listen. You had to be there. I mean it was so straightforward. So I sat there and heard him out. Everything poured out. I felt like a priest at confession". She paused to take a breath. Sarah and Peter could feel the strong emotion of the moment.

"Did you know Morris Glenn had a gambling problem? Evidently that's where it all started. Then Phil Craft at the bank finds out and tells Thomas Lawton. So our slimy, small-town lawyer Lawton gets his hooks into the kindly doctor and begins blackmailing him. But it's not really for money. No, that would have been far simpler. Goodness no! If only it had been for money. My mother would still be alive. No, Lawton gets mixed up with Walton Trent over at the college and this is where it gets really sinister. Dr. Glenn told me that Walton Trent is a crook through and through. He also said Trent is part of a larger operation working out of New York." Sarah and Peter exchanged looks.

Peter asked Cindy. "Did Dr. Glenn tell you anything about this New York connection?"

"No, he was afraid, I think. Not for himself but for me. But he said the New York people made even Walton Trent nervous."

Peter considered this comment and logged it into his rapidly working brain.

"What do you mean 'sinister', Cindy?" asked Sarah.

"You're not going to believe this, Sarah. I can hardly believe it myself. What Dr. Glenn told me is shocking. But after I thought about it, everything begins to make sense. He told me that there is a terrible conspiracy going on at the college."

Sarah sat forward on the small office chair.

"What kind of a conspiracy?" She could feel her hands gripping the cold aluminum edges of the inexpensive chair. Peter leaned in closer to hear Cindy's answer. His presence was reassuring to both women.

"Sarah, this is going to hurt you, but it's the truth. They killed your grandfather for his money. He didn't die of natural causes like they said. He was as healthy as you and me. They made Dr. Glenn do it."

Sarah suddenly felt cold all over. A strange tightness gripped her heart and soul.

"Tell me more, Cindy." Her tongue stuck to the roof of her dry mouth. She could barely utter the words.

"Glenn told me Walton is behind the whole thing. He came to the college to do his dirty business and plans to leave shortly. Trent is the initiator. Cannon hired him to help raise money for the college. Boy, he sure did that. Problem was he did it in a way that hurt a lot of people. Cannon is involved, but is scared to death. Lawton is in deep too. The conspiracy is so simple that no one has caught on. Trent and Cannon get our richest alumni to include the college in their will and then make Dr. Glenn kill them. Oh, and by the way, the amount of money they willed is altered in such a way that most of it is funneled to the Bank of Boston and then on to New York. They somehow change the records at the Bank of Boston so that the actual money willed is changed, with the difference going to the bad people. In every case Thomas Lawton is the attorney of record. He alters the records through his law firm. You see, Cannon and Trent convince the donors to keep their gift secret and so when Lawton changes the actual amount and they make the switch at the bank no one knows."

"What about my grandfather?" asked Sarah quietly.

Cindy turned to Sarah and gently laid her hand on Sarah's shoulder.

"I'm so sorry to be the one to tell you this. You and Martha didn't deserve any of this. Do you know the day before John Phillips died, he went into see Dr. Glenn for a checkup?"

Sarah sat up sharply. "Why yes, I do. I remember because Grandmother was so shocked when he died. She even told me that he had been to see Dr. Morris the day before and everything was fine. She couldn't understand why he had died. But then she trusted Dr. Glenn."

Cindy hesitated. "Dr. Glenn suggested a flu shot for your Grandfather. The flu season was coming so it wasn't hard to convince him. Unfortunately it wasn't a flu shot."

Peter couldn't wait. "What are you talking about, Cindy? A flu shot is a flu shot."

She plunged on.

"Not when it is laced with a slow-acting drug called benzene that gradually stops the heart and is completely undetectable. The drug's full effect doesn't take effect for 12 hours. So Dr. Glenn administers the flu shot to John Phillips late in the afternoon and he goes home for dinner and later that night his heart begins to beat slower and slower. The next morning he doesn't wake up. Then the family doctor and EMTs come and determine his heart stopped, which it did. Cause of death? The heart just gave out. Dr. Glenn knows differently. Cause of death? Murder!"

Sarah emitted a slight gasp.

Peter asked another question. "So, why would Dr. Glenn tell you all of this? And why didn't you go to the police?"

She responded, her eyes softening. "I think Dr. Glenn

knew it was all over. Sooner or later everything would come out. He just wanted the whole horrible nightmare to be over. I must have caught him at the right moment. Besides, I had figured out so much he must have just caved in. As to why I didn't go to the police? Actually I almost did but decided to talk to you and Sarah first. You two were so supportive when Mother died. Plus by then I knew what had happened to my family happened to Sarah's."

Sarah perked up. "Cindy, I can see how they did this to Grandfather but how did they kill the others?"

"That's the genius of it. Somehow Trent and Lawton figured out that my mother, Elisabeth Williams and Henry Townsend all had the same doctor, Morris Glenn. He gave each one a flu shot just like John Phillips."

Peter interjected. "Yes, but Williams lives over by Lake Winnipesaukee and Henry Townsend in Belmont, Massachusetts."

"I checked on that too. Dr. Glenn was their physician even at such a distance. You need to remember Morris Glenn lived in this town for a long time. I discovered that he met Henry Townsend and Elisabeth Williams while they were students and he was the new young doctor. They forged a relationship that lasted all of these years. He was their regular doctor. So Morris Glenn visited each of them the day before they died. He gave them their regular flu shots. He was my mother's doctor too. She adored him. I asked my dad if she had seen Dr. Glenn the day before she died. He said she had gone to see him for her flu shot."

"This is unbelievable," said Peter. Yet he knew every word was true. "Who would ever suspect the trusted town doctor?"

Suddenly Sarah bolted straight up from her chair. "Anne Ashdown, they're going to try and kill her too!"

"Not if they can't find her," replied Peter.

"What?" asked Sarah.

He stood up and said, "Let's go, we're going out to see her right now."

They thanked Cindy for her great help and, leaving her at the college, hopped into Sarah's BMW and drove straight to the Ashdown estate. In a few minutes they were sitting in Anne's living room telling her most of the story Morris Glenn had told Cindy Allen. By 9:00 that same evening, Anne Ashdown was sitting in a luxury condominium in Boston, drinking tea with Martha Phillips. The doorman in the security-conscious building had been told explicitly by Peter that he was to call the Boston Police and then Peter immediately, if he saw anything suspicious. The condominium belonged to Martha Phillips. Trent would never be able to track her down.

CHAPTER FORTY-EIGHT

Monday morning Trent was waiting for President Cannon outside his office in the administration building. He stood up and, without comment, motioned Cannon into his own office. The secretary watched in anger as Cannon meekly did as he was instructed. Trent slammed the door behind him and started in on Cannon.

"Do you know where the hell Anne Ashdown is? Lawton tells me she is missing."

Cannon trembled. "Walton, how would I know where she is?"

Trent glared at Cannon. "Listen, we are this close to finishing our entire strategy. You'd better not be getting cold feet."

Suddenly, unexpectedly, Cannon laughed. "Come on Trent, don't you think I know how deep I am into this whole mess? I'm just as guilty as you."

Trent appeared satisfied with Cannon's answer. What he failed to see was the utter resignation in Cannon's bitter laugh.

"You'd better think that way, Cannon. Lawton's looking high and low for her. I want you to help him. Do you understand?"

"Yes, Walton. I'll call Lawton as soon as you leave."

"You do that. Oh, and keep me posted."

Trent got up and walked out without another word.

Cannon stared at his office door that was still open.

While Cannon and Trent were meeting that morning, Sarah was sitting in Susan Turner's office. Sarah felt nervous being just down the hall from Trent and Cannon's offices. But she had every reason to be there. Part of her job was to work with the Planned Giving Office to audit gifts to the college and match them with the college's annual budget. However her real reason for being there was to keep an eye on Walton Trent while Peter and Jeff visited Walton Trent's townhouse. Sarah could watch his comings and goings and if this failed, she could see his dark blue Lincoln Town car in the parking lot. She felt for her cell phone in her purse for at least the fifth time. Just in case, she assured herself.

Peter and Jeff were just leaving the cottage. With Anne Ashdown safely out of the way they were ready to proceed with their plan. At 9:30 they drove down the long driveway in one of Anne Ashdown's less conspicuous cars. The 1997 Ford Estate Wagon was used by the butler and cook to go into town for groceries. Turning left onto the old country road, they headed east towards Pinehurst. The town soon came into view. Clutching a piece of paper in his left hand Peter consulted the writing on it a couple of times. Before long the Pinehurst Townhouses loomed ahead. Built in 1999, they were the most luxurious living accommodations in town. This was where Walton Trent lived. Peter parked the car in space nineteen, Walton Trent's reserved space. Climbing out of the car the two confidently walked up to his front door. Security in the town of Pinehurst just wasn't a real concern. Most of the residents at the townhouses were faculty and professional people. No old ladies would be peeking out of their curtained windows ready to call 911. Anyway, Peter and Jeff were carrying tool-boxes and had on utility work shirts from New Hampshire Power and Electric. At the door Jeff expertly picked the lock and the two quietly let themselves in. Closing the door they froze for a moment. The enormity of their actions momentarily closed in on them. They fanned out into the townhouse with Peter checking the upstairs while Jeff went directly to the office and Trent's computer. The apartment was lightly furnished. A huge-screen television dominated the living room. A dark leather couch and recliner were separated by a coffee table and lamp. The upstairs main bedroom was fairly ordinary. The walk-in closet contained at least 10 expensive suits and numerous dress shirts and ties. This guy likes his clothes, thought Peter. Satisfied, he went back downstairs to the office where Jeff was busily punching the keyboard. Peter was amazed at the young man's ability on the computer. Suddenly Peter's cell phone rang. He almost jumped out of his skin. Grabbing it out of his pocket, he answered it.

"Peter, is that you?" asked Sarah in a quiet voice.

"Yes, it is and you almost scared me to death. What's up?"

"Nothing, I just wanted to let you know that Trent is holed up in his office down the hall. I'm in the ladies room. I've been meeting with Susan Turner for the last hour. You and Jeff are good to go with the search of his townhouse."

"Good, that makes me feel a lot better. Just keep an eye on Trent and if he leaves the building, call me right away. We shouldn't be too long here."

"OK, bye," and Sarah hung up.

Peter checked the front window of the townhouse just in case. The parking lot was almost empty. He felt relieved. Turning back to Jeff he watched as his new friend worked the computer keyboard. A half-hour later he was done. He quickly inserted an empty disk into the hard drive and began copying the contents. By 11:00 they had what they had come for. They checked to make sure everything was back in its original place and left the townhouse. Walton Trent would never know anyone had been there. His arrogance made him careless.

Back at the cottage Jeff inserted the computer disk into Peter's computer and together they watched in fascination as Walton Trent's bank records filled the screen. He had a small checking and saving account at the Pinehurst Bank. The current balance in checking was $5,000 and $20,000 in savings. More interesting were accounts with the Bank of Boston and a bank in New York called Morgan Savings and Trust. Peter was amazed at the amounts in both banks. One and one half million with the Bank of Boston and three million in Morgan Savings and Trust. So where did he get all of this money, wondered Peter? This was just an idle question. What they were really after were Trent's bank account numbers, which Trent had foolishly left on his home computer. Peter copied the crucial numbers down while Jeff made a duplicate disk, which Peter would hide in his safe deposit box in the Pinehurst Bank.

The next day was a Tuesday. Sarah bade Peter and Jeff goodbye early in the morning. They were headed to Boston and the Bank of Boston. The night before it had taken Peter and Sarah two hours to convince Jeff to accompany Peter back to Boston. He was frightened to death to go back. If the plan was to work, Jeff's computer skills would be absolutely essential. Peter steered Anne Ashdown's estate wagon down the driveway and turned east towards Pinehurst. They passed quickly through town and continued east on the White Mountain Highway in the direction of Lynwood and Concord and eventually Route 93, which would take them south to Massachusetts. As they drove along the quiet rural highway, Peter's thoughts drifted back to last summer when he first came to Pinehurst. The night had been dark that first time he came to town. So much had happened since then. How would it all end he thought to himself? The exit for Rockingham Park loomed ahead. This is where it all started for Dr. Glenn. By 11:00 they were looking for a public parking garage close to the bank. After parking the car on the second level of a concrete garage, they made their way down to a very busy Boylston Street. The bank loomed up ahead. The ornate lobby was not busy at all. Suddenly Jeff's friend Molly was at his elbow. She flashed two visitor passes in their faces and for the guard to see before escorting them through the lobby to the now familiar bank of elevators. She chatted with Jeff as they made their way across the lobby. Pushing the seventh floor button they patiently waited for the doors to open. The ping sounded and Jeff looked like he was ready to pass out. Peter and Molly subtly gripped his arms, which seemed to revive him. The heavy doors opened and to Peter's relief the car was empty.

As they ascended she quietly told them they would go to her office first and wait there until lunch. The computer room would be pretty empty during the noon hour.

"Listen, thanks for helping us," said Peter. "I realize this is a big risk you're taking."

"Yeah, Molly," chipped in Jeff. "You didn't have to do this."

"Well to be honest, I want to do this. Ever since Justin Nichols came to work at the bank, things just haven't seemed right. Anyway, since Bill Rutherford died, there have been a lot of rumors floating around."

Peter and Jeff glanced at each other, but said nothing. They didn't want to see Molly get hurt in any way. The less she knew the better.

"Molly we need about 30 minutes in the computer room," said Peter. "Will people be there?"

"Yes, maybe some, but with the cubicles you will have privacy. Anyway, if anyone is there they will think you guys are bank visitors."

They waited nervously in Molly's small but nicely decorated office until 12:10 before making their way down the long carpeted hall to the stairway where all three walked down to the seventh floor, which housed the information technology department. Molly led the way as they approached the bank's massive computer room. She quickly opened the glass door and all three walked in. To their relief it was virtually empty. Noon had been a good time to come. She motioned them to the corner and a back cubicle where a small computer sat on a desk. Jeff sat down and immediately began keying into the mainframe computer system of the Bank of Boston. He used a password Molly had given him but one which couldn't be traced back to her. Molly and Peter kept an eye on the door and tried their best to appear relaxed and look as if they were simply working. She sat in a chair next to Jeff while Peter sat at an empty desk and began writing on a yellow pad of legal size paper. The steady hum of the climate control system and computers in operation seemed incredibly loud.

Jeff worked furiously at the keyboard. His intensity was impressive. Not once did he look up. It was as if he was lost in another world. The truth was he wanted to do the job and get out of the bank as fast as he could. Every once in a while he stopped and inserted a disk into the tower and then went back to the keyboard. His eyes roamed the computer screen, scrolling up and down with the discipline of an artist working on an oil painting. Peter and Jeff had agreed earlier in the day what Jeff would seek to achieve on the bank's computer system. It would be dangerous and certain to gain the attention of the system's security watchdogs but they believed there was enough time to get what they wanted and leave the bank. By 12:45 Jeff was almost finished. A couple of bank employees wandered in from lunch and were busy at their desks. Neither paid any attention to the three by the back cubicle. At 12:50 Jeff motioned to Peter and after stuffing two more disks into his pocket the three casually stood up and made their way to the glass door at the front. One of the bank employees glanced up at them and resumed his work.

Out in the hallway other employees were beginning to return to work. Peter began to feel more anxious. Jeff kept his head down as the two of them followed Molly to the elevators. They waited patiently for the doors to open. The familiar ping was followed by the heavy doors parting. A crowd of employees surged out, forcing them to stand to the side. Several anxious moments passed before they could enter the elevator. A single lone man stood at the back. He was dressed in a dark blue suit with a starched white shirt and a red tie. He was at least six foot two and weighed close to 250 pounds. Almost completely bald, he had the scarred face of a heavyweight boxer. A thick bulbous nose was the most prominent feature on an unattractive and very intimidating face. Peter heard a barely audible intake of breath by Molly. She turned and stared straight ahead at the closing elevator doors. Who was this guy, thought Peter?

Peter decided to go on the offensive. He looked at Molly and said, "So what do we do with the Anderson account?"

For the briefest of moments she looked at Peter like he was crazy. He willed her to understand. To his relief her eyes suddenly told him she understood.

"I just can't figure it out. I mean the Andersons have been with the bank for over 20 years. Why would they want to change now?"

"Maybe their children want control and see our bank as an obstacle to that?"

Molly considered his response. Peter, who was closest to

the man, could hear his breathing and smelled garlic on his breath.

"You know, that's an intriguing thought."

Peter heard the big man shift uneasily behind him. He felt cold sweat trickling down his neck. Molly's breathing became more pronounced. Jeff simply appeared to be in a trance.

The elevator slowed and soon opened. They had arrived at the first floor. It was too soon to feel relief.

"Excuse me, can I see some identification?" the man asked as all four spilled out into the massive lobby. All three turned to face the boxer, who was flashing a security badge. A slight smile creased his unpleasant face. Peter saw the outline of something heavy like a gun under the man's left side.

The four stepped aside and to the left into a small alcove. Molly took out her bank identity card and also the visitor passes and handed them to the man. He studied them intently.

"Why are you men visiting here today?" he asked Peter and Jeff.

"Oh, we're here to consult with Molly on one of the bank's accounts. We work for a law firm that represents one of the bank's clients." At that moment Peter was relieved he and Jeff had worn suits. He prayed the man wouldn't ask for a business card.

The man considered Peter's response. Everything seemed in order yet nothing seemed in order. He was a very bright man but couldn't see anything tangible to be concerned with.

Molly intervened. "The bank is having a problem with the family and its children. We needed legal advice."

The security man seemed to reluctantly relent. "OK, thank you," he said and then walked away.

"Wow, that was close," said Peter. "So who was that guy, Molly?"

She continued looking in the man's direction. "Wilbur

Guthrie, head of bank security. He's a mite bit intimidating but really a pretty good guy. Actually, he and Bill Rutherford were close friends."

After thanking Molly and telling her to be careful, Peter and Jeff quickly left the bank.

Out on a crowded Boylston Street sidewalk Peter and Jeff made their way back to the parking garage.

"You know something, Jeff?" asked Peter.

"What?" replied a still trembling Jeff.

"That security man is proof the bank is pretty oblivious to what's going on."

"What do you mean?"

"Well, that guy was just doing his job. He wasn't on the lookout like I thought they would be. I can't help but imagine this whole conspiracy doesn't go deeper than maybe two or three people."

"Yeah, but once they find out their precious computer system has been breached they are gonna raise hell."

"I don't agree. If the bad guys raise a stink they will bring the police into it and expose themselves. It's to their advantage to keep it quiet."

"You mean the bank isn't involved?"

"Not really. Look, even Bill Rutherford was surprised and he was high up in the organization."

"So who are the bad guys?"

Peter thought before he answered. "I think it may be just Walton Trent and Justin Nichols and whoever is backing them."

Back in the parking garage they jumped into the car and immediately began heading back to New Hampshire. The time was 1:15.

CHAPTER FORTY-NINE

Back in Pinehurst, Walton Trent was in a rage. He had just gotten off the phone with a very frightened Thomas Lawton, who had informed him both Martha Phillips and Anne Ashdown were nowhere to be found. James Cannon was of no help either. Trent knew something was up. He just couldn't put it together. For the first time since coming to New Hampshire he began to feel real uncertainty. At no other place had he run into such problems. The problem was he didn't like to lose and more importantly he couldn't lose. Too much money was at stake. They had to find Anne Ashdown. He picked up the phone and called Thomas Lawton back and threatened him in no uncertain terms if he didn't come up with Anne Ashdown.

Jeff and Peter were well on their way back to Pinehurst when Peter's cell phone began ringing. It was Sarah. Her voice sounded excited.

"Peter, Mrs. Glenn called me shortly after you and Jeff left this morning. She found something in their basement. So I went over to her house to see what she found. You won't believe it, Peter."

Peter interrupted her. "Sarah, you went over there alone?"

"Yes, I can't just sit here while you guys do all the work. Anyway, I called Connors and he met me there."

Peter breathed a small sigh of relief. "So what did you discover?"

"Well, Mrs. Glenn was going through some boxes underneath Dr. Glenn's workbench when she stumbled upon some medical records and a tape. At first she didn't think anything about it but then began wondering why her husband would have that stuff in the basement. Then she found something buried at the bottom of the box. Peter, she found small vials of the drug benzene. Just like Cindy said."

"Have you and Connors listened to the tape?"

"No, we're waiting for you. Just come straight here. Hurry up. Connors is pretty anxious to listen to the tape."

Less than an hour later, Peter and Jeff arrived at the Glenn home. Sarah's BMW was parked next to two City of Pinehurst police cars. Peter parked on the street and, jumping out of the little sports car, ran up the walkway closely followed by Jeff. Inside they found Mrs. Glenn, Sarah, Detective Connors, and another city policeman sitting in the living room. A small black tape recorder sat ominously on the living room coffee table. Sarah stood up and gave Peter a warm hug and then returned quickly to her seat.

"Peter, we wanted to wait until you arrived before we listened to the tape," explained Connors. He paused. "You have uncovered something here in Pinehurst and deserve to hear what's on the tape."

"Thank you, Detective Connors," replied Peter.

The burly detective reached over and pushed the play button and remained hunched over with his elbows perched on his knees. Everyone seemed to lean forward in anticipation.

A moment later Dr. Glenn began speaking. His voice

sounded tired and on edge. What was once a vibrant and strong voice was now raspy and halting.

"If anyone is listening to this tape I am probably dead. Today is December 1, 2002. I have come to the end of a long road of deception and death. I can no longer tolerate the life I have been living. Beth, I am so very sorry. I truly never meant for it to end this way. Whoever is listening, please take this tape to the police. My story begins many years ago. It all started so innocently. I am so ashamed. I was driving back from a medical conference in Boston when on impulse I took the Rockingham racetrack exit and went into the racetrack and watched the horses running. Right then and there I placed a bet and to my surprise the horse I placed a bet on won. A feeling of exhilaration unlike anything I had ever known swept over me. I was instantly and irrevocably addicted to the terrible pull of gambling. I didn't know this at the time but I soon discovered I simply couldn't stay away. Soon I got into serious debt but somehow always managed to make things right. Beth, I am so sorry for hiding all of this from you. Things were not good but I was able to keep my terrible habit a secret until the day I got a call from Thomas Lawton who had discovered my secret from Phil Craft at the Pinehurst Bank. Craft knew about my debt and somehow Thomas Lawton found out. This is when the real trouble began. Lawton began blackmailing me to do some terrible things for Walton Trent at the college. At first he just blackmailed me for medical information on several of my patients. Then it got real serious. Walton Trent and Lawton blackmailed me into injecting people with benzene. It was really quite simple to do. These were my own patients so I was easily accepted into their homes and was able to treat them without any suspicion. The drug would gradually begin slowing their hearts to the point where the heart stopped and they died. Since they were old it looked like they had died of natural causes. Certainly no autopsy would be called for. I was forced to kill John Phillips, Elisabeth Williams, Henry Townsend, and Phyllis Allen, all in the same manner. Once I had helped them kill John Phillips I was in too deep to back out. Lawton was the family lawyer and Trent represented the college. All of these poor people had bequeathed millions of dollars to the college. So by killing them, the college would get its money a lot quicker rather than waiting for them to eventually die of natural causes. They want me to inject Anne Ashdown, but I can't, I just can't. It has to stop. Beth, I love you, Mark, and the girls. Please forgive me."

The recording ended. A sad silence permeated the living room.

Sarah's face was flush with anger. Everything now fell into place. The silent look between Thomas Lawton and Dr. Glenn in her grandfather's bedroom the morning he died. Leslie Patton's hit-and-run death, and the strange behavior of Walton Trent. She felt Peter's hand gently touch her left hand as it lay still on her lap. The silent touch conveyed sadness and understanding.

Connors stood up and walked over to the little black tape recorder and picked it up and held it under his arm. He then addressed the small gathering of people.

"Folks, this is what we need to do. While it looks like an open-and-shut case, things can get real complicated very fast. First of all, everything stays in this room. My guess is the mountain man Peter killed out at the cabin is the one who took Dr. Glenn's life. But we have a lot of police work to piece this all together. I'm going to call in a forensics team to go over this house. Sorry, Mrs. Glenn, but we need to establish an evidence trail that unfortunately includes Dr. Glenn. I'm going back to the station and talk to the Chief so we can get a lot of officers working on this. We are about to uncover the biggest crime to ever hit Pinehurst. So we have to be careful not to damage any crime scenes as well as to manage this investigation with accuracy and professionalism."

The stunned group of people stood up almost in unison and made for the door. Connors left one of the officers to stay with Mrs. Glenn and walked outside with Peter and Sarah. Once they were on the porch he turned to them.

"Sarah, I am sorry you had to hear about your grandfather's death this way. He was a good man and didn't deserve to die so needlessly. I think it would be good if you told Mrs. Phillips as soon as you can. We don't want her hearing it on CNN."

She nodded, her red eyes rimming with tears.

The detective continued. "Listen, as of this moment Walton Trent, Thomas Lawton, and whoever else is involved don't know we have the tape. I want to keep it that way. We need to get enough evidence to take to the District Attorney. She won't seek an indictment unless she has an airtight case. Trust me on this one. She's good, very good, but doesn't like to lose. It may take us several weeks to develop enough evidence. We will require physical proof and eyewitnesses. I'm worried about the admissibility of the tape. We may need more than the tape. In fact we will."

"I believe we may have what you need, Detective," replied Peter.

The burly detective looked at Peter. "Somehow that doesn't surprise me." His response was accompanied by a slight grin.

Peter told the detective about his and Jeff's most recent trip to Boston. They even told him about entering Trent's townhouse. Connors winced when he heard this but said nothing.

"Do we need to be concerned about Anne's safety?" asked Connors.

"Not now," replied Sarah. "We have her hidden away in Boston."

"That's good. Now I need to get back to the station and get the Chief brought up to speed. Anything else I should know?"

Peter hesitated but only for a moment.

"Well, actually, there is something more."

Peter's tone immediately had the detective's complete attention. He nodded for him to continue.

"We have set Walton Trent up for a big surprise. I mean big surprise." This time Peter showed a slight grin.

"What do you mean?"

"Well, Sarah and I believe Walton Trent is just a piece of the puzzle. We think there are people above him calling the shots. Justin Nichols for one and the people behind Empire Insurance, whoever they are. Sure, Trent is the guy in charge here in Pinehurst but we think he answers to others in Boston and New York."

Connors bit his lip as he considered Peter's words. This was indeed becoming more complicated.

Peter continued. "So this morning Jeff and I got into the information systems department at the Bank of Boston and reworked some of the accounts. Jeff is a genius on the computer. You see the way we figure it, Trent procures the money through the bequests and has it wired to the Bank of Boston, where Justin Nichols immediately transfers it electronically to New York and Empire Insurance. So Jeff developed a reverse rogue program whereby he electronically transferred $3,000,000 back from Empire Insurance to Trent's personal account in the Bank of Boston. Evidently it was easy once Jeff was able to get into Empire Insurance's home page."

The detective's eyes widened. "So why would you do that?"

"Well we hoped this might force the issue by putting pressure on Trent. If he gets in trouble with his bosses, he might make mistakes at this end and we could then expose him."

"So essentially you stole $3 million?"

"Well the way I see it, we recovered three million stolen dollars."

"All semantics, the way I see it," said Sarah. A slight grin on her face too.

Connors sighed. "You two are really something. I just hope you haven't made Walton Trent and his evil buddies too mad. I'm serious. We don't know who these people are."

Sarah stiffened. "Well we know enough about them to know they are killers."

Connors relented and began walking to his car. "Just be careful both of you. Oh, and please stay in touch. We will handle things from here. I'll call you when we know more."

Sarah and Jeff watched the town's detective drive away.

CHAPTER FIFTY

Walton Trent sat at his desk willing the phone to ring and Thomas Lawton tell him where Anne Ashdown was. He was in a quandary. Things were rapidly coming to a close with regards to his assignment at the college. He smiled to himself. Assignment! That's what the big bosses referred to his work at Kingston. If only these stuffy academics really knew what an assignment was. Not some dull research paper that most people would never read much less understand! He desperately wanted to finish the job. That meant Anne Ashdown's death. But people were getting suspicious. Even if he managed to get to her, the cause of death might be investigated. Maybe! Peter Kramer and Sarah Philips didn't have much concrete information, he thought. In his heart he knew he would go to the wall on this assignment. Thomas Lawton knew a lot but was in so deep that he would go to jail for a long time if exposed. He'd keep his mouth shut. President James Cannon was another issue. He was in pretty deep but running scared. It wouldn't take much for him to spill his guts. Randolph Bolles, so clueless that he had been a wonderful pawn in Trent's hands. Bolles had put so much pressure on Cannon that he had literally forced the President to turn to Trent. If Bolles was guilty of anything, it was pure ignorance and unfettered arrogance. Suddenly the phone rang, jolting Trent out of his thoughts. He eagerly reached for the phone.

"Hello," he barked into the mouthpiece.

"Walton, this is Justin. What is going on up there?"

Trent sensed the tension in Justin's voice.

"What do you mean?"

The man's tone changed from tension to impatience. "Walton, the boys in New York are pretty upset. They want to know why $3 million disappeared today and the same amount appeared in your personal account at the Bank of Boston."

Trent's face went white at this news. He couldn't believe what he had just heard. He felt his head spinning and heart pounding.

"What are you talking about, Justin?"

"Come on, Walton. This isn't the time to play games. The boys are ready to pull the plug on you. It isn't just the money. They think the whole assignment is unraveling and frankly so do I."

Trent felt like his whole world was closing in on him. Things seemed to be getting dark all around him. He knew he was close to blacking out. Grabbing a glass of water from his credenza he hastily gulped half the glass. Slowly things started to come back into focus.

"Walton, are you still there?" asked Nichols.

"Yes, I'm still here. Justin, you've got to believe me. I have no idea how $3 million ended up in my account. Obviously someone is trying to blackmail me. You have to believe me!"

"It's not me who has to believe you. You know that."

"I'm about to wrap the assignment up. I'm that close. I just have a few loose ends to tie up. I need three more days. Can't you get them to give me that?"

"I don't know. Listen, I'll make a call to New York. Trent, this better be on the up and up. If I find out you are screwing me around…"

"Justin, don't worry. Just make the call and let me know tonight."

Walton Trent sat back in his plush chair and breathed a long sigh. He dearly hoped Justin could buy him more time. Otherwise he was a dead man. That much he knew for sure. He picked up the phone and began making his final plans. He worked all afternoon on his plan. As he was ready to leave for the day the phone rang. Justin Nichols told him he had his three days.

Peter sat in Sarah's living room reviewing the day's events with her. He was worried about what Detective Connors had said about making the bad guys mad. He hoped he hadn't put Sarah or Anne Ashdown in danger.

"Peter, listen to me," said Sarah, "it's not your fault. If you hadn't come to Pinehurst, none of this would have come to light. We should be grateful."

"Maybe I should have gone to the police earlier and let them take over."

Sarah softly took his hand and looked him in the eye. "Peter, I'm so happy you came to the college. You are smart and brave and I love you very much."

"Sarah, I'm in love with you. It's been a wonderful time for me too. I just hope things work out."

She squeezed his hand. "They will, Peter. Let's just stick to the plan. Now is not the time to deviate from it."

He stood up. "I'd better be going. Jeff is probably wondering where I am. Listen, call me anytime if you need me. OK?"

"You bet I will, Mr. Kramer," she replied throwing her long graceful arms around his neck.

She watched him drive away in his little sports car. She checked all the doors and windows before heading upstairs to bed.

At 7:00 the next morning Thomas Lawton and Walton Trent were eating an early breakfast at the Pinehurst Inn. Thomas Lawton was acting very pleased with himself. Thanks to several discreet inquiries he had located where Anne Ashdown was hiding. For some reason he had asked Phil Craft if Anne had any other residences on the off chance she might be at one of them. To his surprise Craft suggested maybe she was staying with Martha Phillips at her exclusive Boston condominium. It made sense. So Lawton hired a Boston private investigator who had quickly established that both Martha Phillips and Anne Ashdown were indeed staying in Boston. He eagerly passed the news and address along to Trent.

"Lawton, I want you to have lunch with Phil Craft tomorrow and make sure he won't go to the police. Make sure it's tomorrow and at your regular time. I'll take care of James Cannon. Your job is to help me tie up the loose ends to this whole thing." He paused. "Don't worry, you will be well taken care of. Got that?"

"Sure, Walton, it's just that once you leave town I'm kinda left all alone."

Trent's terse reply jolted Lawton. "Listen, like I told you before, if any of this gets out, I'll know it came from you and if so, what some boys from New York do to you and your family won't be pretty."

Lawton's sallow face went white. "OK, Walton, you don't have to worry about me. I've got a lot at stake here too, you know."

"Well let's just keep it that way. Now after you meet with Craft tomorrow, call me on my cell phone. Oh, and make sure you meet at the same restaurant so I know where you are."

The two men left the Inn and headed their separate ways.

Walton headed back to his office at the college for what he hoped would be the last time. Time was running out and he had several tasks. One was to see James Cannon, the second to place a call to Boston, and the final was to take care of Anne Ashdown once and for all. Once the old woman died, Lawton would see to the immediate release of her gift to the college. Upon her death the transfer would occur with the Bank of Boston through Justin Nichols for the last time. He would then disappear, as was the plan. He arrived back at his office by 8:45 and placed two calls. The first was to James Cannon. Ten minutes later the distraught Kingston College President was sitting in Trent's office, almost wringing his hands in despair. Trent started in on Cannon without preamble.

"Cannon, my work is almost finished here. I'm sure you know that by now. Now let's sit back for a few minutes and look at the big picture. Everything you have asked me to do I have done. We have raised literally millions of dollars for the college. Things are starting to take shape. New buildings built, more on the drawing board, and a healthy increase to your endowment. Donor giving is at an all-time high. Now it seems to me you have two choices here. You can go along with the plan and keep your mouth shut or you can go to the police and unload that guilt etched all over your pathetic face. The problem for me is I don't know which way you will go."

Trent's demeanor made the room seem darker. President James Cannon sat frozen in his chair as if he were a wax figure. He despaired with the stark realization that he was finished. There was no way out. He knew it and so did Walton Trent. James Cannon was essentially a weak man outside the protected walls of academia. Inside, his fine mind and intellect prevailed. But that's where his power and strength ended. Outside of the college, he was out of his depth and no one knew that better than Walton Trent. Trent's plan was working to perfection. He then decided to play his final card, the one that would eliminate President James Cannon as a potential problem. A cruel smile crossed Walton Trent's face as he uttered his final words to Cannon.

"You know, James, you wouldn't survive one week in the New Hampshire State Penitentiary. I mean, can you imagine a man with such a great mind as yours in a cell with hardened criminals who would know you were a college president and hate your guts for it. From pin stripes to prison stripes."

The malice on Walton Trent's face matched his cruel heart.

James Cannon abruptly stood up and without even looking at Trent opened the office door and walked out. It occurred to Trent that Cannon had never uttered a word during their entire meeting. It really didn't matter to Walton Trent. He knew what James Cannon would do next.

The door remained open once Cannon walked out. Trent quickly jumped up, quietly shut the door, and reached for his phone. He punched the area code for a Boston number and was soon talking to a familiar person. Trent issued several instructions and hung up. He stood up and looked around the plush office he had occupied for the last three years. He felt no emotion or nostalgia. It was time for him to go. He was ready to leave this place and move on. Probably there would never be a more hated administrator at Kingston College than Walton Trent. Once again, men like Walton Trent didn't care about such things. He picked up his leather briefcase and began stuffing papers into it. He didn't need to be too careful. After all, his name wasn't really Walton Trent. He smiled to himself. The irony was rich. He would travel back to New York and disappear from sight until the next job came along. They could search all they wanted to, but his trail would grow cold within days.

At 8:30 Peter, Sarah, and Jeff were finishing breakfast in

the Phillips country kitchen when the phone rang. Detective Connors was on the other end. Peter listened intently.

"Listen, I have just finished a meeting with the Chief of Police and District Attorney. We are several days away from issuing a warrant for Walton Trent and any others who may be involved. But the evidence is looking strong. The DA won't move forward until she has a strong case, like I told you the other day. I'm calling you to make sure to be careful. The DA thinks Walton Trent may be involved with organized crime and is calling in the State Task Force. You may have stumbled upon something real hot here and we want you to be extremely careful."

"Sure, Detective, we will be watchful."

The Detective sensed a pause in Peter's response. "Peter, I'm not kidding. This is serious stuff. Are you with me here on this?"

"Detective Connors, is there a possibility Walton Trent will get away with this? I mean, he is pretty street savvy."

"Peter, you just let the authorities handle it from here. We now have the State of New Hampshire and federal authorities working together on this case."

Peter hung up the phone and looked at Sarah and Jeff. They had heard the conversation and arrived at the same conclusion. Walton Trent could easily elude the grasp of the police. They were afraid the cautious District Attorney would give Trent time to escape before issuing a warrant for his arrest.

Suddenly the telephone rang again. Sarah picked it up and listened to a voice at the other end. Jeff and Peter could only hear bits and pieces. Sarah's eyes widened in fear. "OK, OK, thanks," she mumbled before putting the phone down.

"What is it?" asked Peter.

"That was Phil Craft at the bank. He's having a conscience all of a sudden. He wanted me to know he told Thomas Lawton about my grandmother's Boston condominium. He's afraid for my grandmother and Anne Ashdown."

Peter leaped to his feet. "That means Trent knows!"

Sarah grabbed Peter's arm. "We better call Cary Connors and get them moved to a safe location."

"Yeah we better." He quickly called the Pinehurst Police Station and was told Connors was in a high-level meeting with the DA and federal authorities. The secretary promised to pass along Peter's message.

Peter looked at the other two. "Listen, we can't wait. We have to do something."

Sarah made a quick call to the college and established that Walton Trent was still in his office. She asked Trent's secretary to call her on Sarah's cell phone immediately when he left. The secretary joyfully agreed to help Sarah. Meanwhile Peter and Jeff loaded Anne Ashdown's car with audiovisual equipment and the three of them headed to town. Their plan was simple but dangerous. They would follow Walton Trent and tape record his every move. If the police wanted evidence then they would get evidence.

At 10:30 A.M. Sarah's cell phone rang. Sylvia, Trent's secretary, was reporting that Trent was leaving the building, clutching his briefcase, and apparently headed to his dark blue Buick in the parking lot. Peter, Sarah, and Jeff fortunately were almost to town. They spotted Trent's Buick turning left out of the main administration parking lot. Jeff quickly hit the record button and an expensive but very discreet swivel camera began recording Trent's progress.

"Where do you think he's headed?" asked Sarah.

They didn't have to wait long. He went directly home to his townhouse where, after parking the car, he vanished inside. Thirty minutes later he reemerged with two expensive leather bags. Quickly loading them into the Buick's trunk he got behind the wheel and began slowly driving out of town. To their amazement he drove up Old Mountain Road in the direction of the cabin in the woods. Since it was broad daylight the three followers had no choice but to stay well behind him. With the camera rolling, they discreetly followed Walton Trent up the quiet highway and observed him finally turn left onto the old cabin road. Peter drove by the old cabin road and continued up the gradually ascending highway before spotting a turnoff where they could observe Trent undetected when he came back to the highway.

"What do you suppose he's up to?" asked Jeff.

Sarah answered his question. "I'll bet he is after some more of the benzene to use on Mrs. Ashdown."

All three became silent. The callousness of such an act being perpetuated upon one human being by another was sobering.

"How can he believe he can get away with this?"

"That's just it. The man's arrogance empowers him in ways we can't understand. He also has no idea how much we know about everything. The same arrogance that empowers him blinds him. The problem is all he needs is one electronic transfer of Mrs. Ashdown's money and the game is over. They win. We have to stop him."

True to form, Trent's Buick shot out of the old cabin road 10 minutes later and began rapidly heading in the direction of town. Peter wisely stayed a safe distance behind. Once in town Walton Trent didn't look back. He drove straight through the old New England town, heading east toward Concord.

Back at the college, as the two cars were leaving town, President James Cannon was walking slowly down the carpeted hallway of the executive suite in the direction of his office. Since his ugly encounter earlier that morning with Walton Trent, he had taken a long leisurely walk around the Kingston campus. He entered different academic buildings and traversed the snow-covered walkways as if a visitor looking over the campus. People would later comment on his solitary walk as that of someone subdued and reflective. He stopped to talk with no one, simply nodding in silent greeting. Elisabeth Rutherford, who was in her office, happened to see the President on his lonely walk but was too busy to give it further thought.

The solitary figure entered his President's office, walking past his secretary without greeting. Closing the door he almost stumbled to his large desk, where he sat in his swivel chair looking over the pretty college campus. His campus! All he ever wanted was what lay before his sad eyes. He glanced at his diplomas hanging on the wall and a framed picture of his wife of 38 years and his two grown children. Reaching into the bottom drawer of the desk, he pulled out a small black revolver, placed the gun into his mouth, and pulled the trigger. The sudden thrust of the explosion severely jolted his head back against the window overlooking the campus. Blood and brain matter spattered the walls and window in a grotesque display of hopelessness and death. Walton Trent had played his final card on the life of President James Cannon perfectly.

The three followers were a mile behind Trent as he headed east in the direction of Route 93. Sarah's phone rang again. It was Sylvia urging her to have Peter call Elisabeth Rutherford immediately. That is all she could say. Peter called the Dean and learned of Cannon's death. Peter was the first person she called. She wanted to know where he was and what he was doing. Being his usual forthright self, he told her everything. She urged him to be careful and promised she would call Detective Connors. Peter and Sarah could hardly believe James Cannon was dead.

"The man is covering his tracks," said Peter. "Elisabeth says it looks like a suicide but we all know who and what probably drove Cannon to take his life."

Soon they reached the turnoff for Route 93 and continued following Trent south to Massachusetts. The traffic increased as they neared Boston. A couple of times they almost lost Trent but managed to stay close. Peter was starting to sweat. What if they lost Trent? In the back seat Jeff was hunched over a small glass dial that kept emitting a small beep every so often.

"What's that?" asked Peter.

"Oh, it's just a tracer. The last time we were on campus I put an electronic beeper under Trent's car. No way we can lose him now."

"Why didn't you tell me? I've been worried we would lose him in all this traffic."

"Sorry," said Jeff sheepishly.

Sarah reached over and held Peter's hand. She felt his stress too.

"Jeff, thanks, that's a great idea!"

The Buick maneuvered through the heavy midday Boston traffic. Clearly Walton had a destination in mind. They followed Trent to Boylston Street and the Bank of Boston Building. He parked his car in a garage across the street and the three followers watched him enter the main lobby.

"No doubt gong to see Justin Nichols," said Peter.

They waited in the car all afternoon. At one point Jeff left to go buy them some burgers and fries at a McDonald's up the street. He hurried back, arms full of food. By 5:30 Trent had not emerged but his car was still in the garage.

Back at the college the campus was in an uproar. President Cannon's gunshot suicide was all over campus and the town within minutes. Randolph Bolles, Chairman of the Board, was frantic. He kept calling Elisabeth Rutherford every 10 minutes for updates. Clearly he was out of his depth for handling such a crisis. In contrast Dean Rutherford handled the catastrophe confronting the college with far greater poise. She quickly assembled the President's Cabinet in an emergency meeting and together they established a course of action. A couple of members of the Board of Trustees were present but it was evident she could effectively manage the situation. A campus-wide community meeting was called for 5:00 that late afternoon over which she presided. Elisabeth forthrightly told the campus community what had happened and gave out as much information as possible. People had a need to know and she knew the value of straightforward communication. The fewer rumors the better. That evening at a hastily called Executive Committee of the Board, Elisabeth was appointed as administrator in charge of the college by the board. She would be assigned the responsibility of managing the college in the interim. By late evening the shocked campus had returned to some semblance of calm. Things would be difficult in the days ahead but the current President's Cabinet was competent and worked well together. The absence of Walton Trent was clearly noticed but no one had seen him since 10:00 that morning. Only Elisabeth Rutherford knew, but she was keeping that fact a secret.

The late evening traffic was thinning on Boylston Street as Peter and Sarah and Jeff patiently waited for Trent to reemerge from the Bank. Suddenly Peter sat straight up as if he had been shot.

"Oh no," he cried.

"What's the matter?" asked a panicked Sarah.

"I can't believe this. I'm so stupid. Trent's not coming out that front door. I'll bet he and Justin Nichols left from another door leaving Trent's Buick as a decoy to throw us off. Sarah we have to get over to your grandmother's condominium right away. I'm afraid that's where Trent might be."

Sarah stifled a cry, her hand covering her face in agony.

Peter started the car, pulled out of their parking spot, and following Sarah's directions headed to the downtown harborfront where Martha Phillips's luxury condominium was located. He silently prayed it wasn't too late. They had waited over three hours for Trent to come out of the bank. So much could have happened during all that time they waited. Peter felt sick to his stomach. Peter instructed Jeff to get his camera equipment ready as he raced through the streets of back Boston.

The gleaming lights of Boston Harbor greeted them in the background as they made their way to the elaborate entrance of the luxury condominiums. A doorman in red and black watched them suspiciously as they slowed to a stop. Security cameras recorded their every move. Peter felt some relief once he noticed the cameras.

Tipping his tall hat, the greeter asked them their purpose in a strong Boston accent. Sarah quickly took out her wallet and showed identification. The man was sharp.

"Certainly, Ms. Phillips. I will call Mrs. Phillips and let her know you are on the way up. What a busy night indeed."

"What do you mean, what a busy night indeed?" asked Peter, suddenly alert.

"Well you aren't the first visitors Mrs. Phillips and her house guest have had tonight."

Peter and Sarah exchanged a knowing look.

"Was it two men by chance?" asked Peter.

"Why, yes it was. One of the men stayed behind in the car while the other went up to the penthouse to see Mrs. Phillips. The man wasn't there but maybe 30 minutes. I must tell you, I didn't like the looks of the man who went up at all. He had dark bushy eyebrows and a real dark look about him. As soon as he came back down the two sped away. Is there something wrong?"

Peter jumped into action. "Call 911 immediately and send them to Mrs. Phillips's place. Do it now!"

The greeter ran over to the phone, while Peter, Sarah, and Jeff took the elevator up to the penthouse floor.

They reached the top floor and followed Sarah to her grandmother's condominium, where they pounded furiously on the door. No answer! Peter felt a panic rise in his soul. Sarah kept yelling for her grandmother to open the door. In the distance they heard sirens. Peter took three steps back and hurled his shoulder at the door frame. It barley budged. He tried it again and again. Soon other residents began tentatively opening their doors, frightened faces peering out. Suddenly two burly building security personnel and four Boston Police officers appeared, guns drawn. They yelled at the three to drop to the floor, guns raised. Sarah refused and yelled at them that her grandmother lived in the penthouse and was in danger. A moment later came three Emergency Medical Technicians from the Boston Fire Department. Sarah had finally gotten through to the Boston Police officers by tossing them her wallet and identification. Soon the door was broken open and everyone rushed in. Peter and Sarah found Mrs. Phillips peacefully sleeping soundly on the living room sofa. Anne Ashdown was also sound asleep in a spare bedroom. Everything looked normal but Peter and Sarah knew differently.

Sarah turned to a tall EMT with red hair and a pale complexion and told him that she suspected both women had been injected with benzene. At first they didn't understand. She continued.

"Someone is trying to kill these women by using the drug benzene. It acts to gradually slow their hearts down eventually to where their hearts stop. Since they are older it looks like a simple case of heart failure. You have got to do something to alter the drugs in their systems or they will both die."

The emergency technicians nodded their heads in unison and immediately opened their equipment and began working on both women. Soon they were ready for transport to the hospital. One of the EMTs was constantly on the radio with the hospital.

The Boston Police took a report from Peter and Sarah, including a detailed description of Walton Trent and a lesser one of Justin Nichols. Back at the front entrance of the luxury condominium complex, two ambulances hurried away with Martha Phillips and Anne Ashdown inside. A Boston Police officer accompanied each ambulance for their safety. The police also got a description of Nichols and Trent, as well as the car Nichols was driving, from the doorman.

Across town Walton Trent and Justin Nichols were headed back to the Bank of Boston in Nichols's dark blue Lincoln Continental. Justin Nichols was furious.

"Trent, I should never have let you drag me this far into this whole mess. There are too many loose ends. I'm telling you, the boys are going to be pretty upset."

"Come on Justin, everything is working according to plan. We just have to wait for 15 more hours. By 9:00 tomorrow morning Anne Ashdown will have died of heart failure. One call to Thomas Lawton in Pinehurst and the money she bequeathed to the college is electronically transferred to the Bank of Boston. We grab our share and disappear."

"Yeah, but how can this happen so fast? Good grief, the women just died. Don't these things take time?"

"Normally, yes, it takes weeks but that's the beauty of the scheme. Thomas Lawton is her attorney and when he approves the release of funds it goes through. Remember, everything rests upon what these people don't know. They trust Lawton and leave everything to him. Anyway, once the electronic transfer goes through, there is no going back. The money is then sent to Empire Insurance, which is untraceable."

Nichols was still doubtful. "What about the doctor's certificate. That's one of the things we used Dr. Glenn for all the other times?"

"That's true, but for this last time Thomas Lawton will release the funds without the death certificate."

The heavyset Nichols steeled his narrow eyes on a dark Storrow Drive. They arrived back at the bank, where Trent got out to go to his car. He leaned into the front window and gave Nichols a few final instructions.

"Tomorrow morning you be at your office at the bank just like usual. At 9:00 I place the call to Thomas Lawton and then he immediately begins the wire transfer of funds. You work your magic at the bank and then we both leave Boston for good."

CHAPTER FIFTY-ONE

The tall, attractive, dark-haired doctor walked briskly out of the emergency room at Massachusetts General Hospital at 10:30 that same evening and approached Sarah, Peter, and Jeff, who were sitting anxiously in the waiting room. Dr. Kim Peterson was 37 years of age and a graduate of Harvard Medical School. She gave them a concise update on both women.

"We ran some toxicology tests and confirmed traces of benzene in their systems. Fortunately the drugs didn't have the time to really do their damage. We gave both women adrenaline to speed up their heart activity, thus countering the benzene. If you two hadn't gotten them medical attention they both would have died during the night. You saved their lives."

Peter paused and, looking Dr. Peterson directly in the eyes, asked if she could keep all of the night's events confidential. She looked surprised, almost offended, but assured them everything would be kept quiet. The two Boston Police officers standing off to the side nodded their heads in approval.

After thanking Dr. Peterson and making sure both women were under police protection, they left the hospital. They stood outside the hospital's emergency entrance gazing across Storrow

Drive and at the dark outlines of the Charles River. Sarah shivered as she reflected upon the night's events. Somewhere out there Walton Trent was loose. She held Peter's hand tightly.

"What now?" she asked softly. She could see a fire and determination in his eyes.

He looked down into her lovely dark eyes and replied.

"We now have them just where we want them."

"What do you mean?"

"Trent and Nichols believe Anne will be dead by morning. If I'm right they will follow their usual plan and attempt to transfer Anne's money to the Bank of Boston using Thomas Lawton. I'm sure this is their final act so we better act fast ourselves."

They walked out into the well-lit parking lot to their car. They had a lot to do that night.

Peter drove the car while Jeff sat in the back seat fiddling with his electronic tracer. They headed in the general direction of the bank. They drove around for thirty minutes. Soon the faint beeping intensified. On Park Street, right across from the old Park Street Church they suddenly spotted Trent's Buick headed west in the direction of the Boston Hilton. Peter quickly did a U-turn and began following Trent. They watched as he slowed his car down and drove into the main entrance. A valet took his car and Trent walked straight into the plush hotel. It appeared he was staying the night. Peter asked Jeff to keep the beeper on just in case Trent left the hotel during the night.

Peter called Elisabeth Rutherford at 11:30 that night and quickly filled her in on the evening's events. She took the news calmly.

"Elisabeth, I need your help. Can you arrange a meeting with the head of security at the Bank of Boston? I think his name is Wilbur Guthrie."

Peter heard her exhale a breath. "Of course, I know Wilbur.

He and my father were very close. Listen, give me a few minutes and I'll call you on your cell phone."

They waited at a Dunkin' Donuts shop for Elisabeth to call back. Peter marveled at how many donuts Jeff could eat. He was just wiping his face after consuming his third chocolate cream donut when Peter's phone rang.

"Peter, Wilbur will meet you at the front of the bank at midnight. He's more than a bit curious but I told him he needed to trust you and that this involves a serious matter with the bank."

"Thanks, Elisabeth."

"Peter. Please be careful."

At 12:00 midnight they arrived at a very quiet and darkened Bank of Boston. Approaching the main doors they glimpsed a massive shadowy figure swiftly move in their direction. Wilbur Guthrie quietly opened the massive doors and ushered Peter, Sarah, and Jeff into the tomb-like lobby. Surprise filled his broad face as he instantly recognized Peter and Jeff. They proceeded upstairs to the bank's security offices, where all four sat down around a large conference table.

"Now, Mr. Kramer, what is all this mystery about? Elisabeth Rutherford has told me there are some serious improprieties going on here at the bank and that I should talk to you."

The giant man sat back in his chair and steepled his hands together to listen intently to Peter.

Peter cleared his throat. "Well, Mr. Guthrie, I'm sure you recognize Jeff and me from the other day when we were visiting Molly."

"Indeed I do, Mr. Kramer."

For the next 30 minutes Peter carefully outlined everything he knew beginning with his first week at the college earlier that fall. He left nothing out. As he came to the part of Bill Rutherford and the suspected misappropriation of funds by Walton

Trent and Justin Nichols, Wilbur Guthrie's face tightened in anger. When Peter was finished, silence filled the room.

"We knew something was going on but just couldn't put a finger on it," responded Guthrie. "Justin Nichols came to us from New York's Chemical bank two years ago. He always kept to himself. Employees never really responded well to him." Guthrie looked directly at Jeff.

"Jeff, I am very sorry this happened to you. We got some really bad information and reacted poorly to it. While I didn't know you, I had heard about your situation. I apologize."

Jeff's relief spread across his young face. "Thank you, Mr. Guthrie. You don't know how much this means to me. All I ever wanted to do was work here at the bank. It's been my life."

"Mr. Guthrie," Peter said, "I have a plan that might help us nab Justin Nichols. It will involve leaving Jeff with you while Sarah and I go back to New Hampshire tonight."

Guthrie stood up, towering over the three young people. "I will do anything to catch the killers of my dear friend Bill Rutherford. Now fill me in on your plan and let's get started."

CHAPTER FIFTY-TWO

Once again Sarah and Peter headed out into the dark New England night and began driving north to New Hampshire. They placed two phone calls from the car. Sarah called Mass General to check on her grandmother and Anne Ashdown. Both were resting comfortably. Peter called Cary Connors and filled him in on his plan. They arranged to meet at 6:45 the next morning at the Pinehurst Police Station. Meanwhile Cary Connors called the Boston Police and arranged round-the-clock surveillance of Walton Trent at the Boston Hilton. The Boston Police also got a grumpy judge out of bed for a court-approved wiretap of Walton Trent's hotel telephone. Things were starting to fall into place.

It was well after midnight. The road was almost devoid of cars. The neon signs and strip mall lights dotting the highway cast their annoying ultra colors over the deserted roadway. Sarah and Peter stopped at an all-night hamburger joint and feasted on really tasty but hardly nutritious food. Sarah sat with her knees hunched up, munching on her burger, while Peter drove northward. Peter's mind was racing as he anticipated the events of the coming day. Soon he hoped the net would be cast and encircle its prey. By 2:30 A.M. they had reached a very dark and quiet Pinehurst. Peter dropped Sarah off at her home promising to pick her up at 6:30 the next morning. She kissed him good-bye at the door after he had checked the entire house.

Back in Boston at the Hilton, Walton Trent was pacing his hotel room. He was nervous. Everything was in order but something didn't feel right. Once he made the phone call to Thomas Lawton in the morning, that would set the wheels in motion for the money to be transferred. Then it would be all over and onto the next assignment. He would prove to the bosses in New York that Walton Trent could finish a job and finish it right. Picking up the phone he called room service and ordered a late-night prime rib dinner complete with a bottle of red wine. By 1:00 he was fast asleep.

Peter's alarm woke him from a deep sleep. The glowing red numbers said it was 5:30. He was amazed at how well he had slept. After quickly shaving and showering, he dressed. By 6:30 he was at the Phillips house, where Sarah was waiting for him. She wore a short skirt with a stylish blue dress shirt under a long-sleeved off-white sweater. Peter thought she looked gorgeous. At 6:45 sharp they were seated in the Pinehurst Police Chief's office, along with Detective Connors, one other detective, two police officers, and an attractive but stern looking woman in her early forties, who was introduced as the District Attorney for Central New Hampshire, Diane Johnson. Following the introductions, Detective Connors asked Peter to explain his plan to the team. All eyes watched Peter intently as he explained the plan in detail. The District Attorney took copious notes, pausing only to watch Peter or ask him a question. It was clear this was one case she wanted to be perfectly prepared to bring to a grand jury. was A long-time New Hampshire resident, Diane Johnson also was outraged at the events at the college.

At 7:00 Sarah placed a phone call to Massachusetts General Hospital and talked briefly with a hospital administrator. She looked over at Diane Johnson and handed her the telephone. The attorney listened intently, pausing to ask questions and once again taking notes. After a few more minutes she thanked the administrator and hung up the phone. A pleased look came over her face.

"That was Dr. Thornton Green at Mass General. He confirmed several things for us and is having their legal staff develop an affidavit. Both women are doing fine. The drug benzene was injected by a Mr. Walton Trent into both Mrs. Phillips and Mrs. Ashdown, against their wishes, last night sometime around 8:00. Both women have identified Walton Trent as the one who forced his way into the condominium. Evidently Trent told Mrs. Phillips that something had happened to Sarah and tricked his way though the door. Once there he overpowered the women and after the forced injections waited for them to gradually fall asleep. He figured the drug would eventually cause their hearts to stop during the night."

She continued. "We now have solid evidence of an attempted murder. Our two star witnesses are safe and sound under Boston Police protection. Once I get the affidavit from Mass General, as well as statements from Mrs. Phillips and Mrs. Ashdown, I can then prepare formal charges. But first we need to continue to gather more evidence. I don't want to leave out any of the other families who have suffered at the hands of Walton Trent. They all deserve justice."

A secretary brought in hot steaming coffee and sweet rolls for the group. At 7:15 two of the police officers quietly left the room as if on cue and went out the front door of the Police Station. At 7:45 they returned with an unshaven, disheveled

Thomas Lawton in handcuffs. He stumbled into the room. His face went ashen white as his small beady eyes took in the scene around him. He began shaking uncontrollably. Peter felt some satisfaction seeing Lawton this way, but honestly regarded the small-time lawyer as bait for a bigger catch.

Cary Connors took over. "Sit down, Thomas. We have a few questions we need to ask you."

At first he was belligerent. "What right do you have dragging me out of bed and down here? I've done nothing wrong. I have my rights you know." The bluster was short-lived.

Connors very calmly told the crooked lawyer all of the mounting evidence against him. He was stunned. When Connors told him Anne Ashdown was alive and well he slumped back in his chair. Thomas Lawton had believed all along that Walton Trent's plan would succeed. With this last vestige of hope gone, he was ready to talk.

"I'll cooperate but I want a deal."

Diane Johnson stepped in. "Mr. Lawton, I can't guarantee anything, but if you fully cooperate I will do my best to see you don't die in prison."

The man seemed to shrink in the plain green plastic chair as he realized the trouble he was in.

"OK, how can I help you?" He knew it was all over.

Connors leaned in and explained what they wanted Lawton to do.

CHAPTER FIFTY-THREE

Back in Boston, Jeff and Wilbur Guthrie had been up since 5:00 A.M. Guthrie had taken Jeff, who had slept at Guthrie's house, to an all-night restaurant for an early morning breakfast. They then went to the bank, where Jeff once again worked his magic on the keyboard for an intense 40 minutes. At 6:30, Wilbur took Jeff to Justin Nichols's office, where Jeff carefully placed two hidden miniature cameras and speakers. Before leaving the office Jeff activated two four-hour long tapes. Back at the computer lab Jeff checked the equipment and was satisfied any activity in Justin Nichols's office would be transcribed as well as electronically documented.

The trap was slowly being set.

At 8:30 A.M. two police officers, Detective Connors, Diane Johnson, and Peter and Sarah sat in Thomas Lawton's law office on Main Street in Pinehurst. The curtains were drawn. A sophisticated recording device had been placed on the telephone. Two other phones had been set up in the room for the District Attorney and Detective Connors. They could listen in on any conversation.

By 8:55 the law office resembled a morgue. There was

nothing left to say nor any further instructions required. Everything depended on Thomas Lawton's performance. Peter hoped Lawton knew how important the call would be to any hope he might have of escaping a long prison term.

The phone rang at 9:05. Lawton almost jumped out of his chair. Not a good start thought Peter. He glanced over at Sarah. She was staring at the phone as if it were about to explode. Everyone seemed to sit up and lean towards the phone. All eyes watched Thomas Lawton, almost willing him to succeed. Detective Connors motioned with his hand for Lawton to wait while he flipped on the recording device. Everything was now in place.

Lawton almost reluctantly picked up the phone. Fear crossed his sallow face. Connors and Diane Johnson carefully picked up their phones.

A familiar voice at the other end asked, "Lawton, is that you?"

"Yes, Trent, it's me."

"Well how are things up there? Anything going on that I should know about?" Trent didn't completely trust Thomas Lawton.

Lying came easily to Thomas Lawton. "No Walton, everything is fine at this end. I've just been here waiting for your call like you told me yesterday."

Walton Trent's relief was evident. "Good man! Now listen carefully. A few more hours and this whole show comes to a close. I'm calling you to tell you that Anne Ashdown is dead." Trent then chuckled as he added, "Oh and Martha Phillips too."

Lawton hesitated with his response. He couldn't believe Martha Phillips too.

"Hey, are you still there?" asked an impatient Trent.

"Sure, Walton, it's just I didn't think we needed to do Mrs. Phillips, too."

Trent's callousness showed through. "Well, when I went to visit Mrs. Ashdown to finish the job, I couldn't leave any witnesses. What do you think I am, stupid?"

Lawton decided to push the conversation further. "So was it the same method Dr. Glenn used on the others? "

This time Trent's hesitation came through. Everyone in the room who could hear feared Lawton had gone too far. Everything seemed suspended in mid air. An agonizing moment passed before Trent responded.

"Yeah, old Dr. Glenn's medicine works wonders again."

An audible sigh of relief filled the small office as Trent evidently failed to pick up on Lawton's leading question.

Peter glanced over at Diane Johnson. She was furiously writing notes. Clearly Walton Trent had just implicated himself.

"Lawton, you know what to do next. Call Ashdown's bank and report her death and begin the immediate transfer of funds to the Bank here in Boston. Hell, I know they may gripe and tell you it's unusual to expedite things this fast but do it. They trust you." A slight snicker followed Trent's last comment.

"OK Trent, I'll get right on it."

"Oh, Lawton, one more thing. I still want you to have lunch with Phil Craft today and call me after you're done. Remember to have lunch at the same place and time so as to not arouse any suspicions."

Walton Trent hung up without any further word.

The team of people in the room sprang into action. The two police officers would stay with Lawton while he made the pivotal call to the Bank of New Hampshire, releasing Anne Ashdown's funds to the Bank of Boston. A court stenographer would record all of his actions. Diane Johnson took off for her office to prepare attempted murder and murder indictments. Peter, Sarah, Jeff, and Cary Connors went back to the burly detective's office to await word from Wilbur Guthrie.

Back in Boston Wilbur Guthrie watched the security monitors from the confines of the Bank of Boston's ninth floor security offices as Justin Nichols entered the bank through the main entrance. Dressed in an expensive dark blue tailored suit he marched into the bank as if he owned it. The arrogance of the man deeply annoyed Wilbur. Bill Rutherford would never have strutted into the bank like this. He deeply missed his old friend. In the computer lab Jeff waited anxiously at his computer screen for the activity to begin. Everything was programmed but he wanted to be sure everything was also recorded. Two bank security guards stood outside the computer lab. No one would be allowed in until after it was all over. Across town at the Hilton, Walton Trent again ordered room service and waited by his phone. He had several calls to make before everything was to be wrapped up.

At 10:00 A.M. Thomas Lawton, under the watchful eye of Cary Connors, called the Bank of New Hampshire and after identifying himself as Anne Ashdown's attorney, informed the Senior Vice President for Major Accounts of her death. A Pinehurst Police officer recorded the conversation. As stipulated in her will, of which the bank had a copy, an immediate release of funds was to be made to the Bank of Boston upon her death. He requested this release be done electronically and immediately. At first the cautious bank officer resisted but upon further pressure on Lawton's part he relented.

The wheels were now set in motion.

At 10:00 A.M. Justin Nichols was in his office awaiting the transfer of funds from the Bank of New Hampshire. Poised to make the switch and redirect the funds to Empire Insurance, Nichols failed to detect the subtle and silent nuances of the special computer program Jeff had set into motion earlier that morning that would catch the redirect order and dump the entire amount of Anne Ashdown's money into an auxiliary security bank account. Once this occurred all assets were automatically frozen until the entire mess could be sorted out. The money was irretrievable. Justin Nichols simply wasn't computer literate enough to notice. He was an arrogant man, technically out of his depth. As if this wasn't enough, the entire proceedings were being perfectly recorded. More importantly the illegal programming scheme was also being documented. For the first time the scheme was captured on tape and Justin Nichols was being exposed.

At 10:10 the phone rang. It was Trent. The transfer from the Bank of New Hampshire was under way. Nichols quickly went to his computer and directed the rogue program to work its magic one final time. He didn't bother to verify the redirected funds. He wanted to get out of the bank as soon as possible.

Nichols began packing his black leather briefcase. Suddenly his phone rang a second time. Expecting it to be Trent, his face went white as he listened to a familiar, angry voice at the other end. A coldness swept through his body. His body went rigid as he listened to the caller's tirade.

"Justin, it's all over. You trusted Walton Trent once too often and he has betrayed all of us."

"What do you mean? I just completed the transaction. The money should be there by now."

A derisive laugh filled the phone. "Justin, you now have three major problems. First, the money is not here. Our computer people tell us the total amount disappeared into an unknown account moments ago. Two million dollars is missing. It never got here! You said it would be here this morning. Well it's not! Second, the boys here are steaming. They don't like to lose money. Third, our computer expert here says someone ran a rogue electronic program at the Bank of Boston and believes they are on to you. You better get the hell out of there."

Nichols stammered to explain but the phone went dead.

Sweat began pouring down the side of his beefy red face. He hastily gathered his things, not even bothering to call and warn Trent. He opened the door to his office in a panic. The long plush executive hallway was empty. He breathed a sigh of relief. There was still time to escape. He ran down the hall, rounded the corner, and approached the bank of elevators. Hearing soft footsteps behind him, he whirled around and faced the angry face of Wilbur Guthrie, who was accompanied by two equally fierce-looking bank security guards. Their guns were drawn.

"Going somewhere, Justin?" asked a bemused Guthrie. He was clearly relishing the moment.

"Yes, I'm late for a meeting over at the Prudential Plaza." He couldn't take his eyes off the guns.

"I don't think so," said Guthrie. "Actually you have an appointment with the Boston Police, who are patiently waiting downstairs in the lobby."

The two security guards grabbed Nichols by each arm and escorted him down the hallway and into the elevator that had opened. Wilbur Guthrie followed a close distance behind, his hand on the small gun attached to his left side. Downstairs in the busy bank lobby, true to Guthrie's word were three Boston Police officers and two plainclothes detectives. People stopped and watched in fascination as the scene unfolded. Nichols was frisked in plain view and had cold steel handcuffs snapped around his wrists. He was briskly escorted to a waiting police car at the curb and driven away.

Across the street a very plain-looking man in a nondescript black suit watched the proceedings intently. As the police car drove away he discreetly picked up a cell phone and after speaking for a few moments turned and continued walking down the busy Boston street.

Wilbur Guthrie stepped into a small office off the bank

lobby and placed a call to Cary Connors in Pinehurst. He told the detective that Justin Nichols was now in custody.

Part of the net had closed.

In his Hilton Hotel room Walton Trent anxiously waited for a confirmation call from Justin Nichols telling him the transaction had gone through. Thirty minutes had passed. He felt a rising panic. Had something gone wrong? He nervously paced the room. He desperately wanted to get out of the hotel and Boston. Glancing out the window at the street below he was stunned to see two Boston Police Cruisers swiftly drive up to the entrance of the Hilton. Accurately sensing he had not a minute to waste Trent grabbed his briefcase and raced out of his sixth floor room. As he rounded the corner and headed for the staircase, he heard the ping of the elevator doors open behind him. He darted unseen around the corner, opened the heavy stairwell doors and began rapidly descending to the floors below. Moments later he heard a shout two stories above him and doors slamming and loud footsteps. At the fifth floor he paused and reaching for a red fire alarm on the wall angrily yanked it. The piercing shrill of the alarm began wailing throughout the entire building. Doors began opening and people started filling the hallways. Soon Walton Trent was just one of hundreds of people all headed in the same direction. By the time he reached the lobby the first fire trucks were pulling up. Amid the chaos he was easily able to disappear into the crowded street. A moment later he was gone.

Back in New Hampshire Cary Connors answered the phone on the first ring. He was expecting good news. He listened to the voice at the other end, an agonized look on his face. He slowly replaced the phone. Peter and Sarah stared at the detective.

"I'm afraid I have bad news. Trent escaped the Boston Police at the Hilton. Evidently he outfoxed them by setting off a fire alarm and escaped in the confusion. We now have a fugitive on our hands."

Sarah gripped Peter's hand tightly. She felt scared. "Where do you think he will go? Are we in any danger?"

Peter bit his lower lip as he considered her question. Cary Connors looked at Peter.

"Walton Trent has no place to go," said Peter. "The bad guys in New York, whoever they might be, have probably turned their backs on him. After all, we fixed it so it looks like he stole their money. No doubt they are going to go after him. Justin Nichols is in custody. Trent has to know the Boston and New Hampshire authorities are after him. I'd hate to be in his shoes."

"I believe you are right, Peter," said Cary.

He reached for the phone and called Diane Johnson to inform her and then began the paperwork for an all-points bulletin. The Massachusetts, New Hampshire, Maine, and Vermont police were all connected for such bulletins. Within thirty minutes law enforcement officers in the four-state region would have Trent's picture flashing on their computer screens. The federal authorities would take care of the geographical areas south of the Massachusetts state line into New York and all points south and west. It would only be a matter of time.

Connors suddenly had a thought. He straightened up in his chair. Everyone turned to look at the detective.

"Hey, do you remember when Trent told Thomas Lawton to call him after his lunch with Phil Craft? Why would he ask Lawton to do that?"

"Maybe he wanted to make sure Craft would keep his mouth shut," answered Peter.

"Yes, but Lawton is telling us all he knows. Trent has to know he couldn't trust Lawton," replied Sarah. "So why worry about that now?"

Connors suddenly shot out of his chair. "Hey, Trent told

Lawton to have lunch with Croft at the usual place and at the usual time. Why is that so important? Only one reason. He wants them together."

The same thought hit Peter and Sarah.

Connors quickly reached for his phone and called dispatch and then the bomb squad. They found Thomas Lawton's car at home where it had been parked all night. After evacuating the entire neighborhood block and cordoning it off with yellow police emergency tape, the bomb squad carefully examined the car. A few minutes later they emerged from under the car with a small package. Wires dangled loosely from the device.

Peter and Sarah stood well back of the police lines thankful the bomb had been discovered. Neither could believe how far Walton Trent would go to keep his secret. When Thomas Lawton heard of the bomb under his car he began singing like a bird to the police.

The time was 3:00 in the afternoon. It had been an eventful day. Thomas Lawton, Justin Nichols, and now Phil Craft were in police custody. President James Cannon was dead. Only Walton Trent remained on the loose.

It was decided to keep Martha Phillips and Anne Ashdown in the hospital and under heavy police guard until Walton Trent was captured. Meanwhile Peter and Sarah left town and headed back to the Phillips estate.

Walton Trent had successfully slipped into the shadowy underlife of Boston. He had changed his swanky suit for heavy work clothes and an old fisherman's hat he had stolen off of a packing crate in the Back Bay of Boston. He carried his cell phone and over $50,000 in cash. At 4:30 P.M. that same afternoon he stopped at an internet café, on the edge of the red light district. He logged onto his computer at home and to his despair discovered that all of his bank accounts had been frozen. Not one dime of his vast resources was accessible. He dialed Justin's cell phone, which went unanswered. He could only surmise that the Ashdown transaction had failed. He walked across the street to a small hole-in-the-wall diner and ordered a cup of coffee and bowl of cheese soup. As he was contemplating his next step he saw a Boston Police Cruiser slow down in front of the internet café and two officers enter the establishment, guns drawn. He carefully slipped out of the diner and quickly blended into the crowded sidewalk. He now knew they were monitoring his computer and somehow had tracked him to the place across the street. For the next two hours Walton Trent walked the streets of old Boston determined to find his way out of the mess he was in. It was unsafe to head south to New York. He was finished with the boys in New York. They would find him and kill him. Truth be told, he was scared to death of falling into their hands. He shuddered at what horrible things they would do to him. The Boston Police were looking for him. The airport, bus, and train stations were all no doubt being watched. He couldn't access his funds at the bank. He was in real trouble. Trent's desperation slowly and irreversibly began a dark descent culminating in an incredible desire for revenge. He was angry. Angry at the futility of his hard work these last two years, all for naught. Gradually his anger found a most natural outlet. Peter Kramer. Were it not for him the entire plan would have succeeded. The man was almost single-handedly responsible for what was now happening to him. Suddenly a clarity of purpose swept over Walton Trent. Like a fresh ocean breeze soothing his face, Walton Trent once again had a sense of sweet resolve. He knew what to do next. A twisted smile crossed his maniacal face.

Back in Pinehurst the town was abuzz with the dramatic events of the past two days. Beginning with James Cannon's suicide, the attempted murders of Martha Phillips and Anne Ashdown, and ending with the arrests of Thomas Lawton and

Phil Craft. The Pinehurst Police had their hands full. Slowly as news traveled across town and the Kingston College campus, the full enormity of the terrible conspiracy began to sink in. By 4:00 that afternoon all the major television network crews were camped outside the Pinehurst Police Station as well as the main administration building of the college. Somehow murder and intrigue on a college campus was big news. Reporters scurried about looking for the latest news and hottest interview. The town of Pinehurst and Kingston College were national news, leading every newscast as the top story. Even Ted Koppel of ABC News was in town to do a special report on the story.

Back at the Phillips estate Sarah and Peter ate a quiet dinner of spaghetti, garlic bread, and green salad accompanied by a nice bottle of red wine. The big house was quiet except for the occasional reporter calling for a story. Somehow they had gotten hold of the number. Sarah politely declined any interviews. With Mrs. Phillips gone, Nellie had taken a few days off. Sarah loved cooking for Peter.

Jamie was sprawled out on the kitchen floor sleeping. She was delighted to have someone home with her since Martha Phillips had been gone almost a week. As the evening wore on, Sarah got more and more tired. Peter called Cary Connors twice during the evening to check on the status of Walton Trent.

"He's probably trying to leave Boston," said the detective. "We have no word from any law enforcement agencies on any sightings. Don't worry, he'll show up."

"So where do you think he may have gone?"

The detective sighed. "Oh, I think he is in such serious trouble with his people in New York that he's probably trying to leave the country. On top of that, we have all the cops in New England looking for him. The federal boys too! The guy is in big trouble."

They said their good-byes and Peter hung up the phone. He

looked over at Sarah, who was almost asleep on the living room sofa, Jamie lying on the floor at her side. Her soft silky hair lightly grazed her beautiful face. At that moment he decided he would stay the night rather than go back to the cottage. He called Jeff, who was now back at the cottage, and told him he would be at the Phillips house for the entire night. Peter went to the closet and selected a dark brown blanket and crossing the living room, gently put it around Sarah's shoulders and legs. Kissing her lightly he grabbed a second blanket and some pillows and lay on the living room floor next to the sofa. The dog snuggled next to him. Soon all three were fast asleep.

BOSTON 11:00 P.M.

Trent knew his Buick would be under police surveillance at the Hilton Hotel so he took a public transportation bus to Logan International Airport's long-term parking garage. He got off at the quiet terminal and made his way through the five-story parking garage looking for a car that appeared to have been there awhile. He found a dark late model blue Ford Escort with a light coat of dust covering the entire car. He quickly jumped in and fiddled with the wires under the ignition. A moment later the small Ford engine sputtered to life. As he drove slowly out of the garage Trent looked for a dated parking ticket. To his relief he found one in the glove compartment. The young parking attendant in the booth barely looked at him as he took the ticket and $50 from Trent. The little Escort sped away down through the Sumner Tunnel and out onto Storrow Drive heading towards I-93. He stopped at an all-night gas station and told the high school–age attendant to fill up the Escort with the cheapest gas they had while he went into the restroom and changed his clothes and trimmed his bushy eyebrows and hair. He came out wearing casual pants, a polo shirt, pullover sweater, and loafers. The effect was startling. He looked years younger and far less imposing. The young attendant stared at him but thought better of saying anything. As he drove away the young man wondered what that had been all about. He was savvy enough to say nothing.

So intent was Walton Trent on his new mission that he failed to notice the long, black Lincoln Continental that had been following him since he had left Logan. Two men in dark clothes sat in the front seat. They were under orders to tail Trent and report in on where he was headed. Never once did they worry about losing him. They were that good and he was that careless.

At 1:00 A.M. Trent reached the edge of Pinehurst, where he parked on a deserted side street, one block away from the downtown. He was impressed with the extensive media coverage. The downtown was bathed in bright television lights even at 1:00 in the morning. Several Pinehurst Police cars were parked around the town commons with officers sitting drinking coffee, obviously enjoying the fame that had come to their town. No one noticed the small car, with the most wanted man in six states watching. The quiet, dark street was perfect cover for Trent. The black Lincoln Continental sat discreetly two blocks back, parked under a giant New England Elm tree. Both men were barely visible to any passer by. After 20 minutes Walton Trent made his next move. He started the car and made a quick U-turn, heading away from the center of town. His lights illuminated the lawn of a New England clapboard house before settling on the quiet street. He passed right by the Lincoln but failed to notice the car or two men inside. One of the men swore under his breath as he saw Trent's car headed their way. They both ducked down in the nick of time.

Walton Trent took the next left onto Old Campus Drive and made a circle around the town by following the old college road that led out to Green River Road and eventually

Anne Ashdown's place. He passed by the deserted athletic fields and soon was out of town. In his car mirror he saw the fading yellow glow of the television lights as he made his way deeper into the lonely, dark countryside. He had been to the Ashdown place once before when he and James Cannon had met with Mrs. Ashdown to discuss her bequest. Ten minutes later he slowed the Ford Escort as he neared the long driveway leading to the country estate. He quickly turned off the car lights and parked the car just inside the driveway off of Green River Road.

The two men following him slowed to a crawl and watched Trent as he got out of his car. One of the men quickly placed a call on his cell phone. He spoke a few words and then listened intently nodding his head in affirmation.

Stepping out of the car Trent listened for any unusual sounds. The bite of the cold winter night had awakened all of his senses. He felt alive and prepared. Silently he made his way up the winding driveway past the silent dark house. Briefly glancing at Mrs. Ashdown's house, he continued to the little cottage at the back. A bitter smile crossed his face as he saw the little green MGB parked out front. The cottage was dark. He found the front door locked. Walking around to the back of the cottage, he tried the back door and found it also was locked. A dog barked in the distant countryside, its echo making the night seem that much more lonely. Back at the front Trent began looking for a spare key and to his surprise found one under a flowerpot next to the door. He grasped the key in triumph and carefully inserted it into the front door. The door opened with a slight squeak. He froze. No movement from inside. He continued on and soon was in the great room. He waited a moment for his eyes to become accustomed to the darkness of the room. Someone was asleep on the couch. The big man moved quickly, drawing a small-caliber gun from his right coat pocket and pressing the cold steel barrel to the head of the sleeping person.

"Turn around real slowly," commanded Trent.

Jeff awakened with a jolt, then did as he was told. When he lifted his head and saw it was Walton Trent he almost passed out.

Trent immediately recognized the young man.

"So it's the little computer guru who has been doing all the damage. Sit up, you bastard."

Jeff complied. He was stunned to see Walton Trent. He wondered if he was dreaming.

"Now where is Peter Kramer? We have some unfinished business. Tell me!"

"I don't know," lied Jeff.

Trent laughed mirthlessly.

"Sure you do. You've been running around the whole countryside with him." Trent's cold eyes bored into Jeff.

Suddenly Jeff was incredibly tired of the entire affair. Somewhere deep in his soul he found resolve. There was no way he would betray Peter and Sarah. He owed them his life.

"You can shoot me right here and now but there is no way I will ever tell you where he is. Go ahead, shoot me, you miserable creature."

Trent grunted in surprise, and then, without warning, reached out and soundly struck Jeff on the right side of his head with the small pistol. The young man fell heavily to the floor, out cold. Trent looked around for some rope and tied Jeff up. He bound his hands behind his back and roped his legs to his hands. Putting the gun back into his coat pocket he ran out the front door and down the long driveway to his car. He never noticed the short stocky man in dark clothes silently watching him from the bushes along the driveway. Trent jumped into his stolen car and quickly continued his journey along the Green

River Road. The man waited for Trent to get into his car before running back to his car. Both men continued their careful pursuit of Walton Trent.

Trent sped up Green River Road until he came to Canterbury Lane, where he turned left. It was 2:00 A.M. The narrow road was bordered on both sides by overgrown trees and wild berry bushes. Deep shadows covered the rural road. Walton put his hand in his right pocket and felt the gun for reassurance. Soon he came to Old Vermont Road and turned left, back in the direction of town and the Phillips Estate. He knew Peter Kramer was there.

At 2:15 A.M. Jamie suddenly stood up, her long fluffy ears standing on end. She uttered a low growl and walked over to the front door and began sniffing around the edges. Peter stirred from his place on the floor but failed to react to the dog's warning. Suddenly the massive front door crashed open and Walton Trent exploded through the opening, eyes wild, gun in hand. He violently kicked the dog aside. She yelped before flying through the air, landing at the bottom of the stairway in a silent heap. Before Peter or Sarah could react, Trent had his gun trained on the two of them. Sarah bolted to a sitting position on the couch, blanket pulled over herself, paralyzed with fear. Peter leaped to his feet but froze at the sight of Trent and the gun he held in his right hand.

"Sit!" commanded Trent. Peter alertly took a chair as far away from Sarah as possible and tentatively sat down.

"What do you want, Trent?" asked Peter.

The man laughed. "Oh, I just want to have a conversation with the bastard who spoiled everything."

Peter replied. "You really see yourself as the victim, don't you, Trent? How pathetic!"

This angered Trent. "Listen, you no good son of a bitch. Everything was going great until you came to Pinehurst last fall. You had to dig your nose into what was none of your business."

Sarah responded angrily. "You don't think killing my grandfather is any of my business?"

Trent kept his gun trained on Peter and looked at Sarah. "Nothing personal, your grandfather was just a necessary casualty in a very expensive scheme."

"Of course, John Phillips wasn't the only casualty, was he?" Peter fixed a steely glare at Trent.

Trent turned back to Peter, his dark bushy eyebrows slightly moving up and down in concentration.

"It's all over so you can stop your silly little investigation. I know what you are trying to do. Frankly, I have to give you both credit. You got things pretty well figured out. But I don't give a tinker's damn what you know now. Once I'm through with you two, I'll disappear for good."

Peter looked intently at Trent.

"You don't really think you will get away, do you?"

"Why not?"

Sarah replied. "Because you are leaving a trail of dead bodies in one of the most sensational crimes ever in New England. The police and FBI will never stop hunting you down."

Peter interjected. "Tell me Trent, what went on at the cabin in the woods. We know you had Leslie Patton, Henry Townsend, Elisabeth Ann Williams, John Phillips, Bill Rutherford, Phyllis Allen, and Dr. Glenn killed, but what was the cabin all about?"

"How did you know about the cabin? You followed me there, didn't you? How long have you suspected me, you sneaky bastard?"

Peter didn't answer Trent's questions.

Trent was out of control. He continued on.

"That's where we had most of our meetings. How would

it look if the esteemed college president, popular town doctor, town lawyer, and me were always meeting? Oh, and a couple of local thugs too. Anyway, that's also where wonderful Dr. Glenn kept his magical potion."

Sarah asked. "So was it all just for the money?"

"Of course. We had it all figured out. A brilliant scheme! Most colleges have wealthy donors. You two should know that. Especially you, Sarah. So with Thomas Lawton as their lawyer and Dr. Glenn as their primary physician, the rest was easy."

Sarah was astonished. "What do you mean? How can killing be easy?"

Trent shifted his feet so he could look more directly at Sarah and Peter. He was enjoying himself immensely.

"Thomas Lawton is crooked. You must know that by now. He would write up their wills and get them to keep their gift to the college confidential. Everything hinged on that. Once it was written into the will no one, not even family members, would see the true amount. Once our donors met their untimely death, with Dr. Glenn's help, Lawton then would notify the bank and the money would be transferred to the Bank of Boston. Lawton would have already changed the document in the will to reflect a much lower amount. That lower amount would go the college. The remaining money would be electronically transferred to, ah, somewhere else. That's where the Bank of Boston came into the picture."

Trent paused. Clearly he didn't want to say any more about where the money went.

Peter stared at Trent. "Oh, you must mean to New York and the Empire Insurance Company."

Trent's face was impassive. "I know you know about Empire Insurance."

"You look a little upset, Mr. Trent," interjected Sarah. "Are you OK?" She was fully awake now.

"You two think you are so smart," snarled Trent.

"No, we just like to cover our bases. So, anyway, who are these people at Empire Insurance?"

"Wouldn't you like to know? Actually if I were you both, I'd pray that I would never find out."

Peter abruptly changed the subject. "Why did Bill Rutherford have to die?"

"Such a stupid question. The guy discovered the electronic transfer program. Your friend, the computer nerd at the bank, figured it out and told him. Sad thing how Rutherford died. Takes a pleasant stroll in the park and gets mugged."

"Trent, you truly are a ruthless bastard," responded Peter.

The man smiled at the two of them. "Yes, one could say that. But on the other hand I delivered the goods."

"So what about President Cannon? Where did he figure into all of this?"

"Cannon was obsessed to put Kingston College on the map. He was feeling great pressure from that bumbling idiot, Randolph Bolles, to make Kingston a top-notch academic institution. They both wanted the college to focus more on research rather than teaching. It was going to cost the college more money, too! I don't know the difference, but it sure created a lot of tension at the board and faculty levels. I could have cared less."

Peter silently reflected back to the faculty meetings earlier in the fall semester. Trent continued.

"In addition, the college struggled financially from time to time. Cannon hated the financial problems, so he kept the pressure on me to generate funds. I did that just to placate him so I could do the real job I was sent here to do."

Sarah asked. "Was Cannon in on the entire plan?"

Trent grunted. "He knew enough. I'm sure that's why he took his life."

"How about Randolph Bolles. Was he involved?"

"No! Bolles is a lightweight. He likes to put lots of pressure on people. His ego is the biggest thing about him. He kept meeting with Cannon and insisting that Kingston needed to become a great academic institution. What does Bolles know about quality? Hell, he was a corporate executive! Anyway Bolles started sounding like a broken record and Cannon got more and more discouraged. Cannon came along with us because he felt the pressure from Bolles and a few members of the board to make something happen. Yet he wanted the college to change too, so I don't feel too sorry for him."

"How did Dr. Glenn die?" asked Sarah.

Trent shrugged his wide shoulders.

"Lawton and I hired some local hillbilly to take him out. He was ready to go to the police. We couldn't let that happen."

Peter could see Trent was getting antsy. He kept shifting his feet and looking around the room.

"So Trent, how are you going to get away with this? I know you don't have all the money you had hoped for."

Trent suddenly stiffened and glared at Peter.

"I know you and that computer nerd friend of yours deposited a lot of money into my account at the Bank of Boston to cast suspicion on me. You tried to get my friends in New York to lose faith in me. Well after tonight that won't be a problem."

Suddenly Peter knew what was coming. He couldn't quite believe it up to this point but now he did. Walton Trent had come to kill him and Sarah. Not just for revenge, but to put him back in the good graces of his bosses in New York. No wonder Trent had told them so much.

"You actually believe your New York cronies will accept you back. You're screwed up, Trent. You didn't even close the Anne Ashdown account. You couldn't. You cost your friends several millions of dollars. I can't imagine they will be too forgiving. They don't sound like the forgiving type. Of course, not that you are either."

Trent stood straight and pointed the gun at Peter. "Time for you to die, Professor." Trent's eyes were black as the night. He stood in the middle of the well-lit room. Peter wildly looked around the living room. Trent raised the gun. Sarah cried out and began moving toward Peter, while Peter suddenly leaped out of his chair and lunged in Trent's direction. They were too late. Unexpectedly and remarkably, Trent paused, and his eyes widened in confusion. For the briefest of moments he stood there transfixed before his head exploded violently in a bursting spray of bright red blood and gray matter that projected across the room, covering Peter and Sarah. Trent's body crashed to the floor, hand still clutching the gun. He hit the living room floor with a thud and landing on his back lay there, sightless eyes staring up at Peter and Sarah, who witnessed the scene in horror and disbelief.

Outside the house, in the middle of the expansive lawn, the small man who was the passenger in the black Lincoln Continental knelt down on the waterproof mat he had placed on the wet snow and methodically began putting the high-powered telescopic rifle back into an elegant carrying case. The car was quietly idling in the lower driveway waiting for him. As he walked to the car the expert marksman reflected on his latest assignment. Walton Trent had been an easy target. His arrogance had been his undoing. How stupid for him to have stood in the middle of the living room, lights ablaze. Walton Trent, the man who had set up everybody else, in his final moment had become the perfect target. The car pulled out of the driveway and headed west, away from Pinehurst towards Vermont. They would use a different route to get to New York.

EPILOGUE

The national news stations stayed in Pinehurst for three more days after the death of Walton Trent. Cary Connors became the police spokesperson to the media. He handled himself well under the glaring lights and incessant questions of reporters.

Thomas Lawton was charged with conspiracy to defraud Kingston College donors of millions of dollars. The charges extended to bank fraud. Connors and the District Attorney kept to their agreement not to charge Lawson with his part in any of the murders. They wouldn't need his testimony since Trent was dead. But Lawton kept telling them everything he knew. He would go to jail for a long time, as well as be disbarred from ever practicing law again.

Phil Craft was charged with misuse of bank records and eventually would be given a six-month jail sentence. The bank fired him immediately after he pleaded guilty. The hit-and-run accident case was revived, but not enough evidence surfaced for an indictment to be brought.

The Board of Trustees at Kingston met in emergency session and in their first act removed Randolph Bolles from his role as board chair. The board's second act was to name Elisabeth Rutherford as interim President.

Jeff Peters was given his old job back with the Bank of

Boston with back pay and a nice raise. He moved back in with his parents. He and Peter and Sarah remained good friends.

Anne Ashford and Martha Phillips were released from the hospital after two days. Both returned to Pinehurst to live. They would have lots to talk about in the days ahead. They had become minor celebrities.

Things gradually returned to normal at the college. Peter resumed his teaching responsibilities. Clearly, he was a celebrity in the classroom as well on campus. The faculty was grateful for his role in bringing an end to one of the most horrific chapters in the history of Kingston College. He and Sarah continued seeing each other. On the day before spring commencement, 2003, Peter proposed to Sarah and they set a date for August 13 to be married. Peter continued to live in the cottage behind Anne Ashdown's country home.

The FBI and other government agencies spent hundreds of hours unsuccessfully looking for the people behind Empire Insurance. One day after Trent's death a team of agents raided the address in New York and to no one's surprise found just empty offices. No trace would ever be found of the people involved in the murder and conspiracy beyond Walton Trent and Justin Nichols.

Remarkably Justin Nichols was able to post bail before he was connected to Trent's death and the bank conspiracy. A very well dressed attorney flew in from New York and was able to get him out on bail thanks to a friendly judge. Justin Nichols disappeared from everybody's radar screen within two hours of his unfortunate release. The final link was gone.

THE END

AUTHOR BIOGRAPHY

Dirk Barram lives just outside of Portland, Oregon, where he is on the faculty of a small liberal arts college. He and his wife, an elementary school teacher, have a son and daughter. He is originally from New England.

CPSIA information can be obtained at www.ICGtesting.com
Printed in the USA
BVOW03s1425140415

396099BV00024B/283/P